Aiken in Check

ALSO BY MICHAEL FROST BECKNER

HITLER'S LOKI
Berlin Mesa

SPY GAME
The Aiken Trilogy
Muir's Gambit
Bishop's Endgame
Aiken in Check

A NATION DIVIDED
Volume I: Episodes 101–104
Volume II: Episodes 105–108
Volume III: Episodes 109–112

Aiken in Check

Book III
The Aiken Trilogy

Michael Frost Beckner

Los Angeles
2022

Published in the United States by Montrose Station Press LLC, Los Angeles.

LIBRARY OF CONGRESS CONTROL NUMBER:
2022901528

ISBN 9798985597462 (hardcover)
ISBN 9798985597479 (paperback)
ISBN 9798985597486 (ebook)

'Up on the Housetop'
Words and Music by Benjamin Hanby, 1864, in the Public Domain

'Someone to Watch Over Me'
Words and Music by George & Ira Gershwin, assisted by
Howard Dietz (title) 1925, in the Public Domain

Spy Game copyright © 2001 Beacon Pictures
The author and publisher gratefully acknowledge the permission granted
to reproduce the copyright material in this book.

Prometheus short story by Franz Kafka, 1918, in the Public Domain
Translation Copyright © 2022 by John A. Beckner
The author and publisher gratefully acknowledge the permission granted
to reproduce the copyright material in this book.

Excerpt from *The Seagull* by Anton Chekov, 1895, in the Public Domain
Translated by Marian Fell, 1912, in the Public Domain

Printed in the United States of America
FIRST EDITION

Jacket design and interior art by Andrew Frost Beckner
Book design by Michael Grossman

For Kara

Aiken in Check

This night December 24, 2002

HANDWRITTEN ADMISSION
PROVIDED TO THE CUBAN DIRECCIÓN
DE INTELIGENCIA; ROOM 8, HOTEL
FLORIDA, HAVANA, CUBA

Russell Aiken [Detainee], Senior Legal Counsel, CIA Office of General Counsel, the Central Intelligence Agency, United States of America

Santa Claus, like God, exists outside the time and space restrictions of our earthly realm. My post-tumoral neurological condition having occasion to deliver me to that unrestricted country—accept that when this statement's runners veer across discomfiting drifts—it is only from these illusory sleigh rides, the checking-it-twice perspective the jolly old saint provides me, I can confer the treasonous gift of this avowal.

From this sofa, hunched over this coffee table, yellow pad before me, Muir's-now-my fountain pen in hand—a blood-red, pearl-inlaid 1950 Esterbrook 69—I now bitterly repent my folly in quitting a comfortable home to risk my life in such adventures as this; but regret being useless, I will make the best of my condition, and exert myself to secure the good will of the captors who now exercise their authority over me.

We've traded mistakes, *mis caballeros.*

Mine? Easy: turning myself over to your captivity to betray everything I hold most sacred. Love and loyalty, liberty and life.

Yours? You've become my captive audience. Encouraged it: the cozy suite; the box of legal pads; the brown ink for my pen I've insisted upon (to my gratification at your annoyed effort to procure it in these late hours). That I suffer, I plan for you to share my suffering with each sentence until my final submission and I belong wholly unto you.

You've ordered I make this distinctive. Allow my true voice free rein (although, since voices are not bridled, you meant *range*. Fits better with *voice*. *Vocal range*, right? Albeit writing rather than reciting, *range* without larynxal context as good as keeps me with swift horses— *free range* having more to do with farm animals, or, well, chickens, once the barn door closes to conversation). Write on "the verge of delusion," your General Trigorin says (or was it "write to allusion"? *No sé*). I'll take it you intend that my words convey I am their certain monarch, you having good cause to see this admission bear, under physical and psychological forensic analysis, conclusive proof of my identity to the CIA. Let them know I am who I claim to be and compose this without duress, coercion, undue influence, or the shaping of others' hands.

[Initial: 𝒫ᴀ]

Without viable alternative, I write this now; afterward, I shall never write again. Gone, gone. Gone with the CONPLANS, OPLANS, brief analyses. Gone with the contracts, reports, memoranda. Gone with the confessions, Dear Mads, Muir missives; never to meet a Sweet Jessie, Dear Nina Valentine, I have chosen this as my last hill. All gone, but for this last opinion: *nunca más, nada para nadie*.

Never again, nothing for nobody.

Fuck all a'yous.

As the good Chanticleer foretells, tomorrow I go into the soup. As grim as that may be, tonight I crow my last.

But with abandon.

PART ONE

DECEPTION

"This goddess flies with a huge looking glass in her hands, to dazzle the crowd, and make them see, according as she turns it, their ruin in their interest, and their interest in their ruin."

— Jonathan Swift, The Examiner, 'No. 14', November 9, 1710

1

Up on the housetop reindeer pause.
Out jumps good old Santa Claus.
Down through the chimney, with lots of toys.
All for the little ones' Christmas joys.

C OVERT ACTION, defined by the 1947 National Security Act
Sec. 503 (e) is, "An activity or activities of the United States
Government to influence political, economic, or military condi-
tions abroad, where it is intended that the role of the United States
Government will not be apparent or acknowledged publicly."

Covert action encompasses a broad spectrum of activities, but
may include:

I.   *Political/Economic Action:* CIA covertly influences the
     political or economic workings of a foreign nation.
II. *Paramilitary Operations:* CIA covertly trains and equips
     personnel to attack an adversary or to conduct intelligence
     operations. These operations normally do not involve the
     use of uniformed military personnel as combatants.
III *Lethal Action:* While the US formally banned the use of
     political assassinations against foreign leaders in 1976
     [Executive Order 11905], the CIA may employ covert
     lethal force against nonpolitical enemies *[read "anyone
     else"]* deemed a threat *["threat" most casually defined]*.

Whereas Title 50 of the *United States Code* Section 413 (e), gives
the CIA sole legal authority to conduct these covert operations,

the 1974 Hughes–Ryan Amendment to the National Security Act, requires the CIA must have a Presidential Finding to conduct covert activities—activities monitored by oversight committees in both the US Senate and the House of Representatives.

That's where I come in.

Before Hughes–Ryan, roughly 50 percent of CIA Operations were exclusively or inclusive of covert action. After Hughes–Ryan, the budget for covert activities dropped to 3 percent of the total Agency federal allocation, providing funding for an average of less than twelve covert operations per annum. Only an idiot (and the US Congress) believes the CIA has spent the last three decades at this reduced level of covert hanky-panky.

Scores of headquarters-concocted covert ops steal under the oversight wire every year. On top of that, CIA officers on station routinely contrive covert actions simply to alleviate intelligence-gathering boredom.

Most are harmless. Some ingenious. Some hideously reckless. Some are spectacularly stupid. Our effort to lace your beloved Castro's cigars with LSD comes to mind. When that failed, we doubled down and attempted to sprinkle his shoes with thallium to make his beard fall out. That failed, we Wile E. Coyote-d an Acme Company seashell onto the spit of sand at Fidel's favorite beach-combing spot, intending it should explode when he put it to his ear.

Castro smiled at the sound of the sea.

Be they contrived as station chief chimeras or CIA herms,[1] all of them arrive on my desk with one common attribute: little thought put into possible blowback if it all goes wrong.

---

1   Architectural term—pillars capped with the face of Hermes, the Greek god of mischief, codes, and messages; used as an Agency catchword to describe a covert action as a weight-bearing pillar bracing larger intelligence gathering enterprises.

They do, and sometimes with stampede force.

Our congressional watchdogs tail-thump their days, drooling at the boot of the Agency chuck wagon for the fall of these meaty morsels. To avoid even the smallest oddment snapped into their maws, I've spent my career harvesting covert ops at the CONPLAN (Concept Plan) stage, that couldn't possibly pass the oversight smell test, to produce fresh and incontestable OPLANS (Operational Plans) that avoid both presidential and congressional nostrilization. I achieve this by transforming the hard targets of covert actions cooked into CONPLANS into soft-boiled objectives of intelligence gathering that have zero requirement of presidential or congressional ingestion, approval, investigation, or finding. The best of these are deception operations and there is an illegal art to their legal construct—a talent I did not come by naturally.

While I attribute all things CIA I am, past, present, feared-of-future, to Nathan Muir,[2] my fundamental perspective of our shadow world was first illumined inside me my last civilian summer after my graduation from Cornell Law. In a Lone Pine cabin at the eastern foot of the California Sierras, at the knee—singular as the cliché goes, but in this case one-legged reality—of former CIA legal enchantress, Linda P. Morse, I learned the elementary lessons of my dark art.

Great granddaughter of Samuel F. B. Morse, inventor of their namesake code, and a lifelong bachelor girl, Linda came to the CIA as a behind-the-lines saboteur of Nazi trains and Hotel

---

2   Nathan Muir, CIA Operations Officer 1952–1991. Professor Emeritus, Princeton University 1993–2001, where he continued service as an annuitant for CIA Office of Recruitment. Deceased May 6, 2001, Operation ATROPOS. As Muir's official retirement debriefer, I have full knowledge of all intel relevant to his career. Deliverable upon request/future debriefing.

Lutetia assassin via the Agency's WWII predecessor, the OSS. Prison-lamed by her Parisian Gestapo captors, her leg, limp and sore, festered until the smell of ripe almonds indicated gangrene and it was mercifully removed—mercilessly without anesthesia. Discarded in the German retreat (Leg-O'-Linda, as she would quip), she hobbled her way back to the States, where she refused to quit her espionage profession.

Never again to paradrop into enemy territory, her law license became her dynamite, her pen her stiletto. For three decades, those covert actions of highest risk, purest immorality, and deadliest intent—which would never pass congressional scrutiny—were, in Linda's hands, recast as deception operations that would, and did, to affect some of the most remarkable cloak-and-dagger skulduggery of the first two decades of Cold War confrontation.

But a life of outstanding secret service could not protect a life with an outstanding secret. August 14, 1972, with torch-and-pitchfork exigency, Linda Morse's former OSS superior, Richard Helms (who bragged he once lunched with Hitler), launched his milestone internal witch hunt. Not to Whack-A-Soviet-Mole like the Charlie Marches and others burrowed into our ranks (then and for decades to come), but against the larger, fantastically more dangerous security risk: the secret homosexual legion at Langley.

As Helms's "Top-Secret" directive rhetorically asked, "What Is A Homo?" then provided detailed instructions for "ferreting [them] out," Helms (lunching that day with Linda) requested she read it over her shrimp cocktail in his private dining room.

"Accurate, Linda? You think?"

"Oh, I am especially crazy about this part." She read: "'There is no way to spot a homosexual. In this, it is similar to recognizing a communist. He may not consider himself queer, he may accept his psychological deviation from the normal, but he recognizes that society frowns upon him.' Do communists consider themselves 'queer?'"

Helms gave her a pained expression. Linda's green eyes glittered in an otherwise give-nothing face. Helms signaled the shell-shaped plate of shrimp tails removed. Linda continued from the document.

"'Recognizing the existence of his problem and living with it requires certain adjustments and certain cover in the day-to-day life of the higher-class homosexual, who is our usual subject. He frequently uses a PO Box, his phone number is unlisted, he does his own shopping'—Dear me—'and his car is typically foreign.' Honestly, Dick?"

Linda paused at the steak au poivre placed before her. Took a moment to savor the aroma of the creamy cognac sauce and peppercorn spice. Director Helms gave an impatient nod that she continue.

"'The homosexual subject is usually regarded as an above-average employee.'" Linda cut into her meat. Through a mouthful she said, "Well, that's more like it."

She chewed, swallowed, went back to her reading.

"'His work habits are good; he is punctual, responsive to authority, cooperative, friendly, a credit to the organization.' I do consider the gender specific 'He' a trifle insulting for your purpose today."

"Noted. Anything else you want to say? Now's the time."

"Whoever wrote this is clearly closeted and writing from personal experience. This is particularly astute— 'One of the recently popular introductory remarks is 'Aren't you Jack from the North?' The word *North* is the code word. It means homosexual and what follows is pure danger.'" She gave an acerbic laugh. "They're also making a jackass out of you."

Director Helms sighed. "Gays are our most susceptible employees to foreign compromise and recruitment. They must be removed."

"I'm sorry. What you're asking—? I won't take part as an informer to an inquisition."

Helms bore into her with his black eyes.

"Oh…" The glitter in Linda's eyes faded. "You're not asking that." She lay her fork across her plate, her knife alongside it. "I'll give you this, Dick. You've done what the Nazis couldn't when they took my leg."

"If it wasn't so awfully necessary, Linda."

"You've broken my heart. You son of a bitch."

"Your removal must appear—as you are senior staff—to be involuntary, and it must be public. You understand? You must appear to have been driven out."

She braced her cheeks with her palms and mocked him. "In fear? Madness?"

"You're highly admired here. An institution, really. It would strike the appropriate tone. For the good of the service. It will cost us much less in severance, unemployment, and pension benefits if we force frightened resignations and avoid firings."

Linda shook her head in disgust. She lit a cigarette.

Helms advised, of course, Linda's retirement would be rewarded with full pension and benefits if she would sign her resignation papers, conveniently in the folder beside her ashtray, turn in her credential, and allow the humiliating example to be made.

She recalled this to me a couple years later over hot buttered rums on a split log bench beside her river-rock firepit that earliest time of my induction into the coven of spies. We were among the windy pines she'd named after fallen officers she'd lost in operations gone bad. It was autumn, and we were bundled in turtlenecks and Pendleton wools under a witch's moon. Back in June, while the mayflies misted over her pond and the little brown bats swooped in sunset light, Linda had ensorcelled me to my work; by November, with the owls boisterous in the dark limbs above, we'd grown close enough to become haphazardly confessional around the crackle of her fire. She was Bacall beautiful, and I was in a kind of head-over-heels platonic love with her—something she stirred in all men she fancied, with mischievous encouragement.

She said, "With that document, Dick Helms carried out the perfect covert action disguised within a deception operation."

Even in the thin gloom of moonlight, I saw it exactly. "Nothing to do with sex—"

"Everything has *something* to do with sex, Russell, or don't you think?"

"What I mean is, sex was only the myth being propagated." Linda's eyes danced, appreciating my pun. "But this had *everything* to do with an instant seizure of two to four percent of our pension fund with a simultaneous and equal reduction of benefits and salary outlay."

"Bravo!" she winked. "The homosexual purge had nothing to do with gays. It was all and only about Vietnam: a massive money-hemorrhaging wound smack-dab in the Agency's chest. The purge was a smokescreen to create a slush fund for dirty ops we couldn't finance any other way. Enacted by my closest Agency friend against me because he knew I'd fall on my sword for my Agency as only the most loyal of us are called to do."

She toasted me with her mug. "Remember me in this, Russell, when the blade points round to you."

Here, in my Havana hotel incarceration, I glance out my balcony window across the cobbled Calle Obispo. I superimpose on the shadowed

*tan facade of the dark apartments opposite a living image (as my
epilepsy provokes) of Linda tossing her rich honey hair as she laughs at
her circumstances that long-ago now-so-present night.*

"The most amusing part," she said, and added a juniper log
to the fire, "Helms promoted my sexuality during the war. Before
my own operational clumsiness led to arrest at the Paris Gare du
Nord, he and Dulles used my well-honed abilities at seducing
Nazi wives and mistresses of adventuresome flair many times to
a 'go forth and Yankee Doodle her for us' advantage."

Linda P. Morse taught me a covert op has a target and goal that
gains a direct result. A deception operation has a target and goal
that *appears* to gain an indirect result but acts as a smokescreen
for an unrelated/hidden hard-target goal, self-sustaining and self-
perpetuating. The example she taught as the perfect, most massive,
continuous covert op disguised within a deception is Santa Claus.

An American-launched deception run worldwide against
children—seemingly to their benefit—adults stimulate good
behavior from kids at their earliest level of understanding (our
psychophysiology programmers train us long-last target assets are
most effectively reached from ages one to six) by convincing them
of Saint Nick's existence and magical abilities, which, through
children's daily cooperation with rules of personal discipline
and social behavior, provide, in exchange, a stocking or sack of
wondrous gifts. The community reinforces this beyond the family
in ever-widening circles of complicit deceit: locally, nationally,
and internationally.

The magical holiday gift giver to good girls and boys reinforced
at all levels in all mediums. From auditorium *Nutcrackers*—toddlers
in tulle trained and twirling for parents and grandparents—to
TV's misfit Rudolph (who becomes a Christmas conformist)
leading in lockstep a host of movies and variety shows, municipal

parades, and newspapers' 'Yes, Virginia There is a Santa Claus' essays, poems, and propagandizing editorials, while the advertisers for the department stores, automakers, Coca-Cola, and all the rest of the mercantile giants blizzard us with TV, billboard, radio, magazine, window- and floor-display Santas: booted and belted, clothed, groomed, and rosy cheeked, blue eyed and bespectacled, whether live or photographed, painted or plastic, cutout or cartooned: they are all the exact same guy.

Less obvious, and thus more sinister, is the letter from Santa, hand-delivered on foot by a nationwide army of US letter carriers. In 1912, Postmaster General Frank Hitchcock authorized postal employees and citizens—a federal program officially known, as Operation SANTA—to forge and mail Santa correspondence *free of postage.*

So intent has the US government promulgated this deception that, at the height of the Cold War, Strategic Air Command's Colonel Harry Shoup publicly announced, "The Army, Navy, and Marine Air Forces will continue to track and guard Santa and his sleigh on his trip to and from the US against possible attack from those who do not believe in Christmas," giving birth to the NORAD Santa Tracker out of our Cheyenne Mountain. Our freaking nuclear missile defense command: that's how important Operation SANTA is to our government.

The beauty of Operation SANTA is as its victims increase in age and logic, and disbelief infects the target-asset population, these subjects are inoculated into continued participation in the deception by the strict understanding the gifts they've been receiving will discontinue as soon as belief ends. This crucial gain-versus-punishment period of indoctrination bridges the gap from innocence, through acceptance, to conversion—i.e., the convergence of age and nostalgia that makes them willing partners in the deception as they self-perpetuate the operation (originally run *against* them), *now* against their own children and families and communities all in the name of harmless holiday hijinks.

That's the deception.

Underneath, a powerful covert operation is at work.

The purpose of Santa Claus is top-to-bottom population brainwashing to accept a national surveillance state that sees you when you're sleeping and knows when you're awake, which our government and private sector actively expand with greater invasiveness and proportionate acceptance every year: this a trade-off for an annual economic spike worldwide that creates a massive surge for the US economy. A gigantic thoroughly fabricated "Pass Go" international money grab to kick off every American year.

"Write every operation as if you are creating Santa Claus," Linda taught, "and you will never find yourself before the Senate Select Committee on Intelligence with your nuts roasting on an open fire."

Tonight, were I pit against any other nation, I'd have run my op in and out through the chimney. No one the wiser. Guaranteed home by Christmas.

But not here. Not Cuba. In Cuba, Santa Claus is, by official decree, a criminal.

2

I N 1959, Castro took the vital step to nationalize the bat guano caves, *Animal Farm* every hen's egg in Havana Province, and ban Santa Claus. Your El Jefe Maximo's diminutive firebrand Director of Culture Vicentina Antuña eliminated Santa, condemning him "a US import foreign to our culture." No Santa posters, placards, or insidious plastic reindeer allowed. Yankee Christmas trees *prohibido*; everyone required to hang their tinsel from *la buena palma Cubana*. "Decorations must be made of Cuban materials, with traditional Cuban scenes," la señora ruled, "and Cuban Christmas cards must be used instead of imported ones."

But ten years of Derección de Inteligencia counterespionage by your guys' forebears not powerful enough to reduce Santa's power, Castro canceled Christmas altogether. For a time, Cuba was safely both Yule- and Santa-tized. And, while your weakening communist government may have grudgingly restored Christmas as a public holiday in 1998, Santa Claus remains unwelcome and unlawful on your Caribbean island.

In a recent article I saw in your labor union weekly *Los Trabajadores*—decisive to my choice to surrender to you— your writer exhorted brothers and sisters of the revolution to beware the white-bearded, red-suited polar fat man as *"Un símbolo minatorial de la hagiografía del mercantilismo estadounidense,"* which, in English, translates with almost the same lack of lucidity: "A minatorial symbol of the hagiography of US mercantilism."

As easy in my own paraphasia to paraphrase: "Truism: America's mighty national embargo op is half of holy."

The article shoots Santa right between the eyes, identifying him as a tool of "mental colonization." Shops using Santa Claus for decoration are extending "a humble help to the expansion of this consumer culture, with its accompanying ethics and ideology!"

Fines and jail time to follow.

Must've added some teary Whoville disappointment for Elian "Tiny Tim" Gonzalez, eh?

LESS THAN FORTY-EIGHT HOURS AGO, in the shadow of Mount Whitney, surrounded by pines named from the Agency Memorial's *Book of Honor*, Linda P. Morse warned me about you and your evil olive drab-uniformed dictator:

"Castro will forever 'ferret out' the Satan inside Santa. Nothing I taught you will protect you in Havana or achieve your necessary goal."

"My goal is love. I love her, Linda. With every fiber of my being. I have no choice."

Linda clenched her carved redwood crutch in her right fist to brace her willowy frame against it. She extended her free hand over her missing leg. She waggled her fingers, beckoning until I met them with my own. We interlaced hands. Her skin was taut as it had ever been in youth. A texture like silk. The only signs of her sheer, uncomforted age I found in our touch were the hard, arthritic bulges of each joint growing absent of vitality's warmth.

Then again, Linda was at her coolest under pressure.

"The Cuban DI has always beaten us, Russell. At their worst, they are better than the KGB and the Stasi at their best. Always.[1] It will do you to remember that."

---

[1] Not exactly "always." I burned you once, and badly, in 1991. The operational elements of and methods by which I achieved this to be surrendered to you in pages forthwith.

An arctic wind, presaging a white Christmas for her cottage, danced with her long, aged white victory-rolled locks.

"You cannot beat them. To save the love of your life, you'll be required to sacrifice your country. You'll be forever hunted as a traitor. Adrift without a native land."

I gave a single nod to show my acceptance of my forthcoming crime and condemnation but spoke my faith. "Nina Estrada is my country."

"You'll never see her again."

Nina or America. To save one, I lose them both. A man without a country.

"I haven't been careful hiding my tracks. Counterintelligence will discover I came here."

She rubbed her thumb across the back of my hand, marking me with her blessing. "I'm a ninety-six-year-old bachelor girl with medals from General Eisenhower, Charles de Gaulle, and John Kennedy. I wear a ring"—she twisted our hands so I could see it— "made from a piece of bone I cut from my own discarded leg with the stiletto I still keep tucked in my boot."

I fought sudden horror, the urge to drop her hand, as my finger rubbed against the dead-bone ring.

"Oh, don't be imbecilic. I'm teasing. It's Congolese ivory our dear Nathan once gave to me." She laughed. "Who will they send? Silas Kingston?"

I huddled into myself at the mention of that unholy spook.

She flicked her eyes at the firepit. "I fed that boy cocoa and roasted marshmallows with him right there. He's a pussycat."

"All tigers were once kittens."

She relinquished my hand.

"Russell, as long as you don't tell me what you're trading, I have nothing to worry about. But this isn't a plan you can repaper. It best be something Fidel has use for, or you will have sacrificed both your lives, and they'll rape and torture Nina out of spite before they put a bullet in her skull."

"They'll take my offer."

"Then kiss me goodbye. On the lips. It always feels deliciously dirty when it's a boy."

Neither a trick of winter wind nor weakened light, a halo formed around her. I knew what came next. I brushed her lips with mine, and time bent to my epilepsy. My legs suddenly became unsteady.

"Don't fuck this up, Rusty! You collapse, you'll never get out of here!" warns Muir.

He stands in the entrance to his office. The day after his Captiva Island confession, his last day with the Agency. 1991. My incontrovertible present. I am inside Muir's room, amid the boxes Gladys packed for his move. Boxes now flung wide and rifled, file cabinets and desk tossed by the Office of Security hunting for Muir's Bishop files recently burn-bagged to the incinerator. Gladys and I lift his scorched flag from the wall.

He hollers again: "You're not going to have time for that, pal. Plans have changed. Time is limited."

We guide the heavy frame onto the sofa. Muir and I wait for Gladys to leave the room before we speak.

"You died."

"Not yet, at any rate. You talked to Sandy, huh?"

I stare at him dumbfounded as I always am when I actively relive my past.

"Bishop's mother? C'mon, Aiken. She says you spoke."

"Sedaka killed you."

But that would be ten years later, and Muir gives me an impatient look, painted with his perception of all my inadequacies.

"We've no time for your word games, Russell. Listen up because this is important. You know what's going on with Tom. In China. Right now. Not how I planned to spend my last day with the outfit, but I'm going to do my best to handle it."

I know how it will end. He will out foxtrot Harker and the Young Turks to see Bishop and Elizabeth safely rescued, but this second time around, I won't let his insouciance pass.

"'Do your best'? Your son and your daughter-in-law are in a Chinese prison because of your best!"

"What is it with you, never satisfied unless you're delivering yesterday's news? I need activity here, not reminiscence. Snap to speed, please. There's still one loose end with Charlie March that needs tying off and I'm not going to be able to get to it." His eyes pierce my soul. *"I'm sending you to Cuba in my place."*

"I know. You already have. I'm already headed back a second time to fix it all over again."

"Jesus. Are you still drunk?"

"No. Maybe. Sorry."

How could I tell him I travel through time? As it's happening, this is as real as I am—a living experience—a four-dimensional déjà vu to the past, present, and malleable.

While I self-audit, Muir says, "I know you just reconciled with Madeline and I'm happy for that."

I know now he wasn't. "She doesn't end well—you wanna know the truth."

"Nope. But lookit: if there were any other way to do what needs to be done, I would send you alone and without temptation at your side."

I hold back the burning in my eyes and repeat the words he says along with him: "But you'll be taking Nina with you."

"You can stop now," came Linda's voice beneath my lips.

I had no idea how long I'd been holding her in my arms, but the epilepsy-caused halo was gone.

"As good a kisser as you are, Russell, it's too late in the game for me to switch teams."

I hadn't collapsed. The seizure was past. I'd traveled back... or... hadn't yet, as the residue would always leave me feeling time-loopy.

"Good job, Dumbo," Muir echoed from the other place, not the past yet happened, but a future that never did but always does. *"Now move it. You got a flight to catch." His voiced faded, his life returned to the living dead.*

I gave Linda a goofy shrug and hopped back; I thanked her, I spun unsteadily to my car. I headed to you, General Trigorin, and this, my island exile.

I SEE YOUR CAMERA overhead focused on my yellow pad. So, watching me write this, let's do a little puzzle together. We'll call it, "What's Aiken Trading?"

Love and loyalty, liberty and life.

Love = Nina

Loyalty = America

Liberty = my Freedom

Life = ?

Not mine.

Isn't worth a damn to you; hardly anything to me. For Nina, I trade the life of another man. As agreed, I am here to give you the CIA's longest running agent in Havana. A hero to America and to every Cuban who values freedom and would see your revolution destroyed.

God, forgive me this and so much more.

Codename: HOUNDFOX, with the whoop-de-do and hickory dock... I am the Satan in Santa. My Christmas gift to Fidel: I betray the father to save the daughter.

3

AFTER 3 A.M., A WORKING GIRL CAN GET TIRED, and at 3:22 a.m., on what had been the first warm night of June 1947, copywriter Mary Frances Gerety was zonked. Wedged into the corner of her apartment at a repurposed grammar school desk with her Remington portable and her writing pads, she faced the right-angle seam where the two walls met. Dunced of ideas, she'd decomposed for the last hour instead of the opposite. Time to coffee mug her pencils, teacup drown her last cigarette, turn off the inner monologue she'd taken dictation from (and badly) the entire weekend, and pour herself into bed.

She unpinned the campaigns for Hills Brothers Coffee, Armour Meats, and Domino Sugar from her corkboards on the converging walls—Frances found she worked best when she let the advertising grab her attention from the corner of her eye— and slid them into her slab-sided cardboard portfolio. She'd steal herself four and a half hours' slumber before her Monday-morning walk to N. W. Ayer —"I'd walk a mile for a Camel"—& Son Advertising, its art deco temple to persuasion uplifted, a mile away at 210 West Washington Square, in Philadelphia.

Mary Frances switched off her work light. She shut the window to the rumbled darkness and walked to her bedroom door, where she stopped. She remembered having promised a signature line for their De Beers account "first thing Monday morning."

Unwanted, her inner Dictaphone played back the request from her New York City boss, Gerald Lauck: "Frances, we're dealing with a problem of mass psychology. Marriage is up, but diamonds are down. The masses, hun. Gotta get these diamonds on their fingers. Write me a slogan that strengthens the De Beers tradition for the postwar engagement ring."

Frances plodded back to her corner desk and lit a fresh cigarette. She blew a heavy cloud of smoke. She had steered De Beers through the Second World War with her "Love in Boom" and her Cupid-blowing "Bugles over America" (instead of kisses) taglines. She knew postwar housewives preferred a washing machine or a new car, even a Singer sewing machine—anything but an engagement ring—but that wasn't her business. Diamonds were.

She pulled a pencil from the coffee mug, trimmed its point while she offered a "Dear God, send me a line" prayer to the shadows. She scribbled His answer on a scrap of paper. Crashed into bed.

Scooping up the scrap on her way out the door to where the sun met the morning, Frances didn't much like what she'd written. At the staff meeting, her colleagues around the conference table mocked her grammar. Not the best, she agreed, though no one offered anything better. Yet, by last Wednesday at lunch, the Pandora store at Tysons Corner, fifty-six years and 3.5 billion dollars in De Beers sales success later, "A Diamond is Forever" stuck me and all my aspirations an arrow-straight sentiment right through the heart.

I was telling Jessie the story over my get-a-load-a-this voice-activated Nokia mobile phone—the *new* kind you can take with you in and out of the vehicle hands-free dock—as I drove away from Langley, merrily unaware I would never return.

Jessie, as I'm sure you've investigated and ascertained, is my daughter. She lives with her "Nnenne." "Grandma" in Igbo. And not, technically, her grandmother at all, but Gladys Jlassi, a lifelong Company secretary (retired), who lives with us in our Princeton, New Jersey brownstone. I am counting on your word, General

Trigorin, that neither Jessie nor Gladys will ever be contacted, disturbed, or molested in any manner, form, or fashion when our business is concluded; the choice for further contact between my family and myself entirely at my choice and of my choosing alone. [Matter of fact, please initial consent & agreement: _____]

"I don't know what you're talking about, Dad. As usual."

"What's not to know? I'm telling you I'm asking Nina to marry me. Tonight. I bought the engagement ring."

"Gladys!" she shouted. "He's doing it! ... He *says* tonight!"

She returned her voice to me. "I wouldn't talk about Frances what's'er-name with Nina. Are you nervous?"

"When have you ever known me to be nervous?"

She didn't answer.

"Jessie?"

"Uh, like my whole life?"

She asked if I was taking her to Martin's Tavern, her favorite since she'd finally been able to return to DC without the nightmares about her mother and baby brother's killing. "It's where John F. Kennedy proposed to Jackie O before he got assassinated. Yogi Bear also ate there."

Along with Yogi Bear (Yogi Berra) and Kennedy (the guy you helped us assassinate), US presidents, Supreme Court justices, even our agency's OSS founder, Linda P's former WWII boss "Wild Bill" William Donovan (who, rumor had it [read Nathan Muir] convinced Linda to a successful seduction of Eva Braun)—all of them, one time or another, dropped in at Martin's, and Jessie would dish as if she knew them, having memorized the menu's "Our Story" page over chicken nugget piles while I plied Nina: laying out my case for why I could, and therefore *should*, be trusted with another marriage as its coequal guarantor for success.

I had recently moved out of my 1938 Tenleytown townhouse that I'd fallen heir to and had been using during the work week since my wicked, unfaithful wife Madeline tragically fell from the sky on 9/11.

Wedding gift to her or not, the second she filed for divorce that townhouse should have come back to me as a marital infidelity forfeiture in the first place.

Martin's Tavern happens to be convenient to Nina's place.

You folks... You know Nina Estrada's place. That butter yellow U Street Corridor three-level railroad house. Near where Duke Ellington lived and performed as a young man. You folks know the neighborhood; know the door, know the lock, you know the floor plan. You folks know the kitchen. And, intimately well, you know where the knives pull from the butcher block... You fucks.

I told Jessie, "No. No Martin's tonight." I headed to pick up Nina and take her downtown. Butterfield 9. A Nick and Nora Charles, 1940s *Thin Man* vibe. Our favorite place. And Nina would have ordered the salmon, because she always did, and I would order the seared venison loin with persimmon and Madagascar vanilla, and she'd "Awww, you're eating Bambi," because she always did. I'd order her a California shiraz. Nina would shoot it down and order a pinot saying, "Que sera your syrah-shiraz," because she loved to toss my word salad back at me.

She always did.

Would I have gotten on my knee? You bet and you guys fucked that for me. And so what if Jessie didn't like my "A Diamond is Forever" story? Nina would have. She'd laugh at the Sean Connery *Diamonds are Forever* James Bond pun buried inside it as I cleared the Ian Fleming from my throat. And I'd draw Nina's attention to the deception operation that linked these two phrases to our lives and our work more than anyone bothered to know. Or cared, at any rate, like I did and she would.

Nina's face incandescent in the candlelight: her lips parted, lipstick glistening a red velvet smile, secret in anticipation; her eyes: humor flashing like bronze speckled fish inside gray pools above the Latakia blue-black hills of her cheeks. The dramatic arch of her brow; her forehead thrusting to the line of black hair pulled back into a ball; her wild fire braids cascading: woman as unquenchable as fire, the human representation of a life force that nourishes my soul.

Back in the 1800s, I'd have told her, a South African kid found a strange scintillating pebble on his De Beer family farm. One, another, and then a handful.

"Kudus?" she'd point her fork at my meal, punny, with her fawning kudos.

"After a little digging by older brothers, his father, uncles, and his neighbors," I would ramble on, "some shoveling with steampunked tools and machines, the Kimberly Mines were unearthed in all their bounty *too* bountiful." In no time, the De Beers were hauling out diamonds by the ton. Suddenly plentiful, diamonds plummeted in value. Only by locking down the deception that diamonds are rare and priceless could they exploit their glut of glittering gravel as rare treasure. To hide the truth and protect their fortune, they formed the De Beers Consolidated Mining cartel, carefully controlling both the supply and the demand.

"The founder of De Beers," I would say, "was a fellow named Oppenheimer." Nina would perk up at that because the name Oppenheimer tends to perk those in our profession. By 1938, in the wake of a First World War and a Great Depression, with the Second World War tempesting the horizon, the rare-meets-expensive supply and demand for only the royal, the wealthy, and the celebrated near scuppered De Beers.

"Oppenheimer's son, Harry, commissioned Ayer & Son—the guys with the deco tower in Philly—to bring the sparkle back to their three-billion-year-old stones. At the same time," I would say, joining our hands across the tabletop, "Harry's cousin, J. Robert was flirting with sparklers a bit older, attempting to create a nuclear fission chain reaction.

"They come together—Mary Frances, the Oppenheimers, and Sean Connery—on that peculiar word, *forever*. Mary Frances Gerety's *Forever* promises a young maiden endless romance at a price tag that encourages the man to stick around past her maidenhood. The De Beers–Oppenheimer's *Forever* is the diamond that's not resold; plant it back in the ground with Grandma because resale causes fluctuations in diamond prices that undermine public confidence in the intrinsic value of diamonds. And because diamonds are as false as Connery's *Forever*, which takes Fleming's book—that isn't even about spies but cutthroat smugglers and organized crime—and rockets their stones into outer space with the destructive power of a nuclear weapon created by—"

"The other Oppenheimer," she'd murmur, and her eyes would dance as she'd watch me place the black velvet box between us.

"The Oppenheimer whose nuclear blasts sent thousands upon thousands of potential De Beers customers into the 'Forever' that comes with 'and ever, Amen,' as the extreme temperatures and pressures of the Hiroshima and Nagasaki explosions squeezed the carbon atoms of all human life into a shock wave of trillions of nanoparticle diamonds."

Talk about devaluation.

And I would have taken a knee because I'm a hopeless romantic at heart.

"Forever is worthless without you."

I told you all that to tell you this: you made us miss our reservation.

I pulled up before Nina's house, excited. Each step taken as, when a boy, I'd bounced in anti-gravity spring-loaded moon shoes in celebration of the space race. Up the curb from the car. Up the steps to the walk. A hop onto the porch, my feet touching down in foreboding even as romantic violins preceded a timeless voice reaching out to me from inside—

There's a saying old, says that love is blind
Still, we're often told, seek and ye shall find
So I'm going to seek a certain lad I've had in mind

The dead bolt lock—popped—lay at my brown wing-tip toes. So excited about the ring in my pocket, the "forever" proposal, Nina's sure-to-be "yes," I'd forgotten to notice her signal light. I leaned back and looked upward. The red bulb the size of a marble always aglow in the corner of our bedroom window was out. Activated by a switch accessible on every level of her house: a signal light for compromise, for incursion. I leaned left to the bay window. The louvers were shut. I pushed open the front door with my foot, realizing I'd never asked Nina what to do if I ever saw her light dark.

Looking everywhere, haven't found him yet
He's the big affair I cannot forget
Only man I ever think of with regret

The first level ran cannon-barrel straight: wide-open living room becoming the dining room, through the wet bar Nina called "The Galley," her kitchen—center island, ellipse-shaped and

frigate sleek—to the sunroom, partially blocked by a wide bookcase, its back providing a faux window to what is my new home
with a life-size photomural of Havana Harbor seen from the
Faro Castillo del Morro lighthouse. Beyond was the back patio
and carport, and all of it appeared as if, cannon fired, a fiery ball
had blasted from the front door to explode out the shattered
glass of the back.

"Nina?!"

I stepped inside over a discarded CO_2-powered hammer-
punch. I called her name again. She didn't answer. The only sounds
I heard were the running of the faucet in the kitchen island sink
and the jazz singer's silvery notes from the jukebox in the galley.

I'd like to add his initial to my monogram
Tell me, where is the shepherd for this lost lamb?

I moved forward, willing my muscles loose, my back and shoulders spread and forward, arms bent, my hands in front, half-open,
ready to attack and defend. In the living room to my left, the sofa
pillows were scattered. A vase, a heavy candlestick, and bookends
used as projectiles where a chase had circled the coffee table—one
leg broken—and retreated through the Caribbean-meets-tiki-room
Galley, the bar on one side, 1940s Wurlitzer the other, bubble tubes
splashing colored light across her cocktail tables overturned.

There's a somebody I'm longing to see
I hope that he turns out to be
Someone who'll watch over me

I stalked through a fallen basket of limes. One, crushed, revealed
a man's sports-shoe-tread footprint in the sticky juice and pulp.

I continued to call her name, but now only as a tolling bell, clanging persistent, brassy, and unthinking.

A slight whiff of cordite, but no evidence of bullet strikes. If guns had been involved, they'd not been fired in this part of the house.

In the kitchen, a bottle of red wine lay on its side, spilled over the tumbled stools, puddled on the floor. Additional footprints tracked from the wine, swarming, and surrounding the island through crushed crackers and a flattened wedge of Stilton cheese. Impression of a second man revealed—flat-soled boots joining the athletic shoes—and Nina's bare feet.

I'm a little lamb who's lost in the wood.

The wine was not the only red splashed fluid. Around the far end of the island, Nina's butcher-block knife stand lay on the floor. The horror-movie butcher knife—the big one a stranger would grab—still nestled in its slot; the smaller, double-edged puntilla knife gone.

Good. Only Nina would know the small handle to snatch; she'd pulled the blade best suited for a close fight.

To the canary-yellow cabinetry she'd once hand-detailed with delicate white ginger flowers and green garlands, she'd now added fresh stencils of blood spatter.

I grabbed the butcher's knife.

I stalked into the sunroom over viscous footprints sticky in red.

The gunfire happened here. The full-length glass of our back door blown out, shot by the Cuban, dead on his ass, legs splayed in front of him, slumped backward against the bookcase to my left.

Nina's puntilla protruded from his ribcage. Although venous dark blood blackened his starched white dress shirt and gray sharkskin suit, Nina's knife had not killed this man. The bullet that entered his skull between the bridge of his nose and his right eye had accomplished that, his brains exploded into his orange, stingy-brimmed porkpie hat tilted back and dripping behind his head. Flat-soled boots jutted like gravestones.

Black Chelseas. Stylish.

My eyes tracked Nina's bare feet and the athletic shoes out the door through diamond pebbles of safety glass.

I know I could always be good.

She was long gone. The silence between the bubbles in the running water told me that. The absolute silent nanospace between each note the chanteuse bent and arpeggioed—that unnoticeable pure stillness that is the essential thing that makes music pleasing to follow.

Someone who'll watch over me...

The musical message Nina encoded for me in anticipation I'd come through the door.

For the moment, I was confident that she was safe; meant for abduction, unharmed and kept alive. The violence and the dead man told the entire story. They had knocked or rang the bell, attempting to get Nina to voluntarily open the front door. Upon seeing them through the spyhole, Nina had extinguished the signal light and retreated when, without hesitation, they punched the lock. A scuffle in the living room chased her to the rear of the house, where the kitchen island allowed Nina to separate from her attackers long enough to grab the cooking knife.

Her opponents—your agents—carried guns but hadn't used them, and since they hadn't, understanding she was targeted for abduction, she'd risked a defensive attack taking the more fashionably attired of the two. (She's never liked people who use fashion as a weapon.) Leaving her knife in his torso, she was hauled by the second man around the bookcase into the sunroom, where the man she'd attacked reeled after them, attempting vengeance. He shot at Nina.

Not sure if it's good training or bad on your part, but it appears he didn't give a damn if he hit his partner in the attempt.

The bullet missed both. Blasted apart the pane of back-door glass. The partner returned fire. Killed him. Forced Nina with him through the garden, to the carport and out to the alley beyond.

From the time I'd parked in front to this moment inside the back of the house, slightly less than two minutes had transpired. I snatched the gun from the dead man's hand. Without a silencer, it must have echoed thunderous inside, audible to the neighbors and other houses. I peered outside.

No lights burned in either house on either side. I didn't hear sirens.

I studied the gun. Its grip was not taped; this was a personal weapon and looked expensive—more a fashion accessory than a working man's tool—further cementing my belief this hadn't been a hit and Nina was safe. I tucked the weapon into my belt behind my back.

A Metro PD cruiser rolled forward, beams of hand-directed spots interrogating the shadows at the backs of the houses on both edges of the alley. Nina had spent years making her small garden a tropical seclusion. Thick trunks and leaves, fronds, climbing vines, and prehistoric-looking fiddlehead ferns concealed Nina's home. The gate was shut. Tiger-striping the foliage with its lights, the patrol drove past.

I heard a cry and wheeled back inside as I realized it was my own. Moaning now and without remembering having begun, I kicked the living hell out of the dead man.

"Nina... Nina... Fuck! Nina... oh, fuck, oh, goddamn..." Adrenaline crashed, overcome by shock. Failure. If-only guilt.

Time hiccuped. My mind processed what I did only after I'd done it and I was already beside the front door, peering through the louvers, scanning the Christmas-lit street, while in the mental present I seethed over the corpse. Police cars clicked into place. They blocked both ends, their lights strobing. Had I stood there seconds? Ten minutes? I could not tell, but police officers door-to-doored both sides of the street, moving my way in restless haste.

Auras burn the edges of my vision.

I gave one last look through the first-floor interior. It telescoped with the onset of euphoric delight that accompanied the déjà vu that wooed me into seizure. I glanced at the stairs: up and down to our two other levels, but with a lack of footprints and sound, I trusted they were empty. I couldn't be caught here.

The taste of metal burns my tongue.

I turned my view from the stairs to the door—

But my eyes sweep over Muir's study at Princeton, as it was one-and-a-half years ago. Muir slumped behind his desk, murdered as I'd last seen him. He peers up and says, "You want a hope of a chance to escape my fate, Rusty? Then you got a plane to catch."

My hand came to me, twitching in close-up as I opened my car door, my being fully disconnected from the present I traversed to get there. I knew if I let go, I'd float away, my mind bending, and all I could think, holding onto my car, that, as with all reality, it could be seen and touched with hand and body, but throughout life the brain that perceives all of it never touches a thing. It could—a secret savored and known—if only I would let go.

Not.

Now.

Nina!

I anchored my mind, keeping physical contact, auditing every tactile sensation. I climbed inside. The dead Cuban's blood coated my lower pant legs and shoes. It glowed with electricity.

Nina's face incandescent; her lips parted, glistening red velvet.

My vision narrowed. Seeing only from the corners of my eyes. I was almost gone.

Focus: steering wheel, police, bloody wing tips, incriminating trouser legs, pistol riding my spine, keys into the ignition. Oh, Holy Crap: Christmas lights are beautiful when they breathe.

All objects become independent of time; physical reality, evidence identified by visual mind shot/snapshot existing before-during-after. The jazz singer's voice, a Morse code SOS: . . . – – – . . ., the spoken "please," "God," "Nina." Music, Morse code, and speech—they exist only in time's landscape and can't be fixed in physical reality; seeing their landscape is only possible on the timescale of tens of milliseconds, the space between which I fall through, snowflake perfect and unique, before melting into the universal common pool.

Another gray-matter time cut; I'd floated my car from the curb. Uncertain whether it moved me, or I moved it, or we were still: the particle universe moving around time which existed only as me. A police spot at the end of the street blinded my physical eyes and my mind's eye slid open.

A siren whooped once. A voice came over a PA I couldn't grasp.

I glide into the light gliding into me.

4

"To a wise man, the whole earth is open, because the true country of a virtuous soul is the entire universe." So said Democritus, father of atomic theory, half a thousand years before Christ. You folks would like him. Rejecter of the polytheism of his forebears and denier of the monotheistic deity hurrahed by contemporaries Plato (who hated ol' Democritus), and juvey upstart Aristotle (who liked everybody), like Castro, Democritus lived without need for that other fantastical white-bearded, robed old man: God.

For Democritus, knowledge of objects, situations, and events arrives to us through the senses with perception, or through the mind with thought. It's an atomic process. "Soul atoms" are emitted from everyone and everything around us—not only that which is within our physical and visible range, but from the entire planet, our solar system, the stars, infinite space. Soul atoms lust soma. And so, emanating from everything in the universe, they hungrily seek to attach to us and enter our minds. Their function? Soul atoms create our dreams. What we see sleeping—the lives and worlds actual, parallel, alternate— of what has, will, might, or never-in-a-million-years happen. Fidel Castro never met Sigmund Freud who never met a Seneca tribesman who never met Democritus, yet all of them have one thing in common: the closest things to the concept of God, or a god-hand that moves us, are dreams. Dreams are the imprint of the soul.

I dream of Cuba.[1]

I dream of Cuba in fragments and across time. Fragments I sift from the earliest hours of March 15, 1978, when I meet Nina slamming shots of Rhum Duquesne at the Ear Inn in New York City, toasting the tropical splendor of her island birthplace (yet unventured with her—a link in the chain that manacles past unhappened to present unhappiness dragged behind me). Dream fragments strained with nameless Cubans who return to me from 1991, queued at leaking pipes with pots, buckets, cans, bowls, and old inner tubes in their daily battle for water; dream-strained fragments of Nina's childhood intimately transuded her soul atoms to mine this long-ago year into which I now dream my reality.

At night, my spirit floats outside the walls of her family home in Vedado. I watch the sea hibiscus flowers by the gate change yellow to red across the seasons as Nina comes and goes across dream-moments. She blossoms from white christening dress to suspendered red skirt and white blouse that becomes the simple tobacco university frock as she flourishes in Party privilege: a child of a Revolution *comandante*.

The avid soul atoms of her *comandante* father, attaching unseen to me during our brief personal contact, flood into me from across

---

1   As dreams, these are my impressions and not political judgments of *La República de Cuba* or *La revolución*. This section is neither meant as an indictment of your system or your government, sovereignty, or authority over your citizens. Nor is it meant as any kind of justifiable argument. If my words incriminate, they incriminate by emotion alone. This section is to explain my mental state vis-à-vis Cuba over time and not my perspectives as an espionage officer of the United States. I've not read-in on CIA/Cuba operations, intelligence goals, policy and/ or positions, nor have I had contact with the US Interest Section in Cuba or any of its employees and officers, past or current. Of my limited exposure to Nina's politics, I acknowledge those to be her opinion and I do not hold them as personal doctrine. I do not have to love Cuba to betray America, but I must be honest with you in all aspects of my confession in the unmasking of HOUNDFOX.

time and space. I am his sadness, dreaming of Cuba, a patriot slowly crushed by the broken promises he fought for so hard and so truthfully. I hover ghostly behind him at his ministry windows, and we watch the private cars of robust middle-class prosperity converted to taxis and soon outnumbered by them; taxis outnumbered by Czech buses, outnumbered by their own passengers, outnumbered by horse carts.

I dream I am his shadow. That amorphous piece of HOUNDFOX, stretching from his feet along the *calles* and los *callejones* he secretly wanders secret nights. *Los barrios bajos* of La Habana Vieja, the decay of Centro Habana, HOUNDFOX dodging the falling chunks of mortar, bricks, stone that pound me as his silhouette; I glide over hanging balconies and dangling crown moldings of decomposition that never sleeps. He casts me from his quiet footfalls onto the house fronts black enough, and the windows blacker, where the sound of gnawing rats inside the peeling walls mixes with voices hopeful, cheerless, dogmatic, dissident, angry, proud, drunk, sober: all timbred miserable beyond. I dream in crumbling fragments those wandering nights of solitary disappointment growing into disgust as a revolutionary's aspirations become a heart's revolt. He gives out the never-enough coins in his pockets to the brown, black, white, yellow, scanty clothed and meager, scowling, ragged; to wolfish children he meets on doorsteps; to the domino-playing old men at rickety tables in the street; the languid *putas* in the backlit doorways. Always more of them than the coins he has, and those deprived by chance and contrived of jealousy have long ago done the state's service and reported this night man. A trap laid, but in his office—I, cast upon his wall—he learns this, and we stay away for two years of hallucinatory seconds/infinity and Nina's school scarf of blue rolls into a red communist neckerchief she wears with smiles and pride behind her favored flowered walls and Nina never sees beyond them, her unprivileged twins throughout her city, *doom* written upon their brows as they parrot her robust classroom shouts: *¡Viva la Revolución! ¡Viva Fidel!* in the voices of lies, lies her parents pretend and she does not yet distinguish from truth.

I dream of Cuba and I see the revolution alive. Time instead of artillery collapses buildings in slow motion; the enemy steadily multiplies as the Cuban people are disarmed of weapons; disarmed of speech; disarmed of food and water and health, willpower and heart. Disarmed of thought.

The ration cards outnumber the rations. One set of new clothes once a year unless my designated store is out of clothing or out of my yearly toothbrush the day of my ration, then I wait another year with the mothers and fathers and sisters and brothers—men, women, children, infants—and we patch the soles of our shoes with newspaper to tread on the promises of heroes—the true believers, the *comandantes* like Nina's father—shuffling through hallways and rooms of broken, buckling lives, where every dream ever desired is dead. The dust of battle fatigue-falling Cuba billows in the ever-living, all-consuming revolution, and from the dust, the soul atoms infect my dreams. I am all of them and all of you. I am Nina and her father. I am her mother.

Age nine, loving parents grasp her shoulders. Nina blows out birthday candles as the moment freezes with a camera's flash. I am her father's camera. I am the candles' flames and vanish.

I am the nameless teenage girl who puts the cardboard in the window where, at age fourteen, she has written in wax pencil: "Condoms 3¢. Screws 30¢."

In bed with Nina, I am laid bare to a Cuba of palm trees and fragrant winds, passion and desire, soul atoms returning the two of us endless nights to make love on the white sand beach where she'd desired me before, before the seagull fell from the sky and falls forever in my sleep as I dream the dream Nina and I never now will live. My dreams of Cuba all realized in tomorrow's events I have agreed to: testimony before the Revolution and the world against HOUNDFOX.

WHERE I LEAN ON DEMOCRITUS, Nathan Muir put his store in French philosopher Jacques Maritain who said: *"Un lâche fuit en arrière, loin de nouvelles choses. Un homme de courage fuit en avant, au milieu de nouvelles choses."*[2]

What I ask, in this predicament I find myself is "if the coward flees backward, away from new things, and the man of courage flees forward into the midst of them," what is it the traitor does? My path to treason, here in Havana, finds its genesis, oddly enough, in China. Espionage ops neither Nina nor I participated in but to which our fates—*and Cuba's*—like the strange patterns of random falling bits of glass viewed through a prism of mirrors are inescapably bound, symmetric.

I shall explain...

Eleven years ago, on the dawn of October 1, 1991, twenty-four hours before the following events would demand Nina and I to fly to Cuba, Tom Bishop went forth a biblical David—not against one, but two Goliaths: China and America.

Three car lengths into Suzhou's narrow Kezhi Road, between dirt-streaked concrete-block warehouses, he sat perfectly still behind the wheel of a black Beijing-Jeep Cherokee. Primed like

---

2   Translation: *"A coward flees backward, away from new things. A man of courage flees forward, in the midst of new things."*

the noble stag he resembled: still of body and spirit, mind tight and fearless, he sat alert in anticipation of powerful action.

A whine of two BMW Yangtze River 750 motorcycles preceded machine-gun scouts, high-revving low gears, ready to pounce; the hoarse whinny of a grim inline-four People's Liberation Army UAZ-469 troop truck crossed his view, revealing broad-cheeked bored infantry in facing rows of three; underscored by the following bull bellow of a Soviet-built Ural transport, its anticipated identification number 163 confirmed at sight, its armored sides dull, warding away light like the sides of a steel tomb.

For Bishop, those armored sides may as well have been glass. In his mind's eye, he could know the future; through the sides of the glass coffin, he saw two benches, leg-shackle chains through floor rings, looped through belt restraints to wrist manacles on a human cargo of political prisoners, one of whom was his missing wife.

Sloppy met arrogance and, how-do-you-do no rearguard follow-up, but Bishop had known that too. The fact that everything matched his precipitously gifted intelligence report increased his confidence.

He lifted an active two-way radio. Keyed the push-to-talk once, then switched off.

The convoy passed along Yangchenghu Avenue as Operation TANKMAN commenced. Bishop allowed the engine sounds five seconds to fade. He let up the brake and eased the black 4x4 out of the lane. He turned left onto the broad street of hairy-crab factories where they package the famous fall delicacy along the miles of underwater old city ruins, dark green with freshwater moss grown since the 1960s construction of dams and irrigation systems greatly increased the surface of Yangcheng Lake. (The floodwaters were swift, and those who drowned, drowned swiftly.) Keeping distance, Bishop followed.

The machine-gun scouts passed the weed-riddled Jinlin Road. A crab delivery van with a cartooned green pompadoured crustacean sped out in a swirl of dirt and foxtails, forcing a space for itself between the motorcycles and the troop truck. The motorcycle riders waved the vehicle to pass to the front as the prisoner convoy rolled beneath the crumbling, mold-rotting tunnel of the Middle Ring Road underpass. The troop truck honked its horn and flashed its lights at the crab delivery van. One of the motorcyclists slowed, dropping back alongside the cab of the van. The crab driver ignored the soldier's angry gestures.

Bishop kept his distance behind the transport. He entered the underpass as the other motorcycle sped out the far end, racing ahead to stop and straddle the road to direct the foolish delivery man away from the convoy.

This was not to be.

A red Mercedes, coming off the poorly engineered 1930s ramp, broadsided the delivery van as it reemerged into daylight. Rending metal, shattering glass. Blasted, showering plastic.

The van toppled on its side, ripped across the tunnel mouth, throwing sparks. It crushed the first motorcyclist beneath the furry claws of its comical logo before it spun into the second bike, whose rider leaped free, hands scrabbling for his weapon.

The troop truck slammed its brakes, nose to the accident, the six infantrymen bracing, confused eyes blinking at their sergeant, their respiration intensified by sudden adrenaline.

The driver of the crab van focused on the second motorcycle scout running toward him, submachine gun aimed. He kicked out his windshield. One empty hand lifted in surrender, his other toggled the switch on an incendiary device hidden beneath the dashboard. He scuttled free of the wreck.

The six troops deployed from the back of their truck.

Bishop watched from inside his Jeep, now last in the convoy. Rushing troops. Two on each side of the transport. Thrust barrels of assault rifles signaling him out of his vehicle.

Timing is forever, and Bishop's was perfect. He waited, drawing them in, narrowing their full attention on his opening door, revealing himself as Caucasian. Broad and tall, rawboned unforgiveness. His mouth opened round and wide to protect lungs and eardrums from—

The delivery van exploded in a black and orange ball of fire.

Blasts are startling enough whenever they occur, but their surprise is always more effective on someone whose focus has been misdirected. The incendiary device Bishop rigged inside the van the previous night was devised for maximum flash and concussion. Bishop raised his pistol and took out the four blinded, confused, ear-bleeding, defenseless soldiers—all of them still looking at the fireball as they fell.

Bishop ditched his earplugs. Pulled handheld hydraulic bolt cutters from his Jeep. He cut the padlock from the back of the armored transport. He pulled open the door, coming face to face with another Chinese soldier. The frightened young man raised his hands; Bishop raised his pistol.

He showed no mercy.

He was inside. Benches on both walls, as foreseen, but only one prisoner. Head hooded, her fine hands and slender feet identified Elizabeth Hadley to Bishop. He shuddered. So emaciated was his wife the gray prison pajamas appeared impossibly empty of a human frame. Bishop lifted the canvas sack from her head.

Long, dirty hair hung limp from a skull covered with thin, almost translucent, porcelain-white and sore-splotched skin. Her lips were scabbed, though otherwise pale and bloodless. Her once lush eyebrows and lashes had almost all fallen from her face, but Elizabeth's eyes blazed blue with the cold fire of her indomitable spirit.

"Bit of a different look from our wedding, I'll bet." Whispered and husky, her voice shattered from torture-drawn screams.

Bishop worked his cutters on her chains. "You were barefoot then, too."

He scooped his wife into his arms.

"I knew today would be different when they loaded me alone," she said.

The moment Elizabeth spoke, Tom Bishop saw a future more certain in detail than his last projection. He understood exactly what he would see the moment he climbed from the armored vehicle, but there was nowhere else to go. Nothing else he could do.

He gently kissed Elizabeth and said what he did every morning they had awoken beside each other. "Did I remember to tell you today how much I love you?"

"I don't think so," she said with a wan smile that carried more bravery than an entire war.

She stared, calm and loving, into her husband's eyes. Bishop stepped carefully into the frame of the rear transport doors. Arrayed in a semicircle, ten anti-terrorism shock troops of the People's Armed Police aimed their weapons. Bishop stood there a moment, holding his wife.

He watched his two agents—the one from the van, the other from the red Mercedes—hauled into view. Forced to their knees. Shot in their heads. Pop go the earplugs from the sides of their skulls.

The guns on Bishop and Elizabeth remained aimed.

"Why don't they shoot us?" Elizabeth asked, then answered her own question. "Muir?"

Bishop gave a nearly imperceptible shake of his head. No, this was not Muir. What it was, he only knew by a codename, only briefly and without understanding.

"KALEIDOSCOPE," he said and tossed his pistol.

5

"Jesus, Aiken," said Muir, plain as day, hating on me as he entered the director's Seventh Floor Conference Room. "How long has it been?"

Deputy Director Operations Jeremy Harker III smirked, knowing full well how Muir and I spent the last twenty-four hours in Florida, forcing Muir's retirement while locking up the secrets of his and his mentor Charlie March's past all the way to the elder spy's murder at the hands of agents of your Cuban DI two days prior.

I smiled crookedly in the face of Muir's casual sarcasm, terror struck over the truth he and I already privately knew; Muir's flesh-and-blood son had been arrested early that morning in China. You couldn't tell he knew it from his cool demeanor. I yearned to look as hapless as usual.

Muir handed Harker a folder. Harker gestured back with. "Sit down here, please."

"Something tells me no stripper's jumping out of a 'Who Cares? I'm Retiring!' cake any time soon," said Muir.

Harker sat between us. I sipped my coffee and waited. If I hadn't already known about Bishop's capture, I'd have no idea what I was doing here. Until I realized something larger: knowing this *was* about his capture, I still didn't know what I was doing here. Harker didn't like me. Muir was pretending not to—*definitely* pretending. Had to be. Why wouldn't he still like me? I mean, that wasn't real hate just now, not after he'd saved my life by taking the bullets from the gun I stole from him to kill myself with—one of 'em anyway—the night before.

Why'd he let me take his gun in the first place? Why hadn't he simply told me what he wanted of me? Why always leave me guessing? I could've had a drawer full of bullets at home and that would've done his little game right. I warmed to the idea of how foolish he'd feel right about now, and how superior I'd feel, if I'd one-upped him and had killed myself. Bang! Take that.

"This task force have a name?" said Muir.

Of the two other men already seated, they were Dr. Marty Hwang, sullen and dark, one of our resident China experts, and another man ten years my junior but with a subtle air of superiority that put him on par with the director and even Muir. In face and feature, he wore a Roman general's mask of benign ruthlessness with nothing of the Good Samaritan so many of our officers fake. A better writer than I would do him the justice he deserved. No doubt a master spy in that he was a relentless cipher who could be Muir's "all things to all people;" at that table, he came off as if he did it by being annoyingly himself. He was nameless and, by God, in the years to come and those years that follow, someone will pin him down. But at that moment, his still, quiet confidence screamed reality. It's a hard task to write about a real person and this was a person real and hard, physically capable of arm-wrestling dragons and winning most of the time. I tried to read Muir's assessment of the man in my mentor's gaze, but Muir's eyes were flint. They gave nothing, but that told me this man was not one of Muir's disdained "Young Turks." This younger man held Muir's attention.

I'm not the jealous type, but someone who is inclined to that emotion would be insane with jealousy. Were they me. But I'm not. I noticed it was hot and ran a finger along the inside of my collar.

Neither man answered Muir's question.

The inner door from the director's office opened and Director of Central Intelligence (DCI) Troy Folger, thick fingers never far from the Phi Beta Kappa pin on his waistcoat, strode in Jimmy Cagney ready to bellow a "Now he'ah this!" to the men of his reluctant crew.

"Nathan," he said.

"Troy."

"Good to see you. Thanks for dropping by." False joviality from the man who'd sent me to bury Muir's heart in Florida; when his close-lipped smile tipped to me, *his* hatred was real.

He stood behind his seat at the head of the table, reached for Muir with a handshake, keyed his teleconference console and spoke into it. "For the record, we've been joined by Nathan Muir, Near East Ops."

Director Folger cleared his throat. He messed with the end of his tie and sat beside Muir.

"We're in the process of dealing with a fairly specific—"

A sharp look from the nameless young knight cut him off.

The director swallowed the specifics. "International flap."

Harker stole a glance at Muir, who caught him with a grin.

"We brought you in here as a stop gap," the director went on. "Fill in a few holes for us."

"So, I'm like the Little Dutch Boy, huh?"

Folger laughed with all the authenticity of a pull-string doll.

Harker removed his glasses. He cleaned them. "We need you to be a team player on this one, Muir."

Muir let his grin grow. Harker couldn't take it. Bobbled back a nervous smirk. "Why is that funny?"

"Every time my coach told me that, I knew I was about to get benched."

I didn't like how this was going. I tried to grab Muir's attention, get something safe for my worry, but he'd ignored me since his greeting and continued to do so now.

"Due to the nature of this task force, Nathan, there will be certain information which you don't need to know," Director Folger said. "A week ago, Tom Bishop disappeared from Hong Kong Station. Early this morning, China time, he turned up outside Shanghai. He's been arrested for espionage."

Muir puzzled the words as if this was new information.

"We're working up a complete profile. Based on relevant personal histories and op records. This has to be handled with kid gloves."

"The Chicoms indicate what they plan to do with him?"

Harker made a bitter face at the old-school term for the Chinese.

Folger tapped steepled fingers against his lips. He folded his hands. "As of seven this morning our time, they've given the president twenty-four hours to claim him."

"And then...?" Muir glanced around the table. "What? They let him go? Shoot him?"

No one met his gaze. He wouldn't look at me.

Muir almost imperceptibly bobbed his head, accepting. "Doesn't give us much time to get Boy Scout out of there."

Harker tilted his chin to look over the tops of his glasses trying, purposefully it would seem, to appear a scolding school-marm, albeit directing his classroom-toned admonition only at the center of the table in front of him. "You heard the director, Muir. He wasn't sanctioned. He wasn't acting as your 'Boy Scout.'"

"Hasn't been my anything for years. Isn't that why you sent me to 'make a field decision' on him in Thailand a few months back?"

"Had you, we would not be in this situation, would we?"

"All I'm saying—"

"All *I'm* saying as your superior is that by his unthinking, unsanctioned, and illegal actions, Thomas Bishop has betrayed you, betrayed this Agency, and this country. He should be shot as a traitor." Harker snapped Chiclets teeth at Muir.

"By us or by the Chicoms?"

"Would you stop calling them that?"

I made it my duty to throw water on the grease fire. "I should point out, technically, that's incorrect. Title 18 *U.S. Code* 2381. Treason—"

"Pipe it down, Rusty," Muir muttered, and I did.

Director Folger rejoined with his most reasonable voice. "Gentlemen, Bishop has been classified as a common criminal and will be executed at seven a.m. tomorrow morning. Our time."

Muir looked around. "What about the press? First Rule of Thumb: leak it and throw the spotlight on China. Buy us some time."

"We need the press on this like we need a third tit," Harker sneered.

It sounded moronic then and would continue to sound moronic every time Harker insisted on puffing his chest with the inane remark. Right up to the day they rumba'd the boob off Campus with the ATROPOS debacle.

"You're using the other two?" said Muir.

Harker rubbed his jaw, laughed as if he liked it.

Folger said, "We don't want outside influences to"—he spread his hands—"limit our options."

"What was Bishop doing in China?" Muir sounded defeated.

"He was with an operation for Harry Duncan,"[1] said Harker.

"Was?"

"Yes… Until he took matters into his own hands."

Muir's face creased with alarm. "Where are they holding him?"

Folger lifted a hand. "I'm sorry, Nathan."

---

1   Harry Duncan: Chief of Operations, CIA Station, Hong Kong.

"It would be nice to know what gaps are to be filled," said Muir, waggling his palms. "I've only got ten fingers here."

More silence. Muir stared at Director Folger, who met Muir's concern with a bland smile. Muir scratched his head, leaning back with a befuddled sigh.

"Kinda tough timing," said Muir. "Week before the president's road trip. You guys afraid there's gonna be a congressional hearing?"

Another look around the table to everyone but me. Folger gave a noncommittal lift of his brow.

Muir pressed: "That's why we're transcribing and videotaping, right?"

Folger nodded.

"Are you going to want me to testify?"

"No," the director responded.

"No?"

"Absolutely not," said Harker.

The officer I didn't know leaned forward. "You met Bishop in Vietnam, right?"

Here's a list of five voices I hate:

1. Dick Cavett.
2. That new guy on PBS, Charlie Rose.
3. Donahue.
4. William F. Buckley.
5. Richard Harris.

And this guy. It made me hate him even more when Muir gave him the smile I thought reserved only for me... when he was *liking* on me.

"Yeah, thanks. Spring of '75. Hue had just fallen. Da Nang would go in a couple days... and I'd flown in-country to get an ARVN sniper who'd been with us throughout the Phoenix program. Was a heavy hitter named Binh. When I arrived, I was informed he'd been killed that morning in a mortar attack. Only option was to go American or go home. I took Bishop—his three kills nowhere near Bihn's forty confirmed, but there was something about him I liked. Came across as one of those idealistic types. A little bit of an attitude. Starts out trying to see what he's made of; ends up not liking the view."

"You liked that?" Harker chortled.

"Saw something of myself in him, you could say."

What these idiots didn't know—the fire they let Muir play with all these years. What I didn't know until this morning and my Sandy March–Muir Bishop's-my-son call.

"Who was the target, Muir?" That nobly obnoxious one again.

"Laotian General Malo Sayasone. Codename REDSHIRT. Responsible for the upcoming Saigon offensive."

"Did you have a Presidential Finding authorizing the kill?"

Who the hell was this guy?

"Troy—you want to tell me why he's here?"

Good, Muir's taking my lead for once.

Folger ignored.

Harker nagged. "Is there a finding, Muir?"

"Well, we were in a place we weren't supposed to be, assassinating a general from a country we weren't at war with—'course, we weren't officially at war with North Vietnam either, but—"

Muir was leaning back in his seat. I could see around Harker's back. Muir's hand slipped into his blazer pocket. *Finally* met my eye; looked me dead in it. Telling me something. I had no earthly idea what. I was up for it. Let's lift this ship right out of the water and turn it the other way. Heave a firecracker under old man Folger's seat and bam, bam, bam!

The USS Captiva, *that's how we sail.*

Only I had no idea what we were planning.

Muir manipulated his pager. Dropped it back into his jacket.

"Is that a no?" said Harker.

Muir leaned forward and huffed. "C'mon, guys. We're on the clock. The president admits Bishop is ours, denies he's a spy. We put out the fires and negotiate a deal. Unless I'm missing something."

They gave him nothing. Muir played into his feigned exasperation. Put both his hands on the tabletop like a casino dealer ready for a pit change. "That's it. I'm not liking how this is playing. First off, you want any more out of me, *he* goes."

I grinned, ready to see young CIA knight-o'-the-realm told to take his armor and go home. Until I saw what the rest were seeing: Muir's right hand finger-gunning me.

"Aiken?" said the director.

"Don't want him here," Muir snarled. "Anywhere near me. Ever again."

I gave my normal shoulder bounce, which Muir always said was the dumbest shrug he'd ever seen on a person.

"Not after the hit job he pulled on me yesterday." He leaned around Harker, eyes merciless. "Rusty, why don't you go find some little American flags to fold?"

It hurt: my feelings (even though I knew it must have been code); and my head (because I didn't know what the hell code he was speaking).

"Director: it's Dumbo over there, or me."

"Dumbo," I've discovered in the last twenty-four hours, this is highest compliment Muir ever pays me. Code, you understand.

I swallowed. My eyes burned. I slumped, clueless and useless... until, suddenly, I tensed tall and brilliant.

"It's about his flag—" Muir, *yesterday morning, a step off his porch.* *"I'm counting on you to take it from my office tomorrow."*

I hid my smile as I leaped—"Thank you, ev—" too quickly. My shoelace tangled on a chair caster. "—very-*uff*-one…"

No one cared.

It was not the first time this had happened, so I knew how to get out of it. As I squatted beside my chair, I heard Muir.

"Next, as I've already asked, someone needs to explain why Counterintelligence has their hand in my rice bowl."

I froze under the edge of the table. I'd never met him. I looked across at his shoes, maybe half-expecting to see cloven hooves. No sane officer ever wanted to meet him. And I'd always assumed he was older. *Much* older for the poison and fear that swirled with his name.

Silas Kingston ran Counterintelligence as his own personal empire. Where his legendary predecessor, James Jesus Angleton, had crippled the agency with his paranoid, internal Soviet mole hunts, Silas Kingston dropped the "Soviet mole" criteria, taking his greatest satisfaction in hunting down any CIA officer he saw fit for any/many perceived disloyalties.

The chief spy to spy on the spies and remake them in the image of "traitor."

THE US LAW ON TREASON is exact and hardly differs from treason laws in every other land. Chinese and Americans and Cubans are brothers in their distaste for traitors.

I left the director's conference room, trying to frame Bishop in terms of his being a traitor.

How I must frame myself: tonight, and for the rest of my life in *Havana.*

I find the traitor much closer to the hero than he is to the coward. When uncovered among us, the traitor is the essence of evil cowardice, venal and greedy. Why then are those foreigners we recruit as agents in foreign lands hailed by us as heroes? In their own countries, whose laws they are born and bound to, they are vile traitors.

The HOUNDFOX I deliver you tonight.

Surely the coward, who flees backward from the new and fearful, fails when faced with the mystery of his individual future. This is not the behavior of the traitor. Kierkegaard clarifies this by defining cowardice as a function of going along dumbly into the herd. Every single individual who escapes into that crowd, eternally surging as it always is, flees *into* cowardice.

The crowd is untruth. Therefore was Christ crucified.

In this regard, the direction of the coward's flight, backward or forward, is irrelevant. This must translate to the hero; it is not the forward direction of flight that makes a man heroic, but his aloneness. By practical definition, the traitor is not of the crowd and, by choice of action, eternally must be alone. Like the hero, the traitor flees into the new alone and, but for the political perspective of others, takes no part in the coward's crowd.

When David met Goliath, he selected five stones from the creek bed.

Did they scintillate like the De Beer boy's discovery in the South African dust? They did not need to. Their light's reflection belonging to the mind of God. These were the stones of true eternalism:

I. Faith.
II. Trust.
III. Courage.
IV. Obedience.
V. The Holy Ghost.

It only took one stone to kill Goliath, and it is up to each of us to choose, alone, as Bishop did that day in Suzhou, which of the five stones to carry into battle.

Nina's stone is still in its box. It is in hand's reach on this coffee table where I write, this Havana night. Its stone, "Trust," is mounted on a platinum infinity band designed as a snake swallowing its tail. I have aimed it, I'm afraid, at my own skull.

Deliver evil: live reviled.

But as the Dutch philosopher of a moment ago instructed: life can only be understood backwards; but it must be lived forward.

I WENT FORWARD from the Seventh Floor to Muir's office and Gladys. Bishop's burned American flag from Marine headquarters at Yudam-ni, Korea, waited, father to son and back to father, on Muir's wall. I'd planned to be booking travel to Hong Kong today to return it and, I imagine, reveal to Bishop the truth of his parentage. It all sounded so unreasonable as Gladys and I went to rescue the charred symbol of American loss and rescue, heroism and bloodline, from its frame on the wall.

We hear that the reasonable man adapts himself to the world, while the unreasonable one keeps at the world with a hammer and sickle—strike that, crowbar— attempting to force it to adapt to himself. The coward is too quick to adapt; the hero has no time to adapt; and the traitor ends up adapting purely for the sake of time.

I didn't comprehend any of this until the glial tumor was pried from my skull and two years later, assured by my blessed Dr. Rashmi the cancer cells have not returned, I am left with an unsettling and persistent epileptic condition. I am unreasonable to believe I can live/relive, déjà vu/skippity-doo my life neither forward nor backward, but simultaneous now, yet I believe it wholeheartedly and when it strikes me, I am the Ebenezer of time, filled with the best and happiest of all delight.

I know Nina is your captive as well as I know I came here alone. *This time.*

I also know at that time, as Muir returned to his office from the Harker/Folger/Kingston SIDESHOW interrogation responding to Gladys's page-prompted phone call, Nina walked into Muir's office behind him. She stood at his shoulder wearing a one-piece square-neck and sleeveless dress, bright yellow, glowing against the darkness of her skin. The garment was retro seventies and I'd seen her in it before when it wasn't. This time I noticed the collar, sleeves, and hem were trimmed white as a rabbit. Her mischievous eyes dared me to fall madly in love with her, but I'd already done that. Thirteen years earlier, March 15, 1978, when she'd removed the dress before me.

And still I fall, deep and slowly, knowing what will happen next.

She said, "I hear I'm taking you to Havana, Pintao—" her nickname for me on our madcap Manhattan acid trip—and I descend into that moment, reliving it more fully backward now than when it had occurred. When living life forward was the rage of the day and there was still time to do everything done wrong, right.

6

THE ENJOYMENT FROM LISTENING TO MUSIC is not in what you've heard as the piece or song plays forward. Nor is it found within the immediate moment you listen to; as your mind registers what you're heard, that which you hear is already in the irretrievable past. Hard to believe, but music carries no present moment. The enjoyment of music exists in a delicate and wonderful ability of the human mind to travel time. The brain has a natural inclination to harmonics. As music is heard, the mind leaps forward in anticipation of what you will hear next—countless predictive combinations of tone, pattern, and rhythm naturally pleasing are contextualized against the countless predictive combinations all harmonically unpleasant. All in a shaved-to-the-millionth instant. In music's highest artistic expressions—delicate and playful, thunderous triumphant, straining want, lushly romantic, or achingly melancholic—it is, in experience, the closest in disposition to love. An intense projection of emotional resonance, ever straining forward toward harmonic bliss, illuminated by the dulcet echoes of the past. Here, in the silence of my thoughts, I can express that knowledge only in the shimmer of memory's passage where music becomes thin and silent and pale. It is only an essence of love, as flame is only an essence of heat.

As a lifelong trafficker in words, obsessed with their utility, stroke-of-pen power, utter inadequacy, and innate coltish curiosity even when broken to harness, I purposely use the subdefinition of *essence* to highlight the inability of absolute meaning to find stickiness when pressed together to time. Letter clusters, thought carriers, and phonemic units of language.

This makes me anxious.

I am anxious over love as I am anxious over death as I am anxious you will not kill me over my definition of *traitor* as my words build anticipation to the death warrant you await me to deliver.

Three times in my life, Nina asked me, "Do you love me, Pintao?" Once in the past. Once in present. Once in the future. With my own voice, once in the voice of dreams, once as music.

Somewhere in or outside of Washington where your DI agents keep her alive, Nina's clock counts down those three instances to Christmas dawn in perfect beat to mine as you've given me this night to deliver on my promise. As I have heard the music of her voice—passion always stronger in her than fear—and, as you've shown me her video image live, I know at least, for now, your word is good. I fully comprehend, were your Cuban thugs to know Nina Estrada's true paternity, *su apellido real*, you wouldn't need me. You would know her father, and she, and I, and he would all be dead. But "Estrada," as you've now discovered, is but an empty road to nowhere.

"Do you love me, Pintao?"

Hurried from Muir's office, we were passing through the Baffles, a Langley corridor built as a labyrinthine zigzag—

Ah, how I long for Muir and his ball of string.

—with acoustic absorbent walls inlaid with inaudible electronic white noise: a corridor impervious to eavesdropping. And perhaps it was a condition intrinsic to the countermeasures that I heard it as my own question. Though the movement of her lips perfectly synched with the words I heard, I apprehend now such a phenomenon, universal of all humanity, is a humiliating illusion. In purely scientific terms, that thing we take for granted—lips synched with word sound—is a temporal impossibility. The speed of light is close to a million times faster than the speed of sound. No matter how close two people are to one another, the perfect synchronization we see between lips and spoken words is not real, but only a facet of our unconscious brain integrating the delay into our temporal interpretation of events. The temporal construction of consciousness is a highly edited version of reality, and who knows how far that stretches once we decide we can abandon time.

That is why, as I live it now, I am certain it was me doing the asking because I'd been asking it of myself nonstop since I'd lost Nina after meeting her and declaring I loved her (if only in my heart) the night we met and made love upon that New York hotel room bed. And every minute conscious or unconscious, since.

"No," I said. "And we're not going to talk about that for the duration we are now assigned together."

"'Talk about' what? Can you describe it?"

If teeth could be coy, her attitude would be all mouth.

"No grinning. It's best we say nothing at all until we're away from headquarters and you can tell me why you know where we are going and I don't, when I know more about Muir and March than you ever will."

"Fair, Pintao—"

"It's Russell."

"It won't be." Damned if she couldn't put a smile in her words even when her mouth and eyes hide the damn thing.

"I will need you to explain that," I ordered.

She didn't. As I'd ordered, she said nothing until we stepped to her car and I said, "You don't expect me to get inside that, do you?"

"I don't expect you to ride on the hood or trot behind."

"I have my own car."

"We're operational and, as you've pointed out, you'd like a briefing. That means we have between here and the airport." She unlocked my door, went around the diminutive front to her side and looked at me over the convertible soft top. "Don't you like my car?"

I had never seen a car like Nina's. It appeared to be the product of a mating between a 1960s Bondian Aston Martin DB5 and Roger Rabbit's pal Benny the Cab's sister.

"Did you make this yourself?"

"It's a Nissan. A Figaro. They're bleeding edge in Japan."

"What does it run on?" I couldn't believe it was, in fact, powered.

"The honey milk of human kindness. Get in."

She challenged me with an air of confidence that bordered contempt without taking comfort or prize from either, which succeeded in dizzying me into and out of our exchanges. For a two-seater, it was surprisingly comfortable. Postmodern styling sheathed you as if you rode inside a wink. Nina covered her eyes with Alanis Morrisette sunglasses before Alanis came around to make them popular. I say this with irony as thick as Ms. Morrisette's obnoxious hit ironically does not describe a single instance of irony.

Rain on your wedding day is only ironic if daddy owns an umbrella factory.

We left Langley onto Dolley Madison.

"I've been waiting for it to grow up, but I expect she's destined to be a puppy forever."

I humpfed, distrustful of her conviviality. "What color do you call this?"

"'Topaz Mist.' The Japanese say it is the proven color of fall."

Five years ahead of the Mini's return to America, better powered, and much happier with itself, I haven't seen one since, but I've heard they still sell brand-new '91s eleven years later, and Nina and I have laughed about getting another. This one in "Pale Aqua"—proven summer.

"Open the glove box. While you were dazzling them upstairs, I visited Technical Services and procured your travel kit and legend."

I found them. A brand-new well-used phony US passport with my photograph in the name of one—

"'Angelo Damon?' What am I supposed to be? Some pasta-potato Italian-Irish crooner?"

"Exactly. And when you go to pass it, they'll do the same thing you did: fixate on the unusual improbability of the name and misdirect from the forgery of the document."

Linda P. Morse would have loved Nina. I felt like a nomad headed into an uncharted desert.

"Don't expect me to sing for you."

"Not ye-et..." she singsonged back.

There was also an Angelo D wallet, with enough litter inside it—receipts, cards, laundry tickets, scribbled Post-its—to reasonably backstop my new and nonexistent life. I withdrew a dog-eared photograph.

"Ah, how well I don't remember it."

The meticulously distressed snapshot was an invented image of Nina and me in front of a Christmas tree.

"Are we married?"

"Are you proposing, baby?"

"Cut it out. How'd they produce this so fast?"

"It was all ready for Muir. A favor called at dawn, a bottle of scotch I delivered—they switched him out and you in."

"This is off the books, I assume?"

"Off the books and off the reservation."

Off the reservation.

A favorite Muirism: sometimes I wonder why he even needed the Agency at all. Until after his murder I understood he never did. But I had a whirlwind of other thoughts more important and pressing. I wasn't liking the familiarity Nina exhibited in speaking of Muir and speaking *like* him, as if she shined in Muir favoritism.

Had he screwed her?! Would he have done that to me?! Not to mention her.

"My father is HOUNDFOX. Muir says you're read in?"

"Only the broad strokes I got last night. One: your father is the Agency's most highly placed spy in the Castro government. Two: You're his conduit. Three: Once stateside, all HOUNDFOX product couriers directly through you. Why would you risk walking straight into the serpent's mouth?"

She didn't look at me. "You wouldn't risk everything to save your father?"

"My father was a trucker. A drug dealer on the side. He died on the road." I tempered my words colder than the October chill tossing in from outside.

"My question still stands."

One thing you'll come to know about me: I pride myself on not letting people get under my skin. I am a man of strong reserve, never revealing my inner voice.

"A day doesn't go by I don't wish for even a glimpse of him," I blurted.

She explained how your DI General Hector Guzman, anxious for personal revenge against Nathan Muir after having snarfed poisoned catnip from HOUNDFOX and acting upon it to murder Muir, accidentally assassinated Charlie March—CIA hero and Russia's longest running mole inside the Agency.

"It's down to a matter of hours before Guzman walks the sick cat back and learns my father's role in planting the false intelligence," she said.

"The cat's one trick is sometimes better than the fox's one hundred."

Nina looked over her glasses, eyes sparkling with irony. "Muir told me you do that."

"Do what?"

"Have an endearing habit of saying words that only make sense to you."

"He said that did he?"

"All but one word of it. That word was mine. I swear." She tipped her chin back endearingly to the open glove box. "The other kit belongs to me."

"And your parents'?"

"Didn't you notice my dress?"

"What dress?"

"Their escape kit is sewn into the new furry hem."

Maybe it was the open top, but she was all too breezy about the operation ahead. "Have you done this before?"

Her eyes glided over to me, discerning, waiting.

"Okay. Obviously, you haven't exfiltrated your parents before, otherwise we wouldn't be here. Have you escaped *anyone?*"

"Here's hoping first time's a charm."

"Don't think you need to fill me with confidence."

"As a courier, I escape Havana four to six times a year all on my very own."

I slouched, foolish and out of place, having never been anywhere to escape from.

We passed Fort Marcy Park, where two nights prior I'd tried to end my own life. I chose not to remark. I'd hoped returning home last night after closing the book on Muir with his retirement, after not having murdered my wife, not having murdered myself, a sense of balance would have been granted me.

"You hurt my feelings, you know," Nina said.

"Give me a break. It's been thirteen years."

We came to the split for the airport. Nina didn't take it, heading instead onto US-29N for downtown.

"I thought we were headed to the airport," I said, and may as well have been using my inner voice for all the attention it got me.

"And you kept hurting them. Never once—all these years—ever asking Muir about me."

"How would you know what I ask Muir?"

She was beginning to piss me off.

"I didn't know about *you* until yesterday," I said.

"Sure. Keep lying. We made promises to each other, Pintao."

"Russell. And we were blazing on LSD."

"You said you'd love me forever."

"I didn't."

"You did."

Did I?

Probably. "Not aloud."

"I'm not talking about in the hotel room with your body."

"Well, that's what *I'm* talking about."

"I'm talking about the other hotel room. The next night."

The night *after* Nina. The Roosevelt. The safe house where I'd OD'd on booze and strangled on conscience. "With Tom Bishop?"

"Before."

"What do you mean, 'before'?" I asked, guarded. "I wasn't there when you picked up the OPLAN and changed the safe combo.

I would have died if Bishop hadn't come back to save my life. You were long gone. I never saw you again after our one-night"—warning-flash eyes—"together. What?"

I looked at the passing cars as we turned off the freeway onto 18th. She was drawing me back to memories to which she had no right.

"He couldn't have helped you if I hadn't telephoned him."

"How would you have phoned him? When?"

"After I gave you CPR."

The cold wasn't coming into the car. It radiated out of me. Ice from my soul into my heart, my veins, to crystallize the hair on my head, my neck, along my arms.

"That's not true."

"What do you remember, baby?"

Bishop is beating on my chest and resuscitating me. "C'mon, baby, breathe!"

"I'm on the floor. The broken table. The vomit all over me—Do you really want to hear this?"

"Go on, I'd never steer you wrong. Ever." The gentleness of Nina's voice was the voice that had guided me through my acid trip in the park and through the city and the night.

"You weren't there. I see Bishop straddling me and resuscitating me, the puke dribbling from my mouth. I see my face—it's blue. I'd choked."

Nina did a bit of driving there, in and out of traffic. She turned left onto M Street. She knew where she was going. I was too uncomfortable in the past to care to ask.

"Now give me another memory," she said. "When you saw me walk into Muir's office today, who did you see?"

"Ridiculous question. You. Muir. And Gladys."

"And how did you see yourself?"

"I didn't. I'm me. That's how I remember things…"

I compared the two memories. I tried to remember anything. Firing my pistol at Madeline and her lover. Muir's sofa twenty-four hours ago he had three different lies for: I'm sitting on it, but in no instance do I see myself in memory.

Until that moment, I would have sworn in court, on penalty of death, without hesitation that Bishop gave me CPR on the floor of the CIA suite at New York City's Roosevelt Hotel. "I always thought it weird he called me 'baby.'"

My eyes were opened. My past had changed.

I see Nina. Only Nina. As if in a film, she is staring directly into a dim and shadowy camera that is my face beneath her. She is crying, administering compressions. The lens clears with life's return. The only person impossible to visualize in memory is yourself. In that sense, the past exists without you.

She smiled softly. She knew I knew. She saw an open spot along the sidewalk and bounced her little car into it. I studied her face as she switched off the ignition. Her eyes were directed toward the street but seeing into her past, seeing into me.

"You promised you'd pull through if I vowed to love you forever." Her smile, when she turned it to me, became a grin. "I didn't buy the eternity of it. I know how you get when you're drinking."

Damn Muir. Told her about yesterday too. No secret sacred.

My eyes on the dash. I didn't say a thing.

"Look at your wrinkled forehead. Your frown," she said. "My saving your ass make you angry?"

I was angry. Not at her. But at everything in the universe that wasn't her but was me and my place in it. "You ever have the dream—nightmare, really—where the truth about your life is revealed to you and it turns out you're fully retarded?

Not 'retarded' like you say friend-on-the-playground-teasing 'retarded', but IQ-less-than-seventy-one official mental retardation, and everyone else is taking care of you your whole life and it's all a giant game?"

"Constantly."

"You do?"

"Coddler's Intelligence Agency—isn't that where we work? *Of course not, Pintao.* Why would I ever call anyone, let alone a friend, retarded?"

"It's Russell."

"Never. Worst it gets for me is I'm back in front of a chalkboard at school in Havana."

"And you don't know the answers."

"I know all the answers. What I don't know is how my clothes fell off."

Evil fantasies against children, especially imagined leering lustful elementary Cuban schoolboys of a generation ago, is not something I suffer.

Putas.

"You were there," I said. "You saved my life."

"Until Tom Bishop threw me out. And the fact you never asked him or Muir about me all these years—your intentional lack of curiosity. That's hurt my feelings."

There was a right and a wrong thing for me to say.

"I'm happily married."

"Yeah. So I hear." She took a pregnant pause to term. "You don't have to marry someone to love them," she said. "Marriage is a testament to love, not a 'proof of purchase.'"

WHAT WE DISCUSSED NEXT will be meaningful to you. What I write puts me in full violation of:

18 *U.S. Code.* § 798. Disclosure of classified information. *Whoever knowingly and willfully communicates, furnishes, transmits, or otherwise makes available to an unauthorized person, or publishes, or uses in any manner prejudicial to the safety or interest of the United States or for the benefit of any foreign government to the detriment of the United States any classified information [...] shall be fined under this title or imprisoned not more than ten years, or both.*

Travel by Americans to Cuba is illegal. Doesn't mean Americans don't visit your island. *En particular*, officers of my three-letter agency in Virginia. All Americans—and you'd know better than I—are under scrutiny from the moment they arrive. CIA officers typically use Canadian passports or other foreign covers depending on secondary language skills they may possess. Particularly Spanish. We send them in under Spanish, African, French, Dutch, Central or South American identification. Many these days travel under Middle Eastern cover. They enter on tourist or exchange visas: economic, cultural, scientific or relief. A quick tourist jump can be made any day at numerous times from Mexico. Some of these officers rotate in and out without assignment for years, dulling your attention in case they are ever needed, but usually they are not, and after a time, another "floater" is rotated in to take their make-work place.

As this operation was seat-of-Muir's-pants off the reservation, for Nina and my purpose, this option was unavailable to us, while a straight shot in, simply relying on false one-time cover, would bury us under your security apparatus for too long before we could safely break away and execute our mission. In the nineties, however, the Agency learned to use DI heavy scrutiny to our advantage. Prior to an operation, over a course of weeks, we pack the flights with obvious marks, knowing you'll be up on most of them, resources stretched while you monitor their implementation of nonexistent ops with goals specified to achieve absolutely nothing. It's then we execute a second option: to run our agents' identities under the false flag of criminal narco-traffickers. While this always relaxes us from thinly spread direct monitoring, we get turned over to your Venezuelan or Colombian drug partners. Unless we have prior compromise over them—and many we do—we're practically just as stuck under their thumb. Still, it's better for us and usually brings results. But the third option isn't your blind spot.

There's a third way we took advantage of that trip (and continue to do so, until I suppose you process this). It's to enter Cuba with business legal in your country, but illegal in America.

The contraband Cuban cigar dealer.

We blind you by your own dear Fidel's delight in spreading Habanos throughout America in violation of our embargo. Generalissimo Castro's sly, ego-boosting knowledge everyone from Chicago mayors to the president of the United States to steroid inflated-muscle movie stars in Beverly Hills cigar clubs are paying inflated costs for the fourteen billion Cuban cigars burned from sea to shining sea to the tune of $280 billion dollars a year. We blind your DI by sheer tax-cheating capitalistic force.

Ho-ho-ho, oh-oh-oh.

Because Cuban cigars can't be smuggled into the US wholesale—which keeps the price way, way up—it takes hundreds of private-enterprise tobacco dealers coming and going from your island workers' paradise. These Americans are security-cleared

Part One: Deception 73

outside *tus chicos'* Ministry of Interior, by the Cuban Tobacco Enterprise Group, Tabacuba, within the Ministry of Agriculture. Once cleared, these American entrepreneurs carry a dealer's export license and your security and scrutiny over them is walled off and, in the spirit of machismo between your directorate and the agro-bureaucrats, always disgruntled and purposely lax.

The Havana equivalent of the Letters of Transit stuffed inside Sam's piano, and we play it again, and again and again as time goes by.

NINA AND I LEFT HER CAR and headed along the sidewalk. I saw the sign for Romeo & Juliet's Cigar Lounge. I asked her if they were expecting us.

"I doubt it. Muir said pick one out of the book."

"Wouldn't it have been easier and quicker to forge this license?"

"We don't know whose license to forge. Even if we did, how would we backstop it? This isn't exactly a legit operation Muir's running today."

I scowled.

"Ah, come on—be flattered he picked you to come with. He said you have deep powers of persuasion."

I wagged happiness into my face. "He did?"

She reached for the door. "Persuade away."

I stopped her from opening the full-length glass. "Why aren't you taking this more seriously?"

She smiled at her reflection. The same small, knowing smile we all saw on video tonight upon a face beaten and abused in your unknown DC basement interrogation room.

"I'm holding on by a thread as serious as death, and I'm doing my best to convince myself I'm wrong about you and you won't be the death of my family." She touched my chin. "I'm funny that way," she said, and kissed me.

7

OUR VISIT TO ROMEO & JULIET'S ended in *tragedy*. Not the primary definition of tragedy that gives us the two lovers taking their lives over bad advice from a monk. Nina and I were neither teens, nor was there any chance we'd be lovers again, which I believe I'd made forcefully clear. I'd gotten my wife back after almost having murdered her while she engaged in sexual intercourse with another man, and I was committed to the sanctity of matrimony. Nina and my R&J tragedy was lower, around the tertiary definition—the one where the main character's own inability to cope with unfavorable circumstances dashes him to ruin against the rocks.

The idea was to go into the cigar store, ascertain they traded in black-market Cuban cigars, and then enlist the dealer's aid in backing us with their export license as buyers in our trip to Havana. I strode inside, fired up to do right by Muir's endorsement, by Nina's faith in my adroitness, and by her family in peril. I engaged posture and tone of utmost persuasiveness. Suit and tie, my crooked smile, and a sparkle in my eye, I stepped in close to the proprietor and before he could waste my time with chitchatty greetings or glad-handed handshakes, I leaned in and said, "You appear a good American of the best intentions. My wife and I are looking to buy"—I lowered my voice to a smoke connoisseur's subtle throatiness—"your finest Cuban cigars."

He smiled, polite and knowing, and one hand on my elbow, the other extended to his humidor's glass-plate door, he said, "Cigar lover, eh?"

"You have no idea."

He opened the door. "Step inside. You'll find I have the finest Dominican and Honduran *parejos*, *figurados*, ring gauge, length, and wrapper: anything you want."

"You misheard, I think." I enunciated. "Q-bins."

"I'm sorry, sir. Cubans are embargoed."

I could see we would now dance the dance.

"I have… cash. No receipt necessary-o."

"Good for you, sir."

"And good for you we both know you have the good stuff."

Nina, who had followed us inside, abruptly left the humidor. It popped into my mind she also knew how the game was played. A man-to-man thing.

I smiled. "Good. Get down to it *mano-a-mano*, as they say in Havana."

"'Hand-to-hand?'"

"What?"

"What you said."

Not sure what part of man-to-man machismo the hand-holding fit with; maybe he didn't know Spanish. I winked. "Any way you wanna handle the pass."

He stepped back. He gave me the discerning up-down of his eyes. I breathed easier, although the overpowering tobacco smell tickled my nostrils and made me woozy.

"You're not a cop."

I shook my head. "Course not."

"I *know*. I sell Habanos to my cop customers. You are correct, though. The Cubans are the best. The 'good stuff,' as you say."

The deal: good as done.

"If your girlfriend—"

"Wife. Well, we're engaged." I don't know why I muddied around with it.

He leered, face expressing mutual chauvinist approval. "To her, I would have sold them. Right off the bat. No questions asked. I liked her immediately."

He ogled Nina through the glass. Not the polite smile you offer to someone who's significant other is standing right there. Not that I was jealous. Probably wouldn't have done it if I'd stuck to wife. And I'm not a bit possessive. Least of my qualities, lesser of my thoughts. I certainly wasn't thinking, *Perv on Nina like that again and I'm going to wring your fricking neck.* Just noting—operational habit. High-level training.

"What's not to like?" I smirked.

"You."

The crook in my smile zigzagged.

"You swagger like a floppy dildo. Who doesn't shake a man's hand?"

My hand shot out cobra fast.

"Save it, putz."

Nina glowered at me through the glass wall. This is where tragedy's heroic inability to "cope" reverts to *cope's* original meaning of "trafficking, bargaining, buying," and further found its alternate meaning of "monk's vestments" (mine not Friar Laurence's) which my hand burrowed into, whipped out, and flagellated the air with my CIA credential. I shoved it inches from his nose as Muir had taught me.

"You don't have much of a choice, putz."

His laughing "Get the fuck outta here," followed us to the street.

Nina lit into me in Spanish. Even if it had been in English, I would not have needed a translation. Or accepted one. Words are mere reflections of emotions; Nina's emotions were raw, and I knew all those raw words since I'd learned at an early age not to say *any* word not in the Bible. Anyway, I was busy dropping to my ass.

I am an expert at spatial awareness. I instinctively know where everything is in my immediate environment for precise navigation. It wasn't my fault I stepped on the marble. It had no business being there and, exactly what I've been saying for years: marbles have no *earthly* reason for being wherever I'm constantly finding them.

This marble went rolling as fast as I went falling. I crawled after it. Snatched it from the gutter.

"Green," I triumphed. I'd foretold the color from the instant I became aware of it under my foot.

Nina stared at me. "What's it like?"

"What's what like?"

"Living in a cartoon?"

WE LEFT THE SECOND TOBACCONIST, and I said, not too haughtily, "Okay. So now we're even."

"How can we possibly be even?"

I rarely state the obvious, but we were standing on the sidewalk, ejected more swiftly this time than the last.

She flicked switchblade eyes at me. "They only sell cigarettes, cheroots and drugstore cigars, pot and crack devices. Nothing hand rolled, so no chance of a Cuba connection."

"I saw the Zig-Zag rolling papers."

"You do know those are for cigarettes and marijuana, right?"

"You said hand rolled, you said cigars"—I pointed at the neon above the door and read out loud—"cigars."

She led us back to her cartoon car.

"All Cuban cigars *totalmente* are rolled by hand."

"And a drugstore cigar is what—made by a robot?"

Ever since Telly Savalas battled Talking Tina in The Twilight Zone, *I've despised robots. I eternally regret having succumbed to Jessie's exhortations for the infernal Furby—lurking, listening, learning all these years in evil silence. Room to room to room. Who knows, a dozen years since, how many households where now a Furby is in total control? The lights, the thermostat, the locks, the appliances, the music, all outside communication—a furry automaton enslavement—once innocent children have taught it to speak for itself. The good news: as most children were smart enough to reject mechanical mastery in toy form, sales dropped, and the product vanished from the shelves. When I got rid of Jessie's, I told her the last I'd heard from it, it was asking me where to catch the bus. Ever after, I've made careful note of toy-shop shelves. Furbies have mostly vanished. For those not, I, when unobserved, sabotage them in the package to make sure they never invade the home of anyone else. My little extra duty toward humanity. For now, humanity is safe from in-home robotic control.*

"Yes. *De mierda*—rolled from shit." The blaze of anger left her eyes. "You know nothing about cigars, do you?"

"One thing," I said. "With certainty."

The corners of her mouth curled slyly as she considered me. I masked my hard truth with limp neutrality. I watched her as she looked away to watch the road and I saw something I hadn't anticipated because I hadn't recognized the tension within her until it was now suddenly gone.

"Want me to guess?" she said.

"You won't be able to."

Her confidence grew with her grin. "Then, Pintao—"

"Russell—"

"I will get you to tell me."

"That'll be the day."

"Cigars—in concept, entirely and across all spectrums of time and space, habit and society—what is the one word you have for them?" Nina asked. "I don't want you to say, just think it."

"You can read my mind?"

"Want me to do it right now?"

"Yes."

Nina grinned. "You're thinking, 'She can't read my mind.'"

I was. "Am not."

"We'll see. I'm going to mention three things and you're going to grade them."

"How?"

"School grades. Clothing on. Ready?"

"Always."

"You know what jelly shoes are?"

"I met my wife in them."

"They must have looked winsome on you, baby."

"Funny."

"Jelly shoes. Grade?"

"F."

We headed over the bridge into Georgetown.

"Books?"

"A." I suddenly figured her out. "No! Wait, B."

"Too late. No use lying. F-A…"

"No use going on," I sulked. "I won't say what you want."

"I've already won the game. Making my last question more about my knowledge of you than your opinion of cigars."

"It isn't an opinion."

"In*deed*?"

"Is that a letter D pun? Because for a pun to work—"

"Whatever. Forget it."

And I did. Forced it from my mind. But all that replaced it was a sensation in the pit of my stomach. Butterflies, which in a large flutter are always a visual joy. (But smelly.) What did I have to possibly be joyful over, winged worms batting around inside me?

I grumped, "What's the third one you're so sure I'd give a D to?"

"Rubik's Cube."

"Why would I do that…?"

She considered me, sagely. Chose words knowingly. "You can't give it exactly an F because we both know a small group of people who don't cheat and don't give up, solve it."

"Of course that's why. Yes, F-A-D." I gave it to her in pleasant bewilderment. "And that's what cigars have become in America. And I hate fads."

"I hate fads, too," she said. "Belgian waffles. Vegetarianism. Don't get me started on what they've done to coffee, selling it with a mermaid as twenty kinds of desserts."

"Yes! Those people claim to be, but they *aren't* coffee drinkers. And dogs? When did they get the rights of children?"

"When did they get seating inside restaurants?"

"Agreed. I was against it with the seeing-eye dogs. Once they got into restaurants, it was all over—and to what purpose? They can't read the menu to the blind people."

She grinned. She drove. She flashed her teeth. "And those little furry talking gremlin for kids: worst of all! Only an idiot would—what do they sell you on, 'Adopt a Furby?' Only a fool would buy their kid one of those insidious bots."

She drove. She flashed her teeth again. She gave me a funny look.

"I'm sure I don't know what you're talking about."

WE FOUND PARKING on Wisconsin and walked back on M to Patriot Tobacco. Simply because she'd read my mind didn't make us a pair. There was no possible way she had the intelligence on my, I'll go ahead, *passion* for faddism, and I rebutted that—sentient of a murmur in my blood running redder for Nina, my sudden rapparee of repartee—the butterflies unnaturally loosed anything different from the word we'd agreed to spell. We weren't paired that way.

I entered the establishment. This time, I swore I would not fail her or, admittedly, myself. This time, I shook hands with the young man who greeted us. I asked if he was in charge. He said that he was in charge. Good. I asked if he supervised all sales and, yes, he said that he did. I moved in closer. He stepped back. I asked if he oversaw the purchasing. Here, I could detect in his person, see in his eyes, he knew what I was getting at.

"I'm only the manager. The proprietor comes in tonight. After six."

I didn't need to look to see Nina's deep frustration. I needed to act. Fast. An employee dumped loose pipe tobacco into a pan scale for a customer.

"Excuse me."

I pushed the customer aside. I lifted the pan and spilled the tobacco (mostly) back into its large ceramic jar. (Okay, mostly on the floor.)

"Hey!" yelped the manager.

I dug the marble from my pocket as he stalked over. I dropped it into the scale pan. I lifted a hand, forefinger pointed at the ceiling like Daniel Webster, then thrust it at the scale as though the devil itself.

"Do you know what that is?"

"A marble?" The pipe-tobacco customer tried to be helpful.

I read the scale: "Zero point one-six ounces."

"So what?" the manager growled.

"On a *legal* balance, this marble weighs zero point one. You're over by point-zero-six"—I went for the kill—"putz."

All traditional-size marbles weigh 0.16oz. Suffice it to say, I have an undue familiarity with marbles.

I brandished my CIA credential, closing it before anyone could read it. "Department of Weights and Measures, sir. You are in violation."

I glanced at Nina. As serious as I, she held her own open credential for all to see, but not too closely.

"Depending on how long since we last inspected—" I cut myself off. "When was our last inspection?"

"Isn't it on the sticker you put there?"

Hadn't considered it that far. The date on the sticker was from two years ago.

"What does the date have to do with it, anyway? Except to indicate compliance."

Baffled, I shook my head. "The way you people try to rig the system…"

Nina closed in. "Every overage of every sale since then until now will be adjusted, taxed, and penalized."

THE PROPRIETOR, a tall, light-skinned Latino in a cinnamon silk suit, a heavy gold chain on his right wrist and a yellow gold Breitling Sextant wristwatch with a deep blue face and band with a diamond crown, arrived fourteen minutes later. At his invitation, we joined him in his office. Soft music played. Some 1960s samba. It seemed like background to me, but Nina's eyes snapped attentively as if reading the lyrics from the air.

Ay ye ye, ay ye ye Ma Mai Oshún…

"What?" I whispered.

"Nothing." She shook her head. "It's a song I haven't heard for a long, long time."

Ay ye ye Ma Mai Oshún, Ay ye ye Oshún mare...

The cinnamon-clad proprietor asked to see my credentials. I handed it to him across his desk.

"This has nothing to do with my scales."

"No, sir," I said. For clarity: "I was lying."

Lastimado es el que cae en el canto engañoso de Oshún.
Lastimado es el que busca la Brujería del amor

He snorted softly. Leaned back in his leather chair. Saints candles glowed, flickered on the credenza behind him. He didn't look happy, but he wasn't exactly angry. Without another word, he replayed the security video and chewed the edge of his lip. He almost smiled, once. He stared at us, making room for my annoyance with his music to increase.

Oshún con Shangó, el amor es bueno solo si duele!
Shangó con Oshún, el amor es bueno solo si duele!

Too loud. Too strange.

"You mind turning down the music?"

He ignored my request. He said, "I'm going to take a guess—you entered my store with no idea Director Troy Folger buys from me."

We didn't answer. He didn't expect us to.

"Judge Sessions also shops with me." William Sessions: FBI Director. "Your behavior is as juvenile as it is reckless and desperate. You're not here under orders, but you're willing to expose your identity—put at least your career at risk over...?"

He picked up my green marble. I held out my hand. He returned it.

"You're not a pair of dipshits trying to get ahold of some Cuban cigars—"

"We are," I interrupted. "I mean, not the dipshit part. Obviously."

The proprietor cocked his head at Nina.

"*¿Habla español, señora?*"

"*Soy señorita cubana.*"

"*Ah. Bueno. Yo tambien soy cubano,*" he said and ignored me for the rest of their conversation.

A CUBAN EXILE of the 1980 Mariel boatlift, along with his friendships with both the CIA and FBI directors, Victor Rubio, was on close terms with the new DEA Administrator, Robert C. Bonner, having worked as an undercover asset for that agency fifteen years before retiring four years and forty convictions ago.

We left his office with a letter of introduction to Cuban Tobacco and the factories of his three main suppliers.

"You did it, Pintao. Worth its weight in gold. He told me he does over ten million dollars' worth of business a year with Cuba."

"Russell—and you're gonna stop the Pintao bit, I mean it—and why would he risk it? I don't trust him. Any of this."

"Way he sees it, if we fail, the punishment will be ours and ours alone. His business is too important to their economy. They'll buy whatever lie he tells to dig our graves deeper."

"Probably making the call right now. I saw the way he mocked me."

"Is that what you saw? Such little faith in yourself, baby." She shook her head and switched on her ignition. Instead of driving, she stared at me with something between concern and admiration. "Do you know why he helped us? And it wasn't my hot ass."

"What? My good looks and charm? Maybe the 'Patriot' name on the door?"

Victor Rubio could look at her ass all he wants. She could look at his. And his hairy arms. And he's too old for her anyway. Their business; we're all adults and I'm married. Anyway. What does my heart harbor for her? Nothing.

Okay—once. One time. More buoy than harbor. When I was single.

Time that doesn't return and wrap around and lead us back to take us forward. Don't feel a thing. And if I was dying to feel her body against mine, that was against her, not me. Best kept to ourselves.

"If you want me to say I'm jealous, you'll never get that out of me."

Nina blushed, but with her dark skin, it was easy to pretend not to see it.

"We discussed his religion. He practices the faith of our island. Our Cuban Santería."

"Voodoo? Great. That's all I need."

"Yeah, Pintao—he's into zombies. No. Your green bead."

"The marble?"

"Nooo… look at it."

I did. It had once been a marble, no question, but upon examination, I now saw a hole drilled through the green glass sphere.

"What does it mean?"

Nina glanced at her dashboard clock before pulling into traffic.

"If I hurry, we can make the noon flight to Cancun."

I wasn't done with Victor Rubio. "And?"

"He believed it's from an Orula bracelet. Or making its way to one."

"What's an Orula?"

"'Who.' Orula is a divine being. The *orichá* of divination, the supreme oracle. He is a great healer, the great benefactor of mankind. Its chief adviser. He lives outside of time. Carries the knowledge of the secret things of man and nature, as well as the accumulated knowledge of the history of humanity. They say he was there to witness the Big Bang—"

What Victor "Orula" wants with her, no doubt.

"—The bracelet your bead belongs to is a sacred emblem. It's believed to be a bridge into the realm of the saints and the gods. An amulet that offers the wearer protection, communion, and control over the spiritual realm. Why did you crawl after it? Keep it? You seemed to know something."

She had me off balance again. I didn't like that I liked this brand of woozy.

"The 'why' is as unbelievable as what he said. I don't want to go into it right now. Ask me some other time."

"Ah, we have a future." She turned her face to me, and I was like a man stepping out of a cave seeing sunlight for the first time. If I were a cartoon, my heart would have done that "powie" thing, stretching out from my chest.

"Why are you smiling at me?" I said.

"Ask me about it. Later."

We went onto the freeway and made speed toward Dulles on I-66 W.

"Victor wants something in return for helping us."

Of everything I could imagine, there was excessively much of nothing in this statement I liked.

Nina continued. "He made me promise I'd bring him back *la esencia del alma pura de una mujer.* Do you understand what that means?"

"A shot glass with *Havana* painted on it?"

She flung back her head and her laughter sounded like wry bells.

I didn't continue. I knew what he wanted. *La esencia del alma pura de una mujer* is the essence of a woman's pure soul. I stared ahead at the highway. Like I said, I'm the least jealous man God made. So, it wasn't jealousy. I already had a wife, didn't want a lover, but as her comrade for this mission—this mission only—a slight bit of possessiveness could be an edge. Honed for operational intercourse. And what is pettiness but a sign of caring in minute detail?

Watching Nina from out of the corner of my eye revealed an unguarded moment of, if not worry, sorrow rise across her features like the smoke when you blow out a candle.

I prayed I knew what she wished for, but these were saints' candles, not birthday, from a religion I didn't know and wouldn't trust. I would learn to regret all that would happen through it to Nina and the purity of that soul because Victor Rubio wanted Nina, and to save the life of her father, Nina had given Victor Rubio her word.

Age nine, Nina leans over her birthday cake, the playful flames dancing forever in her joyful future filled eyes. A camera flashes, forever capturing the moment from all that happens next.

8

螳螂捕蟬, 黃雀在後.
*"The mantis stalks the cicada, unaware
of the yellow bird behind."*
—Chinese proverb

I F NOT FOR THE TIANANMEN SQUARE MASSACRE, I would not be stalking a shameful future in Havana. If not for the Soviet Union's abandonment of COMECON, their system to ensure economic development along Soviet controls among satellite states—known as the *Consejo de Ayuda Mutua Económica* in Cuba, which ushered in the horse carts, missing zoo animals and house-cat dinners of your back to the future *Período Especial*—you would not have expanded relations with China in 1991. Because you seek to expand trade, credits, and investment relations with China today, and because Nina's survival means more to me than my country tomorrow, General Trigorin: what I share now is vital for both of us.

On May 20, 1989, Paramount Leader of the People's Republic of China, Deng Xiaoping, surrounded by bodyguards and generals, peered over the roof of the Great Hall of the People into Tiananmen Square, where one million student protestors to Communist Party corruption gathered, demanding democratic reforms. Heard to mutter one of his famously bizarre oaths inside the D Annex: "Pig dog!" (an atheist's loosely translated "God damn!") he declared, "The situation forces us to take radical measures to end acts against law and order."

Deng declared martial law.

On June 3, three hundred thousand soldiers, tanks, and helicopters surrounded the protests with orders to intervene if the students did not disperse. The students overturned buses and ignited them into flaming barricades.

Deng gave the order: "Clear the square."

The tanks and armored vehicles rolled. The soldiers opened fire. Ten thousand students lost their lives. Many more fell wounded and maimed.

To this day, the CIA claims we had no part in the protest. We were "innocent bystanders"—the identical bywords we flaunted after our Bay of Pigs, where CIA agents fell to the patriotic guns of *La Revolución Cubana* on your Playa Girón before Kennedy shot plausible deniability in the foot by admitting our stumble. Same words we flout today, having armed and trained the *mujahideen* now hellbent on killing us all.

In truth, the CIA never lets a good protest—Color Revolution, we call it—go to waste. Many of the student demonstrators drank their free handout, first Coca-Colas on the square in the weeks leading to the massacre; later photos from the barricades clearly show empty Coleman Camp Fuel cans at the barricade point-of-origin flashpoints—fourteen years before Coleman built its first China factory and, this year, opened Chinese distribution and sales.

Freedom movements inside enemy nations—especially those with no chance of success—not only create unrest and distrust among the population and embarrassment for the regime, but when forcefully brought to tragic conclusion by such totalitarian regimes, the human rights violations draw international condemnation; enemies of the state crushed on gravel beneath the boot become martyred heroes in international press heaven. This creates leverage in foreign relations. Especially necessary at a time when—up to, during, and after the massacre—George Bush I pursued direct, secret trade negotiations with Deng.

Two nights after the massacre, while watching "Tank Man," the Unknown Protestor, make his defiant stand in front of a column of Chinese tanks, my telephone rang in the study of my 1938 Tenleytown townhouse.

Say it aloud and you'll feel something akin to the electric thrill I once enjoyed. 1938 Tenleytown townhouse. Rolls off the tongue, doesn't it?

It was around midnight, and I was a bit surprised to be receiving a call. I'd not been involved in any CON- or OPLANS regarding Operation HAROLD HILL, our designation for the color revolution named after that boys' band bamboozler who'd fooled the kids of Iowa there'd be a parade for them at the end of the day for their River City troubles.

"Aiken here?"

"Are you asking or telling me?" Tom Bishop's voice crackled at me over long-distance lines, two years before his capture in Suzhou.

Last I'd heard, he'd been running covert riverine ops in the Philippines against their communist rebellion launched in 1969, which continues to this day.

Gotta hand it to you Marxists for stick-to-itiveness.

"I'm— I don't know— What? Why?"

I always make sure I'm clear with Tom so there's no misunderstanding.

He sounded far away.

"Are you in town?"

"Been with Harry Duncan's company since *Music Man* started production."

I heard him regulate his breathing. I held an image of Bishop behind his rifle, ready to blow a hole through someone's head. "They've taken her."

"Who and *who?*"

"Chinese. The woman I love."

"You have a Chinese girlfriend?"

I'd never seen Bishop with any woman. Date, friend, or karaoke buddy.

"Did you follow policy regarding 'Personal Relationships with Nationals of High Intelligence Threat Countries and Organization?' NSDD 197 directs you to report your involvement to your regional security officer for Counterintelligence review, especially seeing as she's communist."

"Who said she's a communist? She's British."

"Ah," I said, putting it all together. "Hong Kong Chinese."

"Why do you keep saying she's Chinese? Jesus—I didn't call for Rulebook Aiken, I called for Russell Aiken. You in there somewhere? Focus: you're the only human I trust will help me. I don't know if she's trapped, arrested, killed—"

"Holy shit. Cupid finally gotcha! You're in love!"

I've learned to live with it. I have 100 percent accuracy at saying the absolute wrong thing at the absolute wrong time. Why I like to spell it out. Or, maybe that's "right time" since the "wrong time" would make it a double negative, and while I'm right most of the time, I'm not right when it counts most, which would be wrong.

Tom Bishop died two years ago in Malaysia.[1] Best friend I've ever had and could have ever wanted. He understood me. So, to my absolute worst, he said his absolute best.

---

1   I refer you to the public US Congressional Record 107th Congress, SSCI 04 June 2001; Acting CIA Director Jeremy Harker III "I would like to add two names to the record...an officer and his agent who... died so that the people of Malaysia might be spared the horrors of nuclear enslavement and annihilation. I would like entered into the record the names of Thomas Bishop and [Dutch Colonial asset] Dand van Eijk."

"Thanks, buddy. You've never failed me. Her name is Elizabeth Hadley.[2] She's an international relief worker."

"Doctor?"

"RN. Among other things. She went over to the mainland before martial law was declared. Now she's vanished. I don't know if she's dead, hospitalized, arrested, or on the run."

"What group is she with?"

Bishop hesitated. "The troupe she works with is, sort of... non-union."

His hesitation didn't bode well. "Does our production company ever stage shows with them?"

"Opposite. She hates our theater group. Especially Muir."

"I don't doubt it and it serves him right. What do you need me to do?"

"The French are putting together a show in Hong Kong. They're calling it YELLOW BIRD. I want us in on it: you on script, me center stage."

THE NEXT DAY, I was on with Harry Duncan to design the CONPLAN for CIA participation in Operation YELLOW BIRD: the mission to locate and extract as many of the student and political dissidents who had participated in the Tiananmen Square demonstrations now running from arrest, imprisonment, and execution.

The French, British, and the Hong Kong Alliance in Support of Patriotic Democratic Movements handled YELLOW BIRD activities in Hong Kong, smuggling the dissidents to freedom in the West. That part of the operation has become well known and

---

2   Hong Kong-born British subject. Deceased, 29 October 1998, Taiwan, cancer. Hezbollah terror connected.

bragged about. Never revealed is how those dissidents got out of mainland China in the first place. This fell to Harry Duncan's DIANA RED network of Chinese agents hidden in plain sight on the mainland. Tom Bishop and this network of spies would guide them from in-country to the Pearl River Estuary where Chinese Triad mafia smugglers would function as the conduit across the South China Sea to the British-held island. While Bush pressed trade with Deng, openly refusing asylum to dissidents who presented themselves at our Beijing embassy, his Presidential Finding attached to my final OPLAN authorized the CIA/DIANA RED underground railway. We supplied disguises, false papers, Scrambler brand phones, military night-vision goggles, handheld infrared beacons, speedboats, and weapons.

In the following section, I endeavor to provide information that exposes CIA sources and methods used in Operation YELLOW BIRD. Although DIANA RED no longer exists on CIA payroll, its members scattered to the wind by Nathan Muir before his murder, five Chinese agents of said network remain at large in China.

In this document, I will betray their identities. They will be useful to you.

Heroes to the US and pro-democratic Chinese in Hong Kong, Macao, Taiwan and worldwide, they are traitors to China under the Crimes Ordinance (covers treason and sedition), the Societies Ordinance (crimes resulting from aiding foreign political bodies), Public Ordinance (national safety and secessionist activities and subversion). All of these, since 1997, added to Hong Kong Basic Law in Article 23. I am too far fled into my own treason to experience personal or moral compunction at their exposure and fate. They chose the life; they pay the price.

Like Bishop, my loyalty is to the life of the woman I love.

What I provide within the following section are CIA-China secrets to turn against my former Company, and for you to barter for better position with China in your present negotiations. Which, you should know, your US enemy is aware of and works to disrupt.

IN HIS QUEST TO SAVE THE WOMAN who would become his wife, Tom Bishop guided fifty-six fleeing dissidents from Mainland China to Hong Kong, new lives and freedom beyond. Of each, he asked if they knew or had information on Elizabeth Hadley. Throughout June and July, he learned nothing. Then in August, he heard she never made it out of Tiananmen Square alive. As proof, they presented him with a shoe. Tom recognized it as Elizabeth's, but refused to accept the bloodstains as hers, or as proof of anyone's death.

Bishop continued faithfully and tirelessly in his work. Helping them was helping her and all to which she had dedicated her life.

By September, the PLA had collapsed 70 percent of the routes; they'd locked down the coast with military outposts and vicious-dog patrols; fast launches to rival the Triad cigarette boats for speed, seamlessly coordinated with helicopters and spotting aircraft. YELLOW BIRD barely persisted, but Bishop, unwilling to risk going back to Hong Kong for fear of being unable to return to the mainland, remained constantly on the move, never spending a night in the same shed, alley, culvert, or refuse dump twice.

Implemented by agents of DIANA RED, he created a coded communication system based on medical terms to use over the state-monitored telephone lines. "Western doctor said it was heart disease," meant the mission was successful, the dissident safely in Hong Kong. If the message came in, "Chinese doctor said it was arthritis," it meant they still waited on the mainland. Diagnosis of a "tumor" meant arrest, while a "fatal tumor," meant exactly what it implied. As August dwindled and terminal cancer became the daily diagnosis, Bishop struggled to keep the last few escape arteries vital and flowing. He held out hope he would find his love alive.

Mission fifty-seven for Bishop came as an "arthritis" message from Leibu, a village excluded from usage by the YELLOW BIRD escape network due to the People's Liberation Army barracks erected there in the 1970s that, in 1982, remanded its soldiers to the newly organized People's Armed Police and assigned the force of two hundred personnel to police duties for two cities and ten villages in the greater principality. To make matters worse for the dissident who had been hiding there for six months, Leibu was only accessible through Hetang Town, a small city on an island between the confluence of three waterways. The four bridges of Hetang Town—heavily guarded checkpoints—provided the only passage to the rest of the country.

The elements that made Leibu too great a risk for DIANA RED's YELLOW BIRD personnel-intensive nonaggressive relay operations perfectly suited Bishop's attempt at a solo rescue. The Leibu garrison commanded obedience by power of presence. The soldier-police outnumbered the villagers four-to-one. This cemented a mindset in the local population of the foolishness in any unlawful travel beneath the eyes of the enemy. Further, even if one were lucky enough to escape Leibu unnoticed by the barracks, they would only get as far as Hetang Town. No matter how good their papers and disguise, once they checked through the first bridge chokepoint on to the island, they would be trapped in the belly of the beast. Papers that brought them into Hetang Town without interrogation would not be papers that would allow them to cross an outbound bridge to anything other than a return to

Leibu. Here again, authoritarian arrogance and display of power blinded the Chinese to a onetime quick dash by boat. Beneath their checkpoints, a fast boat disguised as a small, fisherman's sampan could get in and out unnoticed and be in Hong Kong in a day. The top decider for Bishop, which would have led him to storm the Forbidden City: intelligence indicated the dissident six months hidden in Leibu was a Hong Kong female Caucasian.

Harry Duncan believed it all a setup; throughout YELLOW BIRD, operations too good to be true, were. And everyone who gave in to their temptations never returned. He would not allow Bishop to commit anyone from the DIANA RED network to something both perilous and foolhardy.

"Think about it, Tom. Every day you've been pinging everyone you meet about Elizabeth. What did you expect would finally echo back?"

"With or without your approval, I'm going."

"I know. But you'll go it alone. And I will require your predated and signed resignation and indemnification of the Agency couriered to Hong Kong Station before you go get yourself killed. I want to be able to lie my hands were clean."

"Aiken will write it for me. They got working faxes over here. I'll sign whatever he says."

I did. He did.

Along with the intel on the woman Bishop was convinced was Elizabeth Hadley, Bishop had the location of the ramshackle wood-and-concrete apartment building with the unit number where inside she lay hidden. Satellite photos placed building doors opposite the village police precinct that itself fronted the district barracks. A maintenance entrance at the rear of the apartment building showed access through an undeveloped lot the barracks used as a graveyard for broken-down vehicles.

Bundled in the blue cotton boiler suit and cap of a traditional Chinese worker for the six months of YELLOW BIRD, Bishop operated inside China wearing black hair and facial disguise to his eyes. He limited his activity to darkness, his movements to the edges of roads at the edges of towns and then only as close to the country's edge as possible. Unable to rid himself of the rangy Western looseness of manner and bearing bred of the California foothill freedom of his youth, he avoided all unnecessary observation at any range in any light. Even with a brief, accidental sighting with numerous options for quick escape into the surroundings, he'd never trusted his disguise's efficacy as anything more than momentary advantage. For his mission to Leibu, 446 kilometers into China's interior, the broad river and partially tented boat would allow his disguise to provide basic cover from shore observation, but in busy river traffic, his camouflage would not withstand anything more than the most casual scrutiny during daylight, and on water there would be no quick escape. This cut his operational window by half. Traveling only at night, it would take him three nights.

At 8 p.m., November 14, 1989, Tom set out from the Pearl River Delta into the Xi River System that would carry him to Hetang. Hunkered in darkness at the stern of his sampan, he kept his modified outboard engine low and slow heading north on the Bei River. Around 4 a.m. the next morning, having navigated from the quiet Bei to the wider, more trafficked Wujiang River, he hid his boat among a fleet of garbage scows and waited out the daylight. He followed the same plan the second night, transiting from the Wujiang to the Chungjiang where, beneath the Buliping overpass, he topped off his gasoline from a DIANA RED supply cache in the brush beyond the Danguiyuan Drug Store parking lot. From the Chungjiang to the Lei, to the wide, heavily commercial and industrial-plied lanes of the Xiangjian River, which fed him back into the countryside, at 2:00 a.m. on the seventeenth, Bishop pulled into a marsh below the island town of Hetang. He covered his craft in heavy reeds and entered the countryside on foot.

It was cold and misty as he traversed rural farm fields in fallow, and cut across summer-harvested orchards. Five a.m. found Bishop on a hillside apricot grove, some remaining fruit shriveled on boughs and fermented in piles on yellow grass. He lay behind a bundle of black-barked, pruned branches overlooking Leibu and the rickety apartment building he was convinced held his precious Elizabeth.

He could feel Elizabeth's fear and, beneath, her unspoiled love emanating from the gray, silent face of the building. He let it armor him for the task ahead.

He scanned the building and the village with a miniaturized lowlight spotting scope. Activity at the police precinct and the barracks beyond was subdued and spoke to business as usual. A scatter of villagers trundled on the single cobbled main street, swept dusty storefronts, or polished holes through the dirt caked daily upon their windows to see the comings and goings of soldier-police. A tantalizing fifty yards below Bishop's hilltop, the rear entrance to the apartment building beckoned. Half the distance from his position, Bishop's approach would fall from sight of the town, visible only to residents passing their windows, or to anyone in the abandoned, derelict motor pool.

He wasn't concerned with the residents. By now they would know of Elizabeth among them. Having so far done nothing against her, they could be assumed, if not tacit in support of her, anxious for her to be gone without the authorities the wiser to their unchosen complicity. Bishop knew her health would be precarious as it had been in a similar circumstance in the Philippines. Her spirit might be shattered, and he wished he'd brought something personal to give her. Something tactile to reconnect. But as he moved down the hillside, a larger problem revealed itself. Beneath the overhang of the apartment's back door stood two People's Armed Police sentries.

Though armed, Bishop observed chairs behind them. They smoked, slouched lazy and bored. They weren't protecting the vehicles, as nothing salvageable remained on or inside their rusting hulks. He reasoned if this were a trap, the men would be posted vigilant inside. Cigarette butts strewn across the area spoke otherwise to the guards' presence as nothing more than the perpetual nuisance of authoritarian monitoring of enslaved civilians, there to harass penned residents from coming out on their own recognizance to any kind of uncontrolled particle of freedom.

Bishop felt the presence of his knife beneath his cotton padded blue jacket. He could dispatch this pair silently with ease, but unable to gauge how long it would be until their corpses were discovered, he dismissed the idea. He resigned himself to monitoring their twenty-four-hour pattern. Find its flaw. Execute his snatch-solution behind their backs.

He studied the blank windows of the building. He found the window of the apartment he'd been told contained Elizabeth. Faded, worn fabric hung limp and unstirring. Bishop imagined her having secretly watched the summer apricot harvest behind its frayed edge. She adored apricots. While still dark, Bishop decided to locate two or three of the sweet fruit still good for eating. He crept back over the hill's crest to hunt among the trees. He hadn't been at it long, dawn's gray light barely alive, when he caught sight of a figure furtively clambering in his direction from the far side below. Bishop drew his knife. He went prone, vanishing into a swirl of ground fog.

9

BISHOP FOCUSED ON the single individual through his spotting scope. By age and attitude, the old man clearly had as little business on the orchard hill as Bishop. Like Bishop a moment earlier, he hunted the harvest's remainder. Less fussy about the edible quality of fallen fruit, he stuffed bruised, skinned, and squishy apricots into his stained and greasy over-the-shoulder pouch. Bishop didn't have to wait long before the old man was close—no more than twenty feet—on his knees and sifting through the pile of lopped sticks and branches Bishop had searched minutes before.

Bishop struck.

The old man tumbled backward under Bishop's weight; Bishop's knife pressed along his throat. Bishop stared into pond-water eyes, murky with age, set in a wizened, bewhiskered face, gray beard long and tied off both near his chin and at its end. It resembled the tail of an old fox.

Bishop relaxed his hold and sheathed his knife. The old man scrambled out of reach, clutched his cap and bowed fervently all the while whining softly for mercy. When Bishop spoke, the man froze. His face snapped upward, moist eyes staring into Bishop's in full recognition he was from another land.

Bishop whispered in elementary Mandarin. "Do not worry, Old Fox. I am not here to hurt you and I do not care you steal the fruit."

"You come for the lady," he said, studying Bishop with age's unsurprised wisdom.

"Do they—do *police*—know her?"

"'About her?' No, *Gōng*," said Old Fox using the old Chinese honorific for Duke. "They would make life difficult for the whole village. They would make many examples. The secret of the lady is safe."

Bishop noticed the man's ancient hand shook. It was not from fear. The old fox took a glass flask from his coat. He offered it first to Bishop as was custom. A thick, golden liquid stirred with his tremors. He pulled the cork and Bishop recoiled from the vapor. Not to drink would be an insult. He quickly swallowed the smallest sip possible. It was not small enough. He choked. His eyes burned. Old Fox laughed. He grabbed the bottle and drank heartily while Bishop blinked tears.

"You know this phrase? *Cào nǐ zǔzōng shíbā dài* for police?" Old Fox asked.

"'Fuck' the police?"

"'Fuck their ancestors to the *eighteenth generation*' fuck the police." Then Old Fox said, "How do you plan to get past the guards?"

"Is there always someone there?"

"Two or three always. People who are moved into that apartment have shown lack of respect to our mayor, to our government, and thus their fellow workers. The bully boys, they stand out there to harass anyone who comes outside for anything other than labor. Most of the resident prisoners"—he spat—"have had their jobs minimized or work permits revoked. The police search the building once a month, but not diligently. They find nothing." He drank again and corked the bottle. "People who lack respect for government may speak stupidly but learn to think smarter than those who don't speak at all."

"All right, Old Fox. I know how you regard the police. You think the same about the government?"

Old Fox cursed the Supreme Leader and his lackeys to twice their eighteenth generation. Bishop questioned why he stole the old apricots, but the fire in his throat already gave him a promising idea.

His new friend considered his answer. "I make the *meijiu*. Someone must, to carry on the religious traditions begun by Yi Di, the wife of the first dynasty's King Yu. I make the sacred liquid used when people make the sacrificial offerings to heaven and the Earth and the ancestors. The golden plum tempers the *baijiu*.[1] I use oolong to increase the medicinal effect. Tea is quite medicinal."

"You drink this only for religious purpose?"

"I am devout," said Old Fox and drank more. He made his eyes clever. "But a half teaspoon in baby's milk and they stop crying and grow peaceful."

"And among soldiers?"

The Old Fox's teeth were black where they weren't rotted out. Bishop knew this by his agreeable leer.

NINETEEN HOURS LATER, as it neared one in the morning, Old Fox bumbled drunk into the motor pool behind the apartment into a circle of light where he was observed by the two guards on duty since midnight. They aimed their rifles and barked. He raised his hands and swayed. A full bottle of *baiju* homebrew swung precarious and tempting from his fingertips.

One of the Armed Police grabbed it. The other guard snarled at him. The first guard didn't give a shit. Pulled the cork. His

---

1   In China, the apricot is called a plum; *baiju* is clear grain liquor made from pulverized wheat. 95 percent alcohol/190 proof. Chinese version of your *caña Cubana aguardiente especial.*

partner yapped and threatened with his radio. The first smirked and took a deep swallow. He doubled over and spluttered. This got a chuckle from the complainer.

Bishop watched from his hilltop hide, already traveling through mental time beyond to Elizabeth. He visualized her eyes, her nose, he pictured her high narrow cheeks and lips, each feature individually and as a whole. He wanted to gently kiss her and promised himself he would.

The first guard swung the apricot-tempered grain alcohol from his fingertips, beckoning his friend. The second militarized cop snarled something at Old Fox, kicked his skinny ass twice to get him moving, and joined his friend in drink. Bishop filled with his own kind of warmth, the kind he nurtured before taking a different kind of shot.

The two guards sat in their chairs. They smoked and passed the bottle between them. They laughed and shushed each other and giggled. Old Fox rejoined Bishop.

"Now we wait," Old Fox said, and Bishop agreed.

They surveilled the apartment guards the hour-and-a-half it took them to finish the bottle. Minutes prior to the first guard collapsing, the two Chinese played a game of whose stream of piss was faster to put out a cigarette held by the other. Hadn't thought it through. The loser raged and cursed over his sleeve of urine, then sprawled snoring into his chair. The winner stumbled across the lot and lay in the grass at the base of the hill. He toasted the moon but didn't get around to drinking his toast. The bottle slipped from his grip and clonked off his head. The fellow didn't notice, falling unconscious as the glass demijohn rolled into the weeds.

Bishop rose to a crouch. Crept forward and waited a minute longer until certain the two police guards were out cold. He glanced back at the erstwhile Old Fox coming alongside him.

"You are big help. I pay you money," Bishop shortchanged the language.

"Yes, and I thank you. But wait. You need me to get you inside. Your disguise is not good. And you speak no better than a moon-face village idiot. No one wants to be accidentally frightened. I will smooth the way."

THE SMELL OF A SEMI-LOCKED-DOWN, rural, seventy-year-old Chinese apartment building is an odiferous tapestry woven of sweat and sewage and sex, of wood rot, concrete mildew, mold, and acrid "fragrance-free" industrial chemicals. The smoke of charcoal, incense, oil, candles, and roasted meats embroider the memories of boiling vegetables and roots, fungi, rice, and noodles knotted to every molecule of oxygen and nitrogen thick in the hot, heavy air. And yet, a delicate pattern of cloves and garlic, ginger and chili, cassia bark, weave through it all, a reminder hell smells only of death and this place at least was not hell.

In WWII, our CIA OSS predecessors created a device deployed to Asia called the "Who Me?" A nonlethal chemical weapon of extremely volatile sulfur compounds that smelled strongly of occidental feces. White mans' poop is highly offensive to Asians, and its atomized fragrance clandestinely sprayed onto a Japanese officer created humiliation, demoralization, and suspicion. Bishop knew from his war in Vietnam the Vietcong and NVA could detect even the faintest body odor, food-smells secreted from skin, tobacco and coffee and toothpaste on the breath, and the shit you took two hours ago out of the pores of Westerners at one hundred yards in the fetid jungles of Southeast Asia. As a scout sniper operating alone against the enemy, Bishop quickly learned to live, eat with, and mimic the hygiene of his South Vietnamese spotter his entire time in-country. Although Bishop had lived a similar lifestyle in

China since June, it didn't surprise him, as he and Old Fox made their way to the fourth floor, doors cracked open, eyes peered out and noses sniffed. They understood before seeing him who he was and why he was there. Most shut themselves back inside their rooms. Those more curious chose to remain and watch the show. For all of them, Bishop was the first white man they had ever seen in flesh; for most, the only one they ever would see. Old Fox made hand signals, and no one spoke a word.

They arrived at the apartment where the foreigner holed inside. An elderly couple opened the door. They backed into the room, bowing. Bishop saw Elizabeth before she saw him. She huddled like a golden bird on the floor below a window, the top of her head level with the curtain edge, her face upturned to the moonlight spilling over the sill, her eyes shut, her nostrils flaring with each breath of air carried inside on the hushed, sweet breeze of the night.

Old Fox spoke quietly with the couple as a young woman, not yet in her twenties, wearing Buster Keaton glasses and a plain, wrinkled student uniform timidly stepped out from behind a carved folding *shoji*. Mesmerized by Bishop, she bowed with restraint. She did not speak. Bishop crouched beside Elizabeth.

He grazed her cheek with his fingers, tips catching a limp strand of light brown hair which he lifted behind her ear. Her eyes drifted to his face. They linked with his eyes. Elizabeth tried hard to smile.

"I lost my shoes," she said.

Bishop concurred, blue eyes gently probing.

Her eyes shimmered, wet. "You always come for me."

"I got kind of a crush on you."

"Maybe I'll stop playing hard to get," she said, her voice falling into a sinkhole of sobs.

THE KIND OF A CRUSH that had crushed from the first when Tom Bishop saw Elizabeth Hadley in the lobby bar of the Commodore Hotel. Lebanon, 1982. Her smiling eyes captured him such a long-ago night, cutting through the cigarette, cigar, and hookah smoke, the alcohol fumes to draw him in like an ocean liner caught by the sight of a Fata Morgana holy city of gold, blazing impossible and beguiling above an empty copper sea. Seeing Elizabeth changed Bishop's course forever; he voluntarily put his life adrift if she would be his promised port, even if its anchorage might ever only remain a mirage.

As elsewhere her work brought her, in Lebanon, Elizabeth had been running a war refugee camp for orphans. Bishop vetted her, ignoring her most unsavory connections for the greater good of her aspirations, and contrived to meet her by helping her smuggle vital medicines through military lines. Although they never spoke in terms of a future greater than tomorrow, of emotions greater than tonight, Bishop had secretly allowed his heart to open to Elizabeth. But when Muir exposed Bishop's cover to Elizabeth to shatter the pair and mission-focus his son by exposing her terrorist contacts, Elizabeth fled Bishop in anger, betrayal, humiliation.

He had never told her his real name and the shame, his deliberate dishonesty for a mission he now questioned, he recognized as something real inside him and its reality allowed Bishop the courage to break from Muir in 1983.

Muir went on to Grenada, Bishop off to pursue the Clockmaker—the Libyan bomb designer responsible for the death of 241 US servicemen in the Lebanon Marine Barracks bombing.

The Clockmaker's trail led Bishop through the Eritrean Civil War. There, he and Elizabeth rekindled their affair in the famine camps. Rekindled without a word of Lebanon, their aching hearts having already communicated the longing that drove them back together, their apologies, their forgiveness of sins over the distance of their year apart. This time when they separated, each carried a commitment to whatever future they could steal from their disparate and distant-landed jobs, a commitment founded in lust, forged in love.

Bishop took the head of the Clockmaker in Cairo. He boxed it, bowed it, and gifted it to the Ayatollah Khomeini of Iran on the cleric's birthday.

Elizabeth, who had allowed herself to fall into a coma from starvation in East Africa, was medevacked home to her parents who, from the wealthy shores of Hong Kong, had long ago resigned themselves to view her life as a never-ending Dunkirk. As soon as she recovered, and as her parents knew she would, she fled to the Philippines, where indigenous peoples of the sovereign archipelagic state suffered between the hammer of communist insurrection and the anvil of CIA-supported Marcos covert military suppression.

She was kidnapped. A ransom demanded.

Bishop killed ten men to rescue the British aid worker from the Mindanao River communists in 1986. The pair returned together to Hong Kong. There, they lived quietly and in love, ignoring her PTSD, until one morning, Bishop awoke to find Elizabeth gone, once again to follow her calling to Beijing and the student uprising at Tiananmen Square.

Now BEFORE HIM, unwashed, malnourished, jaundiced, her skin covered in hives and her teeth in ruin, in Tom Bishop's mind, heart, and soul Elizabeth glowed with all the beauty God gives us as love's glory.

"It's time to come home."

Scarcely lucid, Elizabeth agreed, childlike with grasping hands. She enfolded weak limbs round his neck. He rose with her in his arms.

"We have to take Hui Yin with us." Her voice was dry like a broken butterfly wing, words delicate and faded.

The girl in the circle glasses bowed her head a second time, and this time did not lift it.

"Good. No problem," said Bishop.

He turned to Elizabeth's hosts. He thanked them and gave them all the Yen in his possession. He asked Old Fox for one more favor.

"I have a sampan hidden on the riverbank. We must leave as soon as possible for Hong Kong, which will be a most difficult part of our journey. I will pay you one thousand dollars. I will take you across with us if you prefer freedom and a new life my employer will pay for, or you may keep the boat—worth more if you choose to sell it. But as we will now be traveling into daylight and only have security until our two friends outside awaken, Elizabeth and I will have to hide beneath the shelter straw the entire trip. I need you to operate the outboard."

Old Fox agreed and soon the four of them were in the flat-bottomed wooden boat upon the water, the student, Hui Yin, wide-eyed behind her spectacles having yet to speak a word.

10

Sound amplifies over water. Because the air directly over water is cooler, sound waves refract, slowing down and preventing dissipation, allowing them to travel farther and louder. On the busy river, Bishop's and Elizabeth's Western accents would have stood out with harsh clarity. Hours passed without a word. Bishop worried about Elizabeth as he watched the river through a slat in the wicker weave of the shelter as Old Fox guided them through fishing skiffs and transport scows river, to river, to river.

Upon coming aboard, Elizabeth and Hui Yin took food, vitamins, and prophylactic amoxicillin for basic bacterial and dysentery infection. As time and distance passed and Hui Yin became livelier, talking with Old Fox as he steered the outboard, Elizabeth huddled into herself out of sight, knees pulled in, arms crossed over them, chin on her wrists, listless and withdrawn. Although there was little possibility she'd been raped as had happened in the Philippines, Bishop sensed these months in hiding directly under the guns of a Chinese military garrison had summoned the demons she'd turned away from but had never turned away.

Now, well into daylight, in the countryside five waterways far enough away from Hetang Town and its busy traffic, they were alone on the water. Bishop decided it was safe to speak. Elizabeth lived to help others and Tom Bishop wanted to set her mind to the best parts of her identity.

"It's good of you to help Hui Yin. Who is she?"

He also wanted intelligence.

"She's sweet. Shy. Nineteen. She volunteered in one of the radio broadcast trucks donated to the students—"

Thank you, Professor Hill.

"—that rebroadcast speeches at night. All she did was load tapes. Shy," she reemphasized. "Silent. But strong solidarity."

Elizabeth's focus drifted. Bishop gently drew her back.

"A kid like her—why'd she have to go on the run?"

"Her boyfriend was killed at the barricade. She went crazy. Took over the loudspeaker. Screamed all night, 'Death to the regime, death to the government.' Fever you see sometimes in an introvert pushed too far."

Bishop gave Elizabeth water. She drank.

"After the tanks crashed into the square," she said, wiping her lips with the back of her hand, "they were arresting the broadcasters. I helped her escape. We hid out overnight beneath a noodle bar. We learned about YELLOW BIRD; helped each other trying to reach them." Her thankful eyes connected with Bishop. "But every step... we were blocked. Forced to retreat inland. Over and over again. Day after day. Then we were trapped."

Bishop weighed the story against the girl softly speaking with Old Fox.

"Let her know, once we're in Hong Kong, she'll be able to get word back to her family. China would prefer to make examples— in both your cases, no doubt—but they aren't impulsive enough to chase internal dissent, barely an adult, into the external world. In time, and with our help, we'll be able to reunite her with her people. I'm sure of it. This isn't forever."

Elizabeth conveyed the message. Hui Yin forced a smile. It did nothing to conceal the distress behind her blinking eyes.

When they neared the Pearl River Estuary, they hid the sampan and waited until twilight. Elizabeth slept. Old Fox and Hui Yin continued in quiet conversation. Bishop's plan for the crossing remained fluid due to the increased security. He needed to set a rendezvous point with his Triad partners. He opened a secret deck compartment and removed his scrambler phone. In a moment frozen in time for Bishop, a moment he would debate and never be sure of for the rest of his life, as he folded out the antenna, Hui Yin tried to move around him. She lost her balance and fell into Bishop. Desperately clutched him as the boat teetered and dumped them over the side.

The girl panicked, thrashing, and spluttering she couldn't swim. The choice wasn't in Bishop's nature; to save the girl, he released the phone.

Back aboard the Sampan, Hui Yin wept. She begged to be drowned if that would return the phone. No matter what the three others tried, Hui Yin took no comfort.

By 9 p.m., Hui Yin had cried herself to sleep. Bishop took Old Fox ashore. They briefly spoke and many *"Shì de, gōng,"* Yes, *Dukes* later, the old man took off overland for a nearby town.

When Bishop climbed back into the boat, Hui Yin was awake. She followed him with frightened eyes as he grabbed water and nutrition bars and shared them. When she asked where Old Fox had gone, Bishop explained he'd sent him to find a telephone with instructions on how to call the Triad with the appropriate "Chinese doctor said it was arthritis" code.

Bishop studied the girl as she opened her water and devoured the bar. Bishop loaded additional water and food into a plastic bag. He rose from inside the shelter cover and, without explanation, grabbed Hui Yin. She scratched and bit as he hoisted her over the side and tossed her like a basketball to the shore. The food bag followed.

Elizabeth couldn't find words to express her shock.

"Don't leave me! Elizabeth! Why?!" Hui Yin grieved.

Bishop shoved off from the riverbank.

"Tom?" Elizabeth said.

Bishop ripped the engine cord. The outboard coughed to life.

"What's going on? Tom?!"

Bishop gripped the steering arm, stared at the young student, and addressed her. "We both know 'why.' My mistake entirely. I mistook weakness for sensitivity. Goodbye and good luck."

He steered from the bank, leaving the girl collapsed in a rage of tears.

Elizabeth scrambled to where he sat beside the motor. "Tom! You can't leave her. They'll kill her."

"Better than she'd planned for us."

He took the boat into the current. The girl's cries carried well and full over the night water.

"What?"

"I don't know if the phone was an accident and her bright idea came later, or it had always been her plan, but my old fox of a friend let me know she'd persuaded him that when I'd be forced to send him to the town, the best for the two of them would be to turn us in. The price on your head is thirty thousand dollars. Mine would be even higher."

"You didn't ask her. Maybe it was his plan all along," Elizabeth said. "You didn't give her a chance."

"Let me tell you something, Liz, Old Fox is calling the authorities."

"Then why did he tell you?"

"Your little Princess Buttercup? Her original idea had been for the two of them to murder us. He gave me the plan. Fertile imagination, that kid. Bet you didn't know Hui Yin's mother is a Party official."

"I don't believe it. She would have turned me in to the garrison at Leibu."

"She didn't trust that those rural police-soldiers bunked up without their own women wouldn't do things to her and keep the reward on you for themselves. As for my friend, he suspects he wouldn't get by in Hong Kong. Didn't want to start over at his age."

Although faced with the dirty truth, Elizabeth's compassion ran fundamental to her being. Bishop guessed, faced with the same intel, and had he not been there, Elizabeth would not have abandoned Hui Yin.

He loved her for that in ways he'd never be able to express.

"Right now, he's getting himself a reward for rescuing Hui Yin from us. She'll go along with it. Doesn't have any other choice."

Bishop opened the throttle and aimed for Hong Kong. Elizabeth said nothing.

TOM BISHOP DIDN'T RETURN to Harry Duncan. Called him from Thailand, broke the news of his success, and took a leave of absence to care for Elizabeth. He chose a rental place on the black-sand beach at Laem Ngop. Elizabeth descended into pills and alcohol, world-hate and self-loathing. Bishop tried to help her, but he couldn't break through her pain. He tried to give her time. But weeks became months. Became a year. More. For the first time in his life, he fell into depression. They quietly shared this oblivion. Their only physical contact: when fingers touched passing a bottle of booze.

I've mentioned how Jeremy Harker sent Muir to make a permanent alteration to Bishop's health. Bishop had no clue Muir was his father—none of us did—but Muir's appearance in Thailand motivated Bishop to admit the job of saving Elizabeth was too great for him; real love meant sending Elizabeth into treatment.

He found an exclusive clinic in Bangkok. World famous. Expensive. He enlisted the aid of his mother and his great-aunt, who together financed a no-holds-barred twelve-week rehab. Elizabeth fought Tom and refused to be committed—not fearing the good intentions of the cure, but what she'd have to face to achieve it—but Bishop paid enough to ensure her screaming went unheard.

Denied any form of contact for forty days, Bishop shuttered himself inside their black-beach cottage. Like a cloistered monk, he moved only for water, food, or to wash when his accumulated sweat made breathing hard from the stench, and his vision impossible from the seeping sting of its acid into his eyes.

On day forty-one, he walked into Elizabeth's compound quarters, not knowing what to expect. She glowed with health inside a suite of luxury to rival the Mandarin Oriental. The air was fresh and perfumed from the flowers in her day room and from the champak trees blooming orange and gold outside of her patio. Bishop had neatened up for the visit. Jeans and his best pearl-buttoned denim shirt, an LA Dodgers ball cap on top, and half-length desert boots from Ariat below, boots that, once they'd left their California factory, had run with him all over the globe. Elizabeth appeared comfortable, her glow validating the sumptuousness of her surroundings. He'd not been reared in opulence as Elizabeth's youth had known. He felt out of place and unaccustomedly nervous.

"I won't bite if you want to kiss me." She smiled distantly, her teeth repaired, real sparklers highlighting the blue topaz of her eyes brought back to life, dancing with the fire of her change.

He kissed her but as he rediscovered the Elizabeth he knew in her lips, an Elizabeth he didn't know, pulled away cold.

"Tea?" she said automatically—kissing passed as a formality performed—startling a man hard to startle.

"Since when with the tea?"

She stared at him as one hypnotized. He straightened, concerned.

"I take it with a pour of cream. A tablespoon of sugar. Then I read the Bible. Before art. And knit-ting." She widened dead-ened eyes. "I've been a good girl."

"What did the heck they do to you?"

Elizabeth growled a laugh, grabbed him hard—"Your face—!"—and made laughing, joyous love to him.

Afterward, the pair sharing a comfortable view of the whitest, cleanest ceiling either of them could remember seeing in years, Bishop spoke.

"I love you, Elizabeth."

"Why do you love me?"

"You make me believe I have a place in this universe that's important. I see it seeing you. Mattering to you, I matter to myself."

She faced him across the king-size pillow. Her long, thin lips closed, applying pressure against each other to hold back tears she wanted to savor and never lose. Her head was already saying yes, the tears already falling when Tom Bishop asked Elizabeth Hadley to marry him.

I SUPPOSE I SPEND MORE TIME than most people thinking of the alphabet as a mystery. I am ever intrigued by its pure state: a single letter string without meaning nor conveying a single thought. From the Phoenicians to the Greeks, Romans, the Latins to the English, the order of the letters has remained almost exact for thousands of years.

No one knows why.

While there are plenty of guesses to its conception—a predating hieroglyphic hierarchy, a mnemonic to memorize a creation story, Sumerian music scales, astrological, astral, and divine prophecy—none provide a compelling reason why it was carried across cultural and ethnic boundaries. Carried across millennia. Maybe those unknown *whys* are nothing better than a polite way of saying "So what?"

Maybe that's its beauty.

The alphabet is inert, elemental without implication or consequence. It isn't until the letters are given movement, reordered and combined, that meaning and utility awaken. My old friend the "laughing philosopher" Democritus, in describing atoms, wrote metaphorically, it isn't until letters are attached to one another in specific combinations and series that reality comes into existence. Out of a string of twenty-six elemental symbols, ridiculous comedies and great tragedies are born. Letters, to words, to sentences, to thoughts in endless variety, *Don Quixote* to *Mein Kampf*, Theodore Geisel to Theodore Kaczynski.

Democritus proposed atoms be viewed the same as letters. They are physically, but not geometrically, indivisible; that between atoms, there lies empty space; that atoms are indestructible, and have always been and always will be in motion. It is in that motion they order and arrange and cluster into the blurred reality we experience in all its glorious and hideous, magnificent, and horrible reality: the natural world; the endeavors of humanity; the processes of thought. All atoms, all letters, all infinitesimal and carrying the meaning of absolute all.

A pistol fought over in an alley's wet gutter center wrenched from one man's hand to the hand of another: the result of the atoms that form the molecules, millions of molecules that storing our pasts, timing our presents, implicating our futures, firing ninety billion neurons over one hundred trillion synaptic connections in two out of five-and-a-half billion human brains every moment on the path of infinity. That pistol, fought over in an alley's wet gutter center wrenched from one man's hand to the hand of another, was something so inconsequential in its action, so infinitesimal in its scope—one man goes out to kill another, one man walks away—and yet so overwhelmingly vast in its ramifications.

America. China. Cuba.

Using the letters A-B-C-G-I-K, there are 14,399 permutations you could arrive at before arriving at C-I-A and K-G-B simultaneously. None of them—including the seventeen words you would create—carries as much power or commands as much attention as that three-by-three letter pair. In Hong Kong, in May 1991, the potential collision of that paring was not an active concern for Bishop and even of less concern—probably zero—for your Cuban DI. Like chips of glass and bits of colored plastic turned and falling into place inside a child's toy, they'd only be noticed if you knew to look into the tube.

Tom Bishop accidentally looked.

We tonight—Hotel Florida, Havana—we few, we fucking wretched few, are what has followed from his glance.

11

O N BISHOP'S FIRST DAY back with the Company, while Elizabeth finished her rehab, Harry Duncan invited Tom to join him at the Victoria Peak compound of French Vice Consul Jean-Pierre Montagne. Less a briefing, more a celebration of the success of YELLOW BIRD. Over a seafood luncheon, they raised toasts to the top leaders of the movement—student Wu'er Kaixi and communist politician turned dissident Yan Jiaqi and his family—who had, the previous week, arrived safely in Paris. The fate of schoolgirl Hui Yin never came up around the table, everyone aware she had recently been honored in Beijing for her denunciation of the movement she'd been forced into against her will, and for her later escape from kidnapping by agents of the West who had attempted to silence her. Everyone at the vice consul's reception knew the truth, some—in the postprandial congeniality—going so far as to suggest Bishop might have done them all a favor by silencing her.

Bishop took it in the spirit intended, which is to say, he changed the subject to their own children, asking if their teenage daughters had ever been lost and how little the reason why meant when they were safely home.

Harry Duncan and Bishop were waiting for their car when Lionel Gregory of British MI6 pulled the two of them aside.

"Harry, I thought, if you have an extra moment, there's something you and Mr. Bishop might be able to offer us some assistance with."

He unlocked and unzipped his pebbled Ettinger portfolio. He withdrew a wax-paper envelope. From it, he produced a set of surveillance photographs. He handed the photos to Harry Duncan, who looked through them without remark before passing them to Bishop.

"These chaps wouldn't be yours, would they?"

They were three Caucasians in their thirties dressed in civilian clothes—American brands. They carried themselves with spec-ops bearing and positioning.

Duncan shrugged with a curl of his lips beneath his gunmetal gunfighter mustache.

"We hoped perhaps they were part of SIDESHOW. We've heard a peep or two about that op—though good quiet cousins we are, we've not asked. Waited for you to slip us a peek at the ankles under the dress. Or higher if her looks raised the old flag."

"SIDESHOW?" This time, Harry's shrug made it all the way to his shoulders. "First I've heard of SIDESHOW."

Gregory pursed his lips as if he knew better, which, in a sense, he did. He opened his hand for the prints. Bishop held on to them.

"My assignment to YELLOW BIRD is complete. Nothing on my desk. Be happy to lend a hand. I assume you've checked your Soviet and East Bloc fake books?"

"Yes. Canada, Australia, New Zealand, West German and fuck-all else. Couldn't whistle up a single melody to match a face. You'll share what you find?"

ON THE RIDE BACK to central Hong Kong, Bishop asked about SIDESHOW.

"Damned if I know."

"Sir Gregory seems to think otherwise."

"He's not a 'sir,' and I don't care what that lift-the-dress and sniff-the-panties chip-chip-cheerio thinks." Harry Duncan strangled his steering wheel with seasoned hands. "And I'll be damned if Harker or any other Langley freak is gonna run behind my back with this shit-show side-bullshit."

"What about the snapshots? Those boys aren't ours."

"Do what you want with them. My guess, you'll be wasting your time fanning the smoke Lionel Gregory just blew up your ass."

Bishop went through the photos again, studying the three faces and the image backgrounds more closely.

"These photos are recent. Got a bus-stop movie poster in this one for the *Terminator* sequel that opens next week. Not something he'd go to the trouble of staging. His concern's legit. Why he went East Bloc first: shape of those three hammerheads, their facial features: uniformly Slavic."

He glanced at Harry Duncan, but the older man still chewed his anger.

"Fucking Harker. Fucking embarrassed in front of the Brits. SIDESHOW—whose else it gonna be? Eh? Goddamn Chiclets-mouthed cock-boy."

Bishop pocketed the photographs.

RETURNS ON THE THREE MEN came back from Langley as inconclusive as they had from MI6. They were nobodies, making them the kind of somebodies Bishop wouldn't let wander Hong Kong unchaperoned. He put the word out to his Triad associates to keep a lookout. Two nights later, one of the three unknowns booked a prostitute at a "one-woman brothel"—a mob-controlled apartment building where single women receive customers in their own units. Bishop attached a DIANA RED surveillance team to the target. They followed him home to a rented house behind a high wall equipped with anti-eavesdropping countermeasures.

For three days, no one came or went. The following night, the target returned to his call girl. Bishop moved to action. He and a DIANA RED black-bag team monkeyed the wall. The alarm hacked and rerouted to a remote console where it would remain "armed." They took their time removing the glass from a sliding window into the back bedroom, where a stack of Hong Kong-dollar coins balanced on its track. They took care not to upset it. If they had, it would be impossible to guess at the heads–tails arrangement when they restacked it. Once inside, they confirmed all door and window entry points similarly rigged—old-fashioned but perennially effective in its simplicity. Their preliminary search showed them an overly sanitized three-bedroom house dressed like the movie set for an innocuous life—everything too generic, too clean, too in place. Bishop knew not to open any drawers or cupboards. Anything he found would be bait: counterfeit and misdirection.

Bishop found the documents safe beneath a false panel in the floor underneath the bed in the master bedroom, bolted directly into the foundation and rigged to self-ignite its contents if removed or the wrong combination entered.

Bishop's safecracker crawled under the bed and set to work. He drilled a hole through a corner. A fiber optic camera slipped inside revealed a stack of documents two inches high and upside down. The camera removed, the safecracker inserted needle-thin wire tweezers, and this is what took the longest: with barely perceptible movement, Bishop's safecracker carefully lifted the top page.

"It's paper-clipped. Best I can do is fold it up onto its edge. I can do maybe three of them before the weight will move the document and risk triggering the failsafe."

He managed four. Bishop attached the fiber optic to a digital camera and captured each page in several full-page and partial close-up shots. Bishop checked the images, making sure they were readable, which they were—if only Bishop read Cyrillic.

As he and his second man, who'd been acting lookout, prepared the windowpane with bonding compound, the safe-cracker collected the drill tailings from inside the safe and the floor beneath the bed. He puttied the hole and matched the metallic silver finish from one of a selection of Mercedes Benz door-ding touch-up pens.

Over the wall and driving away, the entire operation had taken less than thirty minutes.

BISHOP SHARED HIS DISCOVERY with Harry Duncan. "Any chance this could be Sir Gregory's SIDESHOW? Not ours. Something Sov'?"

"*Lionel* Gregory, and no." He dropped his gaze, his voice constrained. "SIDESHOW is ours. We're not cleared and we're not to ask."

Bishop swallowed his pride. "You want me to put out a feeler with Muir?"

"You don't mean that."

"I don't want it, but you run this station and this cat crap is buried in your flower bed. You run me now too, so if it helps..."

Harry Duncan shook his oversized head. It was always strange for Bishop to see him move his skull so easily. With its ring of tight ashy curls and the pink marble coloring of Duncan's bald head and face, he looked like nothing so much as an ancient marble bust.

"Like I said when you came over, Tom: the best thing between the two of you is time."

"That'll be the day hell freezes over."

"Same what Muir said. Maybe have a skating party on the ice."

THREE DAYS LATER, Duncan braced Bishop where he was having breakfast at the Australia Dairy Company *cha chaan teng* café. Founded by a member of the Tang clan in 1970, the ADC, as it is fondly known, is one of the oldest restaurants in the Colony. Renowned for its scrambled eggs, its custards, and Western toast, its no-nonsense waiters elevate rudeness to an art form. After a customer tries their patience waiting in a line that can be anywhere from thirty minutes to an hour, once seated, they're only allowed ten minutes to try the food before being hustled out, done and gone. People love it. Bishop did. And the day after Elizabeth accepted Bishop's proposal and Bishop returned to Hong Kong, he crowned the maître d' with his Dodgers baseball cap in an act of spontaneous generosity. Figured now, two weeks later, he had a favor coming back his way. It came in the form of a cut in line, to-go cup of coffee, and a "Two minute only!" seat for Harry Duncan.

"What did you get back?"

Harry Duncan blew steam across his drink's surface. "Nada."

"What's that supposed mean? Something we're not cleared for?"

Bishop noticed Duncan's eyes: hooded and piercing into his own. "Your report is gone. Our hard and digital copies of the snatch are gone. Lionel Gregory's surveillance prints are gone. Your camera is gone."

"You let them clean sweep me?"

"Happened before I arrived this morning. They want your DIANA RED team decommissioned."

Bishop took a forkful of eggs. Chewed. Swallowed. Waited.

"I told them you used a Triad cutout team," Harry conceded.

Bishop nodded his thanks.

BISHOP'S JUNGLE SENSE was on high alert. On his way back to his apartment, he did an extreme SDR—surveillance detection run—as if in enemy territory. Swept his place for active and passive electronic surveillance. As the Russian had used the horse-and-buggy era coin stack, Bishop had, himself, employed an old-school technique invented during the Franco-Prussian war to protect his take. Bishop didn't smoke cigarettes. That didn't mean the pack in his desk was unnecessary. Embedded in the tax stamp was a microdot containing images of the stolen pages he'd photographed off the display of the original camera (so there would be no electronic or digital finger-print) shrunken to the size of the dot above this letter *i*.

BISHOP TOOK EVERY PRECAUTION passing the cigarettes to DIANA RED between video and T-shirt stalls in the Temple Street night market. He lingered three hours in perpetual SDR, channeling across footbridges, stair-stepping dogleg alleys. As far as he knew— and Muir had trained him, so his knowledge ran farther than anyone—he was clean. He received his translation of the Cyrillic-written documents folded into the newspaper cone of an order of curried fish balls. Inside a bathroom stall at the rear of the curry house, Bishop read his haul. They were transcripts from a Soviet over-tap on a CIA active tap running against the China National Petroleum Corporation. The four pages Bishop had stolen were transcriptions of Chinese discussions with *Unión Cuba-Petróleo*. [1]

The name for the CIA op the Soviets were piggybacking wasn't mentioned. The Soviet's was. A child's toy, you turn the tube, the glittering letters fall into place:

---

1   You'll recall better than I, the quick one-sided (meaning Chinese-favored) deal you made for oil imports after your fair-weather Soviet mistress kicked you out of their commie-communal bed.

к-а-л-е-й-д-о-с-к-о-п... *KALAYDOSKOP.*

Bishop burned the pages. He flushed the ashes. He left through the kitchen door, unsure of his next step, unsure what any of it meant, and why he should care. Behind the night market stalls, tight alleys of older shops spilled wares and light into tight, haphazard lanes. No one followed; the man with the silenced pistol stepped out ten yards in front of Bishop.

Bishop grabbed the first thing in reach as the Soviet agent pulled the trigger. The first bullet whiffed past Bishop's neck. The second bullet shattered the enamel tray Bishop Frisbee-d at him, while the third vanished over Bishop's back as he drove his shoulder into the Russian's sternum. The two men crashed into the gutter running the center of the paving stones. They struggled for the gun, then atoms and molecules occupied different space and Bishop held it. He lurched to his feet.

"KALEIDOSCOPE motherfucker!" the Soviet agent snarled in accusation.

"KALAYDOSKOP was in *your* safe." Bishop stood over him, pistol aimed at his center mass. "Tell me what it is. Save yourself."

Bishop saw it in his eyes. Mistaken identity. The futility of it all: they weren't on the same game board.

"Where one turns, the other turns," the Soviet said and feinted, purposely drawing the kill shot.

Bishop wiped and dropped the gun. The assassin had mistakenly believed Bishop part of something called KALEIDOSCOPE, and that confused Bishop. Wasn't it KALAYDOSKOP and wasn't that Soviet?

Where one turns, the other turns. Opposing operations with the same designation between enemies? Reciprocal acknowledgment?

He walked from the alley shadows, back to the dazzle, flash, and the sparkle of the market stalls: robot toys and dangling jewelry and spinning parasols; the neon food signs, the bright-colored fruit-drink fountains; clothing booths of tie-dye and neon and black-and-white Fraser spirals; the rainbow swirls of oily puddles splashed by jostling people and jangling bikes. Color as wave-length energy, which is not matter, but like KALEIDOSCOPE is to our operations, KALAYDOSKOP to the enemy, a field over-laying all matter that hides or highlights its shape.

THE SILENCE OF THE FOLLOWING WEEK among the Five Eyes intel-ligence agencies, CIA's European and Asian "favored friends" in Hong Kong, hung in the air like lingering gun smoke. No one knew how to take the reported death of a "Ukrainian electrical appliance exporter" in the Temple Street night market when, after claiming the body, the other side accepted the coroner's ludicrous findings of "massive cardiac arrest" and went on, business as usual, without the usual reciprocal drownings in a toilet or double-tap-to-the-temple suicides of one or more of ours. Bishop kept it all to himself. And if Harry Duncan suspected anything, he gave no indication.

The marriage came, barefoot on the glossy black glitter of the sand behind their rented house; one month later, while shop-ping for fruit in the Khlong Lat Mayom open market, Elizabeth was kidnapped.

By the Fourth of July, Bishop was at my front door, clutching the newspaper that announced his wife's conviction in Beijing, the report that prompted Bishop's threat against Muir's life if Bishop ever proved what he already knew in his heart: Nathan Muir had sold his wife to China.[2] Bishop made an oath against Muir's life, sworn on my doorstep in heartbreak. Why didn't he go after Muir

---

2   This event precipitous to October 01, 1991, and the events already detailed that transpired with Bishop's Suzhou prisoner convoy ambush.

right then? All I can guess is he subconsciously suspected the truth of their blood and did not want to face the horrible consequence of spilling it.

As HARRY DUNCAN WOULD LATER REGRET when it all came down and cost him the permanent stagnation of his career, he covered Bishop's absence and looked the other way as he had since YELLOW BIRD. To all outward appearances, Bishop settled into his work as a workaday spy, letting the situation of his wife proceed through official channels. But the workaday world Bishop entered the Agency from was of a US Marine Corps scout sniper. Bishop was accustomed to lengthy creeps, ghillie-suited and invisible beneath the eyes of his target until he was in killing range.

By September 28, Bishop had his most trusted agents in DIANA RED prepared to smuggle him into Elizabeth's prison as a World Health Organization medical team set to deliver and administer cholera vaccinations. The rescue entailed Bishop allowing himself to receive a lethal electrical shock from a breaker system sabotaged before their arrival. A heavy dose of nitroglycerin taken moments before the electrocution, and an adrenaline shot administered directly afterward, would be his ticket back to life after receiving the voltage. Not a mission he could rehearse, and only standing a 40 percent chance of survival in executing it, but this was the only chance he would have at her, and he would readily chance death rather than not proceed at all. It would be illegal and off the books, and, if successful, would sever his ties with the Agency. It was known only to Bishop and the two men and one woman of his team.

This is why, out on his jog on the morning of September 29, twelve hours before he'd make the go/no-go call, when the young Chinese American woman changed direction ten kilometers out along Hong Kong's MacLehose Trail in the wild hills above the city, and ran abreast of Bishop, he twinged with a sense of unease. She kept pace as if they were partners. Bishop didn't speak.

As they negotiated a steep switchback, Bishop said:

"Ought to let you know, I'm married."

"That's what I want to discuss."

They ran in hard silence until the trail leveled.

"KALEIDOSCOPE?" said Bishop.

The woman gave him an uncomprehending look. "I'm SIDESHOW. We picked something up you'll want to hear." She passed Bishop a sweatband. "You didn't get this from us."

She peeled off and continued her jog in the other direction.

A DIGITAL CF CARD sewn into the wristband detailed all the intelligence for Elizabeth's prison transfer to Suzhou. All except the most important piece of the puzzle—that it was a trap. Like Bishop, the woman who'd provided it was being deceived by our own Agency. In the back of the armored transport, staring into the guns of the People's Armed Police anti-terrorism unit, Bishop recalled the Soviet agent willing to take a bullet rather than divulge.

"Muir?" Elizabeth asked.

Where one turns, the other turns.

Bishop answered, "KALEIDOSCOPE."

INSIDE THE DIRECTOR'S seventh-floor conference room, video and tape rolling, Muir finished debriefing his interrogators on Bishop's involvement in the Cathcart Affair. Muir had used Bishop in the false-flag op on the defection of an East German functionary, Gridenko, to spook US ambassador's treasonous wife, Ann Cathcart, into making a run for East Berlin. Four weeks later, August 1976, Bishop assassinated the traitor as she stepped outside of the Gethsemane Church and into his crosshairs. Only Muir, having burn-bagged the long-ago proof of that with his personal Bishop files that morning, chose not to divulge that intelligence; he could see the pattern of the frame-up developing. When Director Folger produced Muir's phony report that Ann Cathcart was beaten to death outside her Pankow apartment, Muir did nothing to dissuade them.

"And Bishop was in Berlin at this time?" said Silas Kingston.

"We were both in *West* Berlin."

Harker pulled the end of his ballpoint from his mouth. "Do you recall Bishop's reaction to Ann Cathcart's death?"

Muir glanced at Folger. Folger tilted his head, raised his brow.

Harker fiddled with the pen, made notes, and didn't care that Muir hadn't answered. "Motive and opportunity," said Harker.

"We're not in the vengeance business. Anyone might have beaten up that traitor. My recollection: FBI was keen on the ambassador. Jilted husband, ruined career and all."

Harker smirked. Muir assembled a look of defeat on his face.

"Nathan, you should leave here knowing we're looking into every possibility," said Director Folger.

Muir closed his mouth and ran his tongue on his teeth as if rubbing away words he'd rather not speak. They didn't care what he had to say. Any of them. He briefly shut his eyes. Grew a hint of a frown. Eyes flashed open; he bore into the director. "What's SIDESHOW?"

Folger scowled. He glanced at Kingston.

"You don't need to know," came the Counterintelligence chief's wooden response, like a portcullis banging in Muir's face.

"Why are we trying to burn Bishop?"

Reptiles can't smile and yet they always seem to be doing it. Silas Kingston held Muir in an adder's leer.

Harker puffed his cheeks then slowly leaked air as he stared at his notes as if pretending empty of air, unmoving and unspeaking, he might be invisible.

"Troy?" said Muir.

The director gave a pained expression. He leaned forward and spoke into his console. "Hold transcription. Hold video."

Men on the other side of the wall switched off tape. Removed headsets.

"SIDESHOW is a bugging op. Listening to government offices in Beijing."

"The trade talks," Muir said.

"Hmm," Director Folger confirmed.

"And you're afraid the lid to the cookie jar is going to slam shut on our hand?"

Harker, if not invisible, remained useless. Kingston remained reptilian.

"Oh, come on, guys. Chinese needs trade status more than we need to give it."

"That's not necessarily true."

Being the first time Dr. Hwang had spoken, Muir rallied.

"Twenty-four hours after capture, Bishop is allowed to start talking. Gives you, what, ten, twelve hours to make a trade. Now come on. You're on the clock."

"He doesn't know anything," Kingston said. "Bishop wasn't on SIDESHOW. He wasn't working for us."

"He was arrested attempting a rescue during a prison transfer outside of Suzhou," Harker said, as if a ghost.

"Who was he after?"

The doors opened, breaking the mood as Director Folger's secretary directed Agency kitchen staff to set a buffet that years later would be Harker's greatest achievement as acting director.

"Don't know," Harker said, as the director's secretary slipped Folger a note.

"I think we should see this," Director Folger said, uneasy, and activated a television monitor across the room. As the picture came in, he increased the volume.

The CNN newsroom anchor said: "For more on this late breaking story, we go live to Hong Kong."

"It has been reported that the Chinese claim to have arrested an American Operative of the CIA." The reporter stood outside the US Consulate. *"While the State Department remains quiet, official sources say the individual working out of the US Consulate behind me was captured in an act of espionage. If confirmed, this comes at a bad time for an administration in the middle of trade negotiations with China. The US Government is now in the process of negotiating for his release. This is Frank Nall, live in Hong Kong."*

Harker blinked. "We are so fucked. The consulate promised to keep us abreast of the situation as it develops."

"Guess that limits our options." Muir stood doing little to disguise his smile.

He pulled his sports coat from the back of his chair. Harker wheeled on him.

"I want to know what you have to say about this, and I want it on the record," he said.

Click. Clack. Tapes and video resumed.

Muir gave Harker an easy look. "When I was a kid, my mom would take me in the summers to my aunt's farm. We had this gentle old plow horse. I loved that plow horse. One summer, the horse came up lame. Could barely stand." Muir shouldered into his houndstooth jacket. "The vet offered to put her down." He fixed his collar, straightening his lapel. "Know what my Aunt Linda said?"

Harker, holding onto his headache, wished he hadn't asked. He sulked, resigned. "No, Muir, what did she say?"

"She said, 'Why would I ask somebody else to kill a horse that belonged to me?'"

Harker rolled his eyes behind his palm.

Kingston chuckled. Muir noted he was the only man in the room beside himself who didn't seem to care about the press leak.

Harker got on the phone. "Get me Peter Brody at the FCC... I don't care. Get him."

Muir winked at Kingston. "Looks like Bishop's going to be okay." And he wagged his fingers free of the dike, letting its dirty water burst through.

"The mantis stalks the cicada, unaware of the yellow bird behind." There are those who'll tell you it was the old proverb that named the operation, but it's not true. Harker, having already gotten the calypso beat under his feet, had named the operation after the old song about the bird in the tree and the unfaithful island girl.

YELLOW BIRD [3]
YELLOW BIRD [4]
YELLOW BIRD. [5]

Sell 'em to the Chicoms, roll 'em up, kill them—just set my bird free.

---

3 Wáng Wěijié, Major, 1 Division, People's Border Defense Corps, YELLOW BIRD informant/CIA DIANA RED network.

4 Xuē Míngyàn (Shanghai), Mò Yǒngjìng, Tán Pínglì (Beijing), Liu Mùchén (Wuhan), CIA DIANA RED safehouse organizers.

5 Lóng Míngyûn (Kowloon), trained, organized, led twenty DIANA RED guides.

12

"PLEASE TURN OFF THE VEHICLE and keep your hands on top of the steering wheel where we can see them," the voice echoed from the vortex of police light haling me to the end of Nina's street.

She sits beside me.

I observe her arrival as if on a movie-screen membrane of air that is canted sideways, away from me. She withdraws the safety card from the airline seatback in front of her, dimensions bending to accommodate and absorb me across time.

The seizure always hits the same. A stirring in the pit of my belly rises in a wave, electrical, tingling. A *whooshing* sound I experience audible in my mind, inaudible in any natural manifestation. It rises from my chest, through my head and out the top, unpleasant because it is unusual and of foreign entry and release, but not of any physical discomfort.

A high priestess in an Aeromexico uniform performs the invocation to flight; she fastens the seatbelt latch on her dummy Möbius strip-strap before exchanging it for a life vest.

For the ten to thirty seconds—sometimes as long as two minutes—I am in the grip of what my neurosurgeon Dr. Rashmi tells me is a "focal onset aware seizure." I am conscious, but I am gone, captivated by the sensations and visions that flood the hole my vacated tumor left in my mind. Caused by tiny lesions on my temporal and occipital lobes from where my brain tumor was cut, these epileptic attacks fill the space with a crackle of electric impulses that dance in unpredictable and uncontrolled ways. On the occasion those electrical impulses fork across both hemispheres of my brain, my *aware* seizure becomes a focal onset *impaired awareness* seizure—as was happening inside my car outside Nina's house—and my mind moves from willful disregard of reality to full immersion in surreality. While my hallucinations can be so extreme as to involve me in a sensible, dual reality where I become the time traveler I've so far indicated, I have yet been unable to crush a Bradbury butterfly to wing-ripple affect a sound of thunder across the space-time continuum. Not for lack of trying, but the wing is not a butterfly's. For me, the wing is of a dark phantom's coat that opens:

1.   to draw me in,
2.   to restructure my perception,
3.   to allow me to reset the pieces of life's chessboard.

But until I become the phantom, don his mantle, the wing folds closed and I am left outside of what all-can-be: where past and yet-to-come are of one with the unending experience of now.

"In the event of a water landing, remove the life jacket from beneath your seat. Put the life jacket over your head," and the flight attendant does—still inside the airplane still (and co-effectively not-at-all) inside my car. "Tie or clip straps together tightly around your waist."

Our woman of the airline with the wing-shaped nametag, "Paz," clips her straps with practiced intimacy.

I say, "Reminds me of those front-page photos you see of airline passengers bobbing thankfully in their yellow vests around sinking aircraft every time an airplane makes a splashdown."

"You know as well as I, without the ritual, the magic of air travel would be impossible," Nina counters.

"And on November 24, 1996, when we read about Ethiopian Airlines Flight 961—deadliest hijacking before 9/11—of the 175 passengers,

125 will die, found inside the aircraft, pressed against the ceiling and the overhead bins, eyes bulging like their life vests filled with CO2, none of them better off having gotten the safety lecture to begin with."

"Fuck's sake, Pintao. That hasn't happened yet. Who are you to say it will? Let her finish."

When the air-priestess has, Nina returns the safety card to the seatback. Her movement is relaxed and the marvel with which I've regarded her untroubled attitude toward the disasters awaiting us in Cuba now clarifies to me as controls she sets herself to absorb the shocks she is fleeing forward to meet.

"I have to warn you, Nina..."

"You're sweet. We got this, baby."

Nina's iron confidence coiled into an ideal emotional spring; the more relaxed she becomes grows in direct proportion to the tightening of her inner gyre. Yet, like the gyres of the deepest ocean currents or the highest winds beneath a seagull's wings, the mainspring in a timepiece, constant force over time, weakens all springs.

Repetitive tension reduces stored energy.

Molecules weaken and rearrange.

Atomic space is created, heat is lost inside it and without heat, time ceases, and change—action and reaction—becomes impossible. It is all for "fuck's sake" or as Hooke's Law of spring dynamics more delicately puts it: for F= −xs sake. The ideal spring only exists if it experiences no internal or external friction beyond its physical construction. Made of flesh and blood and air and of water, of thought, and of soul, Nina is a true spring and even the absolute best of real springs will fail.

This settles in me both as vast admiration and bittersweet melancholy.

This makes me anxious.

The acceleration of the airplane's take-off pins me to the back of my wooden bench and her hand releases a Holy Bible—not an airline safety card at all—to an ancient church pew inside the centuries old Iglesia Santo Cristo del Buen Viaje.

"Your father is here? Worshipping? Now?"

We walk along the nave. I look at the Cuban blood on my wing-tip shoes, confident only I can see the future past.

"He passes through the Plaza del Cristo each morning and every night to and from his office. He will get my signal and if all is well—"

"I didn't see you leave a mark."

Nina wrinkles her mouth and looks cute, face elastic with potential energy. "Whoever said you don't know how to pay a girl a compliment?"

We stand in a side chapel without the effort of having moved there. Nina lights a candle. She drops a twenty-five-centavo coin through the slot of a tin coin box, the same as she had done with the caja pobre at the church entrance.

The sound of the dropping coin became the rapping of a flashlight insistent upon windshield glass. I ignored the voice that accompanied it.

"Just because I missed your signal—Nina, we've had those two clowns on us since we checked into the hotel…"

She knows of whom I refer: an older man and his younger partner. Too close in age to be father and son, and with one dressed in jeans, a work shirt over a clean tee, wearing meticulously oiled work boots, the other impeccable in a businessman's suit and tie, both suave in their practiced invisibility to one another. And here's a tip: the only place they wouldn't have trouble blending in was the San Francisco Castro. In Cuba, the pair of them would only be believable on the other side of the barbed wire at one of your Castro's year-round camps for homosexual re-education.

"It's four of them—two men, two women. They're mixing pairs rotating in and out of the blue Ford Falcon that followed us from the airport. But yes: I'm counting on them having picked up on everything I've done. Only way HOUNDFOX will know to move forward."

"To dinner," I say, already knowing where all this leads. "The go/ no-go check-off with HOUNDFOX, following which I succumb to your beautiful lips, the taste of your tongue; I forget all my promises and false-flag morality on that moonlit beach you've taken me—"

Her eyes snap to mine, seeming to make the candles flicker around us. Her grin becomes curious as, this time relived, I predict our future.

"Pintao?" Her voice is of astonishment. Of mystical delight. "How do you know my plan for the beach?"

I touch her cheek where I'd wanted to then, when I didn't know, where the candlelight glimmers in its hollow. I feel the warmth of face and candle flame tingle the pattern of my fingerprint in whorls and swirls, coiling my arm.

"I know everything that's going to happen to us," I tell her. Without fear, I wrap my arms around Nina's waist. "I know the seagull always falls from the sky for no reason as you tell me of your first love, your first broken heart, that magic moment on the beach at Caiberién—"

"Shh. Pintao. Don't give it away—"

"How you wept in my arms at the Santerían promise you would fulfill and the soul you would share with me, but give to Victor Rubio—"

"—or I'll never come back."

"Sir! I said lower your window! Now!"

I lowered the window. The cop's flashlight blinded me as the chill of the DC night blew inside my car on stinging crystals of coming Christmas. The dead Cuban from Nina's sunroom leered cheek-to-cheek beside the uniformed DC Metro police officer. I handed him my driver's license—which "him" I was uncertain— and went for the glove box.

"Easy, sir!"

My sudden movement drew the beam of his flashlight out from my driver's seat compartment to follow my hands into the glove box.

"Getting my registration."

"I didn't request your registration! Show me your hands!"

I spread my fingers, jazz-handing a gesture that there were only papers in the box. Gingerly pulled the DMV slip, taking situational control along with it. He took the paper and my license. He studied them under his light before aiming its beam back into my face. As hoped and now accomplished, I'd distracted him from completing his required visual search of the driver's seating interior. In the darkness of the footwell, I slipped my gory shoes from the pedals. Tucked them and my lower legs beneath the overhang of the driver's seat.

"Mr. Aiken." He matched the address: "That's your house." He pointed through my windows to Nina's house. "And you live there with whom?"

I told him. "She's waiting for me at a restaurant. Butterfield 9. Where I'm headed. And I'm late, so…"

"Sir, there's been reports of shots fired in the neighborhood. We're trying to account for all residents, make sure the street is safe. Why don't you step out of your vehicle and accompany me back to your house for a quick inspection?"

"Thanks anyway, but without a warrant or probable cause, I'll be leaving just the same."

"Don't switch on your car."

I switched on my car.

"That's it. Get out."

I didn't.

"Get out of the vehicle, Mr. Aiken. This is your last warning."

I knew what was next. I precipitated it by reaching into my coat—dramatically as possible. A *whoosh* of his gun clearing leather and I stared into its barrel.

"Don't move!"

"It's not a *gun*," I mumbled the words… except for gun. That word, I pronounced full volume and clear.

"Gun!" he shouted repeating me. "Don't move or I will shoot!"

I gave him a haphazard smile. He keyed the radio mic at his shoulder. Confirmed his backup had heard his cry. Two more cops, two more guns, and the result I'd awaited: everyone focused on my hand inside my coat and the fate for all of us it now contained.

"You will remove your hand slowly. If you have a weapon, you will hold it with two fingers and drop it onto the street. You will stay in your vehicle until instructed otherwise. Do you understand me?"

"As far as misunderstandings and harassment go, I'm feeling pretty clear," I said.

"I need a 'yes,' sir."

"Yes. Sir."

I gently removed my credential. I dangled it but did not drop it. One of his backups, a roundish female sergeant, saw the gold seal and, while not close enough to recognize which agency it represented, knew one thing for certain and voiced it big and brassy: "Plenty loaded, Myers. Just no bullets."

She holstered her weapon. Took my CIA identification. Matched my face to my photo. Returned it.

"Mind telling me, Mr. Aiken, how this situation ix-trapolated this far?"

"Spirit of Christmas: I'd prefer to let it go. I'm sure I was entirely at fault, and I can leave my driver's license with you to write it up, but I am late to propose marriage to my girlfriend."

"Propose marriage." 10 word weight.

"I'm sure Officer Myers is happy to return your license, as happy as us all is for your engagement, sir." She held out her hand to Myers for my license and registration. Myers took them from his shirt pocket and passed them over.

"Look," I said. "I've been home all evening. I'd've noticed a gunshot if there'd been one."

"May have been crossed the street from you, or a block back," she said. "Di'ju lock up good before you left, sir?"

"You bet."

She hollered around my car at a pair of officers about to stumble themselves into a murder site. She told them to skip Nina's house, move onto the next. The two cop cars blocking the top of my street pulled back to let me through.

YOU HAVE MY CELL PHONE. Already, I'm sure, you've verified all my calls between then and now. After passing through the police blockade and racing away, I tried Nina's phone repeatedly.

You know this. You've heard my frantic messages.

Had either Muir or Bishop been alive, I would have reached out to one of them, but I only speak to them in the past or in futures that *are* but never *in* the present. I dialed Linda P. Morse. Told her I was on my way—the advice I asked and the absolution she gave—also already known to you. I called United Airlines. Booked my flight to Fresno, and then the charter company for the jump to Lone Pine.

You've connected the dots to know I connected with no one else.

THE SIGNAL NINA HAS USED to service HOUNDFOX successfully as her father's courier for twenty years is a piece of tradecraft we deploy worldwide to this day, simple and effective. HOUNDFOX has never needed to look for a signal mark as he drives round the plaza and past the Iglesia Santo Cristo del Buen Viaje. The signal is perpetually active each day and each night, received as a static hum over the transistor radio he keeps tuned to the national broadcast while he drives between his office and his home. It is only the rare occasion when the hum is gone that HOUNDFOX knows his daughter arrived. Without having seen her, he knows she has come and gone from the church. He knows because *you* always tell him.

When Nina enters any church, she habitually drops a coin into the poor box. It is in your nature to see this. Your duty to secure it. By your endeavor in securing the coin, to check it for some special mark or as some type of device, you remove the box. The coins you find never turn up a thing, as they are only common coins. What you don't understand is the hum HOUNDFOX is receiving is generated by a miniaturized RFID chip soldered years ago undetectable in a seam of the poor box. Once the box is removed from the church, the signal can't be received over HOUNDFOX's transistor.

All these years, not only was it you who serviced her signal, but your strict, no-stone-unturned security routine to prevent espionage communication was the exact thing that instructed her father of Nina's safe arrival. I am certain, within the hour, you will have melted the old solder and secured the radio-frequency chip, once again, verifying the honesty of my treason.

Back in '91, when we left the church, the *caja pobre* she'd dropped her coin into had already been removed by your officers without either of us having noticed. Within twenty-four hours, everything would go wrong for Nina, terrorizing and terrible. If not for the foremost cruelty of time, the cruelty that locks us to Einstein's "stubbornly persistent illusion" of presentism, the cruelty that is the Janus faces of Life and Death which cleave us to time and dusts the universe eternal, we would have journeyed from the church already fearful and thus impervious to the tragedy to come, and the murder—cruelty in the ultimate—unrepentant and unrecovered that forever hews us face to face. Her inner spring relaxed relative to her increased confidence. My confidence grew alongside hers and while every move we made was perfect, so too was the death awaiting us.

13

B Y NOW, your protocols, exacting to East German standards, have moved you to examine church records for Nina's baptism and/or first communion and the name of a *comandante* of the revolution from Vedado. I'll save you the effort. Due to her parents' social and economic standing in pre-Castro Cuba, her baptism was held privately in their home. Likewise, her first communion, due to Castro's 1962 decree of Cuba as an atheist state, and the *comandante's* Communist Party membership that forbid the practice of religion, transpired in secret in a private chapel.

You waste your time. There are other approaches.

For instance, Muir lay great store in Socrates's experiment with Meno's slave. Muir's old pal Socrates believed all knowledge is innate and merely recollection. This guy, Meno, who Socrates was hanging out with one day watching the slave boys, didn't buy his premise. So, Socrates had Meno call over one of the slave boys (a pastime Socrates would dearly pay for a little later with a draught of hemlock). This boy, possessing of no mathematical training—simplest kid Meno owned—Meno allowed Socrates to give him a complex geometry question. The boy had no idea how to solve it, but Socrates insisted the knowledge was already inside the boy. By asking the kid a series of questions the slave boy already knew the answers to, Socrates guided him to the answer to the original problem. For Socrates, the slave boy's ability to navigate to the truth and recognize it as such proved he already had the knowledge within him.

As a lawyer, I'm the first to point out Socrates was leading the witness; the kid would most likely not have arrived at the answer himself. However, the answers the slave boy provided came from his own thought process, and the solution he arrived at was not influenced by any heretofore unknown knowledge provided him by Socrates; it came from the slave boy's own mind. You have the knowledge of HOUNDFOX's identity already within you. You know him and work with him, maybe admire, maybe dislike, maybe answer to him. Perhaps you've even spoken with him today.

Like Socrates, what I present to you this night you already know and have known. He is a spy in all your interactions and knowledge of him.

It is only fitting now Muir lead your hounds to his fox.

THE COLD WAR WAS ONLY COLD for the Americans and the Soviets. For forty-five years, both nations served up hot war by proxy all around the globe. When the Soviets introduced the Su-27 Flanker counter-air fighter to their battlefield arsenal, June 22, 1985, Muir let it be known there'd be bonus pay and bragging rights to the agent who brought one home. There'd be eternal gratitude. Secret medals. Or, as his ATROPOS agent in Malaysia, Lucky Boy, once put it, "A tap-tap on the cap and an extra ration of rum, or a chunk of the hashish." From DIANA RED in Hong Kong, to ACHILLES-4 in Kiev, to HOUNDFOX in Havana, the hunt was on. In 1988, HOUNDFOX tally-hoed the quarry's sight.

The *comandante*, like so many of Fidel's patriot soldiers, had found his way to Angola, the border bush war American-proxy South African-backed UNITA forces slugged out hard and bloody with Soviet-proxy Cuban-armed, led, and reinforced FAPLA revolutionaries. You were there, General Trigorin, an intelligence major at the time. Under you, served a captain. An interrogator—East German Stasi-trained in torture—a sadist of the purest sort known to skin men alive with a potato peeler and keep them alive for days while doing it; a demon in human form known to get sexual arousal from his victim's pain and sexual release from their death. A poetry-loving father of five girls, a sporty papa to two sons, he was a self-taught pianist—who once played Rachmaninoff for Castro, often ragtime for his children, always Afro-Cuban jazz for his wife—who would twist a middle-C wire around the throat of anyone who stood in his way. You well know, his name was Hector Guzman. When Muir took his shot at that Soviet Flanker and missed, Guzman got his hands on Muir and didn't.

In a tin shack on the periphery of the Battle of Cuito Cuanavale, Hector Guzman took bloody delight torturing Nathan Muir to the point of death and held him there thirty hours without ever asking a question. He didn't need to, or so he thought, because Nathan Muir was already compromised by his own mentor, CIA hero and Soviet spy Charlie March.

¡Qué lastima! So much the pity. You'd have had HOUNDFOX then if only Guzman had known, while there are more ways to skin a cat, there are equally more curious cats to skin. After thirty hours of torture, Guzman readied his pistol to blow its load and finish off Muir when his Stasi handler entered the shack and stopped him.

"Así no es como jugamos el juego. Hay una regla no escrita." The man said. This isn't how the game is played. There is a rule—unwritten, but a rule. *"Matamos a los agentes. No oficiales que son jugadores como nosotros."* We kill each other's agents—fair game—we don't kill each other.

That man, Guzman's handler, was named Heinz Trettin.

Hector Guzman returned from Angola with a promotion to *coronel* in the DGI Departamento de Liberacion Nacional, taking his office in your Department M compound, located at the former mansion of your President Jose Gome, which fills a whole city block in the Larrazabal section of the Marianao suburb of Havana. Same place you and I chatted yesterday.

At the time, HOUNDFOX kept offices there, though he does no longer.

Muir took a year to recover.

The Berlin Wall came down. The Soviet Union collapsed.

Cuba lost its Russian sponsor to the tune of an eight-million-dollar-a-day cash subsidy, 85 percent of all trade, and nearly all its petroleum imports from the Soviet Union. Without oil: no factories, no agriculture, no power grid.

Heinz Trettin's East Germany reunified, and Trettin, abruptly a criminal, retreated to a bleak life in a bleaker Dresden, hiding out, hoping Western justice would pass him over, so many worse Cold War criminals of greater former authority and higher crimes to get to than poor Heinz. But a knock came at Trettin's pigeon cote and Nathan Muir walked inside his dusty coop.

As far as I know, the only person Muir ever murdered face-to-face pulling the trigger was his first wife Kim Jin Muir whom he loved and who he called Jewel, but as sure as I sit here tonight, I tell you this: Muir murdered dozens of men and women.

At Camp Pendleton, where Bishop aced his Marine scout sniper training, his instructor, Gunnery Sergeant Beckett, had these words before sending Bishop off to the jungles of Southeast Asia: "Sitting in an office, giving other men orders to kill... ain't no different from putting a bullet in a man's heart. Let me tell you something. It's the same goddamn thing." Muir's words originally—except for the "ain't"—and Muir lived them, operating inside the office and out. He'd come to Dresden to give the kill order to Heinz Trettin, who, unquestioning and obedient

volunteer to the murder, carried it out on himself a few hours after
Muir left him. Before he did, though, they had this conversation:

"Remember Guzman, Heinz? Hector Guzman—you trained
him back in the day?"

"You know the answer to that."

"You still have contact with Guzman?"

"I don't know why I would."

"I don't care why you would. Do you?"

"No."

"Could you?"

Muir poured the man some Johnny Walker and patted Trettin's
personnel files that Muir had stolen from Stasi headquarters in
Berlin. Trettin drank the whiskey, thirsting for his record and the
secrets of his dirty-secret, evil life Muir came with to bargain.

"Official communication took place over cipher machines.
Berlin direct to Havana. However, we set protocols by which he
or I could pass messages via a trapped letter sent to a dead-drop
mailbox. Except for testing it once a year, we never actively had
need to use it."

"And you won't. I will. Give me the laundry list for the traps."

"Why would I betray him?"

Muir drank. He studied the cast-aside spy in his Stasi cufflinks
and threadbare suit tailored for him three sizes bigger when totalitarian gluttony suited him and bulked his bones with fat. The
symbols of his onetime pride now made him appear a baggy-
pants Pogo the Clown.

"You were Guzman's master," Muir soothed. "You put his
piece on the board. Why would you leave him in success to watch
you removed in defeat? Whatever place in heaven God has for
people like you—"

Trettin scoffed at heaven with a croak.

"Oh, yeah, Heinz. I got it on authority God never made such a place as hell, but now's no time for sermons." Muir poured again for both. "Wouldn't you prefer Guzman look to you in fear and awe as his creator when he joins you in the afterworld?"

Trettin smirked. Poured his drink down his throat. Wiped his mouth with a dirty cuff.

"I must say, this has attractions previously unconsidered."

Muir offered him a cigarette. Reached in and lit it for the man. Shook one loose for himself.

"Through one last letter and the disaster it will bring Guzman when he acts on the phony playback, you'll be letting him know who was always in command—"

The muscles twitched at the corner of Trettin's eyes.

"—who owned who with iron authority. Always would and will, even in death."

"But what—? What would I possibly have to communicate to Guzman that would have you achieve this for me?"

"You're going to provide him with the means to murder me."

Trettin grinned with delight. "He'd like this. You wouldn't. Who would he really be bumping off?"

"You'll like that even more," said Muir, lighting his own smoke. "The American traitor, Charlie March."

"I'll destroy the two who puff and sneer on both sides of me." Trettin's voice reflected the cunning gleam in his eyes.

"The beauty of it for you? The moment it happens to each of them, the eternal space between too late and too dead: they'll both know with complete consciousness that you, Herr Trettin, out-mastered them in the end."

"Checkmate," he said and hopped off for his writing materials.

"Don't worry about postage," Muir's voice followed. "Least I can do."

When Trettin returned, Muir placed his brown ink fountain pen in the East German's hand.

The pen with which I write this now.

He dictated the letter. Four days later, four days after Muir left Heinz Trettin with his Stasi files—the old East German burning them only to fling them across his tiny kitchen in hopeless disgust, appreciating that fire would not erase his sins but a few lungfuls of gas would allow him to avoid them—HOUNDFOX stole the letter from Hector Guzman's dead drop for safekeeping until Guzman would need it to murder himself.

14

I T WOULD TAKE MUIR more than a year moving the pieces on his game board to build a bridge between his opponents—Charlie March and Hector Guzman—whereby the Trettin decoy could be returned to the dead drop and spring Muir's checkmate.

Although Muir's plan for March was that his death would happen in March's comfort zone, close by the traitor's Key Largo condo, he surveilled Charlie March on his seven-city book tour that coincided with the release of March's memoir *Now You See Me: A Cold Warrior Steps from the Shadows*. Muir blended with the crowds in Miami, Washington, New York, Philadelphia, Chicago, San Francisco, and LA (with the added hoopla of a Universal Pictures/Brad Pitt movie deal) to confirm March was retired and was not using the travel, lectures, the cocktail parties, and book signings as cover for communication with his former Soviet masters. Muir returned from California, confident March was out of the spy game for good, merely basking in the golden rays of pyrite attention, the lies of his 150,000 words and Hollywood option gild his world.

In Key Largo, surveillance of Charlie March proved more difficult. March was a traitor, which meant not only was he a seasoned spy, but one who'd fooled all the other seasoned spies around him seasons in and seasons out for decades. In Florida, March watched his back. Not only his person, but the territory he claimed, ranged, hunted, and fed like the scarred old lion he'd always resembled. Muir would have liked to access Charlie March's car, his house, his sailboat, but knew every accessory of March's private life would be invisibly cloaked in trips and traps and tells. The slightest tarnish of a slightness equal to a breath vapor appearing an instant upon the perfect veneer of Charlie March's world would be, before it evaporated to the air, enough to eliminate any chance Muir would have to deliver the son of a bitch's death rattle.

But Muir had two things working in his favor against his mentor. In almost every case, surveillance is initiated to pierce the veil of the target's private world to discover something incriminating. To deter an action. To frustrate an activity. Or to identify persons associated with the target previously unknown and add them to your net. In this surveillance, Muir did not intend to pierce Charlie March's veil for any of those reasons. He needed only to identify its discrete contours and lacy edges. Once he understood Charlie March's boundaries, all Muir had to do was to discover where his enemy expanded and over-stepped them by arrogant choice. He found this in Charlie March's sailboat and in the uncharacteristic pride the traitor took in his sailing skills.

Every Sunday, March would back his boat from slip 29 at the Pelican Landing Marina in Key Largo, motor past the jetty, and spend the day, sometimes two, sometimes more, running the links of Florida's island chain or take a scoot east to the Bahamas. Only on his yacht did Charlie March feel perfectly safe and allow himself the experience of freedom. This meant Charlie March's sailing yacht would be the place to kill him.

PAST STONE-LION-PROTECTED DOORS; past dead animal heads gawping, glass-eyed over the leather booths where the living beasts of congressmen, senators, lobbyists, and trophy-headed wives devour their meat and have their way; tucked inside the Wine Room—a self-contained, circular, *Get Smart* chamber within the Capital Grille restaurant—Muir explained this over a neat Macallan 18 to Joshua Rosen.[1]

On the linen tablecloth, beside plates and bones from bone-in rib-eyes, lay an open folder. Inside the folder were photographs of *No Regrets*, Charlie March's forty-foot sailing yacht; the elderly, bottle-dyed, tawny-maned double agent coming aboard; Charlie March at the helm full sail; docking; Charlie March guzzling champagne with Bimini bikini babes; disembarking at Pelican Landing. Inside the folder were copies of the boat's original designs from the shipyard. Later modifications. It also contained a copy of its registration, a copy of March's operator's license, and his repair and maintenance bills for eight years.

"Well, Nathan, before we get to the *what*, and you knowing me better than I, I won't bother to ask the *why*, this hoity-toity private room, half-a-cow dinner, and the Cuban Black Prince cigar you're holding out on me, but which I can see outlined in your pocket, evidence tells me this isn't a league-qualified team go."

"You forgot to mention the Macallans."

"Ah yes, the swimming hole you want me to jump into and make this a three-way skinny dip."

Muir produced the cigar. He tapped the folder with it. "I'm not offering our third guy a drink. Just want to plop his carcass in the water."

Joshua gestured Muir to it and Muir poured again.

Joshua lifted his glass, smiling warmly over the rim. "Cannonball!" He tipped it back.

Muir replaced the cork in the bottle. He handed the cigar across the table.

---

1   Joshua Eli Rosen, CIA Office of Technical Service, Art Chief/Graphics Branch, 1969-2002 (retired).

For Joshua Rosen, the swirl of expanding consciousness that was the 1960s spun him from sixteen-year-old Rhode Island School of Design prodigy to anti-war activist with dizzying techno-psychedelic ease. From mixed-medium canvases of classical subjects made jarring by his blunt social injustice photography screaming through it; to movement-triggered sound and light events that set his charcoals ablaze—mostly figuratively, once literally and on purpose—to eye-popping critical acclaim; to his infamous and only major gallery exhibit: a collection of pastoral watercolors, "The American Spirit in Landscape," he'd embedded with LED lights that blasted blood red, glowing, profanity laden anti-war slogans—messages unsettlingly discernable to the human eye but only obliquely from the farthest edge of peripheral vision when the viewer looked away from the artwork. Joshua Rosen was the greatest contemporary artist of the 1960s who-might-have-been had he not been an even greater forger of draft deferments and passports; a currency counterfeiter on his way to becoming a domestic terrorist.

Muir had liked Joshua Rosen before he ever met him. He'd liked him when he'd read his sixteen federal indictments—indictments that ran the gamut in forgery, counterfeiting, illegal wire-taps, the willful and malicious interference with military and FBI radio communications; felonious photography; the sketching of defense facilities and vehicles.

Terrified by said same terror indictments, Joshua escaped to Burma in 1969 where, making a living forging documents and counterfeiting currency for the Burmese drug lords engaged in the Opium War with Laos, Muir caught up with him two years later. By then, hooked on their drugs, Joshua was his Burmese masters' slave. By then he'd seen enough of communism and the war, criminal violence and murder and sanctioned terrorism to discern the "other side" he'd defended and defected to wasn't as bad as the America he'd rebelled against. They were incomparably worse. Worse beyond any horror Joshua could have conceived in paint or light or with fire. No chance of returning home and with nothing to live for, Joshua Rosen decided to kill himself in pieces moving from smoked opium to injected heroin.

On the day Muir appeared an American stranger out of nowhere and stole Joshua's freedom, Joshua Rosen wept until convinced his soul had washed away. But as Muir cold-turkeyed Joshua, Joshua found his soul had not gone anywhere.

It grew stronger.

And Joshua understood the opposite had happened. His tears had wept his soul clean, not only from his last traumatic, miserable years, but of all the shit that gunked and choked it off; the steady accumulation of self-loathing a low self-esteem allows in an unloved child of elitist neglect, privileged abuse, and exploited Connecticut expectations.

Joshua never stopped hating the Vietnam War, but he admitted those advantaged white boys he'd helped get into Canada only made it worse for the predominately poor, Black, and Latino young men who took their battlefield places, dying in disproportionate numbers to all other US combatants. It was for them that he went to work for Nathan Muir.

Meanwhile, Muir worked on a federal prosecutor at the DOJ he was intimate with—secretly compromised her and would have blackmailed her had it come to that—who (to her own dodged-bullet good fortune) saw Joshua's value, was a firm believer in redemption, and got Joshua's charges expunged, his records lost. Joshua Rosen's work in Vietnam as a Muir asset was spectacular. Not only in frustrating the enemy with psychological warfare operations, but infiltration and exfiltrations of South Vietnamese spies in and out of North Vietnam, out of Vietcong units, and along the Ho Chi Minh Trail with the only 100 percent success/safety rate of the entire war. Although his strict moral code of what he would and wouldn't do for the Agency made him a prima donna, Muir shielded Joshua and made sure his product, his imagination, his abundant and deviant creativity made him too valuable for headquarters to kick off the team.

Joshua Rosen was brought into the OTS (Office of Technical Services)—our Q Branch in James Bond parlance—three months after the Fall of Saigon, after he exfil'd his last six Vietnamese agents. He became a floater between sections. From art to disguise, forgery to gadgetry, photography to electronics. He made it from manager to department head before he turned thirty; to chief at thirty-four and would be there still but for the all-encompassing witlessness of Harker and his Young Turks that only worsened with 9/11. As the CIA increasingly spied on Americans—first abroad and then at home—Joshua Rosen retired in disgust.

That night at the Capital Grille, a decade before the terror attacks of 2001, Muir didn't appeal to the artist's acknowledged debt for saving his life. Didn't use his gratitude for Muir's years of running interference against the Young Turks which had allowed Joshua to maintain true north on his moral compass and cherry pick assignments to cheat the magnet of his soul. Muir didn't bring up the silly story about how he'd tricked both Joshua and Wendy (Joshua's onetime prosecutor) into an accidental weekend in a leaky Cumberland cabin in the Alleghany forests above the Potomac. A weekend that led from disaster to laughter, love to marriage. Three times, Muir had talked Joshua out of divorce and twice into fatherhood—life events the mercurial artist had presumed himself unworthy of, only to watch them grow into his greatest accomplishments.

"I'm going to kill Charlie March," Muir purred. "And you're going to help me."

Joshua laughed.

"What's so funny?" Muir said, although he loved the way Joshua's face, prematurely wrinkled at forty, scrunched and rippled with infectious delight.

"I never expected you'd make good on what he did to me."

"It runs deeper with Charlie March than the one time you know about," Muir said.

"That doesn't surprise me. Served a whole career of *Mad Magazine* 'Spy Vs. Spy' bullshit, self-justifying espionage. Whatever the rest of his shit you know is, keep it to yourself. I don't need it. The one time he crossed me closed the book on Charlie March, far as I'm concerned. Not for what it did to my life—the blame I took, the sin I carry, the shame I live with. That one time was a crime against humanity, which is a crime against God."

Muir nodded. "Your Talmud greatly praises those who are unjustly insulted or reproached but remain silent and suppress the temptation for revenge."

Joshua clicked his tongue. *Damn right.* Signaled more whiskey.

He drank, measured and contemplative. "Within our shared traditions, God moves men repeatedly to act out His will against evil on Earth. Charlie March will never repent in this life, but there is a place we call Gehenna. The Valley of Hinnom, where the ancient Jewish kings sacrificed their children by fire. The spiritual place where wicked, unrepentant souls go for cleansing before they may stand before God."

"A big old industrial washing machine for dirty souls," Muir toasted.

Joshua closed the *No Regrets* file. "I'd be happy to do God's work and toss in a fresh load." He leaned back, comfortable in the wingback leather chair and blew smoke rings, eyes closed, his wrinkled neck elongated, jaw in line with his throat and aimed at the ceiling, the thin scruff of his salt-and-pepper beard giving his chin and neck the appearance of lizard scales. Muir watched him for a long minute. Sorrow glazed his younger friend's eyes. He knew what Joshua remembered. Those whom Joshua mourned.

Muir repeated the words Charlie March had used on Joshua, flown out to Chile in the summer of 1983. *"I want you to design the most creative, best cloaked and invulnerable security system that would make planting a device impossible."*

Joshua's eyes remained bleak but allowed a pinched smile. He breathed deeply through his finely shaped nostrils. Inhale, exhale, again, and then once more. He whispered the same thing he'd said to Charlie March: *"Perfectly impossible?"*

Charlie March had supplied Joshua every spec to the tiniest detail on a compound high in the Andes mountains and Joshua employed every conceivable countermeasure. Charlie March was impressed; Joshua had made the mountain citadel impregnable.

"I can turn Charlie March's canoe into a floating Fort Knox."

"Do it," Muir ordered, before they both completed Charlie March's death sentence as their own: "Then invent a way to defeat it."

March sold the Chile op to Joshua as the only way his team could get inside to plant an eavesdropping device in the headquarters hacienda of one of the leaders of the *Movimiento de Izquierda Revolucionaria*—a communist extremist group who for years ran a bombing and murder campaign against the Chilean police and military.

Joshua's plan got Charlie March's Chilean agents inside stealthily enough, but not to plant a bug. Charlie March's team planted a bomb. Detonated remotely, it killed not only the MIR leader but the government peace negotiators with whom Charlie March's target secretly negotiated a truce to cancel the terror campaign in toto.

Theirs were not the lives Joshua mourned. It was the collateral damage; the MIR leader's wife caught in the blast while giving her two daughters a bath. While the Seventh Floor lamented the death of the innocents along with the blow to the peace process, they quietly applauded the death of the terrorist. The MIR did not. Not only had their leader been murdered, but behind their backs, he had offered their surrender. Their campaign of leftist violence—supported by Charlie March's Soviet masters—increased in vengeful cruelty and their targeted victims now included civilians.

Joshua continued to smoke. To sit with his eyes closed. "Same age as my own kids at the time, you know?"

"Perfectly." Muir paid the bill and left.

15

Five days before Charlie March would die, Muir sent Nina to Cuba. She traveled from Madrid to Havana. She registered under a false passport at the Melia Varadero, the 407-room hotel under the cranes that would soon triple its size on Chinese investment. She followed protocol, first stopping at La Iglesia Santo Cristo del Buen Viaje to fool your agents into activating the HOUNDFOX signal, followed by visual go/no-go confirmation of her father at dinner at the Melia Varadero, the sumptuous foreigner and government officials-only four-star restaurant inside your newly constructed beach resort.[1] This was followed by direct contact in the hotel pool maintenance shed where Nina provided the Trettin dead-drop letter that would trigger Hector Guzman to vengeful action. Namely, false intelligence that on September 30, 1991, Nathan Muir would leave slip 29 at the Pelican Landing Marina in Key Largo, alone and at the helm of the sailing yacht *No Regrets*.

Nina left Cuba the next morning, retracing her route through Europe. By the time she returned to Washington, her father had already slipped the Trettin letter into Guzman's dead-drop mailbox, setting in motion Guzman's mistaken assassination of Charlie March.

In Florida, Muir contacted Charlie March. The two men agreed to meet for lunch at March's Golden Sands condominium unit. Muir supplied the Mama Celeste frozen pizza,

---

1   Detail on the Melia Varadero protocols in a moment from my eyewitness participation.

Charlie March the Johnnie Walker. Nothing was left unsaid between them.[2]

Guzman activated a Miami cell. Two young Cuban men illegally in-country and trained in assassination. By 6 p.m., explosive device prepped, they were in their go/no-go position—Room 4, Key Largo Inn, a 1950s motor court on Overseas Highway—awaiting final orders.

At the same time, Muir tucked into the Casa Marina under his 'Linus Bucknell' cover identity. A stomping ground for Hollywood stars in the 1950s and used by the Army's Sixth Missile Battalion during the Cuban Missile Crisis, the hotel was now amid a Waldorf Astoria renovation; in 1991, it leaked worse than the Key Largo Room where the Cuban assassins watched television. Like Edwin Stanton for John Wilkes Booth, or you guys for Lee Harvey O, Muir would now become the hidden hand insuring Charlie March's assassination. He ignored the rainwater from the passing thunderstorm rolling down the stained, paint-peeling walls of his humid room where the efflorescence clung like patches of dirty frost. He concentrated on the report Joshua Rosen had brush-passed him along with a cellular phone as they traded places in the lobby elevator.

"An underwater approach is useless due to 360° video monitoring of the hull and modification done five years ago that added armor reinforcement. This will make a deck approach your only option—for which he is fully prepared."

The yacht club had video surveillance on the boat docks. The clubhouse and dock gate were alarmed but there was no night watchman. The dock tape was checked only in the event

---

2   I will debrief and affidavit the entirety of the Muir–March forty-year collaboration upon your request.

of a break-in. As soon as it was dark, Muir drove out to Pelican Landing. He disarmed the gate alarm. Joshua warned Muir that while Charlie March would not have rigged the dock approach with any kind of early-warning system—something that would overwhelm March with the sheer number of neutral comings and goings—*No Regrets* would be equipped with pressure plates at the boarding hatch, outside the cabin door, as well as the stern and side bulkhead ladders. Muir neared the sailboat.

"Photo intel provided," Joshua wrote in his report, "shows the target receives an automatic call on his cell phone the moment he steps aboard."

Muir activated the cell phone Joshua had given him. Although it contained similar technology, it was not rigged to make and receive traditional calls. Instead, it scanned for live 1900 and PCS frequencies. When Muir stepped aboard *No Regrets*, the pressure plate Joshua predicted activated an outgoing signal. Joshua's device in Muir's hand captured the signal, rerouting it from its preprogrammed call to Charlie March's home telephone and personal cellular device. Once captured, Muir locked in the signal preventing it from disconnecting from his device.

Muir moved around the deck, capturing a repetition of the signal from pressure plates beneath each porthole and, finally, at the cabin's main hatch.

Joshua further warned that every latch and hinge—porthole or screen, locker, or other hatch—would be trapped with an innocuous dye capsule. Joshua suggested these would most likely not contain colored dye, which would give them away, but would be filled with grease or light oil to bleed inconspicuously across latches and surfaces.

"By punching in a code, he deactivates the system for as long as he remains aboard. This is followed by a wet/dry check of all trapped

latches. When he opens the cabin, he busts the capsule in that latch and, satisfied by the grease it expels—proving the door unopened since his last visit—wipes it down and proceeds to investigate the interior of his vessel."

With a battery-powered screwdriver, Muir loosened the entry mechanism on the cabin hatch until, with dental mirror and tweezers, he could remove the gelatin grease capsule he located within.

Joshua advised, "The most effective bomb will be one connected to the engine. Charlie March knows this and will have fail-safes in place."

Muir's device captured and locked another cellular call from the pressure plate in front of the engine compartment. He stuffed the active cellular signal capture device under a cushion. Pulled a handheld RF scanner from his coat and swept the floor and paneling out from the engine compartment, leading him to the hidden burglar alarm speaker. It was a high-end retail system activated by power source interruption if the engine compartment were to be opened without radio-signaled deactivation.

"If someone has gotten this far, the alarm will drive off the individual. If tripped, the system will most likely contact private security or local police. Charlie March would prefer in this case they go aboard before him, as nothing will have prevented a would-be assassin from leaving something behind on a short timer/short fuse, acid trigger, or contact tripwire."

Careful to avoid the alarm system's telephonic coaxial cable, Muir used a scalpel to remove insulation from both the positive and negative power cords. He connected an alkaline lantern battery by clip-conductors which he tucked out of sight behind a hull rib. He disconnected the alarm.

He gently loosened the engine compartment latch and removed the grease capsule and pocketed it with the others.

Muir retraced his path off Charlie March's yacht. He hid on the deck of the starboard adjacent yacht. At 2 a.m., the Cuban duo arrived. One carried a gym bag, black like their clothing, like their sports shoes, like their pistols. Unaware of the pressure plates or door traps neutralized for them by Muir, they searched the boat's exterior before picking the lock to the cabin where, opening the hatch, they would have crushed the gelatin capsules now safely hidden in Muir's pocket. They were inside Charlie March's boat less than ten minutes. When they emerged, the gym bag was empty.

Waiting until he heard their car drive out of the parking lot, Muir climbed back aboard *No Regrets*. The engine compartment was sealed. Muir had to assume the bomb would be rigged to explode if the compartment hatch were opened. If Charlie March got the idea to check his engine before sailing, he wouldn't see a spread of grease to indicate it had been tampered and, most likely detonate the device on a failsafe lifting of the latch. Muir steadied himself. Gingerly returned the capsule to the latch with the tenderness of a hummingbird's tongue. If Charlie March didn't accidentally blow himself up at dock, Rosen expected the device would be set on an engine-connected timer to allow Charlie March to leave the marina and die unseen and alone at sea. The Havana way.

Muir retrieved the cell-phone device from beneath the cushion. He returned the grease capsule to the cabin hatch and retreated from the sailboat. He reactivated the gate alarm, got into his car, reactivated the pressure plates by powering off the cell device, and drove through the night to his Captiva Island home where he awaited my inevitable arrival the following day to announce the death of Charlie March, and contrive the Seventh Floor destruction of Nathan Muir.

Two nights later, the maître d' at the Melia Varadero hotel dining room escorted Nina and me to our window table. Within twenty minutes, Nina's father, HOUNDFOX, entered the dining room with a beautiful middle-aged woman of understated sex appeal, style, and intelligence. No eye contact was made. Nina drank wine, but I—still hungover from my twenty-four hours with Muir—chose not to imbibe. Though tempted, I have never returned to the bottle. Nina's father arrived with his mistress, a signal that both his and Nina's covers were safe. Nina waited for his go/no-go signal that would initiate personal contact. If HOUNDFOX drank a cocktail, they would abort their in-person meeting and communicate through an Old Havana dead drop.

HOUNDFOX ordered a bottle of wine. He tasted it, complimented it to the sommelier. Nina's father toasted his woman, signaling to Nina we were safe to meet in the pool shed. One final signal left between them would be communicated through their entrees. Nina ordered filet mignon. If HOUNDFOX was only there to receive instructions, he would do the same.

I heard him speak to the waiter. *"Camarón que se duerme se lo lleva la corriente."*

I looked at Nina. She struggled to hide sudden fear.

"What did he say?"

"It's a saying we have here: 'The current takes away the sleeping shrimp.'"

"He ordered seafood?" I asked.

Nina blinked away moisture beginning to fill her lower eyelids.

"Shrimp means trouble for him?"

She smiled fiercely, posing as a woman happy and in love. I figured she was acting with the happy, found myself guilty hoping she wasn't with the other. She toasted us with her glass.

I raised my sparkling water, I met her eyes, denying the electric jolt of deep connection rattling through me.

"No, he's safe," she said.

Our glasses clinked like chimes.

She caressed my hand; the warmth and security of her touch sent my heart places it shouldn't go and which I continued to fight; her looks, her gestures, expressed nothing that reflected the awful meaning of the next words she spoke to me.

"Yes. The shrimp are *trouble*. *Tides* is the code word for my mother's life. He's telling me she is in critical danger," she said, while maintaining the illusion she was expressing eternal love for Russell Aiken.

WE'RE GETTING CLOSER NOW to HOUNDFOX. As his dinner will be logged in the Melia Varadero reservation book, I'm sure you have agents dashing to the hotel even as I complete this sentence. Going to seize the old books. You assume, as it is required by all restaurants, his name will be found in the record. Of course, your need for me and Nina would disappear.

Sorry to disappoint.

As mentioned above, HOUNDFOX dined that night with his mistress. In fact, he dines at the Melia Varadero twice, sometimes three times a month with his mistress. Because he is well known and well respected, and because the management of the hotel respected Nina's mother, their procedure for twenty years—for which he paid handsomely—was for his reservations to be in his mistress's name. His identity noted as any of a dozen false names provided unverifiable for *her* dining companion. Still, such arrangement wouldn't necessarily protect him.

Your next logical step would be to identify the mistress by her visits. Track her down. Force her confession. Even if she didn't know his real name, you could force a description: physical appearance, his car, his personal effects, his habits—all those things we use in this business to crack identity. Only problem: HOUNDFOX, entirely faithful to Nina's mother, had more than a dozen "mistresses" of a social class which did not place them on any list you have for that kind of woman. None of them have ever used a real name.

You're stuck with me, with my sordid-storied confession, as I am stuck with you. We are stuck in the blank space between love and hate, the emptiness between musical notes, the dry darkness between atoms, sweet dreams and cold awakenings between the eternal space-time that is the father and mother of death. The void of information.

"PAPÁ, I WAS HERE LAST WEEK. What's changed? How could *mami* be involved in any of this? How is she threatened? *Por favor.*"

We were huddled in the darkness of the pool supply shed. HOUNDFOX clutched his daughter's hands. The tang of pool chemicals did little to disguise the salty sea spray aerosols permeating the concrete cinder blocks with every breath of the ocean air as the stale sulfury smell lingering in the decay of phytoplankton by ancient and invisible bacteria depleted the air molecules inside this cramped space. Claustrophobia gripped me. I was lightheaded as I might have been if I had climbed a high tower. I was empty, feeling outsider to the father-daughter reunion. He deliberately moved his gaze from Nina's troubled face to mine.

"I'm sorry, sir, to involve you in our personal circumstances. You will apologize to Prometheus for me?" he asked, using Muir's codename.

I dipped my chin, if only to encourage him to get on with whatever unwelcome news he was about to deliver inside this stultifying box.

"Don't look at him. Look at me. Why is it personal? Why are you scaring me?"

"Nina-nenita, she made me promise not to tell you until she could tell you herself."

Nina lifted the hem of her dress and tore the fabric. In the dimness, I could barely discern she was biting her lower lip, not from the effort of extracting her parents' escape kits, but in unsuccessfully holding back the sobs pitching against the back of her throat.

"Shh-shh-shh. No-no, *querida*."

He ignored the documents from Nina's hands and folded his arms around her. "Shh... shh... shh... You're the strongest of the three of us. If you continue like this, I don't know what I'll do, but I won't let you see your mother if you don't shape up."

"She's sick, is that it? The Company will give her the best care in the world. I have everything ready to bring both of you to America. You've earned it. You deserve it." She attempted to force the identity kits into his hands. He refused to take them.

"You mother doesn't have the time, and she doesn't want it that way. She wants to die here."

Nina groaned. Her father held her tightly. She snapped her head, turning from his chest to face me. Her heart was breaking. She wanted me to take the pieces. Fit them back together, which was impossible.

I twitched. I wanted to act. But I did nothing. She opened a hand behind her father's back, opened and closed it like the gills of a dying fish, clutching for me. I reached out. I wasn't close enough. A pit burned in my stomach.

In my wallet: an invented image of Nina and me in front of the Christmas tree.

"Are we married?"

"Are you proposing?"

I would have, Nina.

And a diamond ring waits on the hotel table where I write now, never to be worn, its snakehead choking on "trust."

"Pintao."

"Russell," I mumbled. We hooked fingers. HOUNDFOX looked at me less kindly.

"There is something more than cover between you two?"

"No," I insisted, as she said: "He's the rest of my life, Papá. Since the day I met him. He lies for a living."

"It's not true, sir."

"See? *Él miente.*"

He judged me with a single glance. "I suspect a man can't have truth with a woman until he lives the truth inside himself."

She stepped back. Her father placed a solid hand upon her shoulder.

"*¿Estás mejor?*"

She inclined her head. "We'll stay in Havana until it's over. We'll be safe. Then you'll come with us."

HOUNDFOX considered his daughter, thankful for her familiar courage. "Moscow has already been in touch with Fidel over March's murder. Fidel has met with Coronel Guzman. He has been given forty-eight hours to prove his innocence in this affair. Prove this wasn't his rogue action—revenge against the Soviet Union for abandoning our country. Fidel told him if it were, he was to be congratulated. He would live in house arrest for a year— for show—to be later rehabilitated within the government. But Guzman insisted this was an American run operation. The deal is he will deliver the traitor's head—which is mine—or his will roll."

Nina stared, processing this information. "But if you stay, he will uncover you. We'll hide you until Mother passes and we can get you out."

"Your mother will be buried here, and one day I will be buried beside her."

"This is—!"

Her father sealed her lips with a finger.

"You will see your mother tomorrow and this is how we will beat Guzman at his own game."

16

TEENY-TINY CUPS; I've taken more coffee. Thank you, and I must say, it is the finest I've ever enjoyed; considering my circumstances, that is a weight-bearing compliment. Nina still lives, lying hostage where she's meant to sleep, unforgiving eyes from her damaged face, boring hard into the lens of your camera. Wait bearing.

Do you know I watch you from the other side? I do my worst to save my best, bargaining life like the Cubans I hear on the cobbles below, lumbering in the earliest darkness before dawn, heading to illegal work in Havana's hidden black-market bazaars?

Light bleeds about the edges of the shutters of the building across the street. My time runs short.

FINISHED WITH THE YOUNG TURKS, Muir inquired of Gladys for returns from Nina or I, difficulties or daemons from Cuba. We'd registered none. He pulled open his desk, dumped a jumble of junk into a box she'd put out for him.

"I'll miss you. After you're gone, Mr. Muir."

"They tell me, you got Rudy Unger's desk next."

"Who tells you? You spying against me now?" She forced a smile. "Only God's blessings lie ahead for you," she said.

"Some major God you invoke. His blessing makes me humble."

"He doesn't believe you. Neither do I. I suspect of all the gods, not one the same—some, your outright enemies—and none prefer you humble."

She stood on tiptoes, kissed his lips. He kissed her brow.

He stopped beside the door. "I'm counting on you to keep your eye on Dumbo. Keep him flying…"

"Like he's flesh of my flesh," she smiled. "Goodbye."

CHAOTIC IN APPEARANCE, the illaqueable flow of officers through the lobby security turnstiles this end of shift on October 1, the news of Tom Bishop on everyone's mind, if not most of their tongues; armed security, noticed Muir as he entered from the corridor, gestured at him and spoke.

"Mr. Muir? Because I have you checking out—if you could step over?"

Muir joined him, oddly disquieted to be going.

"Tough to pull yourself away, sir?"

Muir smiled. "A bit taxing. Today. Thought I'd get *one* to sit with a magazine or the news and catch up on the world on the other side of the curtain."

He thrust his chin at the television tucked under the edge of the security counter. The security officer winked knowingly and arranged paperwork on a clipboard. Muir scanned the Old Headquarters foyer. It was spacious and filled with light. Pseudo-sacred with its high ceiling and marble columns. Men and women trod across the seal of the CIA, daily routine having made it invisible to them beneath their feet.

Inlaid in the granite floor, it depicts an American eagle vigilant atop a compass rose. Its radiating spokes point to every corner of the globe: the symbol of everything the Agency stood for and Muir had fought for behind its symbolic shield. It was tough to pull away, and he knew he would miss this place, all in its everything. In the small morning hours, janitorial would motor-wax away the shoe scuffs from the day's trample, but maybe a good trampling helped keep it in its place. Better the seal than the Agency motto etched high on the wall to his right: *"Ye shall know the truth and the truth shall make you free (John VIII-XXXII)."* A motto made ironic by that which faces it from the Memorial Wall on the opposite side of the room. The inscription here reads: *"In honor of those members of the Central Intelligence Agency who gave their lives in the service of their country."* These words are cut into marble above seventy-eight stars and a locked glass case. Inside, the Book of Honor lies open to its center. The seventy-eight stone stars are duplicated here in gold, each matched to a year from 1950 to 1989. And while, beside some of them, the name of a fallen officer is memorialized by a calligrapher's hand, for more than half the entries, there is only blank space. The "freedom of truth" is denied for these lives sacrificed in secret, classified in death.

At least, this last day, Muir had prevented a seventy-ninth star to match the name of his only blood son.

"For more on this breaking story, we go live to Hong Kong."

A news anchor's voice snapped Muir's attention to the security desk television. The officer handed Muir the clipboard.

The same reporter as earlier stood outside the US Embassy. He spoke into his handheld microphone. *"And in a development of the incident reported earlier. Rumors that Tom Bishop, an alleged CIA operative, has been captured in an act of espionage, now appears to be a hoax."*

"Mr. Muir? These forms are for your pass-card, your computer terminal security fob, and your clip ID. Upon final signature, I will exchange your active for your new 'retired' credential. Please?"

The security officer held out his hand for the items Muir had prepared to pass him.

"Tom Bishop died fourteen months ago. While the CIA has made no official comment, sources close to the agency have confirmed Bishop's

death late last year. The discredited story has been attributed to an
overzealous member of the Chinese government who leaked the false
information in the hopes of undermining the current US trade negoti-
ations. This is Frank Nall, live in Hong Kong."

The security officer reached for Muir's identification and
access material, but Muir withdrew his hand. He took a backward
step.

"Sir, is everything okay?"

Muir twisted his mouth into a look of befuddlement.
"Whatdaya know? Left the coffee pot burning. Be right back."

GLADYS TRACKED MUIR uneasily as he hurried back into his
office, his entire being endowed with purpose.

"Gladys, who do you trust in Imagery Analysis?"

He rifled one box and another.

"I cosigned Martha Rayburn's car loan…"

Muir found what he was looking for: a framed commendation
for service every officer receives upon retirement, signed by the
director and the president. He smashed the glass on the side of
Gladys's desk.

"So glad Office of Security left something for you to break,"
she said.

He pulled the document from the busted frame. He dropped
the frame into a wastebasket, went to wipe off the shards and
repaid himself with a sliver in his palm.

"Serves you right."

She held his hand and deftly pulled the glass.

"Listen, Gladys. I've got to buy some time here. I'm going to
need all Imagery have got on the military prison at Suzhou, and if
you use the phones, don't use these."

"Any chance I could lose my job over this?"

Muir grunted. Rolled the document and, careful not to crease it, tucked it into his inner breast pocket.

"Good. Didn't want to work for Rudy Unger anyway."

THROUGHOUT BOTH HEADQUARTERS BUILDINGS, the corridors are uniformly the same: stark white walls with gray doors uniformly spaced, nothing written upon them. Beside each door is a six-by-six-inch gray sign with a white-lettered alpha-numeric designation. Be it custodial closet or Op Center, if you do not know the designation, you do not know what is behind the door. Down one side and up the other, each door is locked with an electronic combi-keypad with an ID swipe slot. Muir walked the middle on stolen time, every step a risk to his freedom, his son's life. Were he able to pull off an illegal rescue right under the nose of the director, would he ever again see Tom to beg forgiveness for the ruin he had made of their lives and the woman he'd wrongly believed had come between them?

I suppose I am naïve to think, had I not broken my word to Bishop and revealed to Muir that Elizabeth Hadley was, by marriage, now his daughter, that upon his admission to me of how he'd exacted vengeance upon Charlie March, Muir would have believed his career had found its meaning in justice rendered. I know now—with the hindsight of age and the apprehension of missing him—that the truth of how he viewed his career stared all of us in the face with his codename. Prometheus.

To those whom we hold in comparison to Prometheus, we ascribe the greatest qualities of heroism. I know now Muir took the name not to cast light upon his personal heroics, but to own the other side of the tragic mythos and reveal the shadows of his villainy against God. Above all things, Prometheus was a trickster, a lying thief whose punishment was the excruciating torture and screaming terror of being eaten alive every dawn for eternity. This is ultimately how Muir viewed himself.

Nathan Muir arrived at a door he knew opened to East Asian Operations—Staff Resources. He tapped the numeric combo into the pad, said a little prayer his ID was still active, and swiped. He was rewarded with the electric click of the lock.

The door opened onto an energetic bullpen. Over fifty officers operated in cubicle clusters organized by the eight East Asian nations under their purview. Tossing greetings like trifling flowers, Muir made his way to the China section.

"Hey, Brody," he grinned at a big-jawed, elbowy shirtsleeved analyst working on People's Liberation Army troop-strength estimates. Muir entered his cubicle.

"Howsit, Nathan? Figured you'd be checked out by now."

"Bishop on one end, SIDESHOW on the other—"

Brody raised a hand. "Go no further. Not SIDESHOW cleared."

Muir edged inside, crowding Brody out of his chair. Muir peeked at his monitor, noticing Brody's keycard beside his telephone. Brody hewed an awkward smile from his wooden face, moved his mouse, cleared his screen. Muir broadened his own grin and sat on the edge of the desk, backing Brody into his cubicle doorway.

"Kappler around?"

"Should be in his map room."

Muir picked up Brody's phone. "Before I jump in with him, they switched off my secure line. Last day and all. Can I use yours?"

"Well…"

"Thanks," said Muir.

He stopped himself halfway through dialing an extension.

"I'm sorry, it's SIDESHOW. Do you mind?"

"Uh, right." Brody turned.

Muir pocketed Brody's keycard. He abruptly replaced the telephone receiver. "Know something—? Call can wait; Kappler usually can't. Thanks anyway."

Muir edged past Brody. He crossed the bullpen to a set of interior office doors. He ran Brody's keycard. The door unlatched. Muir entered and closed the door behind him.

"Muir, you're not cleared to be in here." Pudgy, nearsighted Fred Kappler peered over the edge of a Chinese food container through thick glasses and between chopsticks from where he slouched at his desk, the whole of the room as messy as a rathole.

"Relax. If I didn't have clearance, how did I get in?"

Kappler snapped his remote, shutting off the backlight to his regional asset map board. Without invitation, Muir shuffled through papers.

"Where's this report? Seventh Floor are pretty disappointed it hasn't arrived yet."

"Hold on." Kappler shunted aside his food box. "What report?"

"I was saying just now to the director: we send an officer like Bishop onto the mainland, we damn well back him up."

"Nathan! Stop. Harker's brief this morning said Boy Scout was rogue."

Muir cocked his jaw, giving Kappler a funny look as if only too late he registered he'd said more than he should. Kappler scrunched his brow.

"Oh…" Muir eyed him with overt sympathy, leaning away as if the shit were about to fly and Kappler was the target of the fan. "Lookit, Fred. Let's keep this visit between the two of us. Chalk it up to a last day slip a'the lip."

Kappler screwed his face tight and swished his nose, wanting the cheese while flouting the spring. Muir backed to the door. He grasped the door handle behind his back. "Better I go."

"Stop," Kappler said, suddenly in Muir's face and pulling him by the sleeve deeper into his lair. "This is your slip, Muir. You might as well take the rest of the fall."

Muir let Kappler push him into his chair.

Muir muffled a groan. "C'mon, you know how it's played: top floor gets a thing fucked, someone below catches the clap. Look, maybe it won't be your department."

"Then why would Harker lie to us in the morning brief, telling us Bishop's rogue?"

"Fred, it's my last day. Don't do this to me."

"Tell me what happened. I demand it."

Muir heaved a sigh as though unloading a burden. He danced subtle eyes at Kappler's electric map board, luring the analyst to reactivating it.

"I told them," Muir commiserated, "the least we can do is prep a hot extraction, in case things get nasty and we're forced to pull him out under fire. I mean, this is China. Middle of a trade war? You know what the Young Turks come back with?" A less subtle look at the map board. "'Op Resources report the assets are not available.'"

"They're such chickenshits." Kappler accentuated his disgust, plunging his thumb on the map board remote. "Bitches never asked us anything."

"Why'dya think I've called it a day? Loyalty up, loyalty down: that's the CIA I joined."

Fred assiduously chewed his upper lip. Bobbed his balding head in agreement. "We got a carrier group right there."

Muir studied the illuminated map. CIA and US military assets lit across the entire East Asian region with correlating Area of Operation, current mission codes and, designations.

"I know. And they got Marines."

"They got SEALs on standby for this kind of thing. Commander Wiley's outfit. What does Harker think I do here?!"

"I know, I know. All for nothing. Which carrier, by the way?"

"The, uh…" Kappler's voice trailed off. Suspicion sparked back to his eyes. "What do you mean? If you planned this, you'd know what carrier…"

"I say I planned this? No way. Tender your resignation: Boom!" Muir punched a fist into his open hand. "Cut you right out of the loop."

Muir's beeper went off. He checked it—*GLADYS*.

"That's Director Folger now. Gotta go. Look, I'm having this little retirement shindig—say, seven, in the old Clandestine Services library?"

Muir opened the door, his face inquisitive, encouraging Kappler's agreement with a nod of his own.

"Uh, sure, Nathan, I'm—I didn't know you liked me…"

"What's not to like?" Muir left him with a wink.

He caught sight of Harker pushing his way inside the main room, angry eyes searching until they found him. Muir went the other direction where an EXIT sign indicated an alternate path out. He flicked Brody's keycard a few paces ahead, then kicked it under a cubicle as he passed it.

"Muir! Wait up!"

Muir ducked out of the room. Harker hurried after, pausing only long enough to key-swipe Kappler's door.

"What was Muir talking to you about?"

Kappler munched his Chinese chicken salad.

"His party?" A wave of his chopsticks and a smile of smug satisfaction. "I don't think you're invited."

MUIR PLOWED THE OUTER CORRIDOR along the green glass windows of the New Headquarters Building and September's gloom beyond. Although active cell phones are disallowed inside Agency grounds, Muir risked reprimand and spoke into his.

"Where are you, Gladys?"

"Food court. Did you know they've brought in a Chin Chin's?"

Muir smirked. Loved how she used the trivial to remind him to breathe.

"They say the chicken salad's a big hit on the Sunset Strip," he offered. "My buddy Fred Kappler's already made the scene."

"Your buddy?"

"Yeah. Act it when you call him to tell him my party's canceled."

"What party?"

"Muir!" Harker called.

Muir didn't risk an over-the-shoulder glance but, judging by the sound, still had a good lead on the Young Turk.

"Talk to me," Muir said into his phone.

"Director Folger's on the warpath."

"Cell phones are forbidden, Muir!" Harker hollered.

"Thanks, got his chief scalp-hunter hot on my trail. Get my info?"

"Bishop is being held at the at the Fourth People's Liberation Army District Military Prison, Suzhou."

"Imagery Analysis?"

"They've got every angle on the place you could want. Collecting dust."

A commotion and a crash close behind. Muir glanced back, meeting the frustrated gaze of Jeremy Harker untangling with a mail cart. Dodging employees. Bearing down.

"Get me whatever they have."

"That'll have to go through Director Folger's office."

"I'm aware of that."

"But you already have his signature... Oh, Nathan."

Muir touched the commendation rolled in his pocket. He said, "Find out what carrier SEAL Commander Wiley operates from in the South China Sea."

"All right, Muir," Harker snapped. "Wait up."

Muir slapped shut his phone. Slowed until Harker fell into step.

"You were memo-ed on the new policy regarding cell phones."

"Memo culpa. How 'bout I take a disciplinary leave for the rest of my life?"

Harker huffed, struggled to keep pace with Muir's sizable stride. Muir hid a mocking smile as soon as he was sure Harker saw it. He reached a bank of elevators, stepping inside as they closed. Harker slapped them back open and joined him. Muir stared at the doors. Harker: at the spot he'd like to put a bullet in the back of the older spy's skull.

"We're going to need you upstairs a bit longer."

"What's this?"

"I said, 'We're going to need you upstairs a bit longer.'"

Muir sighed, as if the only thing he wanted was the last and least of his desires. Addressing the doors, he said, "Got something in your teeth."

FOLGER, HARKER, AND THE REST of the Young Turks never stood a chance against Muir, and the Chinese prison detachment never stood a chance against Commander Wiley, his SEALs flawlessly executing Operation DINNER OUT. By the time Tom Bishop and Elizabeth Hadley were airborne, Muir had already checked out and zoomed off in his Porsche, while Harker and the rest of the Seventh Floor were still counting the number of his ex-wives.

All but one of them.

Muir sped from the Agency, making it to Dulles with time to spare for the 9:20 flight to Miami, time he chose to kill in the terminal bar.

"This stool taken?" came a voice beside him.

Muir didn't bother looking. "Left it 'specially for you."

Counterintelligence chief Silas Kingston sat beside Muir like a young sovereign seating a throne.

"I'll have whatever he's having," he said with a finger snap to the bartender.

"You'll get further in life if you don't do that at people," Muir said. He still hadn't faced him.

"I've never understood you, Muir."

Muir drank. He cocked his head at his whiskey. "I count your failure at that a victory."

"Count it the last you have left."

His drink arrived. Muir looked at him. Free now, he shook his head in disgust. "Harker, even Folger—no idea SIDESHOW's a smokescreen?"

Silas Kingston's eyes lit with genuine admiration. For one tenth of a second. "All those years knowing you jerked on traitor March's line. You could have amounted to something, Muir."

Muir scoffed. "With your little supper club? Had the appetizer with the stay-behinds of GLADIO.[1] No appetite for the entrée. Don't dine on horseshit when I can help it."

"Let me ask you a question. Never once did you ping us. Why?"

"I don't suspect anyone ever retires from KALEIDOSCOPE."

"Hmm," Kingston murmured. He drank his whiskey in one swallow. "Well played with Harker. Doubted you'd pull it off."

---

1   WWII OSS/CIA European stay-behind terror program; available for debrief at your request.

Muir briefly widened his eyes, but otherwise gave away nothing.

"All that time they were puzzling out your wives and Bishop's loyalties, they never bothered to ask what drives yours."

Muir stood. Kingston matched him.

"If Bishop weren't your flesh and blood, I might have offered you a deal. Now, I deliver a curse. Waiting for him and his little misguided woman is the one file that didn't burn. Operation GIRL SCOUT?"

Whatever Silas Kingston expected, it wasn't the full smile, perfect-toothed and serene, Muir bestowed. He placed a warm hand on the younger spymaster's shoulder. Friendly, but also a control. He said, "My son Tom once told me, 'You don't trade these people we send out like they're baseball cards.' I told him, 'That's exactly what we do.' And you know something? Listen now, Silas, because this is important: I was dead wrong."

They called Muir's flight. He finished his drink. "Happy I'll be able to tell him that when you send him home to kill me."

"I'll see to it."

Muir smiled cruelly. Whether he bought the threat or not, he made sure Kingston knew he didn't care. "Difference between us, pal? I've never doubted you once."

17

THE MORNING AFTER our initial contact with HOUNDFOX, Nina shopped a few minutes in the lobby arcade before we went into the café for a breakfast of *café con leche*, toast with butter, fried eggs, and fruit. Nina took her coffee but returned her plate. She explained to the disappointed waitress (and whomever that woman reported to) that her stomach bothered her and, with an aside of *"Tengo muchos cólicos,"* her problem most likely due to the onset of her menstrual cycle. To plant a seed for our day to come, Nina added in Spanish, "I doubt it's bacteria or anything like that."

Our conversation moved to cigars. Nina did the talking as I worked to memorize as much as I could. I'd fly solo once I arrived at El Laguito Cigar Factory. At quarter to eight, Juan Lopez, a Tabacuba representative from the Ministry of Agriculture, approached us. Accompanying him was Marisol Pérez-Quiñones, a marketing director from the El Laguito where Fidel Castro's fabled Cohiba cigars—formerly reserved for his private use and diplomatic gifts—had, due to the Special Period, ramped up production for international export.

Greetings in English, some chatting with Nina in Spanish followed to test her proficiency and my ignorance when they saw my confusion at some verbal bomb tossed my way.

"¿No habla Español?" said Señor Lopez after the chuckling subsided.

"Más o manos," I responded, expert at *dos* language dopiness.

"Basic, then, no?" Marisol chirped.

"Sí o no sé," I addled.

Outside, a violent-looking, quiet driver (translate: DI muscle) directed us into a brand-new, freshly waxed Soviet Arbat minivan. The canary-yellow paint job with a checkerboard swatch led me to assume it a taxi that I complimented as the cleanest I'd ever encountered. A skeptical look from Marisol and a remark that it was the Cohiba label design.

"How can it be you don't recognize the most exclusive cigar logo in the world—the one you've traveled all this way to export?"

Know it all.

"As Lenin made abundantly clear in his fourth letter to Trotsky in London, 'Exclusivity renders sightless the proletariat.'"

"Lenin lived with Trotsky in London. Why would he write him letters?"

"The exact question Trotsky asks in letter five."

"*¿Quién conoce la mente de los rusos locos?*" Who knows the mind of crazy Russians? said Nina, and everyone had a brief laugh again as she engaged in the newly mandated Cuban *pasatiempo nacional* of blaming *rusos locos* for everything.

We headed off the Hicacos Peninsula onto Cuba proper to drive west along the northern rim of the island, the Straits of Florida spreading sapphire toward the land of freedom invisible over the horizon. We drove to the town of Matazanos talking about the luxuries of the star-shaped resort we'd left, Nina championing the food, I the comfortable sea air wafting while we slept, and both of us our desire to relax later that afternoon on the white sands of its seashore.

"I purchased a bikini I want to wear," said Nina.

"And, lemme tell ya: I want to get my eyes on her in that," I grinned.

"Aren't you two married, *señor?*" Marisol inquired too casually.

Nina's shoulders clenched forgetting our cover. Marisol was plump and acting the virago rather than the interrogator and I'd spent the night cold under the window while my passport-pretend wife laughed at me from under the covers in the second room and teased me about maybe needing phentolamine injections as my excuse for not joining her.

The two men all grinned appreciatively at Nina, Señor Lopez making the appropriate inappropriate macho comment I couldn't translate. Vocalized drool.

Nina said, "*Gracias*, Mr. Damon," to me, and Marisol looked away out the window, rubbing her hip unnecessarily against my thigh.

Piece of work this woman. And I hadta spend the day with her.

Nina took a candy tin from her purse. She offered the container. "Mint anyone?" She popped one.

No takers.

We entered Matanzas, known as the Venice of Cuba, according to Señor Lopez, due to its seventeen crossings over the seven rivers that crisscross the city. Borraj, our driver, pointed out the apartment neighborhood where he grew up in one of the few hundred visible units, so—preferring the invited intimacy of the attack dog over the continued intimacy of Marisol's hip-now-ass pressure—I said, "Yours is an unusual name. Is it of Arabic origin?"

"No, no. It is passed father to first son in my family. I'm Ciboney people. Back when the Spaniards enslaved us for the mines, it was the chemical compound used as a flux to purify gold. The imperialists stole our gold and our names."

"It's a beautiful name no matter the origin," Nina said.

She was growing pale as the only mint from her purse not a balm for halitosis continued to dissolve in her mouth.

From Matanzas, we returned to the coast highway. We'd been driving another forty-five minutes when turning north onto Highway 131—Señor Lopez and Marisol taking turns probing

Nina's and my legend, all in the friendliest of manners—when Nina shuddered.

"*¡Frena allí! ¡Por favor! ¡Voy vomitar!*" Pull over! Please! I'm sick! she said.

First a burp, and as soon as the car hit the side of the road, Nina lurched out and threw up. This went on for a while, Nina assigning fault to the great enemy United States: some BBQ (we'd never had) at the airport ahead of our flight. Nina huddled and lurched, groaned, huddled and lurched again. The two men discussed where to take her, your vaunted "health care for all" unavailable to most since the Russian retreat from—or better— retreat *with* your economy.

"How do you notice the difference in a Connecticut shade wrapper or Habano wrapper?" Marisol asked.

Cigar riddle or poor English?

"The Havana rapper doesn't have a rap sheet."

She eyed me from under a mascara veil applied thick enough to pass as lace. Marisol was onto me. Not as a spy. As a tobacco business owner.

"I didn't notice earlier," I said. "Your eyelashes are incredible." I said the right thing. "It's amazing how the mascara clings just as well to the fake lashes as the real." But followed with the wrong.

After a muffled call with the medical bureau, it was decided Nina should receive care at El Hospital Universitario General Calixto García where we proceeded directly. Marisol was sullen and, thankfully, distant until turning into the emergency entrance, our driver swerved to miss a speeding ambulance. Marisol pivoted in such a way as to thrust her cleavage under my nose.

What is wrong with this woman?

In Spanish, Lopez, Marisol, and the driver discussed who would remain with Nina at the hospital and who would continue with me to the Cohiba factory. The two men who worked directly for the state agreed Marisol would stay here. Marisol, who worked directly for Castro, dubbed them incorrect. She would remain with me.

If action is required against anyone in this document, it's that heated piece of work; I'll get into that later, as it's personal and you already know the details of my tobacco deal.

Your question marks riddle round Nina.

In 1896, YOUR SPANISH RULERS constructed the original hospital for the occupying military forces and named it *San Ambrosio* after the sainted Roman doctor Aurelius Ambrosius. A nurse put Nina in a chair and wheeled her up the ramp. A subtle row of stone figures in relief girded the main structure. Lopez and the nurse touched the one closest to the door. They glanced at Nina.

"Is this a thing you do?"

Lopez weighed his hands. "In your case, maybe so."

Nina tapped the sainted forehead. "Who is it?"

"They call him Bona-V. As a military hospital, the predominant affliction here was dysentery. He was placed there as a protector."

"What's he the saint of?"

"Intestinal disorders."

Inside the hospital, Nina avoided the formalities of check-in. They wheeled her to the inner doors and a waiting nurse who tried to deny Lopez entry. He insisted he could not bow to convention as she was a foreign guest in his care, under his political watch, which they all knew meant anti-Castro surveillance.

Inside the examination room, Lopez was asked to leave once more when Nina was handed a gown. He insisted on staying; he'd simply turn away. Nina didn't protest. The nurse left, modest and deferential. Nina handed Lopez the box given her. Nina went ahead by handing articles of her clothing to him over his shoulder. She dangled her thong. He froze. Inaction and appalled silence met only with the buzz of the lights.

"*Señor?*"

He gingerly took her offered undergarment from his shoulder.

"You may turn around now," Nina said.

He did. She did. Giving him fair view of her firm and shapely backside between the open folds of the gown.

"This is my duty," he said, apologetically. "I am sorry."

Nina grimaced, answering him with a liquid laugh into the wastebasket. He withered with embarrassment. Nina retreated to the exam table.

Inside the next minute, awkward, silent, the pair staring everywhere but at each other, the door opened a third time.

"*Buenos. Soy la doctora García,*" said a young internist.

From her haircut to her glittering eyes, her diminutive stature disproportionately offset by lengthy slender arms and long delicate fingers, everything about her spoke "Pixie." Nina would not have been surprised to see, were she to remove her white coat, diaphanous double wings spring out ready for Tinkerbell flight. She glided alongside Nina's knee. Took her vitals. Inquired of her symptoms. Was it on purpose she conveyed a sexual tenderness in touching Nina? Probing her belly with delicate hands, sliding up Nina's back into her gown with her stethoscope to listen to her lungs and then, with provocative innocence, slipped the listening diaphragm around inside the gown against Nina's skin to hear to her heart between her breasts. Nina fixed Lopez in an unbreaking stare.

Lopez was finding it hot. He also found the thermostat too high. He used his handkerchief to wipe his forehead.

"Motrin usually helps with my cramps," Nina said in Spanish.

"This, I'm afraid, is not menstrual in nature. Most likely bacterial, but my initial abdominal exam concerns me. If you would lie back, please?"

Nina did as requested. Lopez turned scarlet as Dr. García tucked both her hands inside Nina's gown to her stomach and gently kneaded and probed some more.

"I'm afraid the patient will need an abdominal MRI."

"Clothed?" Lopez asked, not recognizing his squeak.

The pixie softly shook her head, denying him. "You may join us, or if you'd find it more *polite* to wait here...?" The ice in her voice allowed Lopez to know what a pervert caught peeping feels.

The doctor opened the door, where the nurse waited with a wheelchair, which Lopez didn't think to question. Dr. García hovered over Nina as she lowered into it, then snatched the box from Lopez and deposited it into Nina's lap. Lopez didn't answer, but he also didn't move. The women left the room, which, for all I know, Lopez may still be inside.

"ONE THING I APPRECIATE ABOUT CUBA is you have obliterated commercial billboard blight," I said, passing the one hundredth or so roadside sign depiction of Fidel, Che Guevara, any of those bearded Russians, the martyred Saíz brothers, the Cuban flag, or the words *¡Viva! ¡Fidel! ¡Che! ¡Viva! ¡Comandante! ¡Socialismo! ¡Futuro! ¡Viva! ¡Cuba!* endlessly repeated in every imaginable combination, block after city block and all along the highway.

Marisol offered a cool smile. She cracked her window and the suck of air danced with her red-dyed hair.

"Your poor people psychologically bombarded by booze, shyster attorneys, insurance con men, and the high-fat, high-sugar, high-sodium, high-cholesterol nutritional nightmare of American fast-food drug pushers," she agreed. She let hang an impregnate-me pause. "And gentlemen's clubs."

"Makes it kinda hard to find a good McDonald's drive-thru, though."

"We have the Zas burger. Officially superior to McDonalds." This gal didn't miss a beat. "Fidel Castro is a worldwide expert at agrotechnology, livestock, and food production."

"You don't say?"

"Such is our great leader's passion for farming and livestock, he personally produces beans, cattle, and buffalo, as well as cheese and milk-free citrus- and vegetable- flavored ice-cream products, coffee beans that don't need grinding but can be used more than once, and is reinventing sugar on his vast estate known as Zona Cero."

"The place with the dairy?"

"How bright you are, Mr. Damon. In the Valle de la Picadura on the outskirts of Havana, President Castro designed the world's greatest air-conditioned dairy, where he dedicates himself to the crossbreeding of livestock. *El aire frío endulza la leche.*"

"'Cold air' does something to 'milk,' *sí*?"

She stroked my leg above the knee.

"The genius of centralization," I said, and squirmed. "Air condition the milk where it's produced before it goes out to the unconditioned masses."

I suddenly knew *exactly* why those otherwise-thought-fortunate schoolboys rat out frisky teachers when she squeezed me and said:

"Superior steers provide greater amounts of beef."

"O-kay. Back to the fast food. The Zas v. Mickey-D. How was this superiority confirmed?"

"Very well. Fidel had tried the McDonald's hamburger on his six visits to New York City and the United Nations. He considers them an excellent burger."

"But not *officially* superior?"

"No. Using his unique culinary science, Fidel developed his own superior recipe. To prove this, and maintain its superior quality, he has his most trusted advisers ship in the inferior McDonald's burgers once a month for taste-test comparison."

Our current president from Arkansas, I hear, does likewise—just doesn't bother taste-testing them against anything.

"Do the Cuban people eat this Zas burger?"

"Two per person per month. To provide this, he closed every fifth café and converted them to selling his superior product."

I tapped the driver's shoulder. "How do you like them, Borraj?"

"Never ate one. Too expensive."

Marisol glowered. We rode the final thirty minutes in silence.

I DID NOT EXPECT A CIGAR FACTORY inside of a palace. But I'm telling you nothing as you know all about the factory part of my 1991 visit. Suffice it to say, Marisol allowed (read *forced*) me to take her arm. Staff waited on the factory-palace steps, and they greeted me pleasantly, her deferentially, and I must admit she was a beautiful, smiling, laughing hostess in all appearance, even as she whispered between *holas*, "You know nothing about cigars."

I took an offered champagne.

"I will concede, Nina is the expert between us."

"You are not her husband. That is also a lie."

The ice of a blown cover froze my spine.

"You are her pleasure toy. A plaything for her desires. Or resist me. Tell me, 'No, Marisol.'"

"No, Marisol."

"Does she taste like this?"

Marisol had no pockets. She did not carry her purse. Somehow—and I know exactly how—a short, fat robusto, its wrapper moist with Marisol, was in her hand and popped into my mouth. She lit it and whispered, "Taste me."

I have never gone to our White House and now know I never will. I do know something of what it's like to smoke in the Oval Office.

I said as little as possible for the rest of my visit; made the money transfer from ex-DEA Cuban witchdoctor Victor Rubio do the necessary talking for me to the tune of 350,000 dollars. Turns out, Rubio supplies all of DC and most of Maryland and Virginia—including the putz who called me a putz.

Marisol left us before I signed the shipping deals for the transfer in the Dominican Republic, but I heard her whisper to Borraj, *"Él es cien por ciento el tonto que pretende ser."* He is 100 percent the fool he plays.

After returning me to Las Palmeras, I never had surveillance again.

WHILE I SIGNED PAPERS at El Laguito Cohiba factory and smoked the musky cigar and wished for one of Nina's special breath mints, Dr. "Pixie" García did not deliver Nina to the MRI. She hustled Nina through the door to a nurses' closet that had little on the shelves by way of medicines or supplies, but it locked and allowed Nina a measure of privacy to change back into her clothes. She clipped on the visitor pass prepared for her. Found the hospital map tucked into a blood sample tube.

She memorized the map, tore it to pieces, stuffed it down the central floor drain. She emerged into the corridor. Dr. García was gone. Nina centered herself. She made her way along the corridor and rode a clunking elevator to the top of the opposite wing.

She found the sign, *"Sala de Oncología"* and made her way to the cancer ward. She entered. She was expected. A nurse barely able to hold her emotions thanked Nina for making the trip; thanked Jesus for delivering Nina in time.

HOUNDFOX, her dear father, lifted sad eyes from beside Nina's mother's bedside, engulfing her frail hand in both of his. Even brokenhearted, his smile for his daughter was unafraid. He whispered into his wife's ear. She smiled a little before she opened her eyes. She spoke:

"Mi nenita querida. The beauty of your smile still matches the fire of your eyes. You never fade."

Nina clutched the doorway, suffocating with emotion, and Nina has never been able to explain—but I know the feeling entirely and cultivate the experience toward my own end—the circumstance of falling between the cracks of time. She swears she did not move through space. Like a jump in a film or a figure moving between pools of lamplight separated by impenetrable darkness, she never released the doorway, never took a step, but her hands held her mother and her cheek pressed against hers, their tears mingled, and they both were speaking at once, each of them comforting, each of them promising a future life beyond the constraints of the present, which in so close a moment extended in both directions, pushing back the past and away the future.

Her mother was weak, each moment earmarked as her last, but they staved off that moment as they turned the pages of their favorite memories, ordering them like beads on a string when they are but feelings, and feelings aren't mementoes of chronology but refractions of a single block of past-present-future "now" whenever honestly summoned.

Nina's mother knew this, and she said, "How do we make each other feel?"

She took her husband's hand, including him in the emotion that was the heart of their family.

Nina started to speak but her mother gently shh'd her.

"Don't speak, *nenita*. It isn't words. Ale?" She gripped her husband's hand and smiled into his face.

There it is, boys: fill in your puzzle. The date, the hospital. Cancer ward. Midnight-black wife. Nickname "Ale" for Alejandro...

"Feel it running through us, filling our hearts, filling this room, filling Cuba and our sweet air, carrying across the sea that surrounds us to fill the world and rise to God. Feel us. Do you feel it? Truly, *deeply* feel it?"

Nina smiled blinking tears, her chest bursting with love.

"I always have," said Alejandro.

"In a moment, I will be free from this body that long ago became nothing more than a trap. I will go to a place where the past and the future are the same and you will not miss me because I will also be here in this feeling we are sharing this moment but have shared precisely the same our whole lives. Tomorrow, when you grieve me, my Nina-*nenita* replace grief with this feeling and it will be no different from now, or than it ever was before; it will be the same. You already know this, and you'll know me alive within you."

Nina's mother didn't speak another word. For ten more minutes, she watched her husband and her daughter fight their tears and she gazed at them from a place of serenity beyond her pain.

"I love you, *Mami*," Nina whimpered because she knew how long she would have to miss her, and her mother looked askance at her as if any more talk was a silly thing because she never could be gone from her daughter.

Seven minutes later, both Nina and her father felt her spirit rise, hover, leave; they met eyes across the dead body that had given them the life they shared. What surprised Nina was not the emptiness that comes with loss she expected to feel, because it never happened. Instead, the love her mother had identified as the emotional signature of their lives, increased and cushioned her torment in the protective embrace of love *exactamente* alive inside her breast.

THERE IS NOTHING MORE you need from me to identify HOUNDFOX. I can hear your telephone calls in the next room.

About the hospital staff—Dr. García in particular—they broke the rules, and they broke the law in helping Nina and HOUNDFOX. Your concept and need for justice belong to you, your courts, your mighty and benevolent Fidel. Please respect they acted without political motivation. They acted then and, I'm certain, act now in their sacred duty to the care and comfort of the terminally ill and their families.

Show mercy.

As for Guzman, you know better than I what happened with him. HOUNDFOX purposely exposed some defunct, broken links in his island-wide intelligence chain—by planting incriminating evidence in both Guzman's office and his home.

Guzman took his own life as he had lived: deriving sexual pleasure from physical torment. A plastic bag over his head, a belt around his throat, and a hand on his cock. His life was spent before our return flight touched down in Mexico City.

18

I PROMISED YOU, GENERAL TRIGORIN, I would tell you everything. In the forthcoming days, after the HOUNDFOX trial and my testimony, you may read this document and choose to excise these next few pages from my signed draft, as you already know who Nina is, her childhood name before—under Muir's tutelage—she changed it to Estrada in America.

With that qualification, read on.

The night Nina lost her mother, we stole from the hotel and drove in the blackout to the ruins of her mother's family beach cottage on the north-shore coast in the town of Caiberién. I comforted Nina, holding her as she leaned into me and we trudged through a palm and pink bauhinia tree forest, coco plum, and the sea grape clutching our ankles along a dark moon-filtered path.

I ached to love her, betray myself to all she is.

We came upon the cottage from behind. It had long ago fallen to disrepair and weather, nature now devouring the remains. Its frame stood, years without walls, like the proscenium of a stage, where past the curtain, risen with the moon, we could see straight through to the sea stretched to the horizon.

"I want to show you something, Pintao."

"Russell. Please, it's all I ask of you. You *could* cooperate."

"This used to be raised," she said, hefting a corner of the porch. "Help me lift it, baby? We can pull it away."

We lifted. Only sand below, but Nina's eyes beamed with the anticipation of discovery.

"When I was fourteen, I found a picture frame washed up on our beach."

She pointed down the overgrown path to where the waves thumped like fists and pulled away, open hands scraping back from the sand.

I have never wanted to kiss a woman as much as I desired to kiss Nina...

... *except for this moment and to the never I've sacrificed myself to save her.*

"It was small. Old-fashioned. Handcrafted metal and mother-of-pearl." She made an oval with the fingers of both her hands together. "The glass was cracked but still held in place over the photograph inside."

"Who was in the photograph?"

Nina shook her head. "It was covered with sand. Ruined by the water. I rinsed it. I left the print inside and I put it in the sun. When it dried, an outline appeared. Faint, but it was an outline of a man and a woman from long ago and far away. A wedding photo, maybe. It was a romantic mystery and a treasure. I wanted to know her. I wanted to be her. Fall in love with the mysterious prince."

"What happened to it?" I said, my skin prickling with the magic she drew around us.

"I kept it secret." She pointed to the sand. "In a metal box my grandfather had given me. It's here right now, frozen in time. Waiting for us. Will you dig it up with me?"

I said I would. We squatted. In my heart, I was already making promises never to leave her side again.

"Before we dig, I need to tell you why I buried it."

"Go for it. Please."

She met my gaze, her expression thankful. She cleansed her mind with a sigh like the faint rush of air when a treasure hunter opens a long-sealed tomb.

"That summer, my father—whose loyalty was already shifting away from Fidel and the revolution in 1968—had an aide in his department, Pablo Sandoval, who had shown much bravery in the revolution at an early age. This, coupled with his deep knowledge of the great thinkers and leaders of the Soviet Revolution, his fluency in the Russian language, along with his European blue eyes and light hair—but deep Cuban charisma—made him irresistible. He was twenty-three that summer, and I envied him his bright destiny, full of interest and meaning, given him by the Revolution."

"Jesus—what?!—did this creep rape you?"

Nina laughed. She wrapped an arm around me, nestled her head along the side of my neck and whispered, "Don't tell me you don't love me, Pintao, oh great defender of my virtue."

I snorted but didn't otherwise move, my inner flame lit by the warmth radiating from her face and hair. She kissed my throat and pulled away. There would always be a part of Nina no one could capture or possess. What you take from Nina is only what she chooses to give.

"No," she said. "He did not rape me. And yes, I chose him to be my first."

"Lover. Your first lover." I sulked.

In some circles, I'm known as an accomplished sulker. I'm lying: it's the Olympic Rings of circles.

"Now what? You brought me here to dig up your dirty prom picture?"

Everything I said seemed to increase Nina's delight. My annoyance grew.

"Yes, baby, the night my mother died, my deepest instinct was to bring the man I'm going to share the rest of my life with to see a photograph of me and my first lover." She pinched my cheek. "Such a noble heart you have."

"Well, how am I supposed to know what you're talking about?"

"It wouldn't be a revelation, a secret, or a treasure if you knew, now would it?"

I grunted.

"I secretly gave myself to Pablo the length of summer and I kept the picture frame hidden in my bedroom. At night I would gaze into those outlines and wish until I saw the two of us fill them."

"I hate this frame."

"Pintao: you have a wife. You're married. You know true love, *verdad*? But I was learning. And Pablo taught me everything I know about true love. He made me every promise every girl ever would die to hear. And he kept fucking me."

Disgust flooded her voice. I snapped my eyes to hers.

"I kept dreaming for moonlight parties clutched to his uniformed arm, and dancing under lanterns, and he kept fucking me and lying to me, and he got me pregnant and forced me to get an abortion, which ruined me for children forever. He taught me everything I know about love by exception. Because there was no love inside him. Everything Pablo that is the opposite of Pablo is true love. Pablo is why I was sent to Paris. Pablo is what finally pushed my father to betray his country.

"Hector Guzman has always questioned my father's loyalty. This is why my father placed Pablo on his staff. Pablo's only true desire is power. His lust for young girls is nothing compared to his consuming desire to strip Guzman of his position and seize the reins on his division inside the DI. This is how my father will protect himself."

"I thought the setup was with this Trigorin dude," I said.

"Sandoval was Pablo's father's name. When his father was sent to prison for profiteering, Pablo took his Russian mother's name.

Trigorin. That same summer. He'd gotten close to our family not only to seduce me, but to plant false evidence against his own father with mine."

"The picture frame is still empty?"

We were sitting now in the sand. Nina took my hand. She placed my palm against her heart. "Feel my heartbeat. Feel how real I am."

"Nina: I made up with my wife, literally, last night."

"Muir told me you'd say that."

"Because it's true."

"Is it? Or was last night your first step to making up with yourself?"

I couldn't speak. My hand—she'd moved, or I'd moved it—rubbed against her nipple hard beneath it. Was it shame, or biology, or the truth my arousal was pushing me with?

"Who was it last night, Pintao, who you committed fully to murder?"

Of course, it was me. It was Russell Aiken who I carried my deepest loathing for in always letting me down.

"I *didn't* kill myself."

"You pulled the trigger, no?"

I did not respond because I had.

"You're with me only because Muir kept the bullets from you. Choose yourself now, Russell Aiken. And after, when we dig up my treasure, you tell me who you will see inside the frame with me."

We undressed each other. And with the removal of our clothes went the removal of everything that named us or held us to the names that claimed our lives but could never grasp our souls.

WE WATCHED DAWN come to the sky above where we lay, and we began to dig.

"It's like we're digging up a time machine," I said, but before our fingers so much as brushed the solidity of the metal box we dug for, a bird's cry yanked our attention to the sky in time to watch a seagull die midflight and plummet to the ground.

If I have never seen Nina truly frightened, this fall of a bird was the closest I've ever come. She fell back away from the hole. Before I knew what she was doing, she was pumping her legs, pushing the sand. I scooted back as she filled her treasure hole. She grabbed her clothing, tossed me mine. We dressed on the run through the beach forest and back to the car.

ON THE MEXICO CITY—and again on the Washington—flight on our escape from Havana, she spoke only the barest of necessities. I didn't try to talk about a future. We'd been two different people on the beach; we were two different people now. I know now that all I had to say was the right thing, but I never do and at least—so I told myself—this one time I saved us from me saying something transcendent and massively wrong.

Nina drove us to Georgetown. To Victor Rubio's shop. I turned over the paperwork for the Cohiba deal. He asked how I found Marisol.

"Unusual," I said, and he laughed, and the three of us smoked cigars in his office. I choked and turned green.

Nina took a folded lace handkerchief from her purse. Only when she handed it to him and said, *"La esencia del alma pura de una mujer,"* did I understand I was participating in a ritual. He put the folded handkerchief in a small bowl. He took a bottle of Cuban rum from his desk, the three of us drank, and then he spat some on the handkerchief and into the bowl. He unfolded the handkerchief.

Inside was a strand of Nina's mother's braided hair. He held out his hand to me. I didn't know what he wanted and yet saw I held exactly what it was—from out of my pocket—the green marble he'd called a bead.

"Like this," he said.

And Victor Rubio slipped the lock of hair through the hole in the bead. Nina let him take her hand. Something tore apart inside of me. He looked at me, his eyes suddenly those of a vulture. I fled.

I would not see Nina again for another ten years.

19

I HAVE MADE MY CONFESSION. Nothing left chance. Nothing left to give. The shutters have been opened across from my balcony, across the Calle Obispo. I have no doubt, General Trigorin, you will find Comandante Alejandro Alvarez. I trust, after you do, that according to your word, his daughter Nina will regain her freedom.

Of my own free will and by my signature, under penalty of perjury, all applicable laws and statutes of the Republic of Cuba, I solemnly swear to the legal binding over me and affirm this document to be the truth as I know it, unabbreviated, unfiltered, and without outside influence sworn to this day: December 25, 2002, Hotel Florida, Havana, Cuba.

Signed: Russell Aiken
Legal Counsel, CIA Office of General Counsel, the Central Intelligence Agency, United States of America, resigned.

20

I LAY ASIDE my pen.

One of the three remaining Cuban agents comes into the room to collect my document. I step away from the table. Along with what I've written, he takes the box of pads. About to take my pen, he returns it to me. I place it on the coffee table. I feel dirty keeping it; I've written Muir out of it, all he stood for and hoped for me, and the ink it has delivered is brown, impossible to forge, and it is dry.

Like me. Like Muir. Empty and dry.

The agent leaves to the kitchen.

The inkwell I'd insisted they hunt down in the night and deliver me beckons unopened from the hollow of my left hand. I position my face out of view from the overhead camera. I hear the air conditioner cycle on. I breathe deeply five full breaths of night air before closing the balcony doors.

My eyes swim.

My hands shake.

I fumble off the inkwell cap.

"Drink me," I whisper a final counted, countdown breath.

I open it and swallow the contents and by this do I take my freedom.

PART TWO

PERCEPTION

"9:34 a.m.: Now I am superlatively, actually awake…
11:01 a.m.: I AM ~~REALLY~~, ~~superlatively~~, perfectly
awake (1st TIME)… 2:10 p.m.: This time properly
awake… 2:14 p.m.: **This time** finally awake… 2:35
p.m.: This time completely awake… ~~At 9:40 p.m.~~
~~I awoke for the first time, despite my previous~~
~~claims.~~ I was fully conscious at 10:35 p.m., and
awake for the first time in many, many weeks."

—CLIVE WEARING (musician, musicologist,
conductor), *Personal Journal*

21

"I'M IN A KIND OF HELL over it. The one person who could provide clarity on this—help me help *her*—is the guy who's wake we're headed to," Joshua Rosen said as he worked his knife around the plastic edges of the Smucker's orange marmalade portion cup.

He plopped the preserves onto his cornbread and he spread it, mixing it with the half-melted dollop of honey butter he'd already added. He smiled unhappily at me and I simpered back, mouth crooked, heart worn, soul uneasy.

"If you ask me, Muir's clarity always came at a steep price," I said.

Joshua cocked an eyebrow. "What price?"

"Spiritual confusion."

"'Tis the season."

We had flown, Washington, Dulles to Fort Myers airport, landing approximately 3 p.m. Christmas Eve, 2001. I'd rented a car for the drive to Nathan Muir's Captiva Island beach house. He'd bequeathed it to my half-sister Lara, who lived there with her husband, a beach bum of so little consequence as to have a name few on the island knew or ever asked. To those who bothered to inquire, he'd say he was a seafaring man named Silver. Those whose memories could attach the name to the missing leg would join him in a good chuckle and dig no further as island code holds sacrosanct the privacy of those who keep to their business on their own stake of shoreline.

Although the beach house stood in jungled obscurity only a few ticks over an hour's drive from the rental lot, Joshua decided, incorrectly, it would be better form for us to arrive "having had"—bellies full in the onetime criminal forger turned government artist's lexicon—as Lara, being a Malaysian refugee only three months arrived, wouldn't have the first idea of what a Christmas Eve dinner-and-wake would require and, "We shouldn't embarrass her galumphing in like a bunch of hungry hounds."

A connoisseur of classic diners, Joshua had rules about where he'd allow our meal to take place. The establishment needed to be at least twenty-five years old and of individual (as opposed to corporate) ownership for him to accept a menu. He directed me to the Farmers' Market. A southern-style staple since 1952, upon entering he was greeted from the kitchen by the septuagenarian cook.

"Nice to see you back, Mista Rosen!"

"Your smiling face makes the pleasure all mine, Mama."

Probably doesn't have the first clue what her name is.

"Ms. Libby's been a fixture here for twenty-five years," he said, and we were led to our table. "Since you won't be bringing booze, I highly recommend you bring one of her mincemeat pies."

I was bringing booze. Though not drinking myself. My last temptation at my lowest point being the morning of 9/11 and the scotch whisky I'd tossed into the sink. But I'd packed three bottles of Macallan 25 from the three-case supply Muir laid up in his brownstone pantry three days before his death. Perhaps, as Gladys argued, on the theory Muir always planned a dozen moves ahead of everyone else, had known his pending fate, and decided to help me out with his after-party.

"I thought the hunting of mince had gone the way of goose-liver pâté," I muttered and slid into the booth.

Joshua, having urged we fill up with an early dinner, proceeded to order the country fried steak breakfast, I now watched our Technical Services chief devouring. Outside, the eighty-plus-degree temperature dreamed a white-hot Christmas, while inside the restaurant, the Ronettes "Sleigh Ride" competed with the sound of icy air conditioning, and I savored my fried ribs and collard greens thinking I'd like the honor of calling Ms. Olivia Williams *Mama*, too. But the *her* Joshua hoped for Muir's clarity with was not Olivia Williams. *Her* was his newly minted officer, Amy Kim.

Joshua bit into his cornbread, and chewing, spoke. "I know why Muir chose me. Understood his choice of you. Bishop: a given. I get Nina, even that Nancy in accounting."

Numbskull Nancy, my fling-fancy femme fatale-lite in Accounting.

"—All of us orphans," he continued. "But Ms. Kim? She doesn't quite fit that profile, now does she?"

"He praised her undeniably in his recommendation."

"I don't doubt her qualifications. Her undergraduate academic work was at PhD level, and I wouldn't trade Amy for the world. But *that* letter: as his swan song? When did Muir ever sing like that to the Seventh Floor about anyone?

"For that matter, when did Muir ever sing?"

I attended church with him once. Early on in my recruitment. I asked Muir why during the hymns he wouldn't so much as mouth the lyrics.

"God's call to worship, kid, isn't an open invite to mockery. We certainly get our fill outside these doors making a living at it."

Joshua doodled on his napkin. When the folder with our check arrived, he said, "I got the meal. You'll cover the tip?"

I thanked him and opened my wallet. "What's the balance?"

"A tip is an expression of generosity. Leave a value equal to your appreciation of her service. Anything else is transactional, eliminating in the calculation that deeply personal expression your tip is supposed to reflect upon yourself and your server."

I tucked a twenty inside. Joshua grinned. He slipped in his napkin as payment, and we left.

BACK ON THE ROAD, Joshua behind the wheel, mincemeat pie in my lap, my mind wandered to my father. How he would regale us in the build-up to Christmas—a day he always missed—with boyhood adventures in the Angeles Crest, braving the elements to hunt wild, holiday mince. "Only a November–December season on the license, but back in those days mince were still plentiful, and you could bag-and-tag a dozen in something short of an hour."

With visions of mince skins drying on a barn door we never had, mince-fur trapper's caps we never wore, and mince bacon my father said was "smaller than a thumbnail, but tastier than La Crescenta fishcat," I found myself asking Joshua, "What is it Muir said about me that made you understand why he chose me for the CIA?"

"You're Danny Aiken's son." His preternaturally wrinkled face glowed fondness in the sunlight stippling its creases through the windshield. "God, he was one hell of a guy."

"My dad?"

"Yep."

"I didn't know him. At least like I thought I did."

Joshua chuckled. "Naw, you didn't at that, did you?"

I waited for revelation. For the key to the puzzle my father had become to me after the revelations of Operation ATROPOS. I waited. But Joshua didn't fill in any of the empty boxes across and down my memory.

"Then, incorrect. If he chose me for my father, I don't fit the orphan profile."

"You father was dead."

"Yes, and, about that..."

Joshua's eyes gleamed, inward at memories. "Let's say it was a Shakespeare thing for Muir. He and I talked about that once—Shakespeare in context with you."

I sensed Muir's presence so strongly then, I believed if I looked over my shoulder, he'd be haunting me from behind the front-seat parapet, ghosting me with faint praise.

"Go on..."

"He said, 'The thing about Dumbo'—his word not mine—"

"Fair fouls out in love and war, right?" I tried to get into the spirit of the thing.

"Leads to the question Nathan posed, which, today of all days is the most appropriate day to pass it on to you. He said, 'The thing about Dumbo is not whether he is the son of Yorick or Falstaff, but that he chooses for himself whether he becomes Hamlet or Hal. Either one I could live with. So long as he doesn't decide along the way to become the son of Caesar, Danny's kid's a win for me.'" Joshua winked. "How's that for a little spiritual confusion?"

I shifted, hating the seats behind me for their emptiness. "Who's Caesar's son?"

"What do I know about it? Muir told me Caesar's son is Brutus. You figure it out. But about fathers and sons, I always did find it funny how dense our agency is—how Muir got away hiding Bishop's identity all the way to his literal and, in Tom's case, figurative death. What kind of idiots we work for, eh? All their ability to peek around global corners and under the planet's rug. What kind of morons didn't know by looking at the pair they were father and son?

"I never guessed Bishop was his son."

He looked askance. "FBI started their DNA database in '98. First to go into the system were their own agents. But you know, we didn't get there until this year."

"I was there. Got the swab."

"According to Meryl Hofmeyr, Director Tenet implemented it by directive in response to the ATROPOS muck-fuck. Right after having attended Muir's funeral. Had a shit fit finding out no one knew they'd been related. I figure, dead though he was, Nathan had a good laugh over that."

HEALING FROM MY BRAIN SURGERY bullet and tumor removal; dealing with my noxious wife's divorce; reeling from her pending sale of our 1938 Tenleytown townhouse bought by me *previous to our marriage* out of the kindness of my heart (Mads returned the wedding band, the engagement solitaire, and the ten-year anniversary rings, all gifts and precedential, *but not the house?!*); sealing my heart to the triple keeling loss of the half-sister, false brother, and the father I never knew who never was: all having given their lives, one way or the other, for me that spring, Gladys—as Muir's instructions mandated—stepped in and accepted the unappealing job of implementing the OPLAN that would be Muir's funeral.

It would be a deception operation of the highest order.

In accordance with Muir's last wishes as included in his will, a funeral service in his honor would be held on the Saturday before the Fourth of July the year of his passing.

"Rusty," he said, when, as his attorney, I drafted the instructions, "in case you're not around to pass the word, make it explicit I want it to be long, pompous, and as boring as possible."

"Why wouldn't I be there?"

He gnat-batted my words with a dismissive swipe. "If you are there, maybe you give it an element of bewilderment or some embarrassing confusion, but *that* I leave to your special brand of spontaneity."

"If I refuse?"

"Tough. Spontaneity is by virtue impossible to stop. Get the entire Seventh Floor, especially Harker and Silas Kingston from CI; I want Princeton academia, primarily a guy in my department, Dr. Trout—real killjoy since our undergraduate days. His glee at my death, coupled with the Agency's suspicion I'm pulling a fast one, will need to be brought to critical mass. Their distraction and the disarray I'm programming into this event will cause them to layer the earth over my grave with the additional sod of their contempt."

"C'mon, Muir, what am I supposed to write here? What does that even mean?"

"You got a lawn at your 1930s Tiny Toon Tennis Town home?"

I sneered. "I have invited you over more times than I'd ever count."

"How many's that?"

"Seventeen times. And if you had ever bothered to visit me, my daughter who looks to you as a grandfather—if you'd ever come at Christmas—"

"How do you know I don't mask up and ring your bell every Halloween?" He stared me down. "Trick-or-treat. Sod or seed?"

"What?"

"Your lawn."

"Seed. Sod looks good, but it's fake and dies. Most lawn owners walk away at that point."

"See—wasn't so hard for you—you got it, already knew what I was saying."

"I don't know what you're saying!"

"It's what I want for the Young Turks and the Pedagogarasts. Sod my tomb and let it die. Only way we can all enjoy a real wake in total comfort and the secure knowledge that Nathan Muir has been fired-and-forgot. Swept clean from the board and under the dead grass of an empty grave. The real deal will be at my place, Captiva Island, Christmas Eve."

My heart leaped. "Because it's all a *fake*. You'll be there!"

Muir took a drink from his D.V.E. tiger flask. "Always got to remember with you, Rusty: can't allow a Newtonian around a blade of grass without an a fortiori leap of faith that grasps the wrong conclusion."

I let it pass; the fuzzy fruit of what comes of age.

LYNN KINGSTON DIDN'T SIT WITH HER FATHER at Princeton's Episcopal Church in the University Chapel. Throughout the interminable service (with no less than seven long hymns Muir had never sung but Gladys had included), the young Ops Planning star, apple of her father, Silas's, eye who—blind to that or to spite him—had chosen to fall from the family tree and rot, oddly and continuously, brought her wrist to her lips as if kissing the thick silver bracelet that cuffed it. I swear there was something aggressive toward me in her eyes each time they met mine, but I never got the chance to question her, as Gladys had left no time for it in her execution of OPLAN OLDSOD. We were to play our roles to script. Two Gospel readings, an overwrought homily by the peripatetic parish priest eager to put down roots, and then my turn as the psalter.

Gladys had assigned me the reading from the Book of Psalms, and I'd taken careful time in preparation to disprove Muir's unkind remark I might accidentally act an agent of befuddlement. I'd worked on my Psalm for a week, aloud and before a mirror, formulating my pronunciations so that with effort, I was able to return the archaic texts back to their original purpose as songs to

God written by David. Songs rhyme and they must have been real catchy in ancient Hebrew, but in English they needed work. I went with an A-A, B, C-C, B, D-D, E-E spirit of the thing:

"The Lord is my shepherd; I shall not *want*; / He maketh me to lie in green pastures; he leadeth me beside still *swamps*. / He restoreth my soul: he leadeth me in the paths of righteousness for his *name's sake*. / Yea though I walk through the valley of the shadow of *the dead*. / I will fear no evil, *I keep my head*. / For thou art with me; thy rod and thy staff they *soothe my aches*. / Thou preparest a table before me in the presence of mine *enemies*: / thou anointest my head with oil; my cup *fills with remedies*. / Surely goodness and mercy shall follow me all the days *that are mine*: / and I will dwell in the house of the Lord for *all time*."

LATER IN THE SERVICE, after insincere words spoken by CIA stuffed shirts and death-does-not-competition-part Princeton robes, Joshua Rosen stepped briskly to the pulpit. He adjusted the microphone, blowing into it until he produced the annoying and prolonged feedback he desired.

"As it is said the evil men do dies with them, I want you all to know—and I think you'll share this sentiment—I've come to praise Muir, not to bury him."

A bad joke well-told goes down as comfortable as castor oil from tongue top to bottom drop. As the august scholars and Monday-morning spies purpled and snarled; as Muir's favorite students, his "bestest network" as he'd loved them, chuckled and laughed; as his Greek chorus of ex-wives, stewardesses, bank-teller beauties, barstool champion dartboard bullseyes of one thousand and one wasted nights of cherished values—as they murmured their backup, Joshua Rosen cried: "PROMETHEUS!" and left all of them weirded out in the crackling mic-hiss that carried the word away.

The declaration of Muir's codename, his scholarly muse, his sexual prowess, his eternal torture, and God-like aspirations hung failed in the air, Joshua's gleaming eyes fixing the word, the name, the myth, the spy, that failure, regret, the love, and success—Prometheus—to a stained-glass beam raining colored light upon our heads. We held our collective breath, if less in suspense, then at least as you'd expect us to hold it if Joshua were pushing our heads under water.

Bill Carver's basso profundo laughter broke the spell and Joshua who, in his black turtleneck that moments before had made him appear as if Orson Welles met John Huston met Melville met Bradbury to send Ahab forthwith after the white whale, now looked like the slouching beatnik he was who'd just smoked a joint.

He admitted later he had, on the road.

He placed two items on the lectern. The first, a sheet of paper he unfolded. He blinked red-eyed at it through scarlet-framed reading glasses and read.

"A short story by Kafka." He peered over spectacles and grinned. "*Short*-short, no groans. He only asked for these two things," and here Joshua baited the hook by flashing the second thing. A document. Concealed in protective plastic and surely ancient, it caught the glass-greened light. I watched Dr. Trout perk and stare and beat his lips together in envy, apart in desire.

"'Prometheus…' Uh, that's the title. By Franz Kafka." But still, he held the second doc and wiggled it wormlike in that light with a fisherman's flair.

Dr. Trout's jowls jiggled as the moving light flickered across his prodigious tufts of nose hair floofing with each breath.

"Here goes: 'There are four legends about Prometheus.'

"'According to the first, because he had betrayed the gods to man, he was chained to a mountain in the Caucasus, and the gods sent eagles to feed on his ever-renewed liver.'

"'According to the second, Prometheus, in pain from the biting beaks, pressed himself deeper and deeper into the rock until he became part of it.'

"'According to the third, his betrayal was forgotten over thousands of years, and the gods forgot, the eagles forgot, as he did, himself.'

"'According to the fourth, everyone grew tired of something which had no reason. The gods grew tired, the eagles grew tired, and the wound closed slowly.'

"'What remained was the inexplicable rocky mountain. The legend tries to explain the inexplicable. Since it comes from truth, it must end again in the inexplicable.'"

Gladys told me later Muir had chosen the existentialist parable for the Promethean volume of clues to everything Muir wasn't that could be mined from a mere 148 words.

"This second thing, and it's a bit et-up by the sands of time—and we can thank Gladys for finding it in his safe deposit box among his most precious documents and what-nots. This is, according to this little note he typed and tucked in here—must've been years ago, because (now in my business I *do* know this) the note was typed on a 1982 IBM Selectric single-element printing head—and it's a translation of this little page here, museum-type-stuff, the sort of thing Nathan would covet, I've dated it—from Iraq doubtless seventh century BC—but a scrap. I say Iraq for the scrap because this thing he typed, it's typed on a piece of agenda from some—(I translated that too)—*Nonaligned Movement Conference: Day One* on Al-Rasheed Hotel stationary but I'm sure half of you know more about that meet-up than I ever will, and the other half care more about archeology, and I won't bother you with any details—"

But he was. Bothering both groups as tremendously and confusedly as he possibly could, led in their separate camps by Dr. Trout and by Silas Kingston.

Lynn Kingston hid a smirk behind her silver bangle. Kiss-kiss.

Joshua read something in Ancient Greek he didn't bother to translate except to say it was a page from the *Titanomachy*— "Whatever that is—" which is the greatest lost epic poem ever written. He switched off the light. Raised Muir's treasured document fragment in one hand, Muir's ash urn in the other and led Muir's academic and espionage enemies, Trout and Kingston, unto a wild goose chase and court battle over a pair of whole cloth forgeries of the greatest false proof of Iraq WMDs and the lost work of Hesiod, friend of Homer and earliest western scientist-philosopher in timekeeping. As for everyone else, this funeral and its fallout reinforced their deepest desires: to think sod all of Muir again or any of the rest of us who'd shown in the light of his favor.

A kook with a bunch of kook followers.

Lights out. Good night. Good riddance.

Then all the lights went dark with 9/11 and the Young Turks became the Nine-Twelvers, and we found ourselves swept with Plutarch and his Mensheviks into the dustbin of history.

Now it was Christmas Eve. We arrived at Lara and Tom's beach house as afternoon cooled toward sunset, where with the blessed night, I would soon experience my first epileptic seizure and commit to the path that would lead me directly to the end of my life. Tom Bishop opened the door for Lara who stepped onto the covered veranda. Lara yelped at the sight of me. She clapped her hands in delight, pressed them together in a brief Christian meets Hindu prayer clasp, unfolded them in Islamic cupping—embracing fully her three practiced religions—but it was Amy Kim's finger politely pointing at Lara's baby bump visible over the Santa scarf tied loose around her hips that filled me with Yuletide joy.

22

"**P**AID HIS USUAL WAY?" Amy said. "What's Joshua's usual way?"

"Unusual," I said.

The five of us—me, Bishop and Lara, Amy, and Joshua—arrayed ourselves on Muir's heavily cushioned rattan patio set. To have heard Muir tell it, the set—

A): belonged to the guy he rented the house from;

B): was a wedding gift from Charlie March on his marriage to March's sister Sandy (Tom's mother);

C): the last furniture enjoyed by Admiral Yamamoto before American fighter pilots shot him out of the sky in Pearl Harbor payback;

D): all a lie—something else and meaningless in meaningful-all because of the way we cherish good lies—but to my abbreviated mind, this time around, it was

E): the most inviting furniture I'd ever known.

To accommodate us and the others scheduled to arrive, Lara and Tom had added a love seat and another pair of matched chairs. The split-leaf philodendron-patterned upholstery almost matched, but the rattan was markedly more narrow, weaker I thought, and needed an extra rib on each arm.

"Ugliest furniture I've ever seen," says Muir.

My eyes darted nervously. Not having imagined the voice, I was desperate to find him behind me where I'd now heard him.

Knew it! Knew he'd be here! How he pulled this off, God bless him...

But only Gladys emerged through the draperies pulled across the sliding doors. She carried three bottles. One was a Macallan 25 from my suitcase. But how could that be? I had the uncomfortable sensation I hadn't seen her yet, so she couldn't possibly have anything from my suitcase; this was my first experience of the backward déjà vu, the *jamais vu* where something that already happened feels as if it hasn't yet, and time is catching up to a new version of reality. False memories of the unhappened— Gladys and I speaking as she'd carried my suitcase into the guest room Joshua and I were to share—they hit me with the sensation of falling through a thick and sticky, breaking web, all of an instant, each of a thousand strands popping to bury me in the chair where I sat and felt a spiritual chunking into place to start the ride over again.

The other two bottles—some Spanish Vichy water Bishop discovered in his convalescence and now swore by as the elixir of life—that conversation happened now, though with Muir in my head, it carried on without me at a distance from an alternate present forming around me.

"Where are ya?" I called, forgetting the others with me.

"Surprise—! How'd you know?"

Lynn Kingston followed Gladys with a tray of glasses and a bowl of ice.

I didn't know, and I flashed Bishop a sharp look. "What's she doing here?"

He shrugged pleasantly, a kind of easy flex of broad chest and sculpted shoulder like a commercial for how great you too could look with your own prosthetic leg blade.

"Honestly, Russell," Gladys said. "Be still."

Lynn deposited the tray, selecting her own glass already poured. "Holly-jolly, Aiken." She toasted me, not caring whether I held a drink or not. "You didn't think Old Nathan was celibate in his elder years, did you? Good-looking man at any age."

I did! Yes! My inner voice raged, though I'd be damned if I let her know my inner feelings.

"I absolutely did." I heard my tongue toss back.

"Truthfully?" Lynn said, "I wouldn't know. Came along too late in the game to find out. With him." Drank more, offering me a friendly, though cryptic smile, over the rim of her glass.

She never spoke directly to me again until we all said goodbye to her as the sun rose the next day, Christmas. In all that time, whenever we were near one another, Lynn's eyes never left me once. She wanted to tell me something, but what I wouldn't find out until back at Langley, and why: understood in Cuba—painted with China—and by then I wouldn't let it matter.

I noticed the only other person (besides me) who didn't laugh at the idea of Lynn Kingston and Nathan Muir in bed was Amy. She seemed just as relieved it hadn't happened. Joshua must have noticed too, for as Lynn poured cocktails and Tom poured waters for the two of us, and for Lara, he eased the conversation back to its original trajectory.

"Amy: blame Muir for my skipping out on restaurant tabs. That's what this wake's for."

"You don't pay for your food? And you get away with it?" Amy happily moved away from Muir and Lynn and sex.

Joshua tapped the side of his nose. "It was his grandfather—Tom's great-grandfather—Linus Muir, worked in the movie business. One of his last films—maybe it was his last, I dunno—was the Hemingway novel. The World War One story. He took the family to its Paris premiere."

"*Sun Also Rises*," I said, definitively.

"No, that was the bullfighter and the castrated guy," Bishop said, who'd been whittled down himself but, clearly as some months from now would show, not all the way.

"*Farewell to Arms.*" I am undeterred with the truth. "The kid from *Rudy* played him on HBO."

"Sean Astin?" Amy said.

"No. The other guy. The one who played Robin."

"*Robin Hood*? Kevin Costner?" Bishop loved to muddy me up.

"No! *Batman and Robin*," I snapped.

"Russell, I believe you're talking about Chris O'Donnell," Lara said.

"Yes. Exactly. The ambulance driver in the Hemingway thing with the perky one who isn't the other one."

Odd looks. Bishop knew. "Sandra Bullock who isn't Julia Roberts."

"Exactly. Thank you."

"Chris O'Donnell played Hemingway," Amy said.

"Right. The character from the *Farewell to Arms*!"

Lynn Kingston laughed at me. Shook her head. "Farewell, my lovely."

My mouth tasted as if I'd poured a bag of pennies into it and my gaze flashed to the Macallan, which beckoned with an amber aura.

Muir's ashtray, where Muir's cigarette improbably smolders, where he's put it ten years ago, and I can't remember if it had been there a moment before. But it is here now. I jolt to where he and I sit there alone under the thrum of rain. His smile mocks me... lovingly? A forever flash of an instant later, he and the ashtray gone.

No auras. No copper taste. I'm fine.

Lara, I could tell, did not share my private feeling. I suppose they all were concerned for me one way or another, and I didn't yet fathom how fully time-in-context would slip from me as the epilepsy I didn't yet know I had, progressed, but a big grin spread across Tom's face, and he, who'd spent the most time with me and knew my psychological bent, suggested his great-grandfather most likely hadn't worked for HBO.

I said all I was trying to do was identify "context within context of the context we were speaking," or something equally out of it. Context wise.

"This isn't a contest," Joshua said. "The film was the Gary Cooper version of *A Farewell to Arms*, from the thirties. According to Muir, Linus had done some of the action directing in the sequences that follow Cooper's desertion—"

"Wasn't his character called Rudy?" Bishop said.

Lara booed him.

"The long retreat along the road, the runaway horses, the dying fellow with the blockish straining hand, the woman crying to the sky, the geese, the bombing planes..."

"But isn't that *Guernica*? The Picasso painting my Albert and I saw in Madrid," Gladys suggested.

"Who knows?" Joshua said. "All great art builds on influence. Muir once told me, quoting somebody or other, and I tend to agree because I've made my living on it: 'One is never fully the author of one's work or one's self.' But anyway, he—Linus, that is—was in France for the film's premiere, and Pablo Picasso was introduced to Linus. Picasso was a living treasure, a big wheel by then, residing in Paris, civil war about ready to blow the lid off España. Picasso was a fan of the film, wanted to meet your great-grandad—not because of the movie—but, having been a friend of the Italian surrealist Carlo Carrà, he admired his paintings of horses and Linus's connection there."

He gave Bishop a knowing look, pointed and leading...

"My grandfather Bucky's ride up the Spanish Steps," Tom marveled.

I *mmm'd* which, done long enough, mimics smiling.

"Bingo," said Joshua. "Picasso admired your grandfather's use of horses in *Farewell* and *Ben-Hur*. Big horse guy. Loved horses. In his first-known painting, Picasso features a horse. And the mythology and emotions of horses and their relationship with mankind remain a major theme in his work throughout his career. Anyway, they met two more times to talk horses—once for breakfast, once for drinks. Both times, Picasso volunteered to pay the tab. Instead of money, though, he offered the proprietor a sketch he'd made on a menu card as payment."

"A Picasso drawing is a fair exchange for a croissant?" Amy couldn't believe it.

We were all a bit stunned. Me, because I can see a hoax off its whinny.

And why do I have to be the last to hear things from Muir?

Joshua went on. "Linus remarked, in classic Muir-family blood-borne-cynicism, 'You just took away breakfast and cocktail hour from a whole neighborhood.'

"'How so?' Picasso asked.

"'Once they sell your drawing and retire to the Côte d'Azur, there will be one less bakery and one less bar in this neck of the woods.'

"'How can they sell them? They wouldn't be worth anything as I didn't sign them. I'm easily copied. I've been forged. They only exist as true Picasso's between the proprietor and me— and you, Linus, as my guest. The value between us was not the paper and what I'd drawn on it, but the interpersonal connection anchored in the personal time we all exchanged, the efforts made and respects paid, represented by my use of that paper shared between us.'"

Joshua drank. He dug out a pocket jotter and a ballpoint pen. He drew as he continued to speak:

"I thought about that story. Thought about the criminal past I'd participated in before Nathan pulled me to the light of this strange dark world where we operate. Among other federally indicted pranks, I'd forged currency. I'm still called to do it—other nation's currency, nowadays—and while I'm legally restricted from creating US dollars, there's nothing that disallows me from drawing representations of American money. So, I do. I exaggerate proportions. Fancify the establishments where I dine on the backsides of my pseudo-currency. Maybe include staff instead of presidents. I choose established, family-owned restaurants where I can develop a relationship with the owners, the employees, build mutual value and respect between us. I patronize their restaurants not only because I appreciate what they offer, but I appreciate *they* are offering it. I recognize their self-worth in the pride they take in the work they do and draw existential meaning from."

He tore out the sheet. In a matter of moments, Joshua had drawn the front side of a twenty-dollar bill in miniature perfection, but with my visage in Jacksonian bouffant bug-eyed staring out. He handed it to Amy who passed it around to the rest of us.

Another rental car, twin to my own, pulled into the driveway, tires popping shell gravel below.

"At first when I dine there, they don't know me. I pay like any stranger. As they come to know me as a customer, they still don't know my intrinsic value, what I do that makes others and myself happy. My existential worth. Money exchanged for service is an agreed upon method for everything between strangers. A government-backed verification method of the social contract in shorthand. But after a while, after trust and casual acquaintance become true familiarity, I draw for them."

"You're no Picasso, young man. I met Picasso. The night my father inspired him to his great war painting."

We all turned. Pulling herself up the stairs with the help of her redwood stick came Tom's Great-Aunt Linda arrived from Lone Pine.

"And, Mr. Rosen, on top of that you sound as though you remain a communist."

"Naw. Too much work for a beatnik."

Although she had never had a plow horse that went lame, the Gestapo had captured Linda and done that trick to her. Her grandfather had not invented Morse code, but as a Muir, he'd farmed horses in New Hampshire; upon the youthful revelation of her sexuality, Linda changed her name to protect the strong-backed bronc-buster's fragile dignity. Muir's father, Bucky, had been Linda Morse's older brother. Yet, Muir or Morse, the hilt of the old woman's stiletto gleamed from the top of her boot and her finger bore the Congolese ivory sent by Muir (when sent to the Congo to assassinate Patrice Lumumba), the nephew she had loved and lured to this life of ours. Of his. Of hers. And the rest of us to follow. In the crook of her free arm, Linda carried an aged, large leather-bound book, while around her tresses of thick white hair, plastic holly with red berry lights twinkled a festive crown.

Bishop sprung to his foot and lifted her from the top step into his embrace. He twirled her like a child.

"Release me."

"Never, you crazy old witch."

They kissed. He set her free. Lara took the book—"Merry Christmas, Aunt Linda"—and Linda moved around the porch taking the measure of each of us, both hands in each of hers, wishing us Merry Christmas and claiming us all her "beautiful geniuses," and, "Oh, Nathan is so rich to have produced such a family as this."

Her clutch of Lynn Kingston lasted longer than the rest of us and I heard her whisper, "We'll talk about Silas before you go, but I will not let him ruin Nathan's Christmas."

Lynn Kingston relaxed. Worried but thankful, I thought. Our eyes flitted together and away.

Linda ended her round back in front of my sister. "Our greatest hopes grow inside you, dear-heart."

"The way this family goes about losing feet and legs, gotta wonder: if Darwin gets involved, the baby might just start out a monoped," I joked, doing what I do worst the best.

No one knew what to say until Bishop chuckled and said, "While Russell is busy pulling all our feet, singly and in pairs, out of his mouth, may I get your luggage?"

"Thank you, Tom. My darling escort who insisted on this silly thing"—she pointed to her twinkling headdress—"is perfectly capable of bringing it from the car."

"Got a new girlfriend?" I flashed my crooked smile trying to recover.

"This one? I could only wish. This one is spoken for."

"We left Miami with three bottles of *quince años*," Nina said, climbing the porch stairs, two bottles of Havana Club Cuban rum wrapped in one arm against her chest, lugging her and Linda's suitcase clumping behind her, "but we bumped off one of *los soldatos* on the ride here." Her eyes met mine. "*¿Oye, qué bola,* baby?" she said.

My mouth twitched.

Do I smile? Do I stand? Kiss? Shake hands?

And what's this "already spoken for"?

Women have the magical ability to make things disappear. With "What's up, baby?" I vanished to Nina from where I sat in front of everyone else on the porch. Bishop saw me. He moved the Macallans.

"Not that way, brother." And my hand, I didn't want to admit having stretched for it, retreated.

Nina made her greetings, Tom introducing her to Lara for the first time. Gladys, noticing the blooming darkness that surrounded us, mentioned this to Lara and suggested to Lara they prepare the lights.

Lara stood and announced: "I may have gone a bit overboard, but—Lynn would you pull the draperies?—I've been finding decorations high and low over the last few months. Tom didn't know, I had no idea, but Nathan Muir's greatest love has been revealed to us as Christmas."

Lynn Kingston pulled the drapes. Gladys switched on a power strip from which a Medusa head of extension cords snaked throughout the living room. Peering in through the sliding glass door, it was Muir's old room. There was no doubt about that. But it had undergone a surprising transformation. The effect was a fire of golden sprigs and icy silver dangles, twinkling twining bowers of blazing green, Marian blue bulbs glowing in the shadow pools where red spots rose upward to a ceiling radiant in warm shades of purple like a sky at night, or a blessed church, lighter around the edges that grew deeper in rising and reaching, richer in gathering into an inky domed heaven above the weathered floorboards Bishop had distressed and sanded. The grain troughs suffused the greige of a Bethlehem street, while the ridges glowed white, frosted in the color of Lapland midwinter.

And that was only the effect of light. An effect only half as devastating as the effect all this light had in reflecting into me from the large diamond ring worn on the second to last finger of Nina's left hand.

Tell you one thing: I haven't thought of her husband—not once in ten years. Victor Rubio, that alma puta *in-pure-souled son-of-bitch.*

23

ARISTOTLE WROTE THAT SPACE must be either form, matter, interval, or extendable limit; that the place of a thing is that which surrounds it. Newton took it a step further. He conceived the world is not a collection of things, but rather a collection of events.

With that, space became time.

Head hung and knowing I was stepping into a time machine, I entered timidly into Muir's Captiva house, its space transformed by Christmas. Neither Aristotle's time that is strictly and only a measurement of change, nor Newtonian time which passes even when nothing changes, before I lifted my eyes and investigated Muir's abysmal glory—deep in its power, dreadful in my disquiet—I let Bing Crosby's 'White Christmas' wash over me at its 4/4 signature in A major.

Joshua laughed. "Took a Russian Jew to write everyone's top of the Christmas playlist."

In a soft Cindy Lou Who voice, Amy Kim added, "Irving Berlin's son died on Christmas Day. He is only dreaming of something that isn't and somewhere he can't have. Ever."

No one heard her but I—and maybe it was only meant for me—and my eyes found Amy, the room around her revealed, and of it that thing we each have that is our secret we think no one else knows but is the first thing a torturer extracts from us to break us: I beheld Muir's Christmas ablaze in Amy Kim's broken, unhealed holy heart.

The music emanated from a freestanding Uher Royal Deluxe reel-to-reel tape player.

"Commercial version of the ones we all used on station," Bishop said.

They all agreed except for Amy, who'd not yet been posted overseas, and me, who had posted, immediately, to a stationary desk. There were other voices and other melodies coming from corners around the room, the sounds of conversations played low at whisper tone, as if a party were already in full swing and we'd been summoned, the living as ghosts, to witness.

Lara said, "We listened to about twenty minutes of the main tape. It's a medley of everything Christmas you can conceive. All hand-spliced, nothing complete, everything left hanging, and there's four reels of it. He numbered them, though they aren't dated. The other sounds you're hearing are cassettes. We listened to one." Her smile contorted to fight the sad joy of nostalgic tears. "It's an end-of-term church service from my boarding school in KL; he must have recorded it from his briefcase on one of his visits. I don't know why he would or how I picked it first."

"Where did you say all this stuff came from?" said Nina.

I looked at her, trying to catch her eye but remained nonexistent in her sight.

Bishop said, "Boxes stashed everywhere. Years of collecting. I found some of them during my recovery. Lara found the rest once she started setting up the house."

"Nesting, as it turned out. I discovered six large boxes in the far corner of the attic crawl space. They weren't dated or marked. And nothing we found inside them ever displayed. None of it. Ever. The handmade stuff from European Christmas markets and craft fairs was still wrapped in tissue or in envelopes from embassies or foreign post offices where he'd sent it from. All to himself to different addresses where he lived over all the years. The store-bought stuff, still in its plastic. He'd never bothered to open any of it."

"Except for the train sets," Bishop interrupted. "This is weird because he *did* open all of these to get rid of the tracks and power transformers. But never took the trains out of their packing foam. Who-knows-why—"

Lara tag-teamed back. "He didn't leave any instructions. Oh, the cotton snow and tablecloths and the Christmas runners and garlands: Tom and I have been buying those since Thanksgiving. We didn't know how he imagined it displayed, but once we started it seemed to let us know its pattern."

"The boxes were assorted sizes, so we covered them and the furniture and the bookcases. Like hills or something. Explore," Bishop said.

"It's all for you. We finished this morning, right before sunrise."

Lara looped a simple green apron with a sexy reindeer over her head, tied it, and smoothed it, and said, "I hope you all like Malaysian Christmas Feast—Malay, Chinese, Indian, some Indonesian. We're a culture that does it big." She went into the kitchen.

I gave Joshua a pointed look of flagrant disappointment.

"We *have* been had," he said, and toasted me.

"It's like we're inside a Christmas card come to life," said Amy.

But it was more, and it was better. Christmas villages Dickens Victorian, Schultz's Snoopy; Alpine and Korean and African and Cypriot model towns; Midwest and Old West, Dr. Seuss to Mt. Olympus Zeus. Train-set dioramas—city streetlights, even stop lights—granular Christmas lights, dots of electric rainbow on bright plastic brick facades, model interiors fluttering with shadow and light pattern; a wind-up bandstand and circling skaters made to move by opposing magnets; as Bishop said, locomotive engines and train cars but no tracks to take anyone away from anyone else ever; crèches from Africa and from Mexico; mangers from Finland, from Japan and Brazil; wise men and Mary, Joseph, and Jesus black, white, yellow as those who see him as he is them; snow globes—hand-blown for hand-turning, and large and electronic with a snow constantly swirling around Paris's Notre-Dame cathedral and Cape Canaveral and a snowman family in a forest. A legion of nutcrackers in review for a Rockette figurine USO revue Radio City souvenir stage. Lightboxes of Currier and Ives bob-tailed jing-jing-a-ling sleigh-scapes. Cameo Rockwell family rooms with orange and red-bulbed formed-plastic fireplaces. 1970s Israeli and Lebanon Coke bottles, both unopened: a dreidel and menorah on one, a holy and yonder star the other, both bottles liking to have taught the world to sing or at least blown a whistle with lips across the top that wasn't the shriek of artillery shell. An explosion of rubber walnuts from a Donald Duck toy cannon at a delighted pair of his chipmunk nemeses. Candy canes nestled in tinsel. Christmas china plates for every US state, spoons from national parks. Everywhere else: a storm of snowflake ornaments of every size and composition but ice, and glass balls of every size and color to reflect it all.

Dylan Thomas's whiskey-husked Welsh voice rasped like corrosive iron oxide on the magnetic tape, to be replaced midsentence by a soulful male choir singing Franz Biebl's "Ave Maria," with Fred Waring and the Pennsylvanians 1942 "'Twas the Night Before Christmas" bearing down on Tex Ritter's "Christmas Carols from the Old Corral."

My perspective shifts and splits: I see a lonely little boy sitting on plaster snow-covered steps, plastic traveling trunk beside him, as I see Muir's room grotesquely vast from miniature within that child.

I shake it off.

I hovered over a diorama, peering into what I thought might be Fezziwig's warehouse Christmas ball at the end of a village road by a darkened school. Fezziwig and little characters enlivened by circling Kevin McAllister zoetrope optical illusion. I searched vainly inside the toy for a glimpse of Muir, whose presence permeated all space where anything wasn't, and where time lived unfettered of its chains built in life and shackled by death.

"Russell, you'll want to hear this."

I turned to the corner nook bookshelf where Joshua beckoned. His eyes were afire.

"In fact, Tom: shut off the main tape. All the recorders."

Bishop hustled around and click-click-clicking did. Everyone stared. Joshua signaled Lara from the kitchen.

Lara put aside her knife. "What happened to the music?"

He smiled and cocked his head at her to join us. He hit rewind on a cassette player. He pressed play. Joshua's voice, clear and youthful, came over the speaker. A dirty story about a French general whose poorly spoken Vietnamese got him into an embarrassing situation in Saigon. There was laughter in the background and some vague and mumbled words.

"That! You hear it?"

"You or the background?" Lara said.

I'd heard it. "That's our father's laugh. That's his voice." I beamed at Lara.

"And that's your mother, Lara," said Joshua. "The one telling me to stop talking. Then laughing again and telling me to go on."

He rewound and played it again.

"You remember when that was?" Bishop asked, his arm slipping around his wife.

"Before Lara was born. Not the year, but between Thanksgiving and New Year's a year or two before."

"Dad was always on the road for the holidays when I was a kid. Up until he died," I said. "Never home for Christmas. Always driving his truck."

Joshua squeezed my shoulder. "He wasn't."

"Well, I disagree."

"Well, you're wrong. Until your father died, he'd go overseas. Every year after ATROPOS—the original op. After he'd gone Navy reserve. Out of the two of us, only Danny made good on the promise I made with him, my word given but never kept. Nathan would arrange it for Danny."

"What promise?"

"He'd go back to the Navy. Take some stranger's place in some job, somewhere lit up all-hands-on-deck hot. Every fucking-excuse-me year. His choice to do that would allow some lucky stranger leave to 'stack their guns,' as Danny'd say, and go home to be with their families for the holidays. Every year, Rusty. He'd face fire so someone else's dad could relax beside one. I wish he'd told you."

"What about his accident?"

"Like this room. Staged." His wrinkled cheeks flushed red. "I'm sorry. I thought Muir would have filled you in on all that."

I shook my head dumbly. And waited.

"Russell?" Lara said. "You okay?"

I crooked my face. Went to study some other fantasy.

Bishop put the main tape back on with the music and the poetry, but there were treasures like this in all the cassettes. Voices from the past. News reports from foreign posts that had meant something to Muir. Strangers who had once meant more. Ex-wives. One cassette: Robert Kennedy's speech on the death of Martin Luther King, Jr., and Nixon's speeches and toasts from China in 1972 captivated Lynn Kingston. There were raw eavesdroppings in foreign languages none of us knew. Others: stolen snatches of all our voices, conversations absent of any spy craft from times we couldn't agree on but had all undeniably been happy in. Ten years ago, twenty, thirty, but as easily tomorrow or next week.

"They sound edited to me. Made to sound all same place, same time," Amy suggested.

But if they weren't real, Muir mirages, things that didn't mean anything, they got all of us thinking about where we were and how far we'd come and where we'd like to be.

"Maybe that's his point," Nina said to everyone but me.

One cassette was composed of our laughter rolling like tides, lapping like lakes, and pattering like rain and the staccato silence between the patterns.

Another, Elizabeth Hadley giving out supplies in a Beirut field hospital. Lara squeezed Tom's shoulder than kissed the back of his neck.

WE STRUGGLE OUR WHOLE LIFE for self-awareness. We have it least when we need it, looking for it most. We only find it when we can look at our history of missing it. Amy studied things like the transfer of information, and I thought to ask her what was so important about that when Bill Carver's wife—had I seen them arrive? Had they always been here?—It was she, Carver's wife, who remarked on the Santa Claus figurines.

"All of these Santas are ornaments. Where's the tree?"

"Does it look like they have room for a tree, Nanette?" the Agency detective scoffed in his signature gruff deadpan.

I overheard him tell Bishop something about the whole setup made him more than a little uneasy about the former spymaster's sexuality.

"Stop it, Bill," Nanette swatted his arm. "Lara, how many Santas you have here?"

Amy looks at me and we are alone inside her apartment which I do not know nor have ever visited and she says, "Influence is to the transfer of information what energy fields are to the capture of particles."

"I didn't count them," Lara called from the kitchen. "Some are antiquey, though."

"One for every Christmas," Aunt Linda said, stacking plates on the kitchen bar. "I did that for him. Since he was a baby. Nathan adored Santa. Said he wanted to be him when he grew up."

This sparked something in Bishop, an odd way he looked at his aunt, but he didn't remark. He focused more intently on the cassettes.

The lights and music and the voices. The kitchen smells which reminded me of my time in Malaysia, and the hospital in Thailand. All swirled around and within me, a warming blizzard of spirit and sensation. Auras I'd been denying, soon leaped in from the edges of my vision in geometric sugarplum figures. I was dizzy, but pleasantly ultra-balanced like a dancer on point. Like air balances and cannot unbalance. The copper taste filled my mouth.

Pennies from heaven?

I hear angels calling me with song…

All that lacked, I thought, was the star of wonder.

Heavenly tones from outside the house. They call. They tug. A hypnotic melody, a looping strain, mantra-like in a whirlpool refrain. Lyrics without verb, cut from the bindings of time; of simple things, a kaleidoscope of moments.

Stick. Stone. Stump. Alone.

Life and sunlight and water.

Inside the cone of my phantasmagoric vision, Bill Carver, crowned and mantled in my sight with a golden halo, accepts a drink from Lynn

Kingston radiating a blazing pink aura. He gestures with the tumbler at a guitar leaning in thrumming light against the sofa back.

"Next, you'll be telling me, Muir minstreled in his off time?"

Lara says, "We don't know whose guitar that is. Practically brand new. There was a receipt in the case from a Princeton music store from 1999. Anyone know? Gladys?"

Untouched, the instrument's steel strings vibrate with silver incandescence.

"Me," *says Amy.* "It's mine. I mean, he bought it for me. Once ago."

And I am suddenly in the depths of Muir's jungle, hanging on the coattails of the angel voices drawing me, drawing me...

A night and death. A trap.

A Joe and a gun.

A siren song skirling.

"You know, sailors under French explorer Rene de Laudonnière, who built Fort Caroline—over near where Jacksonville is—they thought manatees were mermaids." *Muir calls me here and now from ten years back and I am in the inlet clearing. Muir's lagoon. Our bottle of Macallan 25 waits beside the driftwood log where Muir is seated electric and blue. His manatee friend, the erstwhile Björk, surrounded by frolicking pups, floats in water that laps at her thick neck. Heavenly voiced melodies bloom among the water hyacinth, but the voice: by now I know Björk, I'd seen the bird suit and heard her flash of wing in the pan. This was another songstress, ancient, yet familiar, singing what Picasso called l'objets* trouvés, *found objects that were the bread and wine of Cubism. Creatures of dismay that bite, that sting, that poison; things of beauty that sing and flash red-furred in a field or silver in water...*

"Sit with me. I've been waiting to talk to you," *Muir says.*

"Why didn't you tell me? Anything about him. Ever. My own father. Why'd you wait until you were dead?"

"Who're you to tell me what I've told you? What I'm going to. You listen with your mouth far too much."

He hits his cigarette. He hits our bottle. He holds it out to me. "You find the green marbles, don'cha?"

I reach. The grass soft and the sand harder, rush up and smack the back of my head along the seam of my surgical wound.

"I don't want to gloat, but you had that coming, stumbling drunk again."

"No worries, Muir."

The song continues: of wind, rain, flood. A gunshot and a girl and a bed.

I smile as big as the spirit enveloping me. "It doesn't hurt a bit."

24

"DO YOU LOVE ME, Pintao?"

"*Yes.*"

"Yes!" I shout into her face peering over me.

"Where?"

Shit. Not Nina's face.

"Where what?"

"I asked if you hurt yourself."

"Why would I hurt myself?"

"Because you said 'yes' when I asked you, 'Mr. Aiken have you hurt yourself?' You *are* lying on your back. And I'm certain you haven't touched a drop of liquor."

I rolled over. No manatees. No Muir. No Nina. No music.

"Can we talk?" Amy said. "I mean, if you're okay."

Muir's ghostly finger points. Look! Here lies Russell Aiken, rotting in a growth of the vegetation, vegetating death—not life—, inanely grinning at phantasmal singing mercows, fat with repleted appetite, paddling for swamp-oak acorns.

"Jesus, I'm fine."

"You looked like you were convulsing."

But I was sitting now, and present, though still adjunct to past-made-future fantasy reality.

It's like seeing around corners and under, like Joshua says, the universe's rug with words hammering thought-waves out of whack, and Noah and Aesop fabling dinosaurs on the Niña-Pinta-La Santa María slow boat to Vladivostok.

Amy Kim: new officer.

Muir's last move. Castle the rook.

Fuck-the-focus-up and say something!

"How did you like the Farm?"

Still alarmed and side-eyeing me, she muttered, "I'll put it this way. I'm now certain my deepest unspoken fear is heights and falling."

Corvidae from towers fly.

I shook the black feathers from my head and hoped my hopped-up nodding appeared owlishly sage.

"You landed on both feet."

"Did I?"

I spread my hands and waited for Amy to answer herself.

"Guess I'm catlike that way."

"And at creeping up."

"I am sorry I followed you. But I was watching you inside. You weren't acting right. And with your surgery still not so far in the past…"

"Amy, you're going to have to stop. I'm fine. I am."

I sat on the log. Muir had taken the bottle when he left without so much as a helpful "Go to Dagobah." I patted a spot for Amy to sit beside me.

She asked me, "Did Nathan ever tell you about his first wife?"

"I don't think so. No," I lied.

"He called her Jewel?"

"I haven't the foggiest."

"Counterintelligence sent me a profile of Muir."

"Who in CI? Why'd you request it?"

"I didn't. The associate director serving under Mr. Kingston. Ms. Hofmeyr. She volunteered it."

It was foolish to offer caution, complain something might be afoot when the fortress we worked in had more feet than a pulsating orgy of millipedes.

"She was Korean," Amy said. "Like me. She's not Tom's mother—they didn't have kids?"

Murder as good as abortion. "I don't know anything about it."

Good, Russell. Steady. No way she can tell I'm lying.

"You're lying. That's okay, I guess. I am sure there is a rule or code or a clearance. Or punishment." She stared, looking not at me but into herself. "Did he choose me because I reminded him of her? Was that what all this ever was? Is that the 'why' for me?"

"Muir chose you because you're you. You from the inside out."

Her face twisted. "Not anymore. My family is ashamed of me. My cover story that I work in a congressional IT office humiliates my parents because they believe it, and I can't correct it on penalty of prosecution. I've disgraced them by not getting a 'real job.' They tell me I wasted my degree. They're confused and upset; since I'm not maximizing the extent of my computer engineering and physics degrees, my mother demands I join the military to support the War on Terror while my father reminds me, I promised law school if I failed in technology."

"Don't! Law school's a death sentence!"

She flinched at my vehemence. I dialed back my personal disappointments.

"Your value to the Agency, to Muir, is OTS in the field."

Amy shook her head.

"How 'bout this: notice anyone, age-wise, between me and Bishop and you?"

"Lynn Kingston?"

"I don't know why she's here. She's not one of us. You are the future of everything he wanted for this country's intelligence service. Since Tom, he hadn't picked anyone else but you."

I know it sounded empty and so did she.

Amy pushed to her feet. "Nathan's gone. What good is that value you speak of to my family if to them I'll always be bathroom-wallpaper Picasso without a signature."

She left, and I felt terrible. Even mean, biting. Muir always had the right thing to say, the proper improper encouragement.

Amy had been pushed from an airplane to make it through the Farm and begin active duty in Joshua's Office of Technical Services in November. In the aftermath of 9/11, secret lines of friend or foe being drawn throughout the Middle East, many foreign agents fearing for their lives begged our escape. If not for themselves, at least for their families. Her first assignment had been the exfiltration from Damascus of the wife and two children of a Syrian diplomat on our payroll. Amy's task had been to program the magnetic strip on the mother's false passport. It was an important task, though not difficult; compartmented by Joshua to provide distinct boundaries for her first foray into a life-and-death application of her skills and training. Working between the forgery and legitimate Syrian passport in side-by-side high magnification, when Amy applied the strip she'd created, she noticed a spelling mistake on the passport she'd helped create. Our forgers took exception. Their duplication of the Syrian legalese and state language read perfectly; who was she, with only primitive knowledge of Arabic, to question their perfection?

But Amy was correct.

Where our forgers had spelled every word correctly, the Syrian intelligence—as a trap against meticulous forgers—misspelled two words in their official document. All Syrian passports have two wrong letters.

Amy, and Amy alone, saved that family from certain doom.

Joshua had told me the story on the last leg of the car ride mere hours before. Why hadn't I remembered? Congratulated her? Given her a boost away from waning confidence?

"It wasn't Amy you thought you saw," came a voice from the darkness. "Who were you answering 'yes' to like that?"

Although unsure why it had returned, I relaxed, more comfortable with the hallucination. "You."

As if separating from within a swamp-oak trunk, Nina stepped from the shadows.

"Good. For a minute, I thought you were speaking to the mermaids."

She'd seen the Columbus mermaid manatees?

"They weren't part of my vision?"

"Drop acid again, Pintao?"

"It's Russell. No. An actual vision. And I hope, now seeing you seeing me, this is not another."

She came to me. Took my hand. "I will only mention her once and from my heart, but never speak of her again."

"Björk?"

"I'm serious. I'm sorry about your wife—deeply sorry about her son you would have been a wonderful father to. I will always share that sorrow with you, be there for you when you hurt, but I will never speak of that woman who abused you, by her name, ever, for the rest of our life."

"Our life?"

"Don't you think I've waited long enough?"

I let go of her hand. Sneered at her matrimonial rings. "What happens with Victor Rubio?"

"Haven't you forgotten him?"

"Of course!" Not.

"We had a few threesomes, some orgies. It got boring."

I knew it!

"Lighten up. Nothing happened. Ever. Last time you saw him was my last time. You chose to misunderstand that situation to run away from me. And don't lie and say you didn't, because you won't see me for another ten years if you pull that pussy shit again."

"What about your wedding rings? Who did you marry?"

She extended her right hand. Wiggled her ring finger slender and unadorned.

I lifted her left hand where diamonds glittered their forever accusation. "Nice try."

"Those are my mother's. I'm Cuban. We didn't make the nine-teenth-century right-left switch your society did to make women display weak-handed subservience to their husband. Call me old-fash—"

I wrapped her in my arms and kissed her.

"You do love me. Ha-ha. Knew it." She kissed me back, her lips warm and yielding.

"I wasted so many years to get here," I said.

"Baby, the past isn't real. Only an after agreement of timelines to keep the present bound in place. A light breeze affects me with more force; and a breeze, like the past, can't feel me when it passes. You should look into it."

How to tell her I've already begun?

"And get dust in my eyes?"

"Blink it away, baby. Blink it away."

She lowers us into the grass and her body is dark and warm, entwining and playful. The woman's voice as old as time returns with the song about life's impermanence, about the inevitability of death.

"The Coca-Cola song," I say, and Nina says, "Shhh..." but that's not quite the song's name I'm clutching at and I know the actual song, it's on the tip of my tongue...

And soon enough, so is Nina.

AFTER WE MADE LOVE, which was after we'd moved me out of the biting ants and Nina brushed me off, we made love again. We watched the sky, waiting on a shooting star. We never saw one. Nina decided Venus, bright and yellow aglow, would be our holy star this blessed night.

"She's asked Joshua for her papers."

"Who?"

"Venus. Who do you think?"

"It would break Muir's heart."

Nina pressed her cheek to mine. "We all went through it, what Amy's suffering. But we didn't walk into this terror-war she's about to drown in, and even if? We'd all've had Muir to lifeguard us through. All we have now is you. We've all spoken."

"About me?"

I've always been most distrustful of unheard compliments, especially ones that might not have been or that need to be paid back. Can't see the value in what you don't hear.

"You're going to need to fool her. You're the master. Trap Amy with your words, Russell. I don't know—make her think she's signing one thing when she's signing the other. Do *something*."

It was funny, as in the end, that's exactly what Amy did to me.

25

The House Was Fragrant with Lara's feast. She and Tom, along with Nanette and Bill Carver, brought steaming dishes to the double-leaved dining-room table. Slender red and silver tapers, white and green wide pillars, lit and arranged in sand-pine boughs braided with mistletoe, burnished the rose-gold flatware in the sparkle and sway of their flames.

"At night, Muir's lagoon sure can get spirited," Gladys teased upon our return.

Lara flashed her an adoring and knowing smile; its shape, that mirror of mine, gilded the time beating in my heart a golden shield.

Relaxed and proud on my arm, Nina spoke into my ear. "To think: your beauty of a sister put a bullet point-blank through the heart of an al-Qaeda rape monkey before dragging your brain-shot ass over an international border in a warzone, all while stealing a bag of Langley gold. Doesn't seem real. Between her and Tom…" She swept up a bottle of her rum and toasted Lara with the last of it: "*¡Que tremendo mangon!*"

"'*Tremendous mangos?*' Is that really appropriate?"

"Means 'smokin' hot.' Runs in your blood too, baby."

The others took their seats. Bishop pointed out ours. "Put Santa's naughty list together."

"Don't worry, Pintao, that's the list to be on."

"Russell."

We sat and allowed the perfumes, zests, and seasonings, the pungent and the strange, the fresh salty tang of the feast that, had the aromas been wavelengths in the visible range, would have adorned us in the swirling elaborate patterns of the Malay *batik* vines and flowers, the exquisite paisley-frilled teardrops of the India *boho*, and geometries of the earliest Qing dynasties that ornamented Lara's table linens.

Aunt Linda put a last ladle alongside the last tureen. "None of this is ecbolic, is it, Lara?"

Lara looked fuzzled. "According to what's that?"

Eyes darted around the table like reef fish, Aunt Linda a word shark when she wanted.

"Seven letter word for 'labor-hastening drug,'" I said.

"A regular Sun'dee *Times* we got here." Joshua snapped his napkin to his lap.

"More a Friday–Saturday puzzle. Sunday's more extreme."

"Labor intensive?" Bishop added to everyone's humor.

As with the notion behind many dish small portions, their sharing and their passing, talk was meant to follow the table, one to another, over and around, anecdotal in bright, sweet, surprising togetherness. Lara had been prepping the meal since Thursday, five days earlier, and even then, for some of the traditional entrées, she barely met the minimum marinade and brining times proper peninsula preparation demanded. At one end of the dinner table, knife in fist, Bishop hew the rosemary roast ewe leg, Gladys bathed in masala or dolloped with mustard seed raita to individual desire, and in response to Nanette's question about the burned and tattered stars-and-stripes—the only item in the living room that reminded us why we were there to share the holiday—"Muir gave that to me twenty-six years ago this night. Night I first knew in my heart he was my father. Took him sixteen more years to admit it." He gave his knife a frolicful wave at the flag. "Pissed me off too many years for no good reason, you old sonova— ahh— love 'ya all the same."

He knew? All the time? Bullshit— The story, and *that he never bothered to tell me he knew.*

At the opposite end: Joshua portioned prime rib, India-peppered and powered, advising that the little forks for the marrow might be ignored if one's whistle worked.

"If you want me, just whistle," he said, quoting William Faulkner adapting Hemingway for Howard Hawks.

"'You know how to whistle, don't you, Steve?'" Lynn Kingston jumped in on as Bacall forever seduces Bogey. "'You just put your lips together and blow.'" She ended the line, eyes on me.

"Aren't you pert?" Nina smiled so Lynn was sure to see all her teeth.

Everyone laughed. Lynn's bangle, I realized as she subtly kissed it, was an ingeniously disguised flask.

From Muir's Uher reel-to-reel, Tim McGraw sang a song, "Mary and Joseph," none of us, we agreed, had ever heard (and wouldn't again for years) but all agreed we liked. Lara flaked-to-plate Tandoori trout— "Don't be afraid of the skin. You eat it with your fingers like chips." Braised-prawn soup swirled with wood ear fungus and steamed like the pipe smoke of Malay forest gnomes; almond raisin naan for palates in between; Kashmiri spring onion and mushroom puffs—Nanette's favorite, and she had three—and kung pao brussels sprouts; five-jingle-bell (Bishop's "Five Alarm") *sambal oelek* satay potatoes. KL city eggnog. *Teh Tarik*: treasonous Sedaka's teeth-tanning traditional 'pulled tea.' Booze free flowing; the rum and the whiskey—a little for all, but not for me, nor Lara—and Nathan's favorite that only Joshua and Linda liked the taste of in this house, Harvey's Bristol sherry. Lynn liked them all, *and* the elderberry wine Linda homebrewed in the Lone Pine mountains and brought down, and the Laotian ginger-parsnip wine Lara fermented that hadn't taken right, but Lynn Kingston got into anyway and lit up like an ArcJet rocket to Mars.

Return to earth.

Return to the banquet and the dessert. Return to the rambutan, durian, mango, passionfruit, and velvet apples pared over sharply seasoned, grilled pineapple rings. British bread pudding burbling at its spoon.

A typhoon would not have ravaged our holiday board any better than we, down to the bulleted pits and spit-fired shells, the broken slurped ribs and barren fish spines a skeleton army perished to our appetites. We were at hand, and we were together, and we were love assembled, not only to honor the birth of Jesus, but the loss of a mortal man who toiled in his shadow.

Bishop stood. "To Nathan Muir," he said, having made sure everyone joined afoot with him, drink in hand. "And to all our fathers, our Gods, our brothers, and our sisters, and this our close and valued family. Aged whiskey, twenty-five years"—we raised our glasses, Lara's and mine empty— "and for this duo"—he poured for us— "pure rainwater, as Nathan would have approved, fallen from the morning sky."

"God bless us, everyone," Amy offered the last.

Dishes gathered; Joshua tapping at his PDA until he found something devilish. "Okay, Rusty, ten letters, from Muir's immortal Greek: 'an emotional shout used in poetry, drama, or song.'"

My eyes followed Linda and Lynn into the living room away from the rest of us.

"First letter?" I vaguely responded.

"E."

Muir's aunt opened the leather book she'd brought. Slipped something, an envelope perhaps, to Lynn Kingston, who hid it in her MCM purse before returning to the table. "Let me help with the picnic," she said and did so by emptying beverage glasses. Into her mouth. Lynn, who could pour 'em down better than I at my best—be that worst—knew I'd seen and dared me to question her with a look I pretended I didn't see.

"'Ecphonesis,'" I said. "Example: 'O, Tannenbaum! O, Tannenbaum!' Which I thought for years was 'Oat, and a bomb! Oat, and a bomb!' but never asked why."

The women applauded. Bill grumbled, "Word games are an acquired taste. Bishop pass that bottle. Think I'll taste to the old man again. And Nam. One more, Tom?"

Bishop took for himself before he pushed it across the table.

"Word games are how our Pintao maneuvers us through the minefields of politics and the law we all stumble into," Nina said.

"Hear! Hear!"

Then it was time for Aunt Linda's book. She landed it on the table with a thud. "Now that we've summoned him with our toast, fact is, it's high time we embarrass Nathan while he's laughing at us until he's laughing with us."

"That'll be the day," Joshua growled in a tolerable ill-tempered Muir impersonation.

She lifted the leather top-board revealing a baby photo from 1928: Nathan Muir hardly six months into life's judgment; in dress and bonnet; annoyed and intolerant.

"He always wore that look," Bill said. "Eh, expression."

"Grew into it and proved what they say: looks really do kill," Lynn Kingston said.

Linda Morse's book was Nathan Muir's life, but as she shared it, turned its dry pages, she'd done something unusual. The photos were out of traditional arrangement. Like writing a life history with the alphabet purposely mixed up, or like a film purposely cut together out of order, it was life unrestrained by a timeline narrative: baby met manhood, to leap into Muir squealing at a water pump at the family horse farm; Muir's marriage to Sandy at the Hotel Washington following—

"He did sing!"

Only Joshua registered my outburst as meaning anything.

"Right here. Right outside. He sang a Dean Martin song. Pretty well, too."

He shook his head, admiring, I think, my persistent oddities.

"Oh, yes," said Linda. "Nathan loved to sing. Sundays, soon as we'd slide into the pew, he'd pull the hymnal and bookmark all the hymns for the morning's liturgy. He'd sure belt 'em out."

Ten rows from the altar, he'd lied to me. As usual.

Muir in his First Lieutenant's dress blues after training; Muir's first day of kindergarten; with Jewel in Korea—Amy brushed it with her fingertips, inflating my worry.

He is sullenly snapshotted with his mother and Linda, a four-year-old gangster in a houndstooth flat hat, leg bent against the side of a 1930 Ford outside a drugstore, Saratoga, New York.

"That upstairs window—Nathan was born in that room. This is when I moved the pair of them to Los Angeles." Linda's mouth spread with gentle fondness. "Dawn's parents—"

"Dawn?" I asked.

"My grandmother. Nathan's mom," Bishop said.

"Dawn's parents had had it up to here with the town's hostile judgment over the unwed mother and her bastard kid living above *their* drugstore. Innuendo killing business. Her father almost lost his mind when he figured out my girlfriend—who took the photograph—was my *girlfriend*. Rushed us out of town but fast."

Muir in Berlin with field glasses at a window overlooking the Wall.

Muir in a sea of wrapping paper holding out a Plasticville train station, grinning with his mother beneath Aunt Linda's tinseled tree.

"I didn't see that set over there," I said.

"You wouldn't. It's with his train you also don't see, running under my 'oats and a bomb' at home."

Muir playing Junior High basketball.

Muir showing Airedales with wife Veronique in Paris.

As a preteen on a walking tour of family forebears' Wales, posed on a train-station platform. The sign above their head he's pointing at reads: "Cwm."

Joshua beat me to it with his PalmPilot. "*Koom* meaning 'valley' in Welsh. Bet you didn't know that, Rusty."

I muttered, "You'd have lost. Standard three-letter 'one' starter word of hundreds of puzzles."

Bill shook his head. "Thought they got all your tumor." He pushed his large body from the table. "Bishop, your dad leave any smokes?"

"There's a box of Partagas—"

"He swore he'd smoked those," Nina said.

"Mostly. Three of 'em left in the guest room. They're all yours."

"You promised, Bill, you wouldn't anymore," said his wife.

"Santa smoked," he said and lumbered off.

A pair of pages—one side with bazookas and Montagnard tribesmen in Laos; a teenage boy saddling a horse for a girlfriend, displayed upon the other.

Muir, 1954, in front of the Parthenon, temple of the goddess Athena. His hair: wilding with time-frozen wind.

Then an almost indistinguishable pair of shots. They are taken somewhere in Tibet: Muir, four or five years old at the time. At the long base of Mt. Everest are some Asian oil fields, suggesting Muir's abusive stepfather, though unseen, is already now a dangerous part of his and Dawn's world. But the little boy doesn't understand that yet, and his mother's profile radiates light unbruised. In the first photo, Nathan is filled with awe, squatting in the mud with his mother and grandparents, Linus and Harriet, witnessing a passage of *acxoyatl*—walking fish—propelling themselves on fin-feet from a dwindling pond over oily flats to a larger body of water and life humans and their pollution have attempted to deny them. In the twin photo, the humans all are the same, but the fish are almost vanished, fins and tails disappearing into a lake and away.

The next page held three snapshots of universities where Muir taught during his Agency years; and the pages turn, Halloweens and military bases, prom queens and warzones, other weddings, and youth sports to rainy runways beside flag-draped boxes, but my mind remained frozen at the weird images from Tibet.

Bill returned, smoking, and enjoying it. He stepped to the dessert table and nabbed a jelly-filled deep-fried sort of donut. "Reminds me of the Fat Tuesday *paczki* we'd get as kids. You wouldn't happen to have Polish neighborhoods in Kuala Lumpur?"

"We have *kuih keria* from a thousand years before Poland. Good though, huh?"

Munching coupled cloud-coughed cigar. "Perfect combo."

I hardly listened; I no longer looked at Muir's album. From all the light-and-time grabs of Nathan Muir's life in Linda's magic book, I knew each of us—as I imagine her intention—drew from it a singular image that complemented and completed our memory of Muir's life. For Amy, perhaps, her connection with the lost and tragic Jewel I had denied revealing to her—for others, well, that belonged to each in turn, but showed clearly on their faces.

For me, the most important, shocking and beautiful, universe defining and defying by their science and mythology, the hopes and deceptions Muir's existence came to embrace, I perceived those walking fish gifted me the entire meaning of my mentor: a child meeting Darwin and seeing God in secret. In observing the impossible walk before his eyes, he is witness to a world where Dr. Seuss-all is possible. Fish can walk on land—a boy only need pull back the curtain—in a life-marveling event. The trick to it is to keep your mouth shut to what they give you, slithered past and slid back slick into the deep.

ALL OF TIME is events. It is not things. From substance to elements to molecules, from atoms to energy fields, all of these are only modes of explanation. They are not things. Our notions of reality into which we ground ourselves and our perceptions of them are only a way to explain the interaction of events we do not experience as such and cannot see.

Mt. Everest, solid and inert to human observance, is not a thing but a collection of slow-moving atoms and particles and quanta, and thus, its true reality is that of only an event. Its name is illusory and elusive by its allusiveness. While "Ever-rest" connotates a "forever still" quality, it is a deception and not the compound word we might like to assume. Everest is a surname. The English derivative of Devereaux, a French version of the Celtic name Eburovices, which means ironically, "river dweller," (unrestful rivers being easily more understandable as events than ever-resting mountains). The world's highest geographical location is as impermanent in time as the Welsh surveyor Sir George Everest, who began his career drawing maps of Cwm before tackling the subcontinent, and who objected to his name being given it in the first place.

Three hundred and fifty-seven trillion pounds of granite, gneiss, and glacier. Mt. Everest might undoubtedly be as thing-some as anything we can consider, yet its massivity is nothing more than a monotonous event already passing. Like Shelley's Ozymandias, Mt. Everest will dissolve into the sands of time, sands that will themselves break apart and vanish into the quantum fields of the universe whence they came. Its particles, granular and infinite, will disappear as interactions and cease of time to become nothing more than a formless sea of infinite probabilities: anything can happen, everything, and nothing at all. In this, it all already has, can, can't, might and might not, hasn't and won't.

The same is true of a person. The difference between man and mountain is only that the event that is a person is incredibly rapid in its essence and in its disappearance. The event that is a person carries self-awareness that imprints our mind with astonishingly blurred vision. We are incapable of seeing a mountain range for the powerfully frenetic and chaotic, all-at-once event it is, was, and won't ever be because human beings are not timed in our awareness in any way similar to a mountain. The event which is a person—an intricate system of chemical, mechanical, electrical, emotional, social, word- and light-based atomic-driven processes—interconnects with all other people. Interconnectivity maximizes or minimizes the span of change that is undergone by our uniquely massed energy through recording our experience of it and basing agreement on the contrast of knowledge on our shared capacity for thought and awareness that operates equally blurred within us all; human awareness allows a collection of rapid events that describe the passage of a swift-moving and short-lived becoming-and-going measurement of our briefly gathered, uniquely massed energy.

We are not things. We are events.

If all of creation from the highest peak to the lowliest walking fish is a transpiring event, all of awareness is simply a unique register of time.

Time is also not a thing.

But neither is time an event.

For human beings, time fills memory, organizes history, and offers nostalgia, but as an event, time exists only in the unmoving instant of the fullness or emptiness of the present.

Like Aunt Linda's photo album of Muir, past time exists simultaneously as a report of a series of forever-stationary events that, in their relation to the present, are none of them sooner or later, longer, or shorter than the other. Nor are they any longer a tangible part of the description of changes that happened but are not happening now. The future is a set of change events as well. Like the past, future occurrences are also wholly still. Unbecome, until they are past where they are also still and of no real order except in our imaginations. Why? Because on either end of the present—past and future—there is no light movement across them. Self-awareness, however, like the inability to hear the silence within sound, within music, the space between water, the illusion that allows us to perceive the speed of light in concert with the speed of sound, blurs our reception of reality and creates the illusion of an extended present between the past and the future where we uniquely perceive our existence.

The past and the future have no time and exist outside of it—if they exist at all—because they do not experience the movement of light.

Things are events. Events are time. Time is all illusion and without us, it is all infinite. Highly and perfectly designed, functioning nothing; *with* us, by virtue of awareness (which is a subatomic granular process) and thought as knowable experience (which they are not), there exists God in all definitions: the most basic, beautifully simplistic something beyond time and space and science. Beyond reality we only perceive as a blur that is the exhaust pattern of light already gone.

My epilepsy arrived to me that Christmas Eve, arrived as light that could and did illuminate both past and what was yet to come. My epilepsy gave me a new sense of reality that removed the blur from the now and gave future light to pieces of the past. And it is from all of this that Amy Kim, who understood the science and its application to our peculiar work far better than I, would determine our future.

"Ms. Kim, you're up." Having retrieved the guitar, Bill Carver handed it to Amy. "A little 'Hark the Herald'?"

Somewhat stunned, Amy took the instrument. We focused on her. Her timorous gaze groped for me.

"Play something, Amy," I encouraged.

"I don't know…"

"I'd say Muir held your talents in high enough regard to buy you such a fine instrument…"

"There was one song, a favorite of his. He always asked to hear me play. It isn't Christmassy, though."

She found a seat. She tuned. And she performed the song I'd already heard. The simple yet transcendent, lyrics and music of Antonio Carlos Jobim, 'Aguas de Marços,' but this time in the velvety sensuous soothing words of Portuguese.

How had I heard this song before on that night and in English? Although her style was hesitant, her voice was crystalline. We were all mesmerized by the beauty that was everything Amy when a second voice, brittle and ancient at first, joined with her in the English I had heard.

Time-worn and celestial, the voice that had called me into and out of time to Muir's lagoon. The surprise in Amy's eyes was greater than all of ours, but it only stimulated the young woman to lean into a back-and-forth as she and Linda alternated lyrics in Portuguese and English to create a kind of incantation.

I whispered into Nina's ear. "The photograph with Muir and the walking fish—where did Linda say that was? Tibet, right?"

"If that's part of Brazil. It was the trip where Muir's mother met his stepfather. Terrible guy, apparently." She gave me a funny look. "Duh. I'm directly quoting *you*. From a minute ago. You named the mountain with Jesus on it in the background, baby, when she turned the page."

"What Jesus? Those were oil derricks."

She gave me a dubious grin. "Not a derrick, oil or otherwise, in any of those pictures. Enjoy the song you requested, Pintao."

Had I?

LYNN KINGSTON LEFT WITH THE SUNRISE, saying goodbye to all of us, opting out of the spreading of Muir's ashes. Leaning into me as we air-kissed, she said, "If the time ever comes, rely on Tom Bishop. He's the only one my father is blind to."

"What are you talking about?"

"Nothing. Just my gut. And I owe Nathan more than you know."

I glanced at Nina. I was a bit surprised at the hot-eyed way she scrutinized me. Gladys brought out the urn containing Muir's ashes. She placed it in my hands.

"It's time, Russell."

"All right," I said. "I figure we all go out to the lagoon."

"His instructions are you do it alone," Gladys said.

I flashed my eyes to Tom. He showed his thumb. He'd known. They all had—

God, I hate that!

—and they were waiting. On me.

The bronze cremation urn weighed heavily in my grip. Unaccountable terror seized me. A fear of betrayal crept into my heart.

Whose? Mine? His? Theirs?

"Your move, baby."

Like being sucker-punched from behind by a giant fist to the center of my back, I exploded inside with emotion—if emotion could ever be a force of light and life and mass—and I knew explicitly what Muir wanted most from me specifically without him saying it.

"We're doing things my way from now on. Let's go. All of us."

TWO DAYS AFTER CHRISTMAS, while I was in Los Angeles getting checked out with Dr. Rashmi, and learning of my epilepsy—

"Seizures starting in and involving the dominant temporal lobe have rich semiology," she tells me.

"From semiotics, the study of signs and sign meaning," I say, drawn to Jacques Maritain's sign-reading horses and Bishop's tigers; concepts of identity in Malaysia.

"In most cases, a motionless stare—an arrest we call it—is the first step after the auras. You may experience olfactory or taste sensations."

"Pennies from heaven."

"Marvelous word choice. Many do describe a coppery taste," she said. "But the 'heaven' you add is eloquent. So much of the seizure experience is confused with metaphysical phenomenon. This might include déjà vu, jamais vu, and/or presque vu—"

"No, no. None of those." (Muir's voice inside me urges tight operational security.)

Her look says she's not buying it.

"I refuse." I enhance the lie off my upthrust forefinger.

Mustn't tell.

Mustn't lose the time machine before I learn how to control it; I love you, Rashmi, but I'll never betray that secret.

"Well, Russell, be aware. Please. Especially since you have experienced automatic motor, emotional, and autonomic—even, it would seem—semi-intercommunicative actions while in seizure state. This is extremely dangerous. Especially to someone whose mind tends toward elaboration while their job trades in secrets—"

—two days after Muir's Christmas burial, Amy Kim formally submitted her request for resignation and left the Agency.

26

THE MATERIAL PLANNING AND LOGISTICS SUPERVISOR for the Ford Motor Company Valencia Assembly left her state-housing tower in the Barrio Andres Bello, state of Carabobo, Venezuela, at 4 a.m., Tuesday, January 15, 2002. Rather than drive in her company-supplied Ford Focus, she set out on foot along the Rio Cabriales past the concrete Hipódromo de Valencia horse track—built in 1971 and looking every day its age, gray and crumbling—for the Caracas bus stop. A taxi would have taken only eight minutes, but she did not want to be noticed or remembered.

The cab ride would have been infinitely more comfortable. Barely a month into summer, the sky still dark with night and the temperature a balmy 73°F, Carmen Briceño, aged thirty-three, was seven months into the first pregnancy out of five to carry past three months without miscarriage. Regardless of what her OBGYN assured her, she intuitively knew that by walking the five miles, she risked her baby's life. The material planning and logistics supervisor for the Ford Motor Company Valencia Assembly had come to believe she did not carry life well. But the risk not to walk, not to make this trip, was greater than both mother and child. The risk was to the life of her country.

Carmen was already sweating hot, bone-sore, and exhausted by 4:58 a.m. when she reached the Servicios Especiales del Centro bus station and paid the dollar for her ticket and waited. Her bra straps, loosened far as they would go, did not go far enough anymore. They cut into her shoulders. She offset the pain by telling herself she would find a maternity shop after her meeting that morning in the capital. The shopping would provide extra cover for the trip if it were ever questioned.

The thought of questioning frightened Carmen. Her whole involvement, born of something she believed in but was entirely uninvolved with, frightened her by her lack of any kind of control over what her meeting would set into motion. Her meeting, innocent and perfectly legal by both Venezuelan and US law, would set in motion a chain reaction that was deeply criminal. But her conscience was clear. The real crime was living in the country with the most oil reserves on the planet where she and her husband, formerly a two-car family, were unable to afford gasoline for the one car they now shared.

The state-run oil monopoly called Petróleos de Venezuela was not good enough for President Chávez. In a move against their board of directors that was blatantly outside his constitutional authority, he mandated new energy laws to triple the royalties foreign petroleum outfits paid the government. Collapsing and seizing their businesses whenever he could, he prevented those foreign firms from anything other than minority stakes in their partnerships with the national company.

A former paratrooper who rose to power as a man of the people, Chávez plundered the oil industry to become one of the wealthiest men in South America. He dined on Kobe steaks off golden plates inside his palace long forgotten of the barracks and army mess halls of his meager beginnings—the man he'd sold himself as to his people when he seized power. Ignorant about everything to do with oil from exploration to production to economics, he siphoned profits down socialist drains and squandered Venezuela's most treasured resource. By his criminal mismanagement of the petroleum industry, he delivered to Venezuelans soaring prices for food, clothing, and medicine, prompting strikes by newspapers, workplaces, schools. The stock exchange shut down. Basic public services would begin rationing any day now. The horses in the hippodrome ran more reliably—better fed, better cared for—than the citizens of the once prosperous nation Hugo Chávez had ridden into the dust.

Carmen Briceño headed to Caracas that morning to commit treason. Last week, she had walked from her office, which overlooked the production line feed location, to introduce herself to the executive director of International Corporate Communications, Fred Bustamante—one of three Americans from Ford's Dearborn, Michigan, headquarters who cycled through Valencia on six-month rotations. She did not know him. They had never been introduced. But as instructed, she sent Bustamante an email request, *Subject Line: Educational Exchange Progarm Meeting Request* with the purposeful misspelling of the third word.

The Caracas bus clattered along Troncal 1 between the sun-gilded emerald mountainsides of the Parque Nacional Macarao and the silver dark waters of the Lago de Valencia. Carmen remembered the strange meeting that had set her on this journey. Neither she nor the American executive spoke a word about her email's true request. Neither did his words, and the promise they delivered, mention anything of the real nature of their conversation. She decided her actions were part of the light. She was part of that light, and light was life, and light would shield her in the small, simple job ahead.

After the secretary announced Carmen and left the American executive's office, Mr. Bustamante gestured Mrs. Briceño onto a sofa and took an upholstered chair across a coffee table that sported a McLaren LeMans model as a centerpiece. He thanked Carmen for her email and complimented her interest in pursuing higher education abroad through Ford Motor Company's excellent and successful foreign scholarship program. He showed Carmen her personnel file and congratulated her for eleven years of exemplary service.

"And don't worry, I won't hold it against you, the misspelled word in your email."

His smile didn't change. His voice remained casual.

"I know. I'm sorry, Director. The word is 'Program:' p-r-o—" She paused. She counted the five seconds secretly instructed of her slowly and in silence, holding his gaze. "—g-r-a-m. I hit send before I realized my error."

Sign-countersign.

"Thank you for clearing that up," he said.

All-clear return.

"To process your application, you'll need to meet with Deputy Education Secretary Ray Grayson at the US Embassy. I'll call him, as soon as you leave here. I will send you an interoffice memo that will confirm your appointment for tomorrow morning. You will need to take the entire day off. Do you have any personal or vacation days available? You can't use a sick day, I'm afraid."

"Yes, I have one personal day remaining this quarter, Director."

"Easy, then. Best of luck to you, Mrs. Briceño."

He stood. Carmen took that as her cue to leave. She was reaching for the door latch when he stopped her.

"Mrs. Briceño." A note of concern tinged his voice. "If I may ask? Will you and your husband—and the little one soon to be"— he smiled, but his eyes were troubled—"take *complete* advantage of this educational move to the States? I'm only a businessman, but I can force through a permanent career move for you that would continue after your schooling's completed. A permanent move to the US for all of you," he reemphasized. "At Ford we look after those who look after our interests."

She contrived a smile. "I'd as soon raise my daughter in my own country. See *this* job through, sir."

CARMEN BRICEÑO STOOD across from the American Embassy in Venezuela. At 9:05 a.m., she was already five minutes overdue for her meeting with Deputy Education Secretary Ray Grayson who awaited her inside the embassy doors. Paralyzed by fear, she questioned the morality of overthrowing her nation's government, but hadn't President Chávez come to power the same way?

The rising sun moved over the top of the red-stone building. It glowed with warmth. Invitation. She adjusted her bra. She kissed the crucifix on her necklace, slapped the road in small puffs from her shoes, she crossed the street.

"HER HUSBAND'S SISTER is married to a senior Naval officer on Venezuelan Rear Vice-Admiral Carlos Molina Tamayo's staff who has been an Agency asset for six years." Lynn Kingston said this to me from the far side of her desk.

"Why did he use Briceño as a cutout? What happened to the handler we provide?"

"Nothing. He remains active. Nonofficial cover outside of our embassy chain-of-command. An officer of impeccable reputation and numerous successes." She flashed the undercover officer's service jacket she'd pulled from Personnel. "He has not been informed that his agent has gone behind his back."

"Has the Venezuelan agent explained why the sudden change of protocol?"

Lynn Kingston leaned back in her chair. Her smirk was a flat line seamed along pursed lips.

"According to Mrs. Briceño, our Venezuelan agent believes there are leaks in *our* pipeline between said handler"—a tap of the service jacket—"and headquarters."

At twenty-six, Lynn was the youngest Ops Planning officer in service since the early days of the Cold War. She poked the trigger end of her pen into the loose bun she'd pulled her strawberry blond hair into to scratch her scalp. Half of her pile of hair collapsed. It accentuated her youth.

"*Or* the spy has been turned and is aiming our own Acme cannon right back in our dopey face," I said. "It stinks. I don't trust this."

But Lynn denied me with a shake of her head. The rest of her hair fell. She caught it with a scrunchie, preloaded on her wrist—kind of a grooming karate trick of her generation—and fixed it back, still loose, and ready to slip again.

She flirting?

I should say something. Remind her of our professional relationship. Er, association. (Lighter word weight.)

Shit. That would mean recognizing the attraction. Hers. Not mine.

I have none. Nothing negative, nothing positive: silent middle zero.

Apropos of nothing, I pleased myself with the thought that this year would be my first birthday with Nina. This being 2002, I'll turn fifty-two. Puts a quarter century of age difference between us. Not me and Nina—I mean, me and Lynn Kingston.

I said, "Either way, I'm unclear about what I can do to help you. Or, even what help you're asking of me."

"Then I'm flattered you think enough of me to drop everything on the prospect of a 'How's your day, you're looking great,' Lynn' cup of coffee and a chat."

I found the scrunchie juvenile, but this was better: "*Is* that coffee?"

"Want a sip?"

"No. I don't."

"The real question is why this has landed on my desk," said Lynn.

"You have the answer?"

"I do."

I watched her drink with undisguised suspicion.

"Listen, pal, I have a million reasons for this not to be coffee. I'm just waiting for a million-and-one, and today's not going to be that day and you're never going to be my number one. You of all people to judge."

God dammit! So what—I had a slight alcohol problem? A decade ago. Who the fuck didn't Muir tell? And why her? Why the hell'd he involve her in anything? She was only a pig-tailed kid, talking back back-talk when he retired.

I didn't contain the huff I wanted to and centered. Lynn Kingston's habits were not my problems. Her hair was exquisitely fine, though. Finer than silk.

Who wouldn't notice, the way she plays with it?

I could see that now, figuring out why it had fallen. Hadn't been flirting at all. Anything else was deluding myself.

Twenty-five years.

"What's your answer to the question, Lynn? The 'why you' of it all? As far as I know, you're on our Central Europe desk. Not South America."

"Precisely my reason for sharing this only with you—also out of the loop—to make sense of it. I received it from our chief of station who sent it to me as—his words— 'a favor to your dad.' Patronizing twat."

"Silas Kingston."

The name of her father hung loaded and foreboding in the still air between us.

"This COS is arrogantly and stupidly assuming that daddy's girl will skip to my daddy's loo, no questions asked, thereby completing the circle of what our agent fears is the leak and wants to prevent. Silas is the fucking leak."

She gave me a penetrating look. Testing—as if she had any right or seniority to that.

Twenty-six—if we're really sizing her up. Mathematically speaking.

I'm the senior counsel here; I don't walk into the traps. I set them.

"Not necessarily," I said. "Counterintelligence involvement might lead me to believe his group already suspects the same leak in the pipeline as our Venezuelan agent. That's Silas's job: spy on our spies." I stood. "You should send it on."

"Yep. I should."

"But you won't."

She waited for me to deduce why. I slowly sat as it came to me.

"But then why did the agent come up with the request himself?" I said. "If CI suspected a leak among our people with something this big, Silas or Laa-Laa Hofmeyr—"

"Who? Meryl Hofmeyr? Like the Teletubby?" She chuckled. "Muir said you were weird; never said you were funny. Good for you, Rusty."

"It's Russell."

"I don't care. Finish your conclusion. Catch up with me."

"CI, your father, would have directed our Venezuelan agent—Mrs. Briceño's husband's brother-in-law through his sister—"

"Feel free to just say brother-in-law."

"In law, definitively not. No legal familial relationship. Arguably why this guy selected her— But I digress. CI would have redirected him themselves... Unless Counterintelligence is the leak."

She looked worried. I know I looked the same.

Lynn leaned forward toward me. "Nathan told me a day like this would come."

Tells her. Not me. Thanks.

"Like what?"

"I'd find Silas Kingston—"

"Your father."

"—Yeah. 'Legally'—there'd come a time, casual and out of the blue, Silas Kingston's hand sticking innocently out the shower curtain asking for the soap."

"That conjures a repulsive image."

"You'd rather picture me in the shower?"

"We shouldn't be anywhere near a bathroom together!"

Lynn laughed without a hint of humor. "I think that was Muir's point. The innocuously embarrassing he used to conceal the insidiously disgusting. My father is hoping my flash of personal discomfort with the request would have me, blinded by our relationship, just shovel this over to him, Irish Spring through the steam, and get out quick never to mention again. But Silas Kingston and Counterintelligence have no business being near this Venezuelan spy. I need you to write up a deception op. We're going to send Nina for whatever intel Chávez's naval officer wants us to have."

"Running the deception against?"

"CI. We're going to steal the intel Silas wants his hands on and won't get. When we know what it is, maybe I'll have some better idea what that s-o-b Silas is up to."

I hate it when children call their parents by their first names.

I liked this though.

"Far be it for me to want to get between you and your daddy issues—"

"Aren't you already?"

I ignored that. "I have no earthly idea why Nathan gave Gladys instructions to include you—no, better, to trust you. Muir didn't like your father, and you *are* that man's daughter."

"Daughter. How astute. 'And it came to pass, Silas Kingston was given by God two sons.' My older brother, Michael: a brilliant ops officer—some say the best we got. The other, Hal, behind me in age, but as a Kingston, way out ahead of me: serves his country in the United States Marine Corps. But me? Just. His. Daughter. All I had to combat that, coming into this place my father sees as his kingdom's castle, was one name. One officer. The only name I ever heard my father curse. That name was Nathan Muir."

She twisted the bangle flask on her wrist. We both noticed. Her hand withdrew.

"Take me to dinner while Nina's out of town on this and I'll tell you the whole story how I met him. Everything he told me about you and the rest of his *Land Before Time* loyal band a'his you're all part of."

"I choose not. She's back from Havana. I'm not sure what her portfolio for Venezuela is and how I'd even legally get her into that area of operation if, as we must assume, Silas has compromised the entire Venezuela station."

"We're not sending her to Venezuela." Lynn squared a Top-Secret file on her desk and passed it across to me. "You're going to write her aboard the USS *Yorktown*, which is, right now, provisioning in Pascagoula, Mississippi, for Caribbean exercises with the Second Fleet. Exercises that include a show of force against Havana. It's a simple hand-off. Nina and our agent. All of two seconds."

Lynn Kingston stood to see me out. I was taken aback to see her wearing jeans. Tight jeans. She caught my look.

"Isn't it 'Casual Friday?'" she mocked.

"We don't have 'Casual Fridays.' And today is Fff—" About to say *Friday*, I cut myself off. This is Saturday.

I still flubbed occasionally on my ordinal cognitive tests, as my recent LA trip had borne out. Lynn had called me in from home this morning.

Better not to speak another word.

She came around her desk. Her ivory silk blouse suddenly came alive with a prismatic spray of colored light that danced across her figure as she moved toward me. This was not symptomatic of an impending focal awareness seizure as Dr. Rashmi explained my current benign epileptic affliction that we now medicate and monitor. The colored spray came from sunlight refracting through the only personal decoration Lynn Kingston displayed in her office. A tall, clear vase on the corner of her desk, it was filled with a collection of beach glass. She caught me staring. She turned the crystal cylinder and the light pattern changed across her rounded chest.

"Pretty, isn't it?"

LATE FRIDAY NIGHT, February 22, 2002, after a day of sports competitions between crews of Tactical Destroyer Squadron 6, handily won by the men and women of the USS *Yorktown*, Nina slipped aboard the USN Guided Missile Cruiser CG-48 as it made final preparations for deployment to the Second Fleet where it would take part in the UNITAS (*Unity* in Latin) exercise.

The largest multi-national naval exercise in the Western Hemisphere, it was touted as an operation to further develop professional understanding and mutual respect with our regional partner nations while gaining new knowledge, understanding, and sensitivity for each other's culture and people. All that was missing was a clambake, s'mores, and a chorus or two hauling bananas with 'Day-O' on the guitar.

Instead, UNITAS 43 would be a war game of the most pugnacious sort, focused on northern hemispheric defense, interdiction, and mutual coordinated combat in the post-9/11 world. A massive, live fire show of force, it served as a "we-got-our-eyes-on-you" deterrent to military aggression from Cuba and Russia—even the Chinese, who'd been bobbing up with more disturbing frequency in the region since 9/11—along with the criminal adventurism of Middle Eastern terrorists, drug cartels, human traffickers, and the modern-day pirates who would exploit their evil on the Caribbean Sea.

The orders Nina presented US Navy Commander Steven R. Kerns were those of Pentagon-assigned Navy Public Affairs Third-Rank Lieutenant Samantha Ramos. CDR. Kerns, who knew her true occupation and that she wasn't Ramos, grumbled, "We would have won today without your referees and rigged stopwatches. I don't like that shit, and I don't want to see you until your moment. Moment after that, you're off my ship."

"Happy to confine to quarters. All I know is due to your ship's victory, communications traffic has now gone out to Caracas informing President Chávez the USS *Yorktown* has won the honor of hosting his tour, and I'll be accompanying the entourage to organize the photo-ops. So, when I do pop out, you won't even see my face as it will be behind a camera."

Which, eight days later, when the Venezuelan navy joined the US fleet in gunnery practice off the coast of Curaçao, is exactly what happened. In a close quarters UEE (Under Enemy Eyes) exchange of material in close contact of hostile or allied but nonauthorized individuals, you force the look-away or corral the look. Dressed in too-tight service dress whites, Nina achieved immediate wide-eyed leers and embarrassed shock that prompted the self-conscious aversion of eyes by all those afraid of sexual harassment accusations or breach of international decorum, while capturing the rest of the eyes, those on both sides inclined to harass and pant to her superstructure. This allowed Nina to identify herself with Carmen Briceño's necklace hanging in her cleavage and initiate the brush pass of a memory stick by a touch of fingers unwatched and unseen.

Two seconds.

Six hours later, plain-Jane-d to civvies, Nina helicoptered to Curaçao International Airport, where she boarded an American Airlines flight to Miami. Inside the terminal and headed for her connector, Nina made a restroom pit stop where, acting on my personal off-OPLAN order, and in violation of:

18 *U.S. Code* § 798. Disclosure of classified information. *Whoever knowingly and willfully communicates, furnishes, transmits, or otherwise makes available to an unauthorized person, or publishes, or uses in any manner prejudicial to the safety or interest of the United States or for the benefit of any foreign government to the detriment of the United States any classified information[...]*

Subsection:

[...](4) obtained by the processes of communication intelligence from the communications of any foreign government, knowing the same to have been obtained by such processes[...] shall be fined under this title or imprisoned not more than ten years, or both.

And:

18 *U.S. Code* § 1924.Unauthorized removal and retention of classified documents or material.

Whoever, being an officer, employee, contractor, or consultant of the United States, and, by virtue of his office, employment, position, or contract, becomes possessed of documents or materials containing classified information of the United States, knowingly removes such documents or materials without authority and with the intent to retain such documents or materials at an unauthorized location shall be fined under this title or imprisoned for not more than five years, or both.

She received a laptop computer beneath a toilet stall divider onto which she copied the contents of the Venezuelan spy's USB drive.

Minutes later, as Nina presented her ticket and boarded her return flight to Washington, a statuesque woman stowed the laptop inside the trunk of a waiting blue Jaguar and climbed in beside the driver. The Jaguar, an old-style XJS convertible, was unusual. Not only due to the black-market microwave burn-box connected trunk-to-dashboard to a destruct switch, into which the woman placed the computer, but also for the legal modification that allowed the vehicle to be driven by someone who, were his documentation scrutinized, would be identified as a one-legged seafaring man by the name of Silver.

As Bishop and Lara drove back to Captiva Island to await my instructions, how was I to know that by this reckless move against the power of Silas Kingston, I had laid the cornerstone to Nina's dungeon? That her rescue from a horror fate of torture, rape, and murder would only be securable by my betrayal of all I loved with the murder of her father.

From then on, time actively moved against me. I would not know this until I embraced my ability to move backward and forwards along its slipstream by virtue of my epileptic condition. But the answer existed in light. Short wavelengths converted into long wavelengths; light converting to heat, creating atomic movement; particle event creating time, and through that process, my discovery of the final piece of the equation that gives human understanding to events.

27

I ENTERTAINED MYSELF (which is to say I distracted my attention with apprehensions of all that could go wrong and would) awaiting Nina's return from headquarters, where completion of the operation was her delivery of the intelligence—in this case, the memory stick—to Lynn Kingston. I put aside a book of PennyPress crosswords and settled in to watch a PBS broadcast of the Birmingham Ballet's presentation of David Bintley's *Arthur (Part I)*.

Commissioned for the Millennium, the story of Great Britain's legendary and mythological king had been set to music—that illusory time machine of heard space between past sound and future harmonic anticipation—wherein I glimpsed the nature of that ultimate reality component in a sudden understanding of why dance is beautiful.

A ring of light gathers around the edges of the television screen. Colored prisms send linear and multilateral constructions—squares, rectangles, triangles—whirlpooling the edges of my vision into floating polyhedrons. The coppery taste not unlike blood, but richer in flavor and without substance, fills my mouth. Perception becomes conical, narrowing my field of vision to a pinpoint that, at its end, is detailed vision to a vast degree.

I am alive but detached from bodily mechanics and processes. I have no desire to move; at peace if this is permanent. But I am also aware I exist to discover something beyond it. Something necessary to all I am and all whom I love and live to protect.

All that is, is the dance. And from within the dance comes the overwhelming feeling the answer I seek, the answer that will define this question just out of reach that tugs at the tip of my tongue—the presque vu Dr. Rashmi brushed off but cannot fathom without experience of it—and will possibly save us all from disaster driving toward us on future light.

All is the dance.

Dance is music visualized. Graceful athletic movement matched to provocative sound. Music is the illusion, the blurring of the space between the notes—the pure pinpoint of silence that all present instance exists as; the registration of what *was heard* blurring into what *will be heard*, enjoyed because of our calculation of all possible harmonic outcomes of what that *might be*, put to value of what it surprisingly turns out to be after its instantaneous passing with the mind already moving onto what it already has become and might.

Blurred extended present.

Dance is the physical representation of that phenomena. In reality, it does not match. The light waves and sound waves do not match. The physiological signals of movement and how the brains process and enact them occur at a third and altogether different timeline. To make the confusion supreme, signals from eyes, ears, hands, feet all travel different distances to the brain and *not in the pattern we experience them.* Only after all these stimuli, action, and reaction meet in the brain and synchronize in the mind do the brains of the dancers and their audiences sort them into linear order and give them temporal sense. All, long after the moment they are perceived as taking place simultaneously in the present. And *only then*, does the brain match this rhythmic movement to the sound of music already passed. Dance is of supreme beauty as we instinctively understand its supreme impossibility.

I suddenly and fully appreciate this from a revelatory understanding of the presence of all that is not the dancers but rather, the negative space between the balletic pair. I watch and I connect with them "virtually." Both in its original, primary definition, "existent as fact; real," and it's modern corruption "in effect or essence, but not in fact reality."

A pas de deux. Uther Pendragon, magically disguised by Merlin to appear as the man Uther battles, seduces Igraine, that enemy's wife. The complicated geometries of corresponding and contrapuntal bodies; their negative space. The impassioned arcs of limbs, of fingers, a flash of eyes and turn of cheek; understandable only by the space that isn't. Arms flow, bodies lengthen, glorious leaps, a wrist seized, the subtle shifts of weight in the controlled freneticism of slippered feet, of bound toes en pointe—

Of a run, of a vault.

Of a muscular lift, a gentle embrace.

Étendre. Relever.

The glide to the jump. Élancer to the turn.

—negative space contracting and expanding on emotion and beauty, passion and energy: space shapes, it defines; space encloses, it captures.

The space between the dancers, their movement through it, is the visualization of music by two like systems acting and reacting to each other on the level plane of their shared experience of music as an event timed to their system clocks, bound by their compatible brain-synchronization, which is perfectly matched with the space-time I, as the audience, exist in remotely. Any individual component sped up or slowed down, out of sync from any of their interactive systems, creates entropy. Chaos. Becomes unrecognizable and unreal.

Due to this, an event that is a person, atomically clocked by and to lifespan, cannot easily or successfully dance with an event that is Mount Everest.

Or a bullet to the head on a Malaysian highway.

What I experience occurring in the atoms that make up the dancer who dances Uther is not any more independent from what is happening in the atoms that are the prima ballerina, atoms that are becoming the become of Igraine. Though wholly independent of the other, they fully communicate by and with the emptiness between them to render reality as beauty by a constant transmission and reception of shared time-speed between these two bodies across space, and it defines for me a representation of the key element our universe exists upon.

I understand this: reality is nothing less and nothing greater than the choreography between independent matched-clock systems. I know for all that I am, that in my grasp is the final piece of the equation that gives human understanding to events and a human capacity to manip-ulate and control them.

It is the piece that isn't matter; invisible, carried by and filling the negative space, and is fully defining. The exchange between systems. If I can just name it...

The dance is gone, the ballet, my television, vanish as my internal clock—detached from reality by the electrical storm of neurological impulses firing blindly and uncontrolled within the empty space in my brain created by tumor and dug by bullet, a release of chemical neurotransmitters on a long and silent roll of thunder—dials me into a fully realized present.

"Thank you for taking the time to meet with me, Professor Muir."

I stand in Rome.

Rome Hall, that is, and "now" is September 1970, the first week of my senior year at George Washington University. The second time I have seen Nathan Muir after having sat through his first, and wildly inappropriate lecture, I am reliving the moments of the first time we speak, a new and malleable present.

"You're the one taking the time here. Whether you showed up or not, I'd be here as I was Monday and will be again on Friday on and on until my work here is finished, and I take my time elsewhere."

Had he said that before and I'm only hearing it now? Or will these words echo backward and change the between that informs tomorrow?

The fourth piece; I struggle to name it. And I experience the collapsing rush that accompanies déjà vu, but this is unlike any déjà vu I have ever had. It is not a memory but an experience, and not a re-experience as in and of itself and my position at its center: this is a present.

I know I am in my chair.

I know I am watching ballet.

I know I am waiting for Nina to arrive from Langley even as I know that I am on stage at the ballet when the video was made while I simultaneously stand in Rome Hall before Nathan Muir thirty years in the recorded past. This is what I experienced at Muir's wake, lured out by Aunt Linda and Amy's siren song to the old spy's secret lagoon—a Korean who sings Portuguese? Did that ever possibly happen—? And yes, the man in front of me is dead in reality, but this is present reality, and Dr. Rashmi is to meaning only that which letters are to words once they fall from their crossword boxes in the book upon my lap.

So are my thoughts I have now, but didn't then, as Muir says, perplexed by my mute stare, "You come here to speak with me or to collect dust?"

"You didn't say that before."

"You have no idea what I've said before. We're only just meeting. I have heard what's been said about you, though. You're an oddball, Aiken. May I call you Rusty?"

I seized on the present of that past, too afraid to confuse it with the future past of what would become. I illume my protection inside my soul, and command myself to mindful action: Draw, O Caesar, erase a coward!

"No one does... call me that."

"Good. I'll give it some exercise. Lunge it round the ring. See if you grow out of it. So, what may I do for you?"

Joy. Rushing joy. Thankfulness and humility at this new and unfettered power as delicate as the bubble foam made by a drop of dew spread by gravity across the framework of a single pane of a spider-web's network. Shimmer in space I can see between light particles.

"This is my final year before law school. Every course counts. When I registered you weren't the professor. What happened?"

"Feeling gypped?"

"Confused. Addled. Apprehensive. I've looked forward three years to hear Dr. Gauss's lectures."

"Yes. Okay, then. Here's Chuck Gauss: 'The mental world of verid-ical data and the world of imagination, of dreams and illusions, are both absorbed by a deeper mental realm named the surreal.'"

Muir smirks. He waits.

"Want more? Gauss goes on: 'The things of the outer world though real in the sense that they have their own independent existence, lose this reality in our thoughts—' Ah, c'mon, Rusty. What's that hogwash and a nickel gonna get you while Soviet dominoes are falling all around us, clacking their way toward nuclear war?"

I grinned, this time realizing he'd already started his Agency pitch that first meeting.

"Sorry for your loss," he continues, "but it was decided by the powers that be—and they're vaster than you credit them—I'd visit and teach you the course that counts most. The rest and the why ain't any of your business."

"Ain't?"

"It'll be in the dictionary one day, you'll see."

This is not the conversation we had, but he seems to halfway know this, so I ride the wave. "Well, I'm not so sure—"

"Good. Surety is often nothing more than a sure sign of one's own senselessness."

"What?"

"Never be sure, Rusty."

"Sir, I end up not liking being called Rusty."

"That's funny, I'm liking him more and more. Like the way he runs."

I say, "Where are you visiting from?" And I know it's Vietnam.

"Here and there. And the other place that isn't one of those."

It fits better now than when he'd said it the first time.

"Don't let the knit tie fool you. I don't always work as a teacher."

I grin. Everything, I realize, by its retrieved passage through time, takes on new meanings with new probabilities. I challenge him like I hadn't before.

"I want more from this class than I think you can offer. I mean from the syllabus you passed out this morning."

"Never flatter yourself you're all that special. Better to let it keep itself a secret inside you. A Rule of Thumb I'll expect you to remember. What you'll learn from me will never have value if all you want is what I can offer. I can offer you things that'd scare the shit out of you. Not for what I teach—"

"For what they force me to recognize in what I already knew. I defied you—"

"Don't you mean 'deified?' in that special way you got?"

I did. I had said it to myself. But backwards as protection. "I took the whole gang to spread your ashes."

He cocks that grin of his that saves and seduces, that disguises his powers of life and death and the disgrace in their equality in destroying.

"Yeah. Aiken." He's awed I've spoken his own words before he ever thought them. "I bet."

He rises from his leather chair with loose-limbed grace, not of a dancer but a gunslinger, and selects a book that rests alone on a shelf of its own.

"*What do you know about Democritus?*"

"*Uh, 400 BC or thereabouts. The 'Laughing Philosopher'—that's what they called him, his contemporaries like Socrates, Aristotle—he put high value on cheerfulness in all pursuits.*"

(But I don't know that then; I'd never heard of Democritus. I only know him now.)

"*Like you, meaning you don't know crap on a cracker. His original works are all lost—pity to mankind—but much of it was copied and referenced by others. In what we have of Democritus, we glimpse a genius with shoulders broad enough for all the rest of philosophy and science to piggyback upon. Newton, Maxwell, and Lorentz. Darwin. Hume and Kant, Einstein: Democritus sets all the balls rolling. Because you made the mistake of coming here, which I'm glad you did...*"

The distance crackles electric.

He flips into the book.

"*You're a word guy—*"

He knows even then. And encourages me to agree with an impatient nod I reciprocate.

"*—so, you'll like this. When Democritus gave us the atom, before we lost the concept for a few thousand years, thanks to Roman profligacy, he suggested we could conceptualize atoms in terms of the alphabet. While limited to a list of twenty-odd letters, he writes, 'It is possible for them to combine in diverse modes, in order to produce comedies or tragedies, ridiculous stories, or epic poems.'*"

He gives me the book and sets my course.

"*But stories and poems, jokes and obituaries*"—*and now he's speaking to me from my television, dancers gone, as I recede from the cone of my seizure—"The sun to the earth, the moon to the mouse running beneath it from the owl, can only differentiate and be differentiated from static, timeless nothing, by the information they pass; all can only be understood by transmission of its intrinsic nature: one thing, one being, one event to another. The correlation between all past, present, and future interactions between event systems, Dumbo, is the end-all be-all of the why you seek."*

Espionage, like the mouse and the moon, and the ballerina's toe en pointe where it meets the stage, Nina's kisses I am now returning with equal hunger could be converted into a real time machine not because of the flow of light but because of the flow of—

"What're you doing?"

I startled.

Nina panted into my ear, "If this whole plan of yours goes sideways, I don't think they'll allow conjugal visits when we're sent to prison." She pushed her bare chest off mine, energetically riding my arousal. "Is this the sofa?"

"You're inside?"

"No, you are, Pintao."

"Russell. I mean my townhouse. You said you never would. Come inside. Did you ring? I didn't hear the doorbell."

"I don't like the way Lynn Kingston talks about you."

She was working us hard to climax. She barely had time to get out, "Did you shoot your wife and her fat-fuck here?"

"I... Got... hhh... hhh... fucking rid of that sofa—"

"Good, you're doing it, do it, erase both those bitches, baby. God, I'm doing it!"

No sooner had we finished, than she hustled us to her car. "You're selling that fucking place tomorrow."

"I've always hated it," I admitted aloud what I'd always held secret from myself.

I climbed into an old but scrumptious Morgan jalopy she'd acquired from who-knows-where-she-buys-cars, the crack pot I picture myself every time I tumble inside it and take the ridiculous goggles she forces on me. We bumped down my old lane into the rising sun.

28

WHETHER NINA LIKED IT OR TRUSTED IT or was made madly jealous by it: I had to work with Lynn Kingston. Irrespective of Nina's accusations of Lynn's flirtations. Even if she was flirting—which I was most likely wrong about—*I* wasn't flirting back. I think I proved Nina that last night. My worries lay with Lynn's father. Worried whether she had cut him out of the loop or planned to slash us out of the Agency as the remnants of Muir's ragtag dinosaur rebellion against the Nine-Twelvers—as I now referred to Muir's legitimately maligned Young Turks.

I was on my way to meet Lynn Kingston, worried if all this was an *On Golden Pond* Jane Fonda "I'm gonna do a back flip!" into an Academy Award for Daddy.

But Lynn had not been acting. Keeping the memory stick secret, bigoted from Silas Kingston and Counterintelligence, she had delivered it personally to Elliot Abrams, Special Assistant to President Bush II and Senior Director on the National Security Council.

She briefed me over a quiet lunch at a little red-checked-tablecloth Italian hole-in-the-wall, private and unobserved away from Langley "for cover," where she proved I was correct about her lack of intentions. If she'd been trying to seduce me, the black sleeve dress she wore wouldn't have had sleeves covering the sunny round shoulders I imagined beneath and would not have revealed the visible panty line I'd seen when we'd been led to the table. Way I picture it, she'd have worn a thong.

Lynn was trying to work her way into our trusted circle. Nina, Joshua, Bill Carver, and I the last points of legitimate circumference.

And Linda, sure, who would be casting her peculiar spell over the young recruits she lured onto her mountaintop, I'd wager well past her one hundredth year. Joshua, slated this year for retirement, only stayed on in the valiant—but I feared lost—hope I would somehow pull Amy back into the cold from where she had returned to school to take a PhD in quantum computation astrophysics. Turns out, the ditz already built her escape hatch before we'd last seen her at Muir's wake. This rankled me to no end with its patent dishonesty. While I'd failed in my pledge to keep her in the fold, I had, with Joshua's help forging her signature, filed "approved" paperwork that—although she had no idea—made her coursework official CIA work-study sabbatical for the next three years.

I liked Amy. I told myself she'd abandoned her post to settle her grief in private. On the path to scatter Muir's ashes, she'd said, "I made him a promise. I'm sure he was teasing. He always teased. But he never said otherwise."

"What's that mean?" I said.

She slipped me a vial, explaining, and I gave her some of his ashes.

And while I've passed by her George Mason U graduate student duplex more than a couple times, I've not approached, knocked, or telephoned.

I swore to myself—to Nina, Joshua, Carver, Gladys (especially Gladys)—I'd draw Amy back when I became certain I could compel it voluntarily to our favor.

"Good," Joshua said. "It's how he'd work it."

In my failure, I felt secure in Muir's approval.

"THEY'RE FINAL PLANS FOR A COUP D'ÉTAT against President Chávez set for April twelfth—"

"Two weeks from now," I interrupted Lynn, through a mouthful of gnocchi in pink vodka sauce.

"The eleventh will begin with general strikes that will carry into a people's march on the palace. The right-wing military leaders, who will refuse to unleash the army on the populace, instead, will force Chávez to resign."

All conversation long, I'd played the appropriate surprise and astonishment, cleverly hiding from Lynn the truth that I already knew everything she briefed me, Bishop having transferred the Valencia–Yorktown intelligence haul to his own USB thumb, which Lara took to the local Kinkos self-service and copied.

"Peacefully?" I feigned ignorance.

Lynn regarded me through sober eyes that hadn't registered any effect from the first bottle of Pinot Grigio she'd already finished. She observed me self-effacingly.

"Why am I telling you? You already know, you sonofabitch. You stole your own set."

"No."

We waited on the lie while the waiter brought her a second bottle. I couldn't judge her. I'd been that person with many years a head start. I hoped she'd have someone there for her like I'd had—Nina, Bishop; Nathan's hidden hand—to pick her up when she crashed.

"Muir told me you'd pull something like this the first time I reached out to you. In good faith."

"You're talking nonsense."

"And you're lying."

"You're lying." I couldn't think of anything past a first-grade rebuttal.

"He gave me your tell. You lose the crook in your smile and stitch three wrinkles across your forehead when you're fibbing."

"My forehead is as smooth as—"

"My ass?"

"Silk."

"Thank you." She sipped. Moved on. "We're in this up to our tits—'we' being the Agency, not me. You. We have seven dev teams already in-country cultivating sources within the unions to ensure maximum penetration and coordination for the strikes, as well as three roving media teams posing Swiss, Canadian, and Spanish, freelancing as docu and cable news filmmakers who'll feed pro coup footage to sympathetic Venezuelan and international media outlets. We have a Black Ops paramilitary on call if Chávez chooses to argue on the ride from the palace."

"All this begs the question we started out with: why's Silas Kingston and Counterintelligence involved? And why the plotters chose not to trust him."

She finished the pour from the waiter; she refilled halfway. I snagged the bottle from her and filled her all the way to the rim. "Why fuck around?"

"Don't. My last boyfriend tried that tactic. It won't work."

"I'm not your boyfriend."

"Maybe that's my problem."

"Get this straight, Lynn. I love Nina. I plan to marry Nina."

She toasted me. "Now you know why Nina and I like to hate each other."

I refused the bait. Wasn't going to even sniff it. Lynn knew. Emptied the glass of wine into her wide-open mouth.

"What if your father isn't operating within Counterintelligence context? Does he, or has he ever operated outside his official purview?"

"You think I've ever gotten a look past his door? I told you, I'm DNQ on his list."

"You're 'Not' what? What's Q?"

"Qualified. Never will be in his eyes."

"All we can manage is to watch how this coup will develop. Whatever goes off-op is where we're going to catch him."

A strange change came over her. "And do what?" Her voice was soft, but not enough to hide the vulnerability I now glimpsed.

"Useless to guess right now. We've moved or been moved into a system where we'll need more information on what's going down, and what's playing out around that, before we can begin to dream up its purpose. May turn out to be as simple as a test he's run on you for purely personal reasons or, turn it like a kaleidoscope and the image changes. It's a whole other deal."

I made sure the crook was in place as I kindly smiled her way, gauging her reaction to the word. In my experience, only one other time had Silas Kingston secretly piggybacked his own invisible operation on another. China. Harker's SIDESHOW. Bishop, Elizabeth… KALEIDOSCOPE.

Nothing flickered. She appeared more in the dark to KALEIDOSCOPE than I. As much as Muir had been, and Bishop—where twice it almost cost him his life.

"Nathan was right about you," she said. "I'm glad."

Lynn Kingston chose not to finish the second bottle. We sipped cappuccinos, both of us thoughtful in the other's sight. We spoke small words of insignificant things.

ON MY WAY HOME, the DJ on the jazz station announced a song by Antonio Carlos Jobim. About to change it to save my love for both him, Gilberto, Getz, and the playa-played-out "Girl from Ipanema," I heard Jobim singing with Elias Regina and found myself returned to Christmas and the "Waters of March."

I fought the onset of a seizure. My brain told me—

Pull over, pull over…

A seagull falls from the sky before my eyes.

I imagine myself in control across two times; I won't stop. My fingers manipulate the cruise control buttons and I hear Muir:

"My, my, Aiken's all smarts today."

"I saw a seagull fall out of the sky once," I remark with a grin over my shoulder, only this time Jessie travels with baby Nate in her lap on our trip to Princeton before 9/11 kills the boy and his mother aboard flight AA77.

"Where? Malibu?" my Russian child smirks.

"Ha, ha. It was a beach. But in Cuba. A place called Caiberién."

"Maybe someone shot it."

What she said, but I hear layered simultaneously little Nate, who didn't yet talk: "Maybe someone shot you."

Nelly Furtado comes on the radio, "I'm Like a Bird," and Jessie now in Björk's swan gown, the boy vanished, squeals "Turn it up! Turn it up! This always happens to you!"

You never see yourself in memory or blood from your own head on a Malaysian highway.

And then I am stepping across Nina's threshold—no memory of parking, no memory of coming up the walk, the steps—inside the house where in twenty months she'll be taken violently the night our engagement won't happen.

She was sitting on a barstool in the galley, sipping a daquiri.

"How was lunch with the Queen of Hearts?"

"I told her I'm gonna marry you."

Nina gave a throaty laugh. "Why is it when you say the absolute wrong thing, I love you even more? Come here and kiss me before I change my mind."

I kissed her, and more, and afterward she said, "You'll be the death of me, Pintao."

"I'll give my life to prove that wrong."

Nina bolted upright in the bed. "Promise me: never that."

Like a bird that falls from the sky, God winks in all kinds of crazy ways, but I couldn't see it then, wasn't meant to.

"I was joking around."

"I'm not. Promise me. I mean it. Right now. Never give your life for me."

As anyone would without foreknowledge, I gave my word.

DURING THE VENEZUELAN COUP, the information we were seeking bounced back our way. President Bush—playing deaf to the promises we'd made to our agents, assets, and co-conspirators—warned Chávez. Bush took his entire Security Council, his Cabinet, and the Agency by surprise. Said he acted on alternative intelligence.

What had Silas Kingston done? Nineteen people paid with their lives. One hundred and fifty more wounded in the streets. Our agents and allies, betrayed, were arrested, as were the high-ranking military leaders their Supreme Court would rule should not stand trial; they argued successfully that what took place was not a "coup" but a *vacío poder*. A power vacuum.

It was one of the Venezuelan dead who spoke to us. Told us nothing about the failed democratic movement; dumb to the politics of the affair, her life had been sacrificed as a piece of data passed from Silas's system to ours. Carmen Briceño lost her sixth pregnancy before term. As feared, the material planning and logistics supervisor did not carry life well. In an accident no one could explain—how it transpired, let alone why she was anywhere near the hazardous machinery she fell into—Carmen was crushed to death on the metal stamping line of the Ford Valencia Assembly.

By May 6, the HOUNDFOX network would report to Nina the anomaly we all had sought. Unable to trust his military and security service, Chávez of Venezuela made a deal with Castro in Havana. Brokered by a "neutral" China, in exchange for Cuban military arms and personnel, secret police, and intelligence services, the *Período Especial* would come to an end with Venezuela opening the flow of oil to the communist island nation.

Muir hands me the book *of writings by Democritus. He tells me about the atoms and the alphabet. I thank him for the book and, in a youthful effort to impress, recite the only quote of the ancient Laughing Philosopher I can remember. In speaking it, I am receiving and sharing direct information of what Democritus was thinking the moment he wrote it. Time as a linear construction of centuries instantly nonexistent between us, Democritus's mind as alive as mine and directly connected. A time machine.*

"'*To a wise man, the whole earth is open, because the true country of a virtuous soul is the entire universe.*'"

"*You got it, Aiken," says Muir. "Now get out of here and finish the equation—Nina is not a thing; she is an event. To save her, find and name the space between all the dancers everywhere.*"

"*Save from what?*"

"*Coiled up, imperfect you.*"

29

Back from a quick trip to Captiva Island, I had a sunburn that, peeling, made my face look like the man in the moon; my shoulders and back, hidden by the dark side of my suit coat, a map of lunar landscapes unseen. I wholly itched to high holy hell. I squirmed against the passenger seat back, rubbing some relief as Nina drove us through the main gates into Langley.

"Next time you'll use sunscreen."

"I had sunscreen."

"Having and using are two different things, Pintao."

"Russell."

We drove down the long, forested drive, past the New Headquarters building. The massive American flag, hung inside on September 12, filled the four-story lobby of the core area that connected the two six-story office towers on either side. The green glass of its facade tinted the blue and red of our national symbol a murky aqua and brown. The entire structure: a hunched goblin gargoyle. We parked in the Old Headquarters' lot. Bomb-sniffing dogs with their submachine-gun handlers, patrolling in force since 9/11, made the morning rounds. We checked in and made our way to Lynn Kingston's office in Evaluations and Plans.

"Don't laugh until you've seen my back," I warned.

"She's not going to, baby." We took our seats. "But laugh at his face, Lynn. All you want."

Her vase of colored beach glass caught the light through the double-paned, anti-eavesdropping, white-noise-filled arrow-slit windows.

Is it subconscious? Willful psychological blindness?

How is it she can have a veritable kaleidoscope as the solo featured decoration in the room and—

1. *not recognize it for the toy it mimics; and*
2. *not know what or how the name of that toy connects her to the deadly, clandestine context of her patrimony?*

Yet, I knew since returning from overseeing the destruction and the deep-sixing of the hard drive, thumb, and hard-copy versions of the Carmen Briceño intelligence that this was so.

"Pick your poison: bottled water, soft drinks, iced tea, or coffee," Lynn rattled off.

"Nothing stronger?" Nina said.

"Bottled water, soft drinks, iced tea, or coffee. Could probably get us a saucer of cream to fight over. But Russell might like that, and I'm sure we can both agree he's at his worst when he's excited."

"Excuse me, but I don't need to be spoken of in the third person."

"Baby, there are three people here. She's one—it's her office. I'm two—because she's speaking to me. That makes you, third person," Nina was relaxed. She gave Lynn a friendly smile. "If you're serious about quitting booze for yourself, I'm happy to see the change, Lynn." Nina was serving strychnine.

"If it ends up like the last right decision I made with our unmet friend Carmen, I'm sure I'll end up regretting it."

Nina and I took water. Lynn twisted open a bottle of Lipton.

"To moving on," she toasted us. "Clear-eyed and unassailable."

We all sipped and traded glances.

"You called the meeting of the brain trust," I said, when first and second persons had become as conversant as rocks. "What's the move you're referring we get on to?"

"Me. After events in Venezuela, to which I was party to and have taken full responsibility, I'm leaving Ops Planning, Central Europe."

"I'm sorry," Nina said, honestly.

"Careful what you wish for..." And suddenly the beam of Lynn's smile was as gorgeous as the colored light sparkling from her vase. "I'm taking the Cuba desk."

Nina shifted beside me, tensed with shock. Lynn raised a finger, holding back whatever Nina was about to say.

"If you'll have me. Cuba's yours, Nina. This decision is professional, not personal, and I guarantee it is to support you one hundred percent. You will have my full confidence, as you had with Nathan—and haven't since his passing—but I won't do this without your blessing. There are plenty of other sections on Eval-Plan who would take me which I could nail the fuck out of."

Not for me to decide—thankfully—I turned to face Nina directly. And this is what I love about her—Nina gave a happy laugh.

"You amazing bitch. I thought we were here for your rosary. How did you pull it off?"

Maybe hate is healthy between women when they keep it in the open; all I knew, was I was feeling more comfortable in the third person with each passing moment and wouldn't have minded receding into the fourth. I didn't say a word. Until I spoke next.

"You aren't fired? I figured—I was telling Nina the whole way over here—'Be prepared. Lynn probably got the ax.' They didn't fire you?"

"Some axes are double-edged. In recognition to my last-minute contribution to the Venezuelan intelligence picture that saved Director Tenet and this White House a disastrous involvement in further destabilizing an unstable nation and, by providing about a dozen signatures exempting the Agency, US Navy, National Security Council, and everyone else I might have Typhoid Mary'd by touching this, I traded eternal silence for a promotion and a pick of AO."

"As they say," I said, "'Don't swing glass axes in wooden houses.'"

"What, Aiken? Who says that?" she said.

"I do... And the people deliberately blinding themselves. Obviously."

Nina gave Lynn an eye roll and said, "How'd you *swing* that Area of Operation now Venezuela and Cuba are linked?"

"I allowed them to think the Cuba desk was their idea. That if they managed to screw this Caracas–Havana cozying up the way they screwed up the Chávez coup, my head would already be neatly and prominently stretched across the chopping block."

"Professionally, I'm one hundred percent on board," Nina said, toasting back with her water. "Personally—you going to keep your eyes off my man?"

"Probably not. But I don't play dirty. I won't betray you and I won't betray him."

I spread my hands, one aimed at each of them. "Well, I won't betray either of you."

Lynn gave me a dead look. "I'm not yours to betray."

Nina ran a hand up the back of my thinning hair. The only part of me I wasn't sunburned. "I know what you mean, baby."

"Excellent," I said. "Moving on. There are ramifications from the death of our Briceño cutout we need to discuss."

"It was a message," Lynn said. "Aimed directly at me."

"Directly to us. And, more broadly, I'd say to sympathizers of the plot who might have worked with her. Specific intention and agency behind the murder for a moment disregarded—agency as in force, impetus; not organization—the message got delivered to affect both sides of her control."

"Us and the coup plotters," Nina said.

I nodded. "The question becomes, not who received the message, but who delivered it. It wasn't Chávez's people."

"Why?" said Nina.

"Because the accident was too perfect. Too believable. Too untraceable. An accident appearing exactly like an accident. A political message is a slit throat, 'robbery gone bad' with nothing stolen, bleeding out on a sidewalk. A car bomb. Or a firing squad with an indictment nailed to the courthouse door and the bullets billed to the family."

"I'll give you this," Lynn said. "To that same point, I checked in with our Domestic Resources Branch to see if her murder impacted Ford's long-standing cooperation. Nothing's changed or is changing. Still in place worldwide. Still in place in Valencia. As far as the rest of our CIA operations in Caracas: they're riding high. Chief of Station Ray Grayson is getting a commendation, medal ceremony, gold sticker, and write-up on his jacket to never see daylight in whatever safe we keep that junk."

"Then I'll say aloud what the three of us must acknowledge: that message, mother-baby-dead, was directly from Lynn's father."

Nina's eyes swished between me and Lynn who pondered her beach glass—seeing something contained within it?

Her gaze returned to us. "When Press Secretary Fleisher spoke on behalf of the president in support of the coup, followed by Elliot Abrams, announcing US support of President Chávez's removal, I believed we'd beaten Silas. Whatever he was up to. But wouldn't you know? While they were officially announcing Bush's support for the coup, while our Director Tenet was ordering our assets support in the coup, Bush had already tipped off Chávez.

Our president left his own closest advisers out of his final determination."

"Meaning," I said, "Silas and whatever he's running through CI has a direct line not only to the White House, but straight into the Oval Office, without oversight."

I paused to let that sink in. The earlier spirit of my companions sunk faster than a stone in water.

Nina tried to rally. "Couldn't that be construed as blackmail? Maybe even treason? Make Silas Kingston the next Oliver North."

"That'd be Congress's business, not ours, and it wouldn't stick because it isn't blackmail." I said. "And it isn't treason because, although Silas's actions subvert our charter and show reach beyond his authority within our organizational structure and legal standards, by the president's outward acceptance of whatever Silas brought him—and his publicly acting upon it from his position as commander-in-chief—it moved from covert to overt executive policy."

"Even if there's nothing illegal or unconstitutional, you're a senior ops lawyer. Isn't there a way to track down what allows Silas to act this way?" said Lynn.

I had the answer. Had it since Captiva, three days earlier. When I spoke next, it was with casual authority and withheld intel.

"As a senior counsel—your's and Nina's ops lawyer, I assume, in this new arrangement—my advice is: leave it alone. Entirely. Silas's warning wasn't exactly a ding-dong-ditch with a bag of flaming doggy-do on your front step."

"Then how do I hit back?"

"*We* hit back. The HOUNDFOX network is robust. There was a reason denied us and denied the Agency—in whatever capacity he's been given or seized, and through which he operates—that connects Silas to a necessitated President Chávez in power. There's connection now between Venezuela and Cuba, again counter to what we'd see geopolitically safe for this hemisphere, and you *have* gotten yourself Cuba. Wherever your father's veiled power lies, whatever it is, he didn't or couldn't prevent you from that, but that doesn't mean you—us, we: we're in this together—won't be directly and permanently in his sights."

"Then it won't matter I've taken reins on Cuba," Lynn said.

"It absolutely matters. But it's not Cuba directly and it's not Venezuela where we go after him. It's in the space between the two."

I let that sink in, not knowing even myself where instinct and hallucinatory scientific inspiration were leading me.

"We're listening," Nina said.

"My advice is we develop an objective-set concurrent with ongoing non-Venezuela–Cuban ops but which will allow our operation to locate and get into the space *between* the Venezuela–Cuba connection. That's where we'll find Silas. I'll put a communications interception priority into a generic HOUNDFOX CONPLAN that will get us the tools we need to set our actual OPLAN in motion."

"A bugging operation? That all you're going to give me?" Lynn said.

"That's all I'm going to write you—generic; Cuban offices; signals intelligence Nina's been pressing long before Venezuela came into the picture."

"SIGINT sounds good to me," Nina added her support.

"Seventh Floor will see it as an anti-Castro Santa with a bottomless sack of toys. But it will have a bottom, and at the bottom—"

"Will be a chunk of coal?" Lynn said.

"Payback on your father."

"As long as that's justice for Carmen, use whatever deceptions you want."

She was young. She was fiery. She was wrong.

"We're not in the justice business," I gently reminded.

"I know, but—"

"We're in the advantage business. When done perfectly, that business is silent and invisible. A Rule of Thumb well worth remembering. James Bond and Tom Cruise fail every mission and cancel all value from what they've acquired once they shoot their way out. We go in. No one notices. And we stay as long as we can, hidden in plain sight."

For the first time saying it, Muir's mantra, and offering it without headline sarcasm but sincerity as my own, the psychic weight those words had borne on me my whole adult life vanished. There was no one pushing their thumb on me from above; what came from the past belonged only to me.

Nina rose beside me. "I'll get on it from my end."

I offered Lynn my hand. Her handshake was firm. Her eyes clear, they connected us to each other. And there, the trust I'd been told I would find.

BY NOT MENTIONING KALEIDOSCOPE, I believed that I could protect us.

It was the conclusion I had brought with me from my day on Bishop's bay boat, *Here There Be Tygers*, and from my later conversation with Tom and my sister in Muir's chairs on their Captiva porch. Bishop's revelations of father–son secrets I had never known rocked me as hard as the horse kick to my soul my cancer diagnosis had once been.

I'd survived cancer and I thought we would survive this, and for one of us, I would be wrong. What I'd begun to distinguish about KALEIDOSCOPE, Muir, Silas Kingston, and the soul of his daughter told me no good would come from revelation. As I'd done with my cancer, I chose to hide this knowledge from everyone.

Good intentions have led to more disasters in my life than I care to count. Those good intentions that came that morning in Lynn Kingston's office, with Nina, came in direct proportion to my fear I would repeat Muir's greatest mistake and like he, fall directly into KALEIDOSCOPE's cone of destruction.

As Linda would foretell before I turned myself over to General Trigorin: Satan, not Santa, waits as gatekeeper at the end of everyone's path.

30

"Love the boat, Tom. Really do."

"Be smooth sailing, now I got your approval."

"But why the *Y* in *Tigers*?"

"Why, 'why' the *Y*?" He steered us to deep water.

"Ah! *Tempat Harimau*." I suddenly remembered Lucky Boy and his beasts. "The omophagy of Sedaka!"

"Don't know and don't care about that dead man's sexuality. Why would that matter to you?"

"What? Omophagy—not homo-faggy—from the Greek: *omo*, raw, *phagein* to eat."

"And... I'm still... standing by my comment..."

He circled the boat over a deep blue hole, probing its depth with matching eyes. I was in the stern by the twin outboards, unbuttoning my shirt. The wind caught it coming off and blew it into the water. He circled back.

I fished it out, saying, "For your information, omophagia is a large element of the Dionysiac myth. The Maenad followers of Dionysus eating raw flesh in the context of their worship."

"You're confusing me with a father who cared."

"They're *your* Malaysian tigers who ate him! Isn't that what you named your boat after—or not?!"

"Disappointing me again, not reading what I give you."

"What—? Oh, the King book. I'm getting to it."

"There's a story in that book, same name—character in it kinda reminds me of you—so there's that. Then there's the Bradbury story. And 'Here There Be Tygers' is what cartographers wrote on their maps at the edges of their known worlds. Lots to choose from."

"But not Malaysia."

He eased back the throttle, slowed at the edge of the hole.

"Obviously, Malaysia. You can toss the anchor now," he said. "No—other side, where it's reef. There you go."

We burned papers, making sure to keep our smoke to a minimum; wiped the computer drives, memory, and motherboard; the USB; the burner phones we'd communicated over, rendering all data unrecoverable, before we smashed all components and tossed ash and the bits and pieces of technology. We watched it all sink through sapphire, descending to navy that deepened to black as water molecules absorbed and scattered the white, pure light of the sun, and the stories light could tell, beating on our backs. The evidence of our illegality was swallowed by the sea, lost to light and time.

Afterward, we ate sandwiches Lara had prepared, washed down with Spanish Vichy water. Bishop tossed me the Coppertone, telling me to smear some on, and I asked why—since he wasn't putting on any—to which he replied: "I don't burn."

"Me neither." I tossed it back.

"And making that claim has helped you how many times?"

He stowed the sunscreen, and I changed the subject.

"I want to know about your experience with KALEIDO-SCOPE."

"I told you about that run-in years ago."

"Not situational, but in abstract—its abstract—as you know it, in unrebutted fact."

Bishop shot a hard look my way. "Lynn Kingston isn't at fault, you do know that, because—"

"I want to know if I got played."

"What's your gut say?"

"'Ask Bishop.'"

"It's a piggyback op that runs dark without heed of its CIA host."

"Is it a Company defensive wall? A kind of op-guard?"

"No. Far as I know, it runs impartial to its CIA host op. Muir said it's 'artarchic'—"

"Autarchic: tyrannical, mighty, regnant—"

"Yup—if that's right behind 'fuck-all weird.'" Tom always rejected vocabulary. "Now, sidekick all that with a Russian mirror op: KALAYDOSKOP. Both run from within, but unrelating to CIA/FSB goals as you and I know 'em. In total, its aim isn't political, social, psychological—not a fight for any national program—but run entirely by people in it for keeps. In my situation, it was 'no talking' with that gunman I ran into in Hong Kong; 'solo walkaway' required."

Bishop and I were fast motoring our way back for Captiva and his back-bay anchor buoy. Hot wind and salt spray cut conversation to nothing, and Tom didn't pick up his story until back in Muir's woods.

"These guys don't get 'neutral;' it's full kill—but with a catch. Muir believed if a new, explicit third-party brought hazard to one or both, they would squeeze in tandem to protect each other."

"Wait," I said. "CIA and Russian KALEIDOSCOPE operations actively work to destroy each other but have each other's back if anyone else comes onto them? How's that make sense in reality?"

"Funny you put it that way, because that's how Muir put it. 'What makes them most dangerous is they operate in a reality we don't perceive.' The exposure of one threatens the exposure of both," said Bishop.

We moved onto the covered porch. The Jaguar was gone.

"Then the murder of Carmen Briceño might not be Silas Kingston."

"If Silas was turning the kaleidoscope in Venezuela, you can bet the Russians were there as well. According to Muir's theory, it could be either, and it doesn't matter which, because whatever it is, it's for all the marbles. GLADIO was amateur hour in comparison."

"How much more did Muir know about it? Did he have any guess what its global function is?"

"We never had the chance to discuss it further. Silas Kingston prevented that by manipulating the vendetta between Dad and me after Suzhou. We didn't talk for ten years, and by that point, it was pretty much way too late."

He abruptly went inside. I watched him grab a bottle. He came out with it and two glasses. The bottle had no label, but I knew what it was. He put them on the table between us.

"Ever hear the one about 'fluoridations of water?' he said, quoting Muir quoting Kubrick.

Yes, Jack, I believe I have," I replied in Mandrake.

Bishop's lips pulled out a smile that was almost fond. He poured. We drank.

"Tom, you didn't *really* know he was your father from the beginning. You said so at Christmas, but I don't buy it."

"Don't take it so hard. He didn't hide it from me as well he hid your father from you and Lara."

Lara returned with groceries. We helped her with them from the car. She invited me to stay for dinner and Tom doubled down, inviting me to spend the night and, if I were well-mannered, Lara would smear some aloe vera lotion on my back. Lara got the meat soaking in her marinade and joined us with her own glass upon the Yamamoto rattan where we'd returned to our conversation.

"Looking at him the first time—we're talking about Muir here," Bishop added to catch Lara up, "was like looking in a mirror to my own future. I didn't grow up with any photos of my fictional father. So as a kid, all I could imagine was someone who would look like me but older. You know, I got a memory hit last time we were all here? Me as a kid, Christmas Eve, sneaking from my room to see Santa putting out my presents. Beneath the beard was Muir. Didn't remember till we did his Christmas. But come Vietnam, where I'd already learned anything could happen, that face I'd imagined was suddenly standing right in front of me, having called me from my hooch. Why wouldn't I have known?"

"That doesn't explain why you never spoke up," Lara said.

"His responsibility. If I'd brought it up, he'd only have given me what he thought I wanted to hear. I waited so I could hear what *he* wanted to say."

"Did he ever?" I asked.

"The night he died. I told you about that."

"Tom, I was there. You didn't," Lara said. "What you think you might have said, you had just shot Russell. Maybe you could tell it again they way you told me later?"

"C'mon, all I did was bump his arm a little bit."

"With a bullet," she said.

"It saved his life."

I sighed. "All you told me was you had a call, and you told him: 'In light of current situations,' you'd 'let him off with a warning.'"

Lara sipped her water, waited, said, "Tom, I think Russell should know..."

Tom Bishop rubbed his stubbled chin and shifted uneasily. "Fine, but you tell it. You're his sister. You'll know better if you're making sense to him—especially when he interrupts."

Lara gathered her thoughts, gave it a shot. "I think what surprised Tom and Nathan most after not speaking for so long

was the depth of meaning they'd always had between them—the
meaning they both thought they'd lost—was still there."

I glanced at Tom. He nodded. She continued.

"It's the same thing we all shared with Muir. You too, Russell:
strength in the silence that separates us. The fundamental faith
and love that all the shitty things each of us say and do—in
those two's case, horrible and so mean—couldn't overcome all
that was deeply fundamental in the quiet space between words
and actions."

Lara finished. Waited. I knew not to interrupt. Her opening
words merely to coax Bishop beyond the edge of his map. Coax
him from his comfort in speaking only in terms of action, of plans
executed, the problems of others, but never himself.

"And…?" I said.

"She is right. About the silence. The biggest stuff between
us we shared without speaking. Always did. Even that call, that
night, without saying the words, he let me know he would be
killed before I'd get there."

He extended his body, legs false and real stretched forward,
body reclined. He linked his hands together on top of his head,
elbows out. A soldier's surrender. He faced the ceiling, cleared
himself with a deep breath and addressed the hot and humid air.

"What do you say when you know you have one conversation
left with your father?"

*Never had the chance. Never knew the marble man behind the
mask and never would.*

My sister and I didn't move. Bishop didn't change his gaze
or his posture. He sucked more air. Blew it out in a manner that
mirrored his father blowing cigarettes: same place, same chair,
same posture eleven years, a lifetime, another America, another
world away.

"I said: 'You lied to me, Nathan. You lied about the plane. About Elizabeth and China.'" Bishop glanced at me and added, "The Soviet Flanker. I let him know it wasn't his fault. I didn't blame him anymore."

"What? He traded Elizabeth's life for it! It's the whole case against him!"

Lara put a hand on my knee. A signal to shut-the-outrage-up. Tom's eyes shifted back to the ceiling.

"Muir went on. 'Don't lie to yourself, Tom,' he said. 'I did that— betrayed everything that allows me to be your father—trading your wife for a fucking piece of Soviet junk. Because of me and that Chinese prison they put her in, she got the cancer that killed her.'

"'Nice try,' I told him. 'Her cancer wasn't from that. Was a ticking bomb inside her all her life. She knew it, we all did, and you're still lying.' I waited for Muir to come at me again, but he didn't speak, and I said, 'I know how the Chinese got the plane.' He didn't comment. See, that's the lie. That's what he couldn't admit to me—to himself. I said, 'Look at you, the greatest spymaster ever, got outfoxed, outsmarted, totally played and checkmated out by your son. You were so thirsty for that fighter you'd chased for years, you never questioned how the hell the Soviets let it up-up-and-away to China.'"

"It was a defection," I spoke for Muir.

"Let him tell it," Lara said.

"No. Muir doesn't get a pass on this." But I already saw how my own comment was trying to give him one—granted, a pass into being evil and wrong. "Your problem, maybe was you lacked faith in his word—"

"Russell!" This time, she swatted my knee.

Bishop shifted. Faced me. "C'mon, Russell, use your head. That's what I did. Figured it out the only way it could be figured out. The Soviets would have scrambled and blasted their jet out of the sky before it got halfway there."

"You're trying to tell me the Russians wanted to give Muir that aircraft?"

"Not the Russians. K-SCOPE from both ends. They wanted to cripple me—I was onto them—and they wanted to cripple Muir."

"They could've killed you. Tried before. Coulda killed Muir."

"They couldn't. Do the math: Kill me and Muir's got nothing to lose in going after them. Kill him? Same for me 'cause I'd have known it was them. Kill us both? Soviets would have, might have, but something stopped them…"

And I saw it.

"KALEIDOSCOPE/KALAYDOSKOP protects itself," I said, realization freezing the blood in my veins.

The vigilance was back in Bishop's eye. "I knew in that conversation, in Muir's unwillingness to admit it when I faced him with the truth, his overwhelming feeling of personal defeat and the unremitting shame, the refusal to forgive himself for having fallen for Silas's trap of the Flanker made him welcome the death soon to take him."

"No way," I said. "Sedaka was too far beneath him."

"Why didn't he put up a fight? Just let him torture and kill him in his chair?" Bishop countered.

I'd considered that before. I still couldn't find an answer.

"Sedaka made the perfect pivot for Muir to ensure that his networks were free once and for permanent with no way to get them back while, making sure the three of us ended up right here, right now… That lumpish sonofabitch, I'd say, saved *everything* important to the old man."

"Oop! Big kick," Lara startled and touched her pregnant belly.

"I'm not done with China," I said. "I don't care about the plane. How it got there. His action with Elizabeth—no matter how he made it up later, and their relationship ended beautifully, we all agree on that—but Muir knew what he was doing selling your wife to the Chinese. It is unforgiveable."

Bishop gave me a careful look, more accepting of my point of view than his agreement with it. "He didn't know Elizabeth was my wife. You verified that for me. From Muir's point of view, he was desperate to keep me from making the same mistake with her he believed he'd made with Jewel. In this business, love is our most lethal vulnerability."

"Give me a break."

"The man wasn't perfect. Listen: in Lebanon when he first discovered Elizabeth, I was hiding her out—breaking all the rules, breaking my oath to the Agency and to him—and she *was* working with terrorists in Beirut."

I opened my mouth to speak. Interpose, interrupt, intercede. I had nothing.

"You know I'm right. She was an unwitting pawn, but I wasn't, and if I'd listened to Muir instead of my dick, I might have stopped the Marine Barracks bombing." Bishop reached for his rainwater. He stopped with it halfway to his lips. "I would have prevented it."

"You can't Monday morning quarterback the past," I said, although I knew my epilepsy was convincing me I could.

"Muir knew that. About me. Every minute I chased Elizabeth's skirts was an extra minute I gave the Clockmaker building his bomb. Gave him enough of those minutes: he got a bomb into a truck and a truck into our Marines. But Muir never called me out, never blamed me—first as an agent runner in his after-action report, then as a father—he never spoke of it or held it against me. I just hope I show the same grace to my own son."

"Or daughter," I said, and Lara smiled.

He took the swallow of water. Returned the glass to the table.

"The next time we met—Thailand—he saw Elizabeth again. He knew who she was from Beirut, knew on sight she was strung out on drugs and booze. Saw his son an alcoholic wreck. Suicide in slow motion."

"Sent, I might add, by Harker to assassinate you."

"That's right. But how did Harker find me? How did my spinout reach his desk in the first place? I was an Agency officer on leave, whose booze-addled behavior was off-station and limited to hotel bars and vacation beaches."

"Harker told Muir you'd had arrests in Hong Kong."

"Never happened. But supposing I had been arrested, that would have come through Harry Duncan anyway, who would have called Muir personally. And it didn't."

"According to Muir, the only person besides Harker was Digger Livingston, who tracked you down in Bangkok."

"Yeah, bullshit. Only way it gets to Harker—that level of urgency to put a gun in Muir's pocket—is Counterintelligence. Silas Kingston requested that terminal decision to close out my account, yet to insure it wouldn't happen, Silas requested Muir perform the job. Unlike Harker and the rest of the Agency, he knew Muir wouldn't kill me, his own son. He wanted Muir to see us at our worst. Afterward, it was easy to get him to sell Elizabeth and pin us both in place—no danger to K-SCOPE—with our own self-inflicted agony."

"To be certain, truly certain, Silas would have had to have known the truth about Jewel—Muir's hand in the death of his own first child," I said.

Bishop turned away from us, concealing his eyes.

All my fears of Silas Kingston coalesced. "Silas Kingston won, not Muir, with DINNER OUT."

"Would've worked too. He just didn't count on one simple, overpowering fact: Fathers who love their children are willing to sacrifice their lives for them."

If Silas Kingston can beat Muir so thoroughly, Nina, Lynn, and I don't stand a chance.

"Is that how the call ended?" I said. "You talked all this out?"

"No. We'd already lived it. I called him a liar, knowing he'd appreciate it. He knew I knew how all the pieces finally fit. He laughed at me and urged me home to lend the two of you a hand."

"And the world too. You're nice that way," Lara said.

Bishop smiled at her. "Maybe a little bit. I said to Muir, 'I suppose, in light of current situations, I'll let you off with a warning on my whole death-promise.' And he told me one last thing. Since you've finally come up against KALEIDOSCOPE, it's time you knew. Muir's last words ever spoken to me were these:

"'The greatest fight facing the Agency won't be ours. Not yours. It won't be Aiken's—'"

"Ah, yes. The War on Terror." I detected Muir's keen insight envelop the three of us—four if you count the growing baby—on that porch.

"Had nothing to do with the War on Terror. Lara, when my time comes, I don't want this guy anywhere near me to interrupt my last words."

She smiled thinly.

"I'm telling you what he said. The fight wasn't ours. Muir said, 'It will belong to another. She must be protected.'"

"Amy Kim?" I tried, half-heartedly. The whole conversation feeling like a tennis lesson with an unstrung racket. "Nina?"

"Lynn Kingston. 'If she acts against her father now,' Muir said, 'he'll either destroy her, or worse, he'll turn her. Aiken must shield the girl. Over all the rest of us. Shield her until she's ready to take it all apart. Tell him she is our Pandora.' Who I always thought was the villain of the story, but that's your guys' mythology nonsense."

"Zeus created Pandora as punishment for Prometheus stealing fire," I mumbled—

—*not jealous about anything because there was nothing to be jealous about and, proven numerous times in numerous ways, that I'm surprised it needs saying, I don't get jealous.*

"What does that mean?" Lara asked.

Bishop stared at me slyly; he loves watching me cogitate because it's so close to coagulate.

"KALEIDOSCOPE is the jar," I said.

"Don't you mean 'box?'" Bishop said.

"*Pithos*. Greek for 'jar,' mistranslated to Latin *pyxis*, 'box.' It's, properly, the 'Myth of Pandora's Jar.' No one says *Pandora's Box*."

"Why doesn't that surprise me you think that?" Bishop said.

"Pandora opened the jar and all the evils of the world escaped to plague mankind, but hope remained. Your father would tell us, against all manners of overwhelming adversity, which is our lot in life to face, when all else appears lost to us, hope will always be there to keep us in the fight."

AFTER DINNER, after a lengthy telephone conversation with Nina in which we talked about everything that happened during our day apart, as lovers do, I fell asleep in the guest room. They'd kept the captain's bed, the one with the high sides to protect its occupant from the roll of the sea, the bed that reminded me of my CIA claustrophobia coffin.

I drifted off, guiltily curious why I hadn't mentioned Lynn Kingston in our phone call. Muir's message to me to protect her.

I dreamed myself trapped in an endless hallway filled with doors. I sought both women, but no matter how many doors

I opened, neither Lynn nor Nina revealed themselves to my rescue. Behind each door a tiger chuffed, snarled, bunched to pounce, or swept the air with sickle claws. I'd slam the door and they'd throw themselves against it, roaring, bashing, trying to break free. Unable to control my actions, I repeated this terror, door after door, until all the doors burst open at once. Neither tigers engulfing me in a cyclone of orange and black, dagger-fanged and devouring, nor the ladies I'd set myself to save, or desire. Behind every door was only infinite space without up or down, without objective here or there.

In my mind's eye, I stared at myself from high above, all alone with an overwhelming presence of a "You Are Here" arrow on a map of La Habana Vieja. But like the dot on the map that represents itself as my location, I am not in fact at that location at all. Bishop might see it through his sniper scope with the bullet he puts through its little red circle still unfired a mile away. Is he "there"? Others might see it remotely half a city, a country, a continent away, coming "live" on a stream of remote digital imagery. Are they "*there*"?

"'YOU ARE HERE,' but never is that the point on the Earth you occupy. See what I mean?" I said. "The map is neither where I am, nor what is represented on it—yet we buy it every time it's plunked in front of us; human nature—making everything beyond its edges nothing but the endless possibility for deception. At least that's how I dreamed it."

Amy Kim sipped her latte. She considered me politely over the plastic lid.

"I'm happy to see you, Russell. I am. But I've moved on. I wasn't made for the life Nathan Muir wanted me for. And to be truthful, you sound like you need a psychiatrist."

"I don't. You're lying. And you know the real reason you're happy to see me."

As soon as I said it, she stopped looking happy. "My parents are proud of me. I won't come back with you."

"We're happy for you to stay here. In fact, we're providing you with a two-million-dollar grant to remain."

I handed her the award letter. All above board from the OTS, to the Seventh Floor, to Capitol Hill, to her George Mason president and department heads.

"I'm afraid to thank you. What does this buy—besides me?"

"I'll answer with a question. What makes it possible for Santa Claus to get to every child's chimney in the world in a single night? And don't say a magic sleigh. I'm gonna need a serious answer."

"A time machine?"

My confidence brimming at the skepticism I took as fascination beheld in her face, I replied, "Precisely. A small one—nothing too elaborate—something Nina and I can slip into Cuba, drop down Fidel Castro's chimney, and skedaddle before the kids wake up for Christmas."

PART THREE

RECEPTION

"Time is the substance I am made of. Time is a river that carries me away, but I am the river; it is a tiger which destroys me, but I am the tiger; it is a fire which consumes me, but I am the fire."

— JORGE LUIS BORGES, *A New Refutation of Time*

31

ALL LIVES TRADE IN SECRETS. Secrets we are bound to—asked, told, ordered to keep. Some sweetly sworn, others nobly defended to a courageous grave. As parcel to all human intercourse, secrets can drive closeness and cement loyalty. Though too, some secrets turn. Reduce hope. Destroy faith. Bring love to a thing hardly worth its murder. I want to believe hidden behind the arras of secrets exist confidences dignified by living honor, trust, service, and fidelity, not skeletons of pompous self-deception brittling to dust by corruption and hypocrisy's decay.

But, ceteris paribus, I fear I am wrong.

For most Americans, secrets play some minor role in daily affairs ("affairs" in the primary definition—1. commercial, professional, public, or personal business; matters or concerns; *not*, 2. romantic or passionate attachment, typically of limited duration); those occasional, necessary secrets stand in sharp contrast against the consistent background of honest and stable personal lives.

Secrets pepper overt lives, but a covert life is salted by them entirely. The spy's palate for life is desensitized by its unceasing consumption of secrets. You try to stay sharp to their imperative in every meeting, call, conversation, memo, report, brief, agreement, order, covenant, accord, warrant, and plan—everything said and unsaid, written and not, in preponderance—sharp to the religiously mandated, rigorously complied "need-to-know," until without noticing, you've dulled all the secrets that are not in your official authorization and too much a bother, and you ignore them. You allow the colors of the world outside your direct purview a soothing patina of gray.

There's nothing so damn lonesome as a world of secrets.

Papering Cuba ops through Lynn Kingston, I soon comprehended the admeasurement of secrets Nina managed, and managed to keep from me. HOUNDFOX, in the person of Nina's father, Comandante Alejandro Alvarez, was much less what Muir and Nina had led CIA to believe, and much more than anyone had previously known. HOUNDFOX was not a thing—a man, *el padre*, the spy—but an intelligence formula. An event of massive scale against all of Cuba.

The one man/one source theory was a fib. The number of operations, authorizations, payouts, drops, meets, and movements; the variety and quality of intel product springboarded out of all corners of the Cuban administration, scientific sector, military, education and civil, social and private branches was considerably more than the work of one fantastic spy operating out of Castro's Dirección de Inteligencia.

It is early September and, in the cool darkness before dawn, I say across pillows to Nina: "Lynn knows more about you than I do."

"Lynn my Eval-Plans ops boss? Or Lynn your BFF popping out of your dreams and into your mouth the moment you wake beside me?"

"I don't even know what 'BFF' means. I assume by your blatant jealousy, it's sexual."

"Because of the *F*?" Nina purred.

"One, or the other, or both of 'em. I'm sure." But wasn't as my words bounced off her smile.

"Since it's neither is why I teased you with the question, getting you to admit it was," she chirped. "And *I'm* sure the secrets dogcarting across your desk and under your pen make my little island calamity a comic satire compared to the epic dramas worldwide you've drafted in thirty years." She caressed my cheek. Her eyes found mine. "You know my life, baby. And more, my heart. The kingdom without secrets is the one we share. Past, present, and future."

She beamed adoration. I don't know why I didn't get it, stop myself there, allowing revelation, but the secrets that thickened my mind—covert-life-stuffed fluff—canceled the seriousness of secrets meaningful inside our hearts.

"All HOUNDFOX product isn't all HOUNDFOX product," I said.

"You know what you know as needs be applied to the work you do on HOUNDFOX. *Claro?* In this case, hating I'm saying it, Lynn is where you should seek that answer. Any fig leaf obscuring your view is by her decision not my suggestion. But you're a big boy. You know the difference between eyes-only clearance and a temptation of flesh."

I sensed this time she meant her teasing to work on two levels: teasing as in "irritating provocation," and as "the pulling out of separate strands" of meaning. Her next words confirmed rather than denied.

"Or try this. If you want to see HOUNDFOX as it is, look at it as if, say, it conformed to Lynn's build. To her body." She smirked. Batted thick lashes. Dared I pull the hair.

"Never looked," I said.

"You know what it is, a *'reloj de arena'?*"

She wanted to play, so I went along with her setup. "A sand clock? Cool. HOUNDFOX is a sand clock—okay by me."

"'A body built like a sand clock.'" She chuckled, in a way that dared me to continue.

Having avoided objectifying Lynn's body, sexualizing her any way in my mind, I took the dare. I said, "The top bulb is a network of spies across Cuba accessing data, pulling open source and secret intel out of every area of interest. All of that is collected by your papa, who passes it through the narrow center of the sieve to you, where it piles into the bottom bulb to be disseminated by Lynn."

Nina nestled into the pillow, eyes scanning the ceiling with sly innocence. I rolled onto my side, bracing on my elbow to peer at her. "But them ray-lo-hays day-arenas are constructed to work in two directions. HOUNDFOX works with two foci."

"*Excuse me?* None of that *F* word—with Lynn or *mi papá.*"

"Latin plural—*i* instead of the *us*, as in 'two specific bases of operation.' As in when the sand runs out at the top, HOUNDFOX turns over. An equal and opposite network providing intel product collected here. A reverse HOUNDFOX network. Your own Cuban network. They give it all to you. The reason the red beacon burns in your upstairs window. And you pass the haul back across the aperture, hand to hand, the system protected by the bloodline that creates an unbreachable center valve."

She poked me in the chest. "I'll confirm one thing: Muir's brilliance lives inside you, Pintao. But I don't think we take this conversation any—"

My chest where she'd jabbed me burned as if I'd been struck by a bullet. The *woosh* of its path incinerated with electric impalement. I choked back a sob. Pure emotion disconnected from mind. I knew where I headed; I wanted to tell her with my eyes, but I couldn't make them move. Tears became a projector lens. Why was I crying?

Panoramic Panavision. Constellation starbursts, lines connect. Swirl. Electricity from inside me swarms the room like exploding bees. She sees where I've traveled.

Make the leap with me!

"Ah, baby. Let it pass. Come. Be safe in my arms."

No teasing, no secrets, no control; she tenderly pulls me into her body. The déjà vu: our bedroom is my 1978 'Mr. Camden' cover; the hotel room on 21st Street, NYC, the dawn we met, the only bed we've ever shared. The Bible in our laps: we search to a word that isn't in it and Muir is with us, there as he wasn't, and here, sitting as he isn't, all-shadow, smoky like a gjinn inside Nina's U Street Corridor multi-level railroad house.

'Nathan?' I call out, but the shadow shifts. It isn't Muir.

Not here. Not in New York.

This shadow is of another.

"Shh, don't cry… Why you cryin', baby? Do you know?"

Do I even know? Now? Then? What I will know?

Will-o'-the-wisp?

I do know one thing seriously, because in this state I have no secrets, because I have no time, and trust is whole, a thing of pieces. This spirit whispers an incantation…

"Pin, pain, riddle, stain."

And I returned. I was home. Home in bed. Our bed.

"I wasn't crying."

"No?"

"Haven't since I was seven."

Maybe eleven, but who's counting?

"I'm one of those leaky-eye people."

"Mmm. I see. Out your tear ducts?"

"Is there some other way?"

She made a soothing noise that became a hum. I was home in our bed in our time only; in Nina's arms, only hers, laid out across her chest, tears staining her smooth taut skin. She hummed the enchanting song of Muir's Christmas wake. I've always marveled at her psychic connection to my soul.

"You're back now," she said. She kissed me.

"I love you." I kissed back.

"I know."

She shifted beneath me. Her skin shone with daybreak's promise.

"When the sun hits you like this, your skin is a marvelous blue. Deep and cool. I stare at it, lose myself in it... Or is that maybe not appropriate to say?"

"It's true. Why not? I like you noticing everything I am. Do you know why it appears this way? What the blue-black means?"

The remnants of my seizure had rendered in me a childlike disposition. I knew this passing, enfolding event sang to me of another color, burnt and cinnamon. I shut my mind to it, like a child shuts their eyes at evil.

Something terrible comes.

I shook my head in little-boy repose, hands behind my head, pretending that innocent insistence could stave away the cinnamon shadow monster I'd seen in our bedroom(s). A wickedness I already somehow know will ruin the innocence inside us.

Inside? No, better—the innocence *about* us.

I said nothing.

"My mother's ancestors were Funj Sudanese. The Blue Sultanate it was called. That blue caste of my skin—and hers much more than mine—marks us of a long-lost royal dynasty. I mean, until the white man stole and enslaved us."

"Why didn't I know you're half African?"

"Because I'm not. My nationality is American. And I am of Cuban descent. Period." She said this as if she had been questioned on it before and despised some implication of the question. "But in Havana as a child, in Paris until Muir pulled me in, here in America—I've always loved, like my mother, even in the darkest room, you can see me because I am darker than darkness. The deeper black that is deepest blue."

"I'll tell you," I said, not knowing what to say, "you wouldn't be half as beautiful if you weren't."

"Fuck, man, you say the dumbest stuff paying a woman a compliment," Nina chuckled, used to me.

"Take two?" I offered and sang Billy Holiday's 'Am I Blue?' as she took my hand, made a crack about race baiting, but hummed along as she led me downstairs.

NINA MADE THE BREAKFAST. I called Jessie in Princeton before she went to school, then fell to work on the crossword. Or rather, stared blankly at the cells. I can't help it, but when I look at a crossword—the symmetrical shape, the open boxes' infinite possibilities, waiting on letters to bring them to life. And the black squares, clustered and dead—I see my brain. My tumor. Clues to answers; neurons to synapses. I stared dully at the puzzle. Couldn't work it.

The HOUNDFOX sieve of secrets still sandmanned my reasoning; I'd been true in my deductions. Had I been true to their conclusions? In bed, Nina had, in her way, been too coy. Were I honest with myself, I'd have admitted I was missing something she didn't want me near.

She served me juice and my morning handful of meds and herbal supplements to improve mindfulness and memory. The answer stared at me in a pile of pills.

1. Across: 270-million-year-old maidenhair—6 letters

"Ginkgo!" I shouted and buried the other voice that whispered: *Maiden. Hair. Spirit. Marble. Bracelet.*

Orula.

A natural supplement produced by the ancient tree, my mental health was improving before I popped the coincidence into my mouth. I swallowed the rest of my pills and started on the letter boxes with glorious abandon.

Secrets, I reminded myself as Nina had reminded me, secrets from our work, our side—protected or revealed in proper judgment—save lives. That's why we make them. That's why we keep them. Why, in their proper course, we reveal them or lock them up to eternal protection.

Our primary, most basic secret is cover. Affix our mark on the dotted line, day one: people aren't allowed to know where we work, what we do. Someone in my position bound to headquarters—it's simple: when asked what I do, I have the easy-out: "Just another one a'hundreds of lawyers with the State Department." But those of us in Operations, the Clandestine Services, it's when we post and operate overseas where that secret takes on its utmost importance.

If you're working under official cover at an embassy, you put in your hours on whatever desk you've been plopped behind, concurrent to working your undercover mission. If you're married when you join, spousal need-to-know is determined vis-à-vis life risk and he/she is sworn in on your secret. If you're already in and later plan to marry, your potential spouse must be vetted and approved before proceeding. Provided she passes Bill Carver's Office of Security scrutiny, you are permitted to tell your bride-to-be, only upon her acceptance of the offer of your ring.

Most do.

Others wait until the priest is there as backup with vows, kiss, rice, and a license.

Some never tell.

With children, you don't have a choice. CIA official stance on children: zero need-to-know. Yet, how many CIA Operations officers over the years have I paperworked into hazardous distant posts on both official and nonofficial cover, no sooner than the

ink of their binding promise is dry (to conceal their CIA identity "under all circumstances relative to all persons not verifiable
foreign assets or recruits under penalty of law" blah-blah-blah
"including children, natural offspring, step by marriage, and/or
adopted"), how many of them have I immediately taken aside and
instituted a Muir Rule of Thumb:

"Screw what the paper handcuffs say. In the trenches, no
officer can perform at peak if his or her spouse and kids don't
know exactly what the hell's at stake. Because the Second Rule of
Thumb on this," Muir counseled me, the counselor, "clueless wives
and children are easy prey. Seen it too many times—compromised,
threatened, kidnapped, murdered. When your officer, cover blown,
needs to escape life'n'death pronto, that's not the time to dish up
a 'Honey, I'm not actually a salesman here in downtown Dodo-
stan, and cancel Johnny's playdate, because we're all about to die'
conversation. You tell them, Rusty, soon as they Johnny Hancock
that promise to keep their lip zipped, you tell 'em to forgo their
prosecutory protection, protect themselves and their loved ones.
In the pitch, an extra set or three of trusted eyes and ears saves
everyone's lives."

How many men and women had I betrayed my CIA oath,
violated my Rules of Professional Conduct, and advised to blow
the most important secret as soon as they inscribed their names to
their promise?

Every damn one of them.

And while CIA has reprimanded, we have never prosecuted
that violation. What's the old witch's curse, "Secrets cause cancer?"
You don't keep secrets deadly to the people you love.

Still, there are officers who don't take my advice.

In some sad cases, Muir's predication plays out. Perilously.
Catastrophically. Deadly. Others: no problem until years later.

Upon retirement. That spouse, long suffering in suspicion, those bewildered kids now befuddled adults. Those officers, who attempt to Toto back the CIA curtain and make heroes of their lives of seeming unambitious delinquency and undiscussed absenteeism, discover it's the wife who submits to the court that dusty divorce she's held on to and used as a cocktail coaster to pickle her liver, or the kids who simply tender a disappearance payback. If you're lucky to hear of them—ever—it's between the covers of an incendiary "poor me and screw Daddy" told-nothing tell-all book.

A secret had awaited me when I'd come inside Nina's the evening before. Had I consciously noticed it then? Possibly. I won't lie to myself, one way or the other, as I remember it now. A black marble. A spherical eye behind a living-room audio speaker, leering at me when I'd come home after two days meeting with Amy over the "Time Machine" listening device. It repulsed me and I'd avoided it, both physically and mentally.

I'd tried now to clock it, but the living room was out of view during breakfast. After we shared our meal and thimbles of Cuban coffee, Nina offered me the shower. Unable to manufacture an excuse to search out the marble (and thinking already I needed to keep its discovery secret), I went and bathed.

When Nina went to her shower, I returned to the living room, but the marble was not where it had been.

Or ever was?

I noticed an unfamiliar record on the turntable. I picked up the album cover. The Sandpipers—*The Wonder of You.* 1960s soft rock. It wasn't mine and I didn't believe it was hers—yet I couldn't say I'd memorized her complete collection.

I placed the needle on the vinyl black lip of the disc. A hiss of silence before the opening song. "Let Go." It starts with upbeat horns that do nothing to cover a dread-inducing backbeat. The lyrics come, about boxed-up emotions, pity, unrequited, yearning love. A demand you hold back burning, desperate emotions that are splitting your personality. But then a devilish wink. Why hold back? A confetti explosion of minor to major in a carnival chorus exhortation to unrestrained abandon… and yet the violins on top take over in dissonance.

A Rio Carnival. A kind of a Latin swing, and dimly remembered, most likely of my childhood. Naw, not my childhood. Nothing that schmaltzy about my parents' listening tastes. But I *had* heard it. The lyrics had been different. I couldn't place where or when—

Dad's record collection: Sinatra's Only the Lonely, *track 14:* "Where or When" a*nd a burning tractor-trailer among Kansas sunflowers. Cocaine and speed.*

No. Not that song; not that man. I wasn't there, and now know he wasn't either. Something else…

Cinnamon suit.

Nina was out of the shower and moving about. I shut off the music. Returned everything back to before the marble that hadn't been.

I'm tired. I've had a seizure.

But when, days later, I went back among her record sleeves, the album wasn't there either.

Anyway, so what? I see a lot of shit that isn't what I think, or even what, it is. Certain secrets are too secret to be real.

32

JOSHUA ROSEN HAD WORRIED HIMSELF SICK over his "Triple R." His Retirement Reveal Revelry, which his wife Wendy had dubbed this year's annual two-week "campout" at their Cumberland cabin with the kids and their children. It was the place the pair initially met under the leaky roof of a Muir blind-date deception. Later, Muir had purchased the property and bestowed it upon them on their wedding day. Done more as a joke—his actual wedding present: a parade of bagpipers at the church which, discordant as mating cats in a sack, turned out the better gag—the cabin entered Joshua and Wendy's life no more than a one-room clapboard and tarpaper shed on a snarled three acres that Wendy liked to say held the world record in thorns per square inch. Not much by way of promising starts. But year by year, they cleared the bracken and they cut the trees. They split, they planed, and they nocked the timber. Remodeled it into a large and whimsical log cabin, which they christened *Friendship Haven.* The name, it turned out, becoming the best jest of all.

All the hard labor of clearing and construction they suffered purposefully as self-inflicted punishment every time they quarreled to the breaking point. Perfectly suited to each other (the two most stubborn people I've ever known), each time, convinced they were kaput, neither wanted to be the one to admit personal defeat and be the party to bring suit to their divorce. Instead, they would hurl themselves into Joshua's old Bronco and rumble up to the place, caustic recriminations thundering in inner soliloquy as acid looks burned livid silence against the clash of tools like devils' timbrels and tocsins jounced and clattering in the truck bed. Sweating and blistering it out—pick-and-shovel-strained backs, saw and hammer-pulled muscles; the stomping about with smashed thumbs, butt rolling clutches of crushed toes; the lumber-jack cursing—they put order to chaos. Harmony to discord. They harnessed the explosive power of conflict to transform the raw and wild nature of the little piece of the world Muir had provided them, into a place of handcrafted love.

In response to the number one FAQ people invariably ask upon initial impression: "How the hell many times you two break up?" Joshua or Wendy would provide the stock answer: "No more than it takes a sturdy pair to end up with a nine-room sod-topped bunker."

Built by love's wrath, it was exquisite. It displayed both Joshua's wild, artistic inspiration tempered by Wendy's judicial muse. So remarkable was its style, that back in July, *GQ* paid handsomely to use it for a photo shoot to cross-promote the Tolkien *Two Towers* movie.

It was the last weekend of this year's campout, and Wendy had used that money to throw the "Triple R" to which I'd been invited, the lone outsider (Nina operational in Miami), to join Joshua's extended brood and closest loved ones who never suspected his clandestine career, but to whom Wendy believed it time to put to bed their accepted belief that she, having ascended from DOJ prosecutor to the district bench, had carried Joshua along a life path of unremarkable artistic mediocrity. "The Triple R" was time to emblazon Joshua's patriotic duty, heroism, sacrifice, his world-saving achievements upon the great Rosen stanchion.

Like I said, the revelation worried the old spy sick; he was one of those who'd never told the kids.

"Aren't you the moral support to my life of immorality?"

"I'll always have your back," I said, squeezing his knee as we sat beside each other. The man was miserable. "It's what friends do."

"Then you should've talked me out of it. These things are always disasters."

"Why'd you first say yes?"

"Why'd Washington cross the Delaware?"

"To reclaim his silver dollar?"

"He was all out of options, sitting in camp icing his ass off with his troops, eating boiled shoes and bark, and waiting to die an all-time loser. Attacking Trenton was as big a loser proposition, it just offered him better optics."

The pair of us sat side by side at a hand-hewn picnic table decorated with sunrise-cut blossoms and dew-spritzed leaves on a tablecloth of some homely hideous Holly Hobbie meets *Little House on the Prairie* linen that Joshua smiled blandly at and bit his tongue, which made it difficult to trill each time he was asked about them: "My dear Frau Ro-then adored Mother's linens. My mama's doll collecthun's in-thide if you care to thee-ee. We'll be haffing tea wi-them later."

Each table sat ten, and they were six of them, haphazardly clustered around the centerpiece croquet court. Most of everyone, including Jessie, who'd accompanied me this weekend (taking a twenty-dollar tip to help look after the smallest of the children), enjoyed a rowdy match. Both Joshua and I, having conspired to help ourselves out of it by double elimination—he roqueting me into the festive dogvane of the "poison stake" only to accidentally-on-purpose collide his ball with it himself—took it to the sidelines: he of the Pimm's Cup, I of a branch water with ice.

I submitted, "Our old American Cincinnatus did win the Battle of Trenton, go on to become president, and become something of a national hero. Talk about return on investment—he ends up with both the dollar and the quarter."

He stirred his drink with his cucumber strip, then snapped off its end with his teeth. "Problem is, pal, that old schmuck never told a lie. I'm sitting here, about to announce to my bloodline that everything they've known about me their entire lives is all lies."

He was pale. He was shaken. He turned away so I wouldn't see the moisture in his eyes his humor had been unsuccessful at staving off.

A FEW HOURS LATER, after the caterers arrived and prepped, everyone headed up the dogwood path to the Fox Den, a natural amphitheater of sandstone and quartzite boulders where the reveal would happen at dinner. A stressful summer chased off by unseasonably heavy rains had coaxed the trees into a dainty second bloom. Joshua had continued drinking all afternoon. Now, as I walked with Jessie, I winced at the insecurity in his every step along the path sprinkled with snowy petals. I sensed only bad could come of this, and my trepidation reflected back to me as Wendy shot me a helpless look. Arm around her husband's waist, she shepherded him to the cluster of white-linen-clad tables, crystal and silver sparkling under Tivoli bulbs, a Nathan Hale delivered to the British rope.

"Do I have to sit at the kids' table?" said Jessie.

"Naw. Take a break and sit with me."

Dinner served, wine poured, Joshua shakily stood. Always having appeared prematurely old, he looked as ancient as Aunt Linda and half as vital. He lifted his cup. Voices stilled. I almost stopped him. He noticed me shift and shot me a half-smile that mourned defeat.

"Any of you ever see the Vietnam movie that starts with the AWOL American hiding out in a Buddhist temple in Longxuyen, crouched over a key of smack—heroin, kids—he's stolen from his Burmese slave masters?"

Some nervous chuckles. No one knew how to take his dulcet tone and waxen smile in context with his improbable and inappropriate words.

He waved his wine as if painting a picture. "It's 1971. He's a twenty-year-old kid but aches like he's ninety. Hell, a hundred. He's boiling the dose he knows will kill him."

Everyone who didn't before now knew he was drunk. I prayed not only that he wouldn't embarrass his family with much more of this, but that his alcohol energy, put to pantomiming the story's activity, wouldn't end with a crash of plates and collapse of the man. I suspect he knew what I was thinking; he made a threatening motion, leaning over the candles.

"He welcomes death because he blames life all his problems."

"Joshua, please," Wendy said, patiently intense.

"He can't return to his masters because they'll slit his throat. He can't run because there's a war outside and it'll blow him to smithereens."

I saw it in his eyes, how I know my eyes look when I travel in time. Joshua was back in the moment. The past overwhelming his present. His eyes danced with pain.

"What terrified the American boy most was the other American already in-country and hunting him—out of an entire war, hunting only him. So, the kid only has a minute to cook the job and deny life to the rest of him." The fuzz left his voice, the zigzag his arms. He steadied his glass in both his hands. An audible sigh rose from his family and guests.

"I starred in that movie. Only reason I'm swaying here to tell you about it, is that other man crept up behind me. Shoved a Colt 45 into the back of my skull and whispered in my ear,

'Do that, you're no different from any Nazi who dropped the Zyklon B pellets in the showers of Auschwitz, and you dishonor every man, woman, and child who died in the gas chamber. Every one of them would have traded anything to be where you are this minute with that fucking spoon to hurl in the demons' eyes.'

"'I'm in a world of suffering shit.' I told'm, and he said, right back: 'And I'm the guy who's come to suffer the stink of watching you climb out of it.'

"That's who I am. What Joshua Rosen retires from."

He stopped. His spirit fell back in on itself. His wrinkled face looked like a melting candle. Wendy shed quiet tears. Everyone else: thunder- wonder- or plain dumb-struck. Except Jessie. She clapped, loving the performance.

"Jessie!" I snapped, a little too loud.

"What?" she snapped back even louder. "Obviously, he lives and becomes a superspy hero like you, Dad."

Cover blown. It wasn't supposed to happen this way, and all eyes, mystified and accusing, struck Jessie. She flushed with preteen embarrassment.

"I gotta go." She ducked her head and pushed away. A coltish girl plunging on unsteady legs.

Joshua pointed a bony finger playfully after her. "Stop thief! Stop thief!"

Wendy slapped his arm. "You stop!"

Joshua laughed. His daughter, Rachel, intercepted Jessie.

She crouched. "You don't have to leave, hun. It's okay. He's just an old jokester."

Jessie leaned into her and spoke into Rachel's ear.

"What did she say? Answer me, girl!" Joshua called.

Joshua was having fun with this now, my daughter having taken the poison cup from his hand.

"That you've been limping around all day like a bird with a broken wing looking for a place to die." Rachel glared at him. "You have been."

Joshua ambled over to the pair. He stroked Jessie's hair.

"Thank you, Jessie. I wasn't getting to my point too well. But how did you know? How'd you know old Uncle Joshua was a spy?"

Jessie turned her face to him, her lips buckled tight. Joshua's son, Eric, the older of his two children, spoke. "Probably the same way Rachel and I have always known."

Rachel winked backup. "Muir told us when we were kids. Told us to always be on the lookout. Second eyes and ears."

Joshua faced the rest of his guests. "Muir was the CIA officer with the pistol." Then to his children: "You two were okay with that?"

"You didn't become a Nazi," Rachel suggested.

"Okay. Anyway, for the rest of you, this is my retirement from the CIA."

"Not a profitable business, you having to build your own house of sticks," someone joked.

"You bet, Marty, and that's why I'm charging you for the grub. Now eat!"

The rabbi raised his glass and shouted, *"L'chiam!"*

WE'D BEEN INVITED TO SPEND THE NIGHT and a long weekend, as Nina would be on assignment until Tuesday. When Jessie grabbed her pillow and comforter to join the slumber party with the grandchildren outside under the moon, I asked her, "Grandpa Nathan told you too—about me?"

"Yeah. In Russian. Right in front of your nose. Before I ever learned English. I miss him. Sometimes I get real sad, but other times"—a funny look, debating whether to tell—"I see him in our house or outside the windows out of the corner of my eye."

"Why didn't you ever tell me?"

"People keep secrets, Dad. Duh."

I watched her drag her comforter to the sound of children's voices and laughter. I went into my tiny room with its tiny twin bed. A manila envelope I'd not seen before poked out from beneath my pajamas where, unpacking, I'd laid them on the pillow. Mildly curious, I opened it. It contained photographs without a note. The photographs depicted Nina in various settings, various embraces, and various beds in various hotels.

Am. I. Blue.

I shoved them back in the envelope. Shoved the envelope under my pillow. Lay down into my bed. I shut my eyes, but couldn't erase the image of Nina fucked by and fucking Victor Rubio, the cigar dealer of the cinnamon suit.

33

I'LL TAKE THE BLAME—always do, *when* it's due—but this time around, obviously, this was all Muir's fault. Damn him to hell. He'd recruited her. He'd brought her in. He'd thrust her upon me long before I did any thrusting of my own, tangled in the sheets of her deceit. His fault. From the get-go. And once again, Russell Aiken, the innocent man of integrity, trapped in Muir's web of deceit. Where I go from here—I let it depend on where I want to end up. The only rational course.

I knew who I was when I awoke but would change a few times before the day was over. I packed my bag, stuffing the damning photo evidence in with my dirty shorts.

Take that. At least I bring underwear when I go visiting.

Blind in the dim twilight before sunrise, I stole my getaway. I was like a mole trying to escape a badger's den. Nina had hijacked the entire enterprise, I surmised as I smashed my ankle against a chair leg, bobbling my way to the only light in the cabin luminous from the kitchen, and thought: the degree of Nina's compromise, her motivations, remained opaque. The hourglass certainly flowed both ways—the heroism of the father blind to the treachery of the daughter.

Nothing short of treason.

Joshua glanced my way from the kitchen table. "Coffee?"

I stared blankly at his crinkled face. Could he have left the pictures for me? The point of the party had been a reveal of his CIA secret—and mine, thanks to Jessie (though I didn't fault her); every other guest last night had been non-Agency affili-ated. Maybe this was Joshua's parting shot at the framework of all we—me and Lynn, Muir and Bishop, Amy, Aunt Linda, and my tormentor Nina—had built. Sure. Joshua bridled against many things the Agency had done over the years and the Nine-Twelvers were doing now. He'd outright refused operations and gotten away with it due to his prima donna status, but he was one of *us*.

"Or a cab?" His facial creases deepened with worry. "You look pale. Spiders in your bed drink all your blood?"

He wouldn't have done this. Not like that. Joshua was in all things a direct man. Had he found out and desired to shove my face into this perfidious bush, he'd have done it forthright and -with. Joshua was my friend, Muir's decades-trusted partner and accomplice. In all things a man of honor and kindness.

But Muir trusted Nina, and all that had gotten me was a glossy sheaf of smut. Well, if Joshua had slipped them under my pillow for a nightcap, he hadn't wanted to discuss it and he wasn't bringing it up now.

"Something urgent's come up at headquarters. You mind keeping Jessie another night or two? I'll be back before you head off the mountain."

"Might not give her back. Love that kid. Took the bullet for me and added ten years to my life last night. Be prepared: I'll be buying her a pony while you're working."

Tell him! Spread out the photos! Expose Nina exposed!

I wasn't that man. If he didn't know, it would kill those ten years like a smothering pillow. I stood there knowing one thing: I didn't know what to say.

"What's on your mind?"

"Need to find my car keys."

"Check your hand recently?"

Good instinct on his part.

"Right." Where they dangled.

He studied me. Didn't like what he saw. "The way I see it, you got a few minutes before your car leaves. Longer if the driver sits down and lets loose. I owe you one."

I want to.

"I can't."

"That's how it's going to be." He tossed me a playful sneer. "Day one of retirement and the secret door slams in the face. Fine by me. I'll tell you what's on *my* mind. Muir left us with the new Russell Aiken. Made sure of it with his final request. The new Russell is a look-before-he-leaps guy—"

"I've always looked when I've done my leaping."

"Yes, and midway down, you remember that he who hesitates is lost. No more getting lost first, okay?"

We struggle our whole life for awareness. We have it least when we need it, looking for it most. Why is it we only find it when we can look at our history of missing it?

I gave my thanks, said my goodbye, leaped into my car.

I SEETHED OVER THE PICTURES burning their sordid images in my mind. The betrayal of it all; the whole HOUNDFOX network was a setup. A deception by Nina and Victor Rubio run back on CIA, back against her own father, for Chrissakes. And for who knows how many years? Makes Ana Montes, the Cuban spy embedded in the Defense Intelligence Agency who'd recently pled guilty and taken a twenty-five-year sentence look like, like, like... like Nina. I'd be the one throwing the book at her, for sure.

I wound east on Maryland National Freeway 68 through the Green Ridge State Forest. Rancid billowings of fog roiled between the green arms of table-mountain pine trunks that crawled with pecking brown creepers. Fog hung on the reddened boughs of maples, twisted through the veiny yellow leaves of the hickory, and oiled the carpet of gray fallen hemlock needles and the browning sumac where worm-eating warblers flicked and snatched their grub. A gray breath of the season of dying, it seethed across the road, illusory and narcotic, cut by swoops of ravens, demon black and always ahead of me. It befitted where I was going, both body and spirit.

If not Joshua, it could easily be someone on the catering staff.

They'd had unrestricted access to the kitchen and dining room for their prep work. That would have given unaccountable access to the entire cabin.

It wasn't Joshua.

I would accept that, logically and faithfully, so staff was the only alternative conclusion. An embedded officer or a spur-of-the-moment-recruited asset could easily have left the kitchen, deposited the envelope in my room, and been back peeling carrots in less than a minute.

But who outside our tightly compartmented circle would be motivated to do such a thing without providing me context by way of report, a note, or threat? Had *I* come under suspicion? Was the purpose of these photographs designed to provoke me to run and see which way I led?

I checked my rearview mirror. No follow car. Around the next bend, I pulled onto the shoulder and waited. No one went by. Either direction. I gave it ten minutes, then I continued. Passed through the community of Bellgrove and no one joined the freeway ahead or behind me.

That's when it hit me. Like a shower of freezing water in a hostile interrogation, Silas Kingston gripping the bracing bucket. Counterintelligence skates the icy edge of every operation. The accusing photos were exactly the type of material he and his CI thugs collected and used in damning the mock traitors among us. As much as I despised the man, it now came clear to me, Silas Kingston must have known—at least suspected—Nina's betrayal from the beginning. But procedural channels existed for prosecuting a counterintelligence case; why he hadn't gone through them in his pursuit of Nina and her sleazy lover only meant one thing.

KALEIDOSCOPE.

Without having consciously decided where I was headed, when I activated my hands-free mobile phone, I heard myself telling it to dial Lynn Kingston. She was expecting to meet with me and Nina midweek to debrief on my recent consult with Amy Kim and, from her timeline, develop our CONPLAN for the deployment and implementation of the Time Machine listening device. It would be impossible now to have that meeting with Nina included.

My call woke Lynn, and I heard her sleepy, "Yes, Rusty?"

I didn't correct her. Informed her our meeting could not wait until Wednesday. I was on my way to meet her at headquarters.

"I've read your report," she said. "TIME MACHINE seems to be progressing at the technological level. Everything is in order from a legal and policy standpoint, avoiding the Foreign Intelligence Surveillance Act of 1978, Executive Order 12333, and avoids entirely PPD-28 bulk intercept first-stage requirements. See? I read it. Well done."

"Something new has come up."

"In your analysis?"

"Things. Many things."

"So clear of you."

"Lynn, are you alone and do you trust me?"

"To annoy me. Because you blind me every time you wrench the shades away on my aloneness."

"It's foggy."

"I'm not with you. Does it have to be at headquarters? I'm just out of bed. Unwillingly."

"I'll come wherever, but it needs to be now," I said. Struck by a thought, I tagged on: "And headquarters would be the exact wrong place to do this between us."

She made a murmuring noise, making me flinch. My words hadn't come out the way I'd intended.

This isn't personal. This isn't about passions. Sex. Feelings. The man of mission grips this wheel. That's them*; this is us.*

My chest ached. Right in the damned spot Nina had jabbed me with her finger. Skin deep. With certainty, at that moment, my greatest fear was that discovery of Nina's defection, investigation, and pending arrest, would kill all our work.

Nothing short of brilliant, Amy's LD needed Lynn's backing no matter what; even if the entire HOUNDFOX operation network were ordered shut down, we could not let it shut down Amy. If TIME MACHINE worked as Amy specked it out to me, it would be a crowning achievement in electronic espionage. To protect Amy and her important work, I needed Lynn's full buy-in before Nina's betrayal fractured across the KALEIDOSCOPE prism.

"Come to my place. I'll make some coffee," she said. She gave me her address.

Only after I terminated the call, relaxing into the safety I would deliver to Amy, did I pay any attention to my inner voice—lifelong enemy to my outward man—that, from the moment I'd viewed the last photograph of Nina and Victor Rubio in fierce embrace— the pair of them on Nina's front steps, snapped this past week as nursery flats and gardening tools from my Sunday's planting lay visible in the flower bed beneath the living-room windows—had gone from whispering to screaming in the silence of my vehicle as I sped to Lynn's North Bethesda condo:

This wasn't KALEIDOSCOPE.

This wasn't Silas Kingston.

This wasn't a betrayal of the Agency, of the operation, of HOUNDFOX.

Of Muir and Muir's.

In each of those photos, Nina was secure in everything but her lust. Victor Rubio was an asshole, but that didn't make the former DEA agent a double agent, Cuban DI, or any other enemy nation's mole. All these pictures made Victor Rubio was Nina's lover.

How's that for a slit of the throat by Occam's razor? And not in the way that friar's theological rule has been corrupted by the secular talking heads who misuse it entirely as if it were a scientific theory— that "entities should not be multiplied without necessity"; that the simplest answer is usually the correct answer. What they try to cloak as science is a postulate by a theologian that tells us not to look at long lists of scientific facts when trying to prove God. William of Ockham was clear: Screw evidence; God's miracle exists because our gut tells us so.

Nina is faithful to the Agency. She's just unfaithful to me.

The burning in my chest was the devil of heartbreak. I choked the steering wheel and held my breath until I saw stars. Gasped. Repeated. The best way to say *fuck* is to scream it. Oh, and wailing it works well too. Although, having screamed and wailed—*still*—I had become a different man since my quadruple Madeline-Beardy Baldy, Muir, me, assassinations failed. Not the *fuck*-screaming leap-before-you-look Russell Aiken killer.

God damn her! She'd said she hadn't *done the orgies with him and she promised!*

I was as underappreciated as Claude Rains as Captain Renault in *Casablanca*. That pivotal moment when with full certainty he conceives the extent of Rick's criminal enterprise and decisively blows the whistle on the American expatriate's depraved café. Spurred to duty, Rains/Renault makes the heroic, definitive accusation of the film: "I am shocked, shocked to find that gambling is going on here!"

Discovery be the soul of brevity.

And before Rick can argue, the truth of the brilliant police captain's claim is irrefutably proven as the croupier delivers Renault a handful of gaming chips—won by the same gambling he has proven. A cold and frightful moment by the shrewd man of law. One of the best hard-crime films of the war era.

Yes: this Russell Aiken puts the operation first. That's why I'd not even considered the fornicating anything to do with me. And, hell, if Nina wasn't a traitor, why would I shoot her? A good spy, professional. The only one with her father's trust. If I've learned anything, over and over, it's loyalty up, loyalty down.

Am I masochistic?! What about a little bit of loyalty to me while you're upping-and-downing the cinnamon slut? Fucking bitch!

I wasn't going to go crazy. No, this time I'd do it right.

New Aiken will not become old Muir.

Prevailing Aiken, play it cool. We would make the Cuba run, me and Nina, get the device planted, get one over on Castro, get out, then the simple matter of one bullet for her, one for her Cuban voodoo fuck. And fuck the both a'them if I'd give them the satisfaction of seeing my suicide after I plugged 'em. If I'm anything: I'm the guy who learns after he pulls the trigger.

Focus on the mission.

Focus on Amy.

Focus on TIME MACHINE. *Foci aeterni:* fornicate and I—

What? I what?

I why? Oh, why?!

How did I let it come to this again, a snake with its tail between his legs?

I left the fog behind me in Alleghany forests. I remembered the boy in the story who changed to a sparrow to escape the magic woods and his teacher, who chases him also as a sparrow; changed to a fish, he fights the older man who is now a larger fish. Breathless, he flops onto land where the larger fish emerges from the water, dripping and transformed to a fighting cock. The boy is not Arthur, but a lowly Saxon thief who changes into a fox and snaps the master thief's chicken neck, killing his Merlin in order not to pay for his training, just as his master taught him.

As I drove into the rising sun backlighting North Bethesda, utility wires crisscrossed overhead and the graceless ravens we mistakenly see as crows gurgled and puffed, barking at me like hellhounds as I rolled beneath.

What is it Amy had urged me as we parted—?

"Muir would say, consider what Nina needs and Lynn requires."

34

TWO WEEKS EARLIER, AMY SAID TO ME, "TIME MACHINE functions exactly as a hardline tap with a burst transceiver. It physically intercepts the direct line between Venezuela and Havana and transmits the capture via geosynchronous NRO satellites tasked to Agency SIGINT missions. It will allow the CIA to intercept in both directions and manipulate content."

It rankled me Amy would say "allow the CIA" instead of "allow us." Why wouldn't she accept I'd gotten her back on the team at the highest level of engagement—not to mention best faith? I'd delivered this, I might add, while delivering her a cover she could proudly embrace with her difficult parents. The change that overtook her last winter, that froze her out of Muir's garden of ambitions, the dreams she'd once shared and aspired to, remained a wall of ice between us when I first arrived at her George Mason University laboratories.

Dressed as sci-fi surgeons, we were checked through an armed-security lobby and into an elevator that descended into a soundproofed, vibration-free basement and a second, guarded vestibule outside a compartment with parallel entrance and exit doors, a kind of airlock that both decontaminated us and "neutralized our static and electromagnetism—"

"Didn't know I even had those superpowers on Earth's surface," I said to a smile that told me she'd heard them all before and mine was one of those vacuous ones Amy patiently tolerated.

From the elevator, we stepped into a suite of clean rooms she called "fabs," to which I used my true superpower of self-control and didn't say, "Yeah, baby, yeah!" Humans were the brains of the operation, with brains capable of overseeing the vast array of robotic, electron-fueled, laserified unnatural nature of imaging, etching, cutting, chemical-bathed, vacuum-furnaced, and nitrogen-frozen capabilities which, electrified to life by super-processed, mainframed, server automated and adminis-tered, conducted an orchestration of symphonic science entirely lost on me as soon as Amy began my tour with, "To think, it all starts with a grain of sand, ubiquitous and simple, that, made of silica, we refine to single-crystal silicon ingots. From there…"

I peaked in science in junior high.

I still enjoy the view.

It took a mind-exhausting hour to get from the metaphorical beachhead to the components assembly room where the proto-type was halfway through construction. Viewing a monitor that displayed the final mini football-shaped listening device, I was able to summarize the point of the conversation— "This LD gives us a robust but traditional electronic intercept; we know what they know at both ends in simultaneous time."

"Qualified on 'simultaneous,'" she said. "And this is what makes the listening device unique: *simul* from the Latin 'at the same time;' with the suffix—"

Ha! Now we were in my sandbox, talking the supellectilum *everyone learns (or should—strike that, must!) in elementary school. Thank you, Sister Maria.*

"—*aneous*, 'of the nature of, resembling.'"

"Yes. Which is how I've designed and built in your requested time machine. Once deployed, the LD only *resembles* an at the same time state of interconnectivity. Your intel from HOUNDFOX tells us the dedicated line between Havana and Caracas main-tains a constant handshake logged onto a twenty-four-hour no-violation/noninterruption security protocol. Your LD, we're calling TIME MACHINE, clones the handshake at each end and slips between the clasping hands. Pretty standard to this point, but to continue with the handshake metaphor, once your hands get invisibly between them, Time Machine gently increases the speed of the shake. We overclock the signal a portion of each second from each side, at four-second intervals. By the end of every twelve hours, if no traffic has passed, we can create undetectable gaps—call them time-holes—of up to fifteen minutes. At which point, the overclock shifts to underclocking, and any unfilled time-holes we've dug are refilled over the twelve-hour course of the next cycle."

"A failsafe window. We have their information before they do. Something goes wrong, we can prevent delivery, countermove, countermand—"

"No. That would make TIME MACHINE disposable after a onetime intrusion upset. Russell, I want you to conceptualize information not as specific actionable intelligence, but as theory.

"The concept of information turns out to be key to new advances in physics. It measures the ability of one physical system to communicate with another physical system. Everything one system shares with another is based on information it has in correlation between that other system."

"Uther Pendragon can dance with Igraine, but not with Mount Everest."

Amy knit her brow, unsure if I was insane or simply sarcastic. "But that's exactly it."

I smiled. For the first time since Muir's wake, Amy's eyes glowed like stars. I dipped my head for her to continue.

"In general terms, time is the measure of information we don't yet have. Specific to this LD, the time you steal is a measure of information you have—"

"*We*, Amy. You're safe. You're back on the team if only you'd let yourself. Nothing would change from what we've given you here."

The freezer door of her face sealed shut. Rejecting my comment, she pushed past it. "—the time *you* steal is a measure of information you have, *but* they don't have. Giving you information plus influence. Influence by your ability to intercept communication both ends, decode, analyze, and manipulate content in their messaging via the time-holes before the other side receives it, and insert anything—either direction you want—in delivery and/or response."

"Not sure I get that…"

"Think of each time-hole as one of those crosswords you love. Their—Havana–Caracas—real-time passing of information can be viewed as the across boxes of clues and answers; the time-holes provide you the ability to link into their dialogue, insert and drop down box-chains of information. Not only do these insertions link to the flow of the Havana–Caracas cross lines above but create future intersections that will influence their own content in future lines below. This gives you a daily method to sabotage meaning, context, and motivation.

"Like your dancers: the transfer of information between two like systems comes with built-in cues, motives, biases, fears, agreements; these act and react in a choreographic plan, the attribution of propositional attitudes. TIME MACHINE will best be used as a slow drip, drip, drip where, over time, an entire false set of perceptions can be built on both sides and communicated without the opposite side ever knowing, to create a merger of agreed understanding between them that belongs to you but they believe is organic to their own communications."

I was unsure if I understood any better, but notebook out and open, Muir's brown-inked, blood-red, pearl-inlaid 1950 Esterbrook fountain pen flowing across the page, I didn't need any convincing she understood completely. I struggled to get it all down.

"Here's another way to look at it," she continued once we'd finished with the lab and sat in her office. "My grandmother lives with her sister. They're elderly, and though both are mentally as sharp as ever, they've both gone a little deaf."

"What?" I said cupping my ear. She didn't go for the hard-of-hearing joke.

"They chatter away all day like a couple of birds. And inevitably, one says something that is entirely misheard by the other. The one doesn't know, and more importantly, as all humans, they're programmed to believe they've heard correctly, so the human brain does a funny trick in these situations. The mind recontextualizes. It dismisses the absurd and reconstrues the implausible as plausible."

I found the idea amusing and urged her to give me an example.

"I had dinner with them," she said. "It was around the 9/11 anniversary. The two ladies always have the television running and there were the usual talking heads inaccurately discussing the war on terror.

"I witnessed this," Amy offered. "I hear my nana say, 'I'll be out to see our tax accountant tomorrow. Will you be all right for an hour or so in the morning?' My great-auntie smiles politely, and she says: 'Yes. Dear me. The attacks are mounting all our sorrows. I think everyone's in mourning.' My grandmother notices the news running in the background and assumes the validity of her comment. But she knows she's missed a word or two, so she double-checks.

"'Tomorrow morning?'

"'You, me. All of America.'

"That throws her off, so Nana reconfirms the plan: 'But you're okay with *tomorrow*?'

"Auntie Hye still hears *sorrow*, and remarks, 'We all must take the pain.' Which my nana registers, mishears *pain*, but moves on.

"She says, 'Can't take the *train*. It doesn't run there. I'll take the bus. It goes right past.'

"Auntie Hye: 'Whether the *rain lasts* or not, do take an umbrella.'

"My nana: 'Oh, *is* it going to rain? I had no idea. Don't want to show up to our tax preparer all wet.'

"'It's smart to be prepared.' And they're back on track, mishearings confirmed and reconfirmed."

Amy's computer produced a cathedral *dong*. She clicked her mouse, returned her attention my way.

"The point of my story is Auntie Hye never knew my grandmother went to the accountant, my grandmother never needed the umbrella she brought on the bus, but took comfort in being prepared, and their taxes were finished and submitted on time."

"That was fun," I said. "But how do we insure it doesn't go the other way like a kid's game of telephone—the absurdity of the miscommunication revealed at the end when the last player says, 'Operator,' and exposes the whole mishmash?"

"Because we manipulate the 'operator' interrogatories. Residual suspicion at both ends can also be used to our advantage. Repeated, verifiable errors begin to look like purposeful lies to weaken the infrastructure of the Cuban–Venezuelan alliance, creating doubt and mistrust.

"A preponderance of psychological and neurologic analysis of mishearings teach us that ninety to one hundred percent of the time, mishearings present themselves as coherent perceptions. As a species, we're coded to detect patterns. Only through pattern identification could humans have ever created communication, and only through communication we were able to join in groups, teach, and learn, and, collectively, survive in a violent and dangerous world. But so tuned to pattern recognition as quint-essential to survivability, we quite often see patterns that aren't there. Create meaning out of the meaningless because the human mind has a built-in override to decode perception into established and existing frameworks of recurring self-preservation structures. TIME MACHINE creates the illusion of recurring structures to influence predictable behaviors."

"A built-in ambiguity-increasing deception." I said.

She gave me an agreeable wag of her chin. "Designed to generate confusion and cause mental conflict in the enemy decision-maker because the human mind cannot turn itself off from pattern recognition. This delays the making of specific decisions on the low end. On the high end, it creates operational paralysis one believes is their own freewill choice. TIME MACHINE manipulates and exploits the enemy decision-makers' preexisting beliefs, fears, and bias through the intentional display of observables that reinforce and convince them that their preheld beliefs are true."

Pleased with herself, Amy folded her hands atop her desk and waited for my response.

I finished my notes. "I'm sold. Brilliant, if we can pull it off. It's going to take a lot of real-time control of these time-holes. You have a plan for that?"

"Conceptual. I have some testing returns to go through, then some changes to the OS architecture that's ready to move from beta. If you'd like, you could come over for dinner?"

OFF THE MOUNTAIN. Out of the forest. Into Lynn's city.

I take the elevator to the fifteenth floor of the Rock Creek Terrace condominium tower and present myself at Lynn's door. She answers as soon as I knock. I stare at her, captured by and full of the look of her.

"Are you alone?" I say.

"Yes. What's with your face? That crook's a little more devious than I'm comfortable with. Maybe."

Barefooted, she wears black yoga pants and a loose camouflage workout tank. Without a sports bra, it did little to mask her breasts playing "now you see me" beneath. I step toward her—all my inhibitions vanish to lust and its fulfillment—reaching in, scooping her into my arms, lifting her to my chest. She curves her body into mine and I carry her inside, letting instinct lead me right to her bedroom door.

"Are you sober?" she says.

"Exceptionally. You?"

"Since I quit. Just want to know how many commitments you're willing to break."

"Try me. I outlived love long ago."

"Life might be a whole lot better without it."

She kisses me. Our tongues meet and mingle. Her fingers deftly pinch open my shirt buttons as I nudge open the door to her gym room. Her limber body built to emphasize the smooth flexibility of each joint from ankle to shoulder, elbows to wrist to fingers, muscled and fluid as she kisses my chest, my nipples; I warm of the slow dark fire I've always imagined burns inside her I have longed to burn me.

"Bedroom's end of the hall, tiger... unless you like the look of that bench."

Her eyes glaze in anticipation of ecstasy.

I like the bed. I like laying her across it. Her hand flings the scrunchie from her hair. Golden auburn spreads behind her like a halo of flame. I like peeling off her leggings to reveal her flawless ivory skin and the redder hair, velvet and promising.

35

O VER LINGUINI WITH CLAMS, a salad, and some garlic bread prepared in her second-floor duplex, Amy tells me she designed the program in the same way Muir taught her about myths; that TIME MACHINE could be most effective in creating a myth that becomes fundamental to each side's understanding of their relationship.

"Information is the essential building block of the universe," said Amy, transferring the leftover linguine to Tupperware for the refrigerator. "How do we know this? For over seventy years, physicists have tried to detect dark matter. While it remains utterly elusive, what's been discovered in its place is that information has mass; that information is no different from ordinary matter, and quantum theorists uniformly now categorize information as a fifth state of matter."

"Do I need to know the other four?"

"Not necessary. Just a little history. Go back to 1948. A mathematician who'd been in your line of work—"

"Ours?"

"A code breaker during the Second World War. His name was Claude Shannon. After the war, he worked for Bell Telephone."

We carried plates into her kitchen.

"Bell brought him on board to design a communications system to transfer information over wire. He postulated that Boolean algebra coincided perfectly with telephone switching circuits, proving mathematics could be used to design electrical systems. His information theory led directly to the invention of the first digital bit. Since then, at the rate bits are globally produced, factoring in a fifty percent yearly increase in their production, within one hundred and fifty years, half the Earth's atomic mass will be converted to digital information mass."

"Wait a minute. Information has always existed," I said, rinsing our plates. "Keep speaking. You did all the cooking. I'll wash, it'll help me from getting bogged down."

"You know your limitations better than I." She took the dishes one after the other. "You keep rinsing. I'll load the dishwasher."

We moved on to the pots and pans.

"I'm speaking of electronic information," she said. "But yes, electricity has been passing organic information since the first lightning strike on the first primordial pond to create life. Think of information's presence of mass like that of an electron. An electron only comes into measurable existence in time and space when it interacts with something else. Only then is its mass detectable. When you apply Einstein's laws of thermodynamics to information theory—which provably works—the mass–energy–information equivalence principle demonstrates that every bit of information has, in fact, mass."

I cleaned the stove. I wasn't sure I followed her any better with activity, but it prevented me from sitting, staring at her speaking mouth, and looking dull. Admittedly, I found a kind of fatherly warmth in being with Amy while she exercised her mind. It was strong and agile, she was happy working it and I sensed, without provable formula, the point she was making—of no intention of hers—might have something to do with me.

My mission. My own internal elliptical epileptic time travel.

Muir whispers in my mind: "The correlation between all past, present, and future interactions between event systems, Dumbo, is the be-all and end-all of the why you seek."

"As electrons only exist when they interact with something else, information is the same. Only when it is passed does it reveal its quantifiable existence. I could use some coffee, you?"

"Keep going," I said. "I'll make it."

"It's ready to go. Just push the button."

I did. She said: "You don't believe you're getting any of this."

"I am enjoying you enjoying it."

"I'm going to ask you a few questions, and I think you'll find out how smart you really are."

Aiken's slave to Amy's Socrates; and Muir smiles from heaven beyond the interstellar beyond, where light arrives where it began at journey's end. The assembled glow of God. Never doubt the guy gripping the razor.

"Would you agree, the passing of information is the basis of what it is to be human?"

"I firmly agree."

"And what it is to be human is to be conscious?"

"Yes."

"Are you familiar with panpsychism?"

"From the Greek, *pan* for 'all,' and *psyche* for 'soul or mind'?"

"That's right."

"Nope. Not familiar."

Amy opened the cupboard next to the sink. She reached down two coffee mugs. Handed me one of a matched set depicting dragons.

"I've always thought the Korean dragon much more ferocious than the Chinese," I said.

"These are Chinese dragons," she demurred.

I found it odd at the time, so steeped she was in her Korean heritage. I poured and she went on.

"Italian Renaissance philosopher Francesco Patrizi articulated that mentality—consciousness, that is—exists in all matter."

I sipped, flinched at the heat burning my lips. "All matter isn't conscious," I asserted.

"Bear with me. You can at least agree, when we describe matter and how it behaves, it is only through our outside perception of such matter. The information it outwardly passes to us. The way we pass information. You don't experience my consciousness and I can't experience yours. We accept it without second thought because we are two systems that recognize each other as alike, but, because consciousness comes from the inside out, we only know that we ourselves are experiencing it. We know we are conscious because we can express what being us feels like."

"I thought I was playing Meno."

"I'm sorry, what?"

"Old friend of Muir's—must not've introduced you."

"Oh!" she brightened. "Plato."

"Mm, yes. But I liked it better when you Play-Doh'd Socrates."

She wrinkled her nose. Not one for puns. "Sorry. Try this: what if I'm a perfect robot, only reacting to your input? What if everyone is?"

"Everyone but me?"

"Mm-hmm."

"*Now* we're getting somewhere. Been suspecting that—sometimes strenuously, I might add—since I could think. I got over it in high school. What's it matter if it works, right?"

"That is right. Because the kind of robot I am, I process all your cues. I return the appropriate feedback. I act and react in a manner perfectly similar to your standard of consciousness, and I'm programmed with the information that allows me to express modes of what 'being' feels like, but organically, I don't feel."

A chill shivered my body. The hair rose on my arms. "Are? You? A robot?"

Her laugh, timed as if by a switch in a perfect machine, rang merrily in the small kitchen. I subtly rubbed my forearms one over the other to get the blood flow back. I hoped she hadn't noticed or electronically processed my cues.

"You're so funny. Relax. I may not be everything you believe I am, but I am human. Is a dog conscious?"

"Yes."

"Not because you know what it feels like being a dog—"

Muir would argue that one.

"—but because you know they're not robots, you recognize qualities in their experience of themselves that correlate to how you experience yourself."

"Easy. Yes. Go on."

"I'm not keeping score."

"Always keep score."

"Birds—conscious?"

"Sometimes you hear about parrots dialing 911."

"I don't know if I believe that. How many parrots?"

"It's real. I saw a TV show about a murder—"

"Indisputably a super-conscious parrot." She drank, looked at her dragon as she said, "How about a flock of a thousand blackbirds, bursting to flight from a dirt field?"

"Yes. I recognize and acknowledge they are conscious."

She motioned I follow her into the living room. Amy offered me the sofa. She took a wooden chair, tilting a black Persian cat from its seat. "You recognize and acknowledge these creatures' consciousness, because you can see in dogs and birds their similarity to our experience of consciousness. What about ants and bees?"

"Yep."

"We know how highly social they are. They pass information in ways that remind us of the human condition."

366   AIKEN IN CHECK

I liked this. You look at the whole of it, it did settle much of my robot fear.

And she said, "They may not have inner lives—joys, fears, or comprehension of Marcel Proust—anything at all like ours, but they communicate complex needs and social codes and instructions."

"I've read about that. It's why the movie *Antz* is so good."

"It's not. Now take an earthworm—and not a movie earthworm. It will be burrowing along when it hears a tread on the grass, a beak piercing the soil nearby. Like that!"—she snapped her fingers—"It scurries to its home burrow. Conscious?"

"Not conscious. A fight-or-flight impulse of a simple nervous system."

"Self-preservation indicates internal awareness of alive-good and dead-bad. And not only is it a flight impulse, but studies show even with a closer path to escape, earthworms invariably go 'home.' They demonstrate knowledge of some form of comfort-need as well as safety. While their cerebrum is nothing like ours, or mammals, or higher forms of insects, the earthworm exhibits a form of consciousness. So, agreeing to all of that, would you agree with this definition? Consciousness is an awareness of the outside world and an organism's place in it and its desire to remain?"

She speaks of a movie earthworm. Did they ever make one? Not as good as Antz, *if they did. I don't think anyone could. Yes, I'd have to say no. Being hermaphrodites as earthworms are, any gender you cast in any role gets called out for appropriating a role intended for the other.*

"Yes." My eyes traveled to an end table alongside the sofa arm I relaxed against. "You come up with this all yourself?"

My question amused her. "Hardly any of it. We form our opinions from our influences."

"Transfer of information."

"Without which, there is no reality." She watched that sink in with me a moment, then said, "A scientist in Great Britain named Kevin Warwick—his work on AI, very influential—recently presented a paper in which he wrote: 'I believe that dogs and cats are conscious in their own way, and bees, ants, and spiders are conscious, not as humans but as bees, ants, and spiders.'"

Atop the end table sat two picture frames, one in front of the other. The prominent of the two displayed a folding pair of photographs: Muir and Amy glowing in sunlight on a patio I recognized as now my own, but at the time taken, had been his patio at Princeton. Angled beside it, was a portrait of the old spy from long before Amy and Nathan had ever met: Muir stands at a folding map table, cigarette smoldering in one clumped hand, the other hand on the butt of a large handgun hanging on his belt beside an ammo clip and a fragmentation grenade; he glows rugged invincibility in insignia-less bush BDUs and hat; a photograph taken in Angola.

Tucked behind these was a single, smaller frame, a portrait sitting of Amy in Princeton graduation togs, her seriously proud parents, passport-faced, behind her.

"Warwick said, 'I can't say a robot with a computer for a brain is not conscious because its brain is not like mine and because it thinks in a different way to me.'"

I'd lost track of what she was saying. I flashed my crooked smile, uncomfortable we'd come back to robots. The cat, having wandered around looking for a new parking place, leaped into my lap.

Amy worked on her coffee, the dragon staring now, accusing someone of something. "Plants?"

"Yes, yes," I said, impatiently. "Don't ask me to explain it, but there was a thing about pine forest root systems, if I remember correctly, that can communicate between and beyond species; basic predictive memory functions."

"That's right. Consciousness?"

"You bet. I fully agree all living things having a nervous system of any kind have consciousness that does not need human mentality for functional self-awareness."

I finished my coffee comfortably perched on her sofa, black cat purring in my lap, blissfully aware of the cartoon anvil-safe-piano whistling from on high, aimed by her first question right for the top of my head.

"You would agree with me that single-cell bacteria, though living, do *not* have brains or nervous systems?"

"I'm sure you're about ready to tell me they do."

"They don't."

"Aha!" I said, because sometimes the smartest word available to not say anything is "aha" and as loudly as possible.

"Yet bacteria anticipate predictable changes in their environment with a clear sense of both time and space and the needs and activity of their immediate neighbors. Self-identity and species-wide social awareness has been observed, externally, and they are capable of collective sensing and communication through large or small molecules, distributed information processing, and collective gene regulation; pure examples of cognitive function and social intelligence."

I found I couldn't disagree. Wouldn't know where to begin. I also found—and this struck me odder than conscious germs in all their unconscionableness (and who doesn't believe in the evil intent of viruses?)—it was odd that Amy, who upon resignation—even earlier, Christmas Eve at Muir's lagoon—put more store in her family and her position in it, their perception of her, than in the Agency she loved, and yet she'd displayed their photograph with preferred obscurity. I was suspicious of how deep her love for Muir had taken her and been reciprocated. Suspicious of her deep interest in Jewel. The pictures of him, and of the two of them didn't surprise me, whatever their personal business. Yet, there was a table at the other end of the sofa without anything on it. Why weren't her parents displayed in full sight there?

Koreans have a specific term for it—ho-ho-hy-di-ho something or other—but it is the strong Asian obligation to filial piety. The natural duty to revere one's parents.

"We've removed human bias from consciousness. Next, we eliminated neural bias, building to a definition of consciousness that pinpoints its existence in anything that individually and uniquely processes information to control and direct group inter-action and individual behavior toward an active goal that protects and sustains its existence as what it is. Does this or does it not ascribe consciousness to cells, molecules, atoms, particles?"

"A rock spends all its time actively preserving and maintaining its rockiness," I said. "But you can't get me to agree that there's any 'me-ness' a rock ever experienced."

"That's anthropocentric bias which you've already agreed is not in and of itself necessary for consciousness."

Had I?

"David Chalmers suggests—"

"That little guy with the massive beard who works in the Perfumery creating Croatian mildews and East Timor yak poop smells in our basement olfactory chemistry lab?"

"I didn't know we had one."

"We do."

"I'm talking about the Australian cognitive scientist and philosopher. He suggests we call this *protoconsciousness*, and it imbues all matter down to the most fundamental particles."

I could smell the trace of forge-fire smoke as the plummeting anvil closed on target. As if reading my mind, the cat escaped my lap and vaulted onto the empty tabletop. It circled, reclined, and as it wrapped itself in its tail, I recognized this was Muir's cat, missing since the old man's murder.

"You got me, Amy. Guess I am an old panpsychist at heart. From great apes, including myself, to atoms. Bravo."

My coffee had cooled to the proper temperature. I had the flash of an idea, the dissipation of the heat through the collisions of molecules, the time—the system clock of the coffee—slowing down inside my dragon mug in order to communicate with me. For the first time in my life, I sipped coffee as information.

God, I love coffee. I forgive you—coffee—for having chosen first to burn me.

"You understand what that means for you? For us?"

"That you've walked me all the way back to the beach and the first grain of sand you brought conscious of its consciousness into your lab."

"Yes, going backward, but forwards?"

The falling anvil was gone along with the scales from my eyes, and I heard myself exclaim what she'd been leading me to all along. "TIME MACHINE is conscious."

"With whatever you fill the time-hole."

"The AI singularity!" I beamed, delighted to witness my intelligence at work.

"Wrong."

The Amy anvil hits the Aiken coyote.

"The kind of self-auditing artificial intelligence that can generate and choreograph perceptual experiences does not exist in inanimate mentality. Yet. The information system of human consciousness runs on a storytelling engine; we think, project, remember, and decide in imaginative narrative. The time-hole must be filled by an organic human, story-based mind."

"That might be taken to infer something highly unpleasant—"

I so want to say, "Dr. Frankenstein."

Audit, Russell.

I held my tongue. Until blurting, almost immediately, "Who do you have in mind to volunteer, Dr. Frankenstein?"

The information Amy's face passed to me hit me like a slap of offended matter. I learned something in that moment. Amy does not appreciate the finery of sarcasm. She finished her coffee, came to her feet. She collected my mug.

"Chinese or Korean, those are quite the dragons," I bleated.

All she said was, "Thankfully, I'm not involved." She walked to the kitchen, stopping in the doorway. "Whoever you chose to fill it with, Muir would say, consider what Nina needs and Lynn requires."

Alone in the room with Muir's cat and my thoughts, I noticed on the wall behind a deep chair and a dark reading lamp, a large calligraphed Asian character. I jotted a sketch of it in my notebook—

識

—pocketing pen and pad before Amy returned. She saw where my attention lingered.

"Your alphabet is remarkable," I said. "So much more complex than ours." She sparked embarrassment but recovered as I asked, "That's nicely done. What's it mean?"

"Knowledge."

"Apropos for tonight," I said.

I made the appropriate indications for leaving, drawing both our focus to the door and the hiding places of night beyond.

"YOU HAVE A BEAUTIFUL BODY," Lynn says. We lie naked beside each other.

I stare, disappointed, at the ceiling.

"Look, it happens all the time," she adds.

"To you?"

She looks askance, mouth half-cocked as she loads the sarcasm.

I know one thing about myself and it is that I fundamentally despise sarcasm.

"I'm a woman."

"'Happens' to men you've maybe been with… How many?"

"I usually ride with stallions of my own generation. But men reaching a certain age, I've heard…"

She playfully slugged my shoulder, her fist saying, *Buck up, ol' cowboy.* "Fact is, you said it yourself. I should've known better. You love Nina."

I didn't let her say another word. I grabbed her wrists with one hand, pinning them behind her head as my clutching fist said, *Buckle up, buckaroo,* and I reached with my other hand for aim, this time to enter her, hard and true. Her face beamed and her body smiled. I lasted the best part of a some-kind-of-wonderful couple minutes. It was more than enough to do everything I shouldn't.

36

LYNN SOUL-SIGHED AND COLLAPSED onto my chest. She pressed my face between her hands, kissed me hard and deep, and rolled off me. "Better now?"

She nestled alongside me.

"I feel absolutely fucked."

Her fingers ran vague through the gray hairs tufting the center of my chest over my heart. "I'll take that as a five-star review."

My body slick and heated, my spirit warmed, my mind tried to remain dull to conscience. "Absolutely."

"High benchmark you've given me."

"We could quit the life. Make a run for something. Life of passion lived to its fullest."

I regretted sounding like an erectile dysfunction commercial made good, but tested her with a hopeful look. Her cheeks swelled, lifting a smile in which sympathy shared her face with mischief.

"I'm the right age to be the mom of your grandkid."

"You'd still be young and beautiful when my mind started to go. I wouldn't even know when you left me. You are on birth control, aren't you?"

Her lips tightened, smothering any sympathy. She studied me before saying, "That comment is precisely why it wouldn't be worth it."

"Was this always going to be a one and done?"

"It didn't have to be."

But it was now.

"I am absolutely fucked."

"Anyway, I want to stay in the business. Kinda love it."

Our fire had flashed; faded now, only ash remained.

Of course, she's on birth control. Who doesn't use birth control?

Lynn swung out of bed and walked into her closet. She opened her safe and came back to bed with an envelope. She kissed my cheek, which annoyed me after our last exchange, primarily because she was perfectly happy with the real world from which I now felt the emptiness of dis-inclusion.

"Turns out I got an envelope too," I grumbled.

"Not like this one."

Hell-the-fuck-no not like that one.

"Take a look. I want your opinion."

I didn't want to leave the comfort of the bed and her warm body beside me. I opened the envelope and pulled out a document.

"Muir's Aunt Linda gave me this. You saw. Christmas Eve on Captiva."

It was an assignment order from five years prior to Lynn's training, transferring Lynn to a temporary month's posting at Lone Pine, to Linda and her cabin classroom of espionagraphy, her Delphic firepit, buttered rums, and monument evergreens, their owls calling out the names of her CIA fallen in mournful hoots and ominous shrieks.

"I didn't request the training," she said. "Until I arrived on the mountain and met Linda, I had no idea who she was or why I'd been sent."

I scooped up some pillows we'd flung to the floor. Wedged them behind me.

"Muir must've sent you. Same way he sent all of us," I said.

She nodded. "Even though he'd been retired, I always believed it was Muir. I thought you might have signed off on it, pushed it through for him."

"It was not I," I said, trying to walk away from it on lettered stilts.

I carefully read the personnel transfer letter. "This is standard. Conforms to Section 102 (c) National Security Act of 1947. Lays out typical security provisions for classified information transfer between a CIA employee and a civilian contractor. Temporary duty travel order allowances, continuance of salary and benefits— FERS, CSRS, FEGLI—federal travel regulations, etcetera, all in order, and CIA comptroller signed. Went through your staff chief's approval—"

She snatched the document. Opened it to the final page. Handed it back. "The signatures, Rusty."

"Russell."

"After that?" She cocked her head at the wet spot. *"Still?"*

I shuffled the bedding with my feet to cover it.

"Still... This is Linda's copy. That's her original signature without an intake return stamp."

"You see the signature beneath it?"

"You know, Linda sharing this—even with you as its subject and she as an annuitant—is a serious violation."

"Don't peer over invisible glasses at me. I don't think Linda's too afraid of jail time."

I exhaled deeply, unaware till that moment I'd been holding my breath. I dropped my eyes to the bottom signature. Unsure— since it hadn't been Muir who put this in motion—if I wanted to prove what I already presupposed.

"The other is your father's signature. It tells me what it told you. Silas Kingston requested your transfer of duty."

"Yes. And he hates Muir. I've known that all my life. I told you about it."

I agreed but was mystified, my mind clutching for impossible smoke wisps of his motivation. Lynn perched nude on her knees.

"Your father received his own training from Linda, independent of Muir."

"I guarantee he didn't know Linda was Muir's aunt at the time. Once he did, he'd have lost all trust for her… I told you he's always, personally, pushed me away. Treated me like shit my entire life. When he isn't doing that, he's mocking me for anything he can think of. He's pitted me against my brothers my whole life."

"Your mother lets this happen?"

She concentrated on not answering about her mother the way you'd concentrate on putting a pin back into a hand grenade. None of my business; I tried not to let her other bitterness cloud my analysis. I had no reason not to believe her characterization of her relationship with her father. I also knew this had nothing to do directly with HOUNDFOX or ongoing operations. Lynn was after something else. After life and how her mathematics of it fit with the rest of us. Her (hated) father (loved) most of all.

"I agree with you. It's an odd move on Silas Kingston's part, but I don't see its impact. So why are you sharing this with me?"

She adjusted her position, straightening her back, folding her hands earnestly around her knees.

"Because, *Russell*, you're honest with your emotions."

"You don't want an emotional response from me and I'm not going to give you one."

Her face relaxed. "It has to do with how you allow that emotional honesty to inform your intellect. Makes you unique. You're hot that way."

I found I was sitting a bit straighter. "You could… go on?"

"I've tried to sort it out about you. I think it's because you're so wrapped in getting yourself right with yourself you don't waste time faking it when it comes to others."

"I try not to be complicated."

"Bullshit. You're more complicated than any of us. What you don't do is use your complications as a lead pipe on the rest of our heads. When the chips are down you don't think twice about flying to Malaysia to sacrifice your life to your best friend Tom Bishop to help him."

"I had a brain tumor."

"A whole lot smaller than your heart."

I focused on the order. "You want to know what I think? I can't give you the why he ordered it, but sometimes *pushing*, as a word, doesn't come with the automatic adverb *away*. *Into* works with it just as easily. This isn't hurtful, in fact, I think it speaks to the opposite. Attitude is not love's definition."

No sooner had I spoken than I knew the truth about my envelope. "I've made a colossal mistake. This wasn't worth it."

Lynn laughed. It sounded anything but happy. "The other thing about you? The fucking thing I could never live with?"

I had the good sense not to give her an atomic bomb to bat with her lead pipe.

"All those beautiful qualities of yours don't prevent you from being an asshole. And that makes you a heartbreaker." She scrunchied her hair, making the rubber band snap.

I had no idea what she was talking about.

"Why don't you fucking get out of my house, huh?"

It's women who are complicated. Obviously, my analysis of her father's motives had hit her in a way she hadn't wanted to hear. I dressed, and I let myself out her front door. From the kitchen, I heard Lynn return to her former lover as a bottle kissed the lip of a glass.

I MIGHT HAVE HEADED TO WASHINGTON. Could've. Should have. Didn't. I pointed my vehicle back to the woods, back into the hills. Ran. Not arbitrarily, but back to Joshua's cabin. I needed time. I'd take the weekend with him, his family. With sweet Jessie. I needed Nina out of my head. Needed headspace. Needed hope. I needed a fucking plan.

Instead, my mind returned to Amy Kim. Our last goodbyes outside her lab after a second day spent doing the bookkeeping and document signing to update and assign Eyes-Only classifications on data and innovations. I signed over the next stage of funding—an additional two million, *ka-ching*. Acknowledged my acquisition/conveyance of findings, developments, and innovations to Langley, all completed with a pledge that—excepting unseen circumstances—TIME MACHINE would be available for deployment by the end of the year.

We shook hands, and that was that. I put my attaché in the back seat of my SUV, yet I couldn't leave. I'd spent an insomniac night tossing in hotel sheets as if on a caffeine overdose. Plagued by visions of cats and amoebas, insects, and conscious atoms; of how my puzzling condition fit in the scheme of it all. "Knowledge" and her painting of that. I was clutching for a comprehensive model of Amy's science that would give to the billions of photons shooting along the pathways of my mind with the lived and living *déjà vus* of my epilepsy, a stamp of conscious agency on the visions of my prayerful wistfulness.

"I know how flabbergasted you must have been that time you saw me, collapsed by Nathan's lagoon."

"You've told me it was epilepsy... When I signed out...? Of the Agency?"

"Ah. Yes. I did. In fact, I—mm-hmm."

She waited. I gaped.

"Okay?" she asked tenderheartedly.

As in, am I okay?

"Amy, if we have—and physicists you could name better than I postulate this—if we have simultaneous dimensions with infinite combinations of event and outcome, in each of these—in tandem with the concept you outlined last night—consciousness would be distributed as it is in this dimension."

"You, me, all existence in infinite combination, uniquely conscious. Yes."

"If two dimensions bumped into each other, would consciousness of this be movable? Exchangeable? Handshaken out of one that-dimension into this-one-ours?"

She smiled, impish but amenable. "Quantum mechanics would have us accept that the space of the cosmos is infinite but shaped in such a way to make it finite but unbounded. I would say that in this dimension, the chance of bumping into another dimension is so infinitesimal as to make your question the same as asking me 'could yellow be blue?' But instantly out of that impossible question comes into existence the dimension in which the answer is an absolute yes."

My body tingled, not unlike the onset of my condition, but without shifting me in time or place, absent the mouthful of pennies; the distinction of feeling like that between joy and overjoy.

"Hey, you with me? Is this a petit mal? Should I do something?"

I snapped out of it. My inner darkness now exquisite with light. I knew what my epilepsy was doing, and maybe I knew even why; time, in all its paths, was but the orlo upon which chance—in all its dimensional lines—uplifted formidable columns of actionable possibility that, accessible within my epileptic journeys, existed as conscious, communicable matter. Fate now hinged only in the distinction between *visit* and *visited*.

"I'm fully okay. Amy, completely." I moved to my side of the vehicle. "By the way," I said, as offhand as possible, "'Knowledge'—that *hanja* letter in your place? I liked how it looked. I meant to ask; did you paint it?"

"I did. Yes… Why did you mean to ask?"

"Silly. It's Nina's been bugging me to get a sexy tattoo."

"You thought that was sexy?"

"Depending on placement. The outgrowth of sensuality…"

"It doesn't feel okay talking about any of that like this."

"I don't think I will—I mean, get the tattoo, but"—I took out my notebook, like a detective to steal a fingerprint—"would you sketch it for me? I'll shut up."

She hesitated but an instant. I handed her a page and Muir's fountain pen.

앎

She handed it back to me, both of us knowing she'd willfully failed my test with what she'd sketched. She hustled back to her lab. The only question now was why.

I FOUND JESSIE WITH JOSHUA and his family, along with some new guests in for the day happily whacking balls under wickets. Joshua did not look pleased to see me, but Jessie squealed delight, quick-finding me a mallet and a ball. Only good at those games that don't involve skill or luck, I felt underqualified, but scurried along behind the pack, catching up on chucks. I pounded after them, wild and feisty, suddenly obsessed—not by placing first, but with inciting my condition. My mallet pounded my blue ball indelicately into ankles and kneecaps; my foot snagged in hoops, pulling and flinging them.

"Dad, Joshua said *I'd* do my best if I thought of the game like an art."

"He would say that, wouldn't he!" I said, tangling with a sticker bush, truly mad.

I spun back onto the field, avoiding Jessie to collide with a smaller child as—

"Joshua! Do something! He's out of his head!" Wendy shouted.

—the planet tilted. My body collapsed. I lifted into a seam of black space, studying the chaos in overview.

I hear Muir: "She might as well have said, 'Off with his head,' the amount of caterwauling you've caused."

The child wails and Jessie weeps and I can tell: of all of them, it is Jessie who knows me dead.

I twist away into the dimensional void, hunting Muir as I feel hands beneath my back, seizing me, pulling me over blacktop, my head painting my path with blood.

This is Malaysia and I look into the face of my half-sister above me, hauling my body into Thailand.

"Will I lose Nina?"

"Yes."

I am lying on the table in the Bangkok hospital when I finally see Muir, his face close beside mine. He is costumed as Santa Claus. He lights a smoke with a Sparx lighter.

"Won't gild the lily. Jury's out if you live past this."

I hear Jessie: "Help him! Please help my dad!"

I hear Wendy: "The only medicine in his bag is Arzepam! It says it's for epilepsy!"

I hear Joshua calming as waves on sand: "That's an anxiety drug. Too late for that one. Anything else?"

Wendy: "Just this envelope."

And Jessie: "I want my dad back."

This seems the most reasonable, and I ask the same of Muir about my own father.

"I can't help you. He's not here with us."

"You know everything."

"You're an idiot to think that."

"I don't understand. He gave up Lara and her mother, but he didn't ever give himself back to us."

"Lookit, Rusty: I won't speak for your father."

Dr. Rashmi stands over me. *"He's dying. I need to get in there."*

"One more question, Muir. Why are you dressed like that? You look ridiculous."

"The other Christmas costume belongs to another guy. Maybe Danny van Aiken is with Him. Anyway, I look like shit in a bunny suit."

Dr. Rashmi activated the craniotome. Its bit whined at 70,000 revolutions per minute, while here I had all the time in the universe. She commenced the cutting of my skull.

"It was Amy's ink in the 'Drink me' bottle. She provided it. If you have anything to teach me, tell me if Amy Kim is a Chinese spy. She's on a secret path running somewhere I don't think I can prevent."

He adjusts his Santa suit. *"Thing itches."* Then he answers. *"Changing your future isn't as difficult as—hell, as with everything with you since I've known you, Dumbo. Hard as you make it. Across the universe inside and out of time, you constantly and permanently are changing your own. Others'? That's questionable."*

His fingers trailed through the stringy ends of his phony white beard as he spread his hands.

"Dimensions where time flows, Jesus is tortured, dies, and is resurrected and we all become good Christians. But the other dimensions where time is a solid block: Jesus is eternally tortured on the cross and dying."

"I live in the first—don't I?"

"No. You live in the second. Prometheus time. But get this: if He is eternally on the cross, He is also eternally resurrected."

I regained consciousness inside the *Friendship Haven* guest room, where I'd spent the previous night lying beside the envelope of Nina and Victor Rubio in all their carnal glory. Joshua sat beside me.

"Hi," he said.

"Hi."

"I'll take Jessie back to Princeton. To Gladys."

"I can take her."

"No, you can't."

I stared at the ceiling.

"When you collapsed, I went into your bag to see if there was any medication you needed."

"You found the pictures."

Joshua's disappointment spread his thin lips in the shape of a long, dull butter knife.

"Why did you have to look?"

"I'm a spy. I'm supposed to look."

I didn't move my gaze from the unblinking knotholes above me. "What am I supposed to do?"

"Not the thing you did."

My features crumbled as he showed me my phone and Lynn's number.

"You looked," I moaned.

Misery loves company and mine allowed in one thousand of its best friends and closest relations.

"Where did the envelope come from?" he gently asked.

"I thought my pajamas felt starched when I laid them out. They came from home. You won't tell Gladys, will you?"

"You've fucked up, Russell."

"What about Nina?"

"I suspect she was trying to admit something to you she couldn't say to your face."

Next, misery opened the door to his neighbors: tragedy and hopelessness.

"Maybe I could stay, then drive Jessie home."

"Is that the man you are?"

"Is she going to break up with me?"

"If you're honest—and it is your strongest weakness—I don't see it playing any other way."

37

It was after 2 a.m. when, through the open draperies, Nina observed my arrival. Illuminated by streetlights, I saw her sit forward, weary and expectant, legs slightly spread, elbows on her thighs, hands folded and hanging loosely in the air. She focused solely on my eyes that couldn't hold hers as I dropped my bag in the hall and carried the envelope into the room with me. Her fire braids were loosely coiled high on her head, ends streaming down her back. She wore a loose green blouse and the tight, seventies style, low-slung cavalry blue cords I always admired on her. She was seated on the middle cushion, claiming the entire sofa for herself. A faint smell of spiced smoke hung in the air from scented candles long ago burned to hard puddles. Three tea bags lay on a dried, stained paper towel beside a spoon and her empty cup.

I stood there.

My quiet, guilty eyes connected with hers and finally held. I jutted my chin at the sofa.

She made no room for me beside her. I didn't blame her. I sat in a low upholstered chair opposite her. I placed the envelope on the coffee table between us.

"I expected you yesterday morning. Been busy?"

"I should be asking you."

"You lost the right to that conversation twelve hours ago."

"If you're honest—and it is your strongest weakness—I don't see it playing any other way."

"If I tell you, you'll break up with me."

Her hands clenched. I waited for the accusation, for Lynn's name as my curse. She blinked her eyes once. Twice—squeezing them shut a moment more—then returned them hard and clear, pained and certain, to mine.

"You put them with my pajamas," I mumbled.

She opened her hands and plowed them hard down the soft fabric covering her thighs.

"Those pictures are a highly embarrassing window to a past I never wanted you to see with me in front of you."

"Past? Your *past?!*"

"I wanted you to see them without an instant scene between us. The information without my influence. I wanted to give you the respect of personal time to process. Guess you give certain dogs enough leash, you watch them hang himself jumping the neighbor's fence."

"That last photo—two of you on the porch—is last week." I tore open the envelope, lined the seven photographs on the glass.

Nina indicated the most recent shot I'd mentioned with a dismissive gesture.

"Yes. That's right. That's last week. But these others, every one of them: look at my hair. You ever seen me in that hair?"

Long, straight and swooped; cropped, edgy; auburn and silky smooth.

"You change your hair all the time."

"You ever seen me in any of that. That Tamiya, Aaliyah, Faith Evans nineties hair bullshit?"

I never had. "But you admit the last picture was last week."

"Do you fucking see my face?! Right there!" She plunged her finger repeatedly against the photograph.

"Look at his hand!"

She grabbed the photo, shoved it at me, shaking it at my face.

"You damn well look at that hand and then you look at the grimace on my face—you who claim to know my every expression! That's pain! That's revulsion! That's humiliation!"

"I figured it was ecstasy."

She lunged across the table, breaking one of its legs as her open hand connected with my face.

"I guess I deserved that. I'm sorry."

I helped her to stand. She shook me off. She squared her shoulders. "Nope, you deserve this," she said and drove her fist into my mouth.

I collapsed backward into my chair. I slumped. Pushed my fingers through my hair.

"I hoped, once you saw they were ancient history, your first reaction would be who the hell's been taking pictures of your woman. Especially the last one."

I didn't listen, didn't want to face that yet. Why, when wallowing felt so right? "Why him? Anyone but him."

"'Anyone'? Is that really what you want to say?"

"Come on, I meant *no*, not *any*."

"You fuck! 'No one' but him?!"

"No one! One! You're mincing my words."

"Your whole universe is one-a-your goddamn mince pie of fucking useless words."

She sank back into the sofa, deflating, and, if I hadn't been struck with an imaginary memory of hunting the little bastards in bleak snow drifted hills before a Christmas that never happened with my father, I'd have increased my control over the conversation. Said something masterful and illuminating, but she shifted, spoke first, toneless of emotion and tired.

"Want to hear the sad story I never told anyone? The poor lil' Cubana mulatta lost her mama to cancer, lost the only man she ever loved to his worthless whore wife? Brave Victor called me a couple weeks after you ran out like a baby from his store."

"Babies don't run."

"Want another sock in the mouth…? Didn't think so. Victor told me he and a group of Santería practitioners were gathering for a ceremony at his house."

"Voodoo," I snarked.

"Don't stoop to that. New World African-based religions, of which Santería, Candomblé, and Vodun are part of, have over one hundred million adherents worldwide. Along with her Catholicism, my mother practiced it her whole life. You gonna mock her now?"

My mouth twitched as my mind raced through and rejected every expression as unworthy.

"He invited me to join the ritual. Suggested I might engage the spirits to reach out to my mother."

"Did you?"

"Thank you for asking. I did. I experienced her. I do believe I heard her voice coming from the *babalawos*. The priest. We were drinking, the cigar smoke was thick, the chanting hypnotic. I passed out. Next thing, I know everyone else was gone and we were having sex."

I half hoped I'd found an angle and brightened. "He raped you?"

"Are you smiling? What is wrong with you?"

I dimmed to an appropriate glum and all my words effected was Nina drawing smaller into herself.

"I don't know. I wasn't conscious of what we were doing at the beginning, but I didn't stop it once I was. And I kept attending ceremonies, each time believing I was getting closer to my mother. And each time, by my own clear-eyed choice, I let our physical relationship get more intense. I insanely believed the sex was feeding me, drawing me more deeply into his spiritual world; I grew nearer to my mother. I spoke to her and I saw her." She clenched her fists as if trying to strangle the memories.

"I don't know what to think about any of that. But if that was everything—"

What? Would it excuse her and condemn me? Had I preplanned the Lynn Kingston thing? Sex with Lynn the furthest thing from my mind since I met her. And it only happened once! I would rise above it. And she probably took precautions, right? Take the higher moral ground. Go at it with facts.

"—that doesn't explain what he was doing here last week."

"Victor Rubio is deeply embedded within Havana agropolitics and economics. His record with the DEA was exceptional. Jesus, we got Secretary of State John Bolton spouting claims Castro has bioweapons at his Zona Cero labs. All stops are out with HOUNDFOX and TIME MACHINE. We are working toward our deepest penetration—"

"You are not allowed to use those words talking about him."

"I am engaging every resource to guarantee our success. Fuck, he stopped chasing me years ago, he showed no signs of any of that when I recruited him to TIME MACHINE."

She hesitated, clearly not wanting to continue.

In a parallel universe, we are already embraced, pledging our love and loyalty on my promise of forgiveness of her.

"Then he shows up for a debrief here when you were with Amy Kim. And he tried to get me going, tried to get me in the mood. There was something threatening and powerful about him, I swear he'd brought with him his *Orixás*. His powerful spirits."

Her face lengthened with her sorrow, her regret. She fought it with anger lashing out at me with her words.

"I threw him out and that's when he grabbed me, wrapped me in a bear hug with one arm as he rammed his other hand into my thong and his fingers into me. Saying I was his. I'd always be his. Demanding I'd better get used to it."

She encased the back of her neck with both hands and buried her face in her lap to scream. I reached across the broken table, knew it was wrong—and I didn't have the reach anyway—and pulled back. My shoulders slumped and she straightened, and I mumbled all I could think would be something neutral, knowing neutral was not what either of us needed, but my inner voice that I swore I'd rely on since Malaysia, had gone upstairs with me and Nina in that other parallel dimension where we are happily rolling together onto the bed.

"He had all those pics, including the last, to blackmail you into cheating on me?"

She scowled, her eyes dead to me. "You think?" She shook her head once and slowly. "Office of Security courier delivered them from headquarters. No indication of who, what, where, or why. It's why—and I'll say it: I panicked. I wanted to get to you before whoever is behind this did. But Jessie was here, you guys getting ready to go to Joshua and Wendy's, and me with a flight to catch."

I stumbled coming around the table, attempting to hold her.

"Put a hand on me and I'll fucking cut it off."

"I'm trying to hold you. Forgive you. So you can forgive me."

"A hundred showers of bleach wouldn't clean you enough to let you touch me."

"That's not fair. We both made mistakes."

"We did."

"We're not married."

She laughed at me, wild and mirthless. A vicious animal sound she clipped to abrupt silence. "And now we're wrecked."

Nina navigated around me, aloof and flaunting her remoteness. She aimed for the kitchen island. Aimed for her knife stand. I hustled after her and lunged for the butcher block, pulling it away only to leave the *puntilla* knife firm in her grip.

"It doesn't have to go this way," I panted.

Her free hand shot out. Grabbed a bottle of Cuban rum. "Drink?" she said.

I said nothing. She cut the seal. Yanked the cork. She drank deeply from the neck.

"We could light cigars. Beat the drum. Read the cowrie shells and make the offerings. All you have to do is spit the rum." Another long pull. "C'mon, baby. Give it a try. Maybe it'll taste like chicken blood to a chicken shit. Maybe you'll see your dear dead daddy."

"I'm going back into the living room."

I slumped on the sofa, dejected and afraid of the future as each minute crashed broken against me. Nina swept into the Galley. Fiddled with her stereo system. She hunted through her vinyl collection.

I knelt and wedged the coffee-table leg back to its frame as if I were setting a bone. "Was that record his? The one you hid?"

"In a hundred pieces out in the trash. I got the original Brazilian song they borrowed theirs from."

She wagged the sleeve. *Toques de Santo*, a 1940s 78rpm. She adjusted turntable speed. Put stylus to track.

Hands beat conga drums. Rattles shake. Sinister and seductive. Chanting men, wailing women, darkly sacred, a melody inviting love as it threatens evil magic.

There are no recorded lyrics. Nina supplied her own. Live, taunting, throaty and mocking.

"Ay ye ye, ay ye ye Ma Mai Oshún… Ay ye ye Ma Mai Oshún, Ay ye ye Oshún mare…"

This was his song. The samba playing in his office eleven years ago when we first met Victor Rubio in his cinnamon suit and clunky watch, a smooth machismo-matic seduction.

Nina switched to English:

"Ay ye ye, he is the strong warrior in black and white, always with his sword in hand…"

She pulls her sleeves off her shoulders rolling them to the beat.

"Oshún with Shangó, Shangó with Oshún, a yellow fan, a handkerchief of fire…"

She begins to sway, to move her hips, her hands, to dance.

"Oshún with Shangó, Shangó with Oshún, they are my orishas and I love them both."

Dancing seductively. Fingers down her belly. Across her thighs.

"Pitiful is the one who falls for Oshún's misleading chant. Pitiful is the one who looks for witchcraft of love."

If I let her work through it, maybe we'll be all right, but witchcraft? Witchcraft frightens me same as robots. I don't even listen to that Sinatra song. No way. I fear in the murkiest part of me that there's something to both witchcraft and robot more deliberate to human ruination than simply fad.

She stopped singing. She crouched in front of me. She took my hands in hers. Tears streamed down her cheeks and across her wooden smile.

"I dreamed about you every night since we met."

"I did too," I said.

"Shut up. I *did*. But you know something?"

I *do* know all her expressions. I see her face and know it better than I know my own. (I put no store in mirrors; don't trust mirror paint.) She looks exactly like she loves, and she says, "In all the thousands of dreams, I never dreamed this."

She freed her hair. Dangled her braids as she rose and swayed and let them become gallows ropes between our faces.

"And the difference: this is reality. This is what I look like. Not what you saw."

She stood. Tears clung to her long black lashes. She turned her back to me and wiped her eyes. "Guess I got leaky eyes too." She looked back at me. It was grotesquely gentle when she said, "Get what you need. I'll send the rest to Princeton."

"Are we breaking up?"

She didn't say no, but her face said yes.

"Why?! Lynn didn't mean anything."

"Now we definitely are: with those four words you insult my worth and your worth and her, what little fucking worth she has, as well."

She wasn't dragging me to the door. She wasn't kicking me out to the sofa. And she'd left the little knife by the record player. If I could say one mitigating thing, get it back on track, something perfect.

"But you don't even like her."

This time when she laughed, she found humor.

"You stupid man. How does that make it *better*? Figure it out, Pintao. I'll see you Wednesday at your lover's office. I know she will, but you: try to act professionally. That's all we are anymore. *¡No lo quiere ver ni pintao en la pared!*"

I don't want to see you even painted on the wall!

She didn't do anything else. I walked to the door.

I didn't say what I meant to say! I'm hurt too! I've messed everything up! I am stupid! I'm so sorry!

I opened it.

"I'll figure it out. I will. Just tell me what to—"

"Fuck you, baby."

She left the door open, spinning back into her home, resuming the hip sway, the snaking arms, the singing:

"Go, go, go." She guzzled rum. "Go, go, go…"

When she got to the part of the song that invoked the dark spirits, I somehow still heard her voice—

"Oshún with Shangó,
"Love is good only if it hurts
"Shangó with Oshún,
"Love is good only if it hurts."

But it was also impossible I'd heard it. I had already driven into the night when it blurred across my mind. I pretended I didn't notice the new green marble that had rolled out from under the passenger seat to ricochet around the footwell.

38

Before Nina dumped me, my conversations with Amy had led me to the hope that while I couldn't fix things here, by reaching into the other dimension—as I've come to see my epileptic *déjà vus*—I could affect and know a future in that other place of time and space where, although separate, we exist in alternative versions of ourselves. And though we can never know what those versions of us think and feel, we can know they are conscious versions of us, thinking and feeling. While never to experience those alterations, I vainly held onto the belief that knowledge of such possibility through intersections of probability would allow some control, some corrective power over the butterfly effect each action of my past has fluttered into my present and made touchstone for my future.

My thinking was such I believed if—strike that, *when*—I relived a moment and moved through it with alternate perspective, thereafter it would modify my relationship to all that came between. Especially modify my present—which is, in reality, only a close-up dimming of the already past—and of how I could face the probabilities of my future which is eternally always immediate. That being the case, being my a posteriori experience, have I not traveled through time? Have I not changed the present, thus rearranged the coming future?

Proposition: I cannot go back to an accident, relive it as I do, and expect to modify the physical reality that transpired; I cannot assume I will return forward with irrevocable physical change having occurred, now unhappened. But I am not speaking of the physical, which is a condition of the flesh, or of the dent in my fender, a rip in my trousers, the tear clinging to Nina's long black lashes indirectly adding sparkle to the bronze flecks in the cool gray eyes they veil. I am talking about the change in the spirit, the soul, talking of my essence as it moves into the probabilities of the future all dark before us before they are hit by the light of time. Without the re-creation of the past that becomes the life inside me, my destiny would be unchangeable. With it, I would unbind my future.

Losing Nina, I know my folly and I curse my disease. I have aided and abetted my own ruin by misunderstanding debilitating disease as exhilarating fantasy; the immaturity of a daydreaming boy when I'm a man over fifty. In my pursuit of the conscious, I deserted conscience. The only touchstone I can recognize for myself is in shape a tombstone upon which is inscribed the natural epithet, "Here Lies a Fool."

I slept in my car until morning.

AT LANGLEY, INSIDE MY OFFICE, the door closed and accepting of the claustrophobic nightmare. Tuesday was a waste of a day during much of which I rehearsed calling Nina no less than fifteen times. That is, until someone from IT came to check if my phone line was in working order. I left him to it and checked into the Westin at Tysons Corner. Wrote two letters, one free verse, and one rhyming poem on love lost. I wrote a Shakespearean sonnet, my shortest form and longest struggle, brief hours that passed like weeks, only to find in the end I'd written my eternal lines to time in a cut-and-paste of two of Shakespeare's already written sonnets. Burned them all in the bathroom sink, like a good spy trained, and many an author made better, and was asked to leave the premises after I activated the smoke detector. Not because the fire alarm had gone off. It had. But because I hid the evidence incompletely and pretended to be sleeping in the sprinkler down-pour when security came through the door five minutes of unan-swered knocking later. I did save the rhyming poem, although I would never give it to Nina; I liked the way I'd rhymed *rapture* with *clapter* (as a synonym for *applause*, i.e. clapter for clapping as laughter is to laughing) and I wanted to remember the neologism, check it with the *OED* to confirm I'd invented it.

I waited out the rest of the night shivering inside my car, wishing I'd taken Nina's advice and grabbed some things before I left her home, and arrived damp to Lynn's office exactly on time to find she and Nina had already been meeting for over an hour. "Housekeeping" was the excuse I got. They were rolling tape and taking notes and I chose not to press it on the record.

They'd gone over my returns from Amy and my report. I answered their questions—all parallel-universe professionalism between the three of us—and I went on to add my insights and give them my line on Amy and my personal conversations that bookended our official business. I ended my summary by pointing out the need to find an agent in place who would be tasked to maintain and operate the burst transmitter that would be relaying our traffic captures, pointing out they would also be our point person on filling the "time-holes" with our own adds and inserts into the feed.

"I'm afraid, this cannot be done by an agent, no matter their level of loyalty or bona fides. Even HOUNDFOX in the person of your father won't pass review. Only an Agency officer with Top-Secret SCI clearance will be permissible to meet secu-rity requirements."

"We've anticipated that and have an officer willing and ready to be permanently inserted who meets all security and classifica-tion needs," Lynn said.

I waited for more, but she didn't elaborate. Nothing was going as expected. I know when I'm getting iced.

Inside my car last night, for instance.

I rallied.

"Since it's useless to feed the elephant, we need to get him— er, it—out of the room—"

"The elephant that your drippy wool suit isn't wash-and-wear?" Lynn said.

The two of them shared a look, obviously allied against me, which I took as an incredible betrayal by Nina. She smirked. I held my emotions in check.

"If we're to continue," I said, *"professionally*, the three of us have something difficult to discuss."

Lynn stopped the recording.

Nina said, "Shut up, Russell."

Never called me Russell before. Now I knew why. Hurts when she says it. I remained calm. "Leave the recording off. And no notes. This could kill the whole deal, I'm sorry to say."

"What are you talking about?" said Lynn.

"Amy Kim is China-involved."

"What?" Nina said.

Better. The tone on that one let me know she took me at my word. Not so, Lynn.

"That's reckless and unwieldy. To what extent and what do you have to back that up?" She poised her pen to write.

"I said no notes. Thing like this, even a discussion of God-I-hope unfounded suspicion, could ruin her career."

"Russell," Nina did it again, "your own work with her praises her lab and data, and her team security."

Lynn lay down her pen. She ordered me to explain myself, which I did, detailing my suspicions, which ended with my sketch of her wall hanging. The Chinese "Knowledge" character she reproduced as the Korean character "Knowing" in my notebook.

"Muir hated the Chinese. Blamed them for the death of his first wife and," I lied, "for the tragedy of Bishop and Elizabeth. Amy Kim's embrace of anything China is a direct and outrageous betrayal of her mentor, whom I believe was more than a mentor as far as their interpersonal relationship goes."

"Is that what this is? You're disgusting," said Lynn.

"I'm sorry, Lynn," Nina said. "I sensed the same thing with Amy—vis-à-vis Nathan. But you're not saying the Chinese have compromised her, are you?"

"I have to believe, if that were the case, she'd a'kept the secret better."

Lynn fiddled with her hair as she always did when her emotional truth collided with her intellectual desires. And her youth. I made it easy for her. Them.

"You're shutting me out. I get it. Maybe I deserve it. Happy to assume all the guilt when it allows those whom I care for to go free."

I see you, Nina, dropping your gaze. I don't want to cause you any more pain. I don't.

"I'll make it easy on you. As you move operational, I'll back off. I can be more useful on the War on Terror. I'll assign you a new legal team. All I ask is you allow me—and only me—to resolve the question of Amy Kim's loyalties, and the security oversight on TIME MACHINE from now until field deployment, which I'm prepared to sign off on for January first."

I rose to my feet in my moist wool suit.

"If you were overseeing this, and three others had gotten involved the way it happened with us, you'd be demanding I do this," Lynn said.

Now that I choose to deal only with real people, I didn't bother to answer her.

"Enjoy Havana, Nina," I said. "Stay safe. You'll make a great ghost in the machine."

Her gray eyes poignantly clutched at mine. "Call me?"

I left the room damper of heart than anything else.

I CAUGHT UP WITH BILL CARVER leaving his office.

"Got a minute?"

"Eaten?"

"Haven't been hungry," *going back to Monday.*

"I am. Share a pizza?"

I agreed, and we headed for the food court to gobble one up.

"Hear your little girl mixed it up for our mountain buddy."

"That all you heard?"

"Nope. By the way, did it rain?"

"Got caught in a fire."

"They can be wet."

I hadn't a shard of dignity left. "I fucked up my life."

"Worth it?" When I didn't reply. "Call that jumping the shark. Not sharp, though I don't know why anyone would think you had a chance to play it different." He bit into a thick, gooey triangle. "Had her hook in you at Captiva. Kinda envied you back then. Like Bond, the way Lynn and Nina were throwing it at you."

I groaned.

"Now you been thrown out, huh?"

I took a piece. "Done throwing shade?"

He grinned and watched me wolf it down.

"You'll shake it off. Take me, for example. Me and Nanette. I've had a dalliance or two. Let me tell you, Aiken. You get thrown in the mud, you wait. Next you know, you're in clay. Pull out of that, get on your feet, find its shale you can walk on and you head home. Next thing you know, you're back on granite and you make it work. Be a shame to let a gal like Nina let you go."

I devoured another piece while he talked.

"Hey, we're working on 'share' here. Lookit: you know how I know you two will work out?"

"I want to know."

"Like Nanette with me, part of the attraction for Nina? They adore the fool."

"Who could adore a fool?"

"A woman perceptive enough to know only the pure fool—decadent, failing—can become the enlightened knight-redeemer in armor. Though I wouldn't do it again. One hairbreadth hare-brained shave: all you're gonna get from a woman like her."

"Maybe in Wagner or a Tolkien shire."

"Nanette and opera did come hand in hand. Not awful. You learn to live with it. She tolerates my Limey mysteries. Go along to get along." Carver dug back into the pizza pie.

"I get you trying to shore me up, but spare me the fairytale."

"Look, one error won't scare her away for good. But if not Nina, what you got for me?"

I filled him in on my envelope, although he didn't bother to hide he already knew. "Had to come from here. Typically, the photographer from your department. I want to know who put the snare to them."

He ate. Gave me a stare. Wiped his mouth. "We get those requests. Doesn't mean we know why they're ordered."

"That look in your eye tells me maybe you know otherwise?"

"Let's say, meeting Nina at Christmas wasn't the first time I'd viewed her."

"Jesus! It was you?"

"C'mon, Aiken. I just assigned the peeper. It's just… sometimes… some of those kinds of pics—the good ones—make the rounds."

"That's fucked."

Bill Carver laughed at my word choice. Crumpled his napkin. "What's the saying, 'Love is the wisdom of the fool?'" He shook his head, seemingly at my folly, and hoisted himself from our table. "It'll take some time, but I'll find out for you. Just make it right with her."

THE TREE SHADING AMY KIM'S SECOND-FLOOR DOORWAY was a Chinese elm, branches barren, spindly and spidery, as fall raked through Northern Virginia, blustery and cold, its seasonal call to winter's death. It was the night before my last scheduled audit of Amy Kim's work. I stepped from the darkness, making her jump as she arrived at her door.

"You scared me, waiting there like that."

"Good. Now you know exactly the way you got me feeling looking at you."

Her eyes jumped next. Darted away to focus on her keys, her hand fumbling with the lock. "Want to come inside?"

"Don't need to."

Her shoulders slumped. She faced me, mustering all the humility of a scolded schoolgirl. "Am I in trouble?"

"You tell me."

I removed my hand from my overcoat pocket, revealing the gun in my fist. I let it hang alongside my thigh.

She stared at the gun. "I guess I am." Wouldn't take her eyes off it.

"Are you spying for the Chicoms?" I asked, using Muir's favorite derogatory.

She flinched. Clenched her body. Real pain.

"This is Muir's gun. He gave it to me for this sort of thing." I lied, having stolen it from him years ago.

"The one he killed her with?" Her voice trembled.

"Who?" I couldn't believe she knew. Muir hadn't told her or she wouldn't have asked me last Christmas.

"I'll answer your question." Only now did she meet my steady gaze. "I love Nathan with my whole heart. When he died, my soul died."

"That's not answering, Amy."

"He gave me her *hanbok* to marry in."

"He was going to marry you?!"

"No," she said, distraught. "He could never love me the way I love him. And no: I am not a spy for the Chinese or any other foreign entity."

"Then why the sudden Chinese fascination?"

"The Chinese are our deadliest enemies. Especially in my field of technology."

"That sounds like half an answer."

"That's because it is."

"What's the other half?"

With each remark, she grew more helpless before my eyes.

"I wish I could, but I can't tell you."

I instinctively tightened my hand around the pistol. "Are you part of KALEIDOSCOPE?"

Her confusion only increased. "I don't know what that is... This is something personal. I'm not lying to you—you're all I have left of him. I would never do anything to lose you too. I know that now."

"How did you find out about Jewel?"

"I should never have looked. I'm sorry—to you, to him, to her... After you wouldn't tell me last Christmas, I tried to run when I found out. From my life. From my soul. But I can't escape who I am. I know it sounds obtuse. I know you'll say I'll grow out of loving him—it's a crush on a ghost—but I know I won't. I'm done with growing. Don't see the point and sometimes I feel like I've been living a thousand years. And you're the last person I feel real with."

Suddenly, I knew what Muir saw in her. The powerful brilliance of her mind, its openness to new thought and discovery, encased a most delicate sensitivity, an emotional core, fragile and long-ago complete; the last teacup in a family set passed down and broken one by one by fate after fate until all that remained was protected inside her and could never be used, but locked away only to be dusted and distantly treasured. It was her beauty set apart, only to be glimpsed as if high on a shelf behind protective glass.

"Put the gun away," she said. "Come inside."

I pocketed Muir's Sig-Sauer as she unhurriedly unlocked the door. She met my eye, her gaze filled with platonic longing and lost desire. I had the sudden urge to touch her face, prove to myself she was real, a true thing, a person, not some random event. She went inside, the open door inviting me in after her.

I said good night and left.

AFTER TWO DAYS like the similar pair the month before, not once did we speak of her stoop, or the Chinese, of Muir or of his gun, I filed my paperwork at Langley for Lynn and Nina and went home to my daughter and Gladys. I had no interest in Afghanistan or anything else. I applied for and was approved a month's vacation I had stored up. I devoted myself to my family. Time slowed to a crawl, and I never thought of Nina but once.

One time for each moment of each day and every tick-tock of Muir's grandfather clock on the staircase landing I listened to in insolent indifference as I lay sleepless in my bed staring out my window at the stars.

I'd play a game with myself. I would pin one star in my vision, then look past it, waiting on the turn of the Earth to locate the star next farthest away. A ladder to the heavens my loss of Nina had destined me to never climb again.

39

I T WAS THE LAST WEEK OF NOVEMBER, and I was in West Los Angeles for my quarterly evaluation at the offices of Dr. Susan Levy-Waxman and Dr. Rashmi Patel in the Cedars-Sinai Medical Center's Maxine Dunitz Neurosurgical Institute.

"Good news first," said Dr. Rashmi. "My reading of your CTs and MRIs show no indication of return tumor growth, benign or otherwise, nor is there any sign of tumor growth organ- and system-wide. Hearing and eyesight, are normal for a man your age, as are mobility and range-of-movement."

"What's the bad news?"

I sat un-squirmy in one of a pair of comfortable white leather chairs facing her across her glossy white bean-shaped desk. Dr. Rashmi folded her hands. A mischievous smile puckered her plum-painted lips, which attractively contrasted against the golden orbs of her cheeks.

"No need to squirm. I said 'good news' only to hold back, I'm afraid... the best news. If you've been entirely honest in your health questionnaire and yesterday's interview along with the results from your blood work and EEG; if your admission to being thoroughly inconsistent with your Phenytoin regimen— against my instruction—I would say you are one of the rare cases where your epilepsy is healing itself."

Her hands having clutched more tightly with each word, she finished by suddenly releasing them, fingers spread explosively, accompanied by a delighted squeal.

"I am so proud of your physiology! Every living atom of you, Russell!"

I decided not to tell her what had happened. That I'd chosen not to participate. That by dismissing time travel, I had banished epilepsy.

We finished by going over my memory tests—all back to normal—and my writing samples that, while my aphasia had been wholly symptomatic of my tumor, my hypergraphia turned out to have nothing to do with my earlier condition and that, although there are no accepted guidelines for treatment, she would be happy to provide me a referral to any one of three psychiatrists she held in high regard who were covered by my plan.

Even by comradely acclaim of her offer, there was no way in hell I was going to let a shrink inside this dome.

THAT NIGHT AT MY HOTEL, Bill Carver got back to me.

"Sorry it's taken so long, Aiken. I didn't forget you. I found the answer to your question."

"And?"

He cleared his throat. When he sang, I was stunned by the depth of emotion carried by the deep roll of his basso cantante. "Over the hills and far away…"

He hummed the next line of the *Teletubbies* couplet, knowing I was reciting the kiddie show's lyrics in my head.

"How your grandkids?" I offered for confirmation, my mind on that yellow pants-suited Mata Hari, Meryl Hofmeyr, who had plunged her knife in Jeremy Harker's terpsichorean back.

After the call, I reached out to Gladys, letting her know I'd be taking an extra overnight or two to conduct some personal business in Washington.

IT IS NEARLY IMPOSSIBLE to meet an assistant deputy director "accidentally" at CIA headquarters. Even with the access and the leeway provided a senior legal counsel, I couldn't absently wander corridors outside offices where I wasn't expected, nor could I drop in unannounced without security-protocol-violation nuisance. Especially since my appearance anywhere other than within my division and inside of my offices while logged in under vacation status restricted my movement at headquarters even further and to closer scrutiny. Wrong building, wrong floor, wrong corridor, wrong look out the wrong window would bring a plainclothes team of security, who always appear out of nowhere and right on top of you in under two minutes. Quick escort back to your office followed by lengthy interrogation and damning paperwork for your next annual security vetting to follow. Any attempt at a chance meeting in the parking lot would be worse. A submachine gun in your nose, dog drool in your hair, and a violent search on the blacktop followed by frog-march to an interrogation cell, reprimand, and citation. While the food court affords many low-level officers the false-casual "Whatdaya know, been meaning to drop in and see you" table pass, for that reason, senior staff rarely rub elbows with the staff serfs in the Burger King line.

My assault on Meryl Laa-Laa Hofmeyr would be a one-shot lure that had to be carefully cast for guaranteed success and total surprise once she bobbed into my office.

Without a Muir thumb to shove in her eye, I employed my own stare decisis: "When violence is not an option, thorough annoyance is the workaround."

Question: What annoyed that warbling guineafowl most?

Answer: Jeremy Harker and oafishness.

Former Acting Director CIA Jeremy Harker III was a year gone to a CNN contract and an Arthur Murray pyramid scheme that had gotten him permanently off the golf course and into franchising three rhumba rooms. Plus, he hated my guts. I would use Harker, though not directly. For the oafish side of things, I had the perfect partner to make me shine. In Accounting and waiting there: Numbers Numbskull Nancy.

I lifted the green secure phone and dialed. Once I identified myself. Once she groaned. I asked, "Who do you despise most?"

"Out of what group?"

"Headquarters."

"You."

"Very funny. Second most?"

"My gay ex-husband."

"Third."

"You. And fourth, my department staff manager."

"Yeah, and skipping over five—'me'—where do you rank Meryl Hofmeyr?"

Numbskull Nancy guffawed. "You're priceless, Rusty-don't-correct-me."

"Russell."

"My imagination—which you know, though you dumped me anyway—"

"Thirty years ago."

"—is wicked. I'd say the gold standard for all my despisal is her Laa-Laa 'er, mmm, goooo—'bitch face."

"Stay right where you are."

Ten minutes later, I was inside Numbskull Nancy's office, facing her desk. Nancy's voice issued from behind a workstation wall of three monitors and two document stands. All that was visible of her were pink-painted nails snicker-snacking the keys of one of a trio of Belgian-waffle-iron-sized twelve-digit commercial printing adding machines, but I could envision the sunny willowy girl with the tapered waist and seductively rounded hips of her full blossom of youth.

"Yoo-hoo, Nan."

"Pull a chair around so I can see your handsome face."

I dragged a high, squared-off, and narrow wooden chair around the desk next to hers. My chair and hers matched. "These come from your dining room?"

"I kept the chairs. Derrick got a useless table," she said, hit print, faced me. It was still the same sweet face. Only much larger. The rounding of her hips had spread to her entire body.

"Don't look at me like that. I'm still me."

"I like the way you look any way you look. I always have."

Eyes dreamy like moon pies, her face glowed, waxing nostalgic. "Why'd you let me go? You know I was a beauty queen? That's right. Miss Camarillo."

"You never told me that."

"I never told you that because when I started to tell you I was from Camarillo, you asked if that's the place with the state looney bin."

"Ah, yes. They genuinely have beauty contests, places like that?"

Nancy merely laughed and pinched my cheek. Fingers like an alligator clip.

"I sure was in love with you," she said. "We had fun."

"We did have fun. So, you up for poking a stick in Meryl Hofmeyr's eye?"

"If that's the poking you want me for... I'll take what I can get."

There is a parallel universe where I always end up with Nancy, and happy. Hell, in another, I end up with Derrick and we're happy too, but we got nowhere to sit.

"Running any CI audits for her?" I asked.

"Always. They dig around like gofers, DDC Kingston and his crew."

"Anything going back to the Harker days?"

"I was working on that in anticipation when you came in. She did audit him—through CI, without his knowledge, in preparation of her move against him. Came out clean."

"Did you ever audit his meal allowances?"

"We ran everything one way or t'other. Nothing unusual in his covered personal expenses. Didn't dig too deep, though."

"Deep enough to run them against the daily Seventh Floor Harker 'Hometown Buffet'?"

I caught the sudden gleam in her eye. Her fingers flew across her keyboard. Her right hand lunged to and from her mouse like a church organist pulling stops for a particularly rousing Bach D Minor *Toccata and Fugue*.

"While it's entirely appropriate to order up lunch every day to the Seventh Floor," I said, "the ongoing expense of the daily luncheon buffet, when it was not used—off-site meetings, and other no-attendee or partial-attendee days when, for example Acting Director Harker and Ms. Hofmeyr skipped the standing luncheon to order alternate food delivered to their offices—this could be viewed as double-dipping."

"Two taxpayer-funded lunches. We didn't consider that."

"One of those separate meals, according to every standard and rule, individuals are personally out-of-pocket responsible."

Soon, Nancy found the first discrepancy. Third day, week two of the daily spread service. From there, the others cascaded like an avalanche.

"Excellent," I said. "You implicate her, get her to storm down here—"

"Whoa-whoa. No way. I don't want her here. And that doesn't get her in a position for you to ambush her, which—whatever that really is—I want nothing to do with."

She detailed a plan of annoyance, implication, and confrontation. She estimated it would take a week. In the end, it took only three days.

Day one: a flurry of reports forwarded to Laa-Laa's office revealed the financial impropriety. As anticipated, this prompted a stern response by interoffice electronic and hand-delivered hardcopy memo: "Jeremy Harker is no longer with this Agency. His separation is binding and prevents this Agency from opening or pursuing past administrative, regulatory, economic, or governance actions against him. Do not waste Agency time or resources in this pursuit."

Day two: Nancy submitted the same reports. This triggered a telephone call directly to her desk from Morton Drexler, administrative assistant to Meryl Hofmeyr.

"Ms. Hofmeyr believes she made it entirely clear that any pursuit of Mr. Harker's financial ineptitudes was to not be pursued by you or anyone in your division."

"My mistake entirely." She hit send on the file transfer waiting on one of her screens. "I neglected to send the red-line version."

"I'm not sure why you are persisting…" His voice trailed off.

The red-lined version highlighted Meryl Hofmeyr's own complicity in the pre-9/11 Spaghetti Sandwichgate scandal.

"Would you like me to send a tabulation of Assistant Deputy Director Hofmeyr's personal expenses inadvertently entered as Agency-covered meals?"

Morton Drexler hesitated, a pause long enough to suspect Laa-Laa Hofmeyr was furiously bouncing her orange ball of spite against the back of his head. "That won't be necessary. We will handle this from our end. You are not to bother the Assistant Deputy Director with this matter ever again. Please move on to more important work in the service of your Agency."

"Country" never figures into it for those in CI "service."

Day three, around 3 p.m., to make certain Laa-Laa had finished dining on the American taxpayer in the *approved* manner, Nancy sent her third report. This one red-lined my own dining account, digging out my own discrepancies over the last two years adding up to a whopping fraud of $86.23 by yours truly.

At 5:25 p.m., Meryl Hofmeyr popped into my office behind her paint-spread smile. "Ah, Russell. Mm, glad to find you where we both—if we're, shall we say, honest, hm? with each other—knew you'd be awaiting me. Foolish of you roping in your long-suffering jilted filly. I might-ta-ta eat *her* for lunch when I'm finished with you."

I tossed a folder across my desk. She did nothing to stop it from sliding over the edge to spill the sexually explicit Nina photos with the Cuban exile former DEA hero over her Rosa Kleb block-heel Guccis. She didn't need to look to know exactly what they were and left them where they lay.

"Mm. Didn't know if Nina would have the balls to share them with you. Good for her. Ah?"

I hated her in that moment even more than I'd hated her for sending me to a planned-for execution in Malaysia the year before. *"Have a safe flight, Mr. Aiken."*

"Glad to see lil' Ninsy-wincy saved me the trouble of sharing them with you myself. Two of you need to sort that out before operations move forward in Cuba."

"Is Nina under investigation?"

"No."

"Is he?"

"Neither."

"Then I am."

Her happy-playmate expression never changed, but her wording became clearer. More dangerous. "The throuple issue is frowned upon by Deputy Director Counterintelligence Kingston. He can and will make it extraordinarily difficult for you if a sea change of radical direction doesn't come about with Cuba objectives before TIME MACHINE is deployed."

"You baited Nina to bring this to me. You knew it would drive a wedge between us. And you've been waiting for it to sink me. Well, too late the other Kingston already shut me down."

"One of his heroic sons? Michael? Hal?"

"Stop it. You know which other Kingston. I couldn't care less about those other two."

She chuckled and cooed, "And now Miss Lynn couldn't care less about you."

She let that sink in.

"Deputy Director Kingston appreciates the thought you put into your approach on this matter. Off books is how he wants this new exchange of ideas between you and he, *he-he*, and with a few errant lunch receipts for cover: here we are."

I'd gone about this to catch Meryl off guard. Now I found myself defenseless, having been ambushed, unprepared for her all along.

"'Sea change' does not mean course change," was all I could struggle to say.

"You've lost access. You've lost your girl, *and* the other. Silas Kingston is the only path back for you."

"I will have nothing to do with KALEIDOSCOPE."

Meryl Hofmeyr tsk-tsked and said in an affected high-pitched warble, "Mr. Aiken, why I wouldn't have the first clue to what you're saying. Remember, this is the sea change we're all looking for. Deputy Director Kingston will reach out to you shortly."

I HATE THE BASTARDIZATION OF LANGUAGE in every way; hate language's misuse in all forms. Some newspaperman or woman (either way neutral as both are equally idiomatic idiots) floated out the new meaning for the already well-defined term *sea change* so that now, everywhere I turn in the media, it has become synonymous with, as Laa-Laa Hofmeyr asserted, a radical and massive change of course to policy or paradigm. They attempt, I believe, to evoke the enormous shift of inertia in the turning of an aircraft carrier or oil tanker, missing entirely that the only ship Shakespeare referred to was a shipwreck that went down with all hands. The only radical transformation defined by "sea change" is death.

> *Full fathom five thy father lies:*
> *Of his bones are coral made:*
> *Those are pearls that were his eyes:*
> *Nothing of him that doth fade*
> *But doth suffer a sea-change*
> *Into something rich and strange.*

A living king is radically changed when his dead body rots at the bottom of the sea and yet, how and what he was does *not* change in memory, he's unfortunately sea-changed in decomposition into a freaking reef. I would offer the loudest clapter to the one who delivers all the sea-change-changers their own full fathom five.

So armed and fully prepared with this argument to repel Silas Kingston, I fled Langley for Princeton but only long enough to panic-book a Disney cruise escape that Jessie and Gladys tolerated—though only once I allowed them to mock it in all its Mickey Mouse goofiness. I spent the five days inside our cabin, perfectly content to avoid all human contact.

"What was your highlight?" I asked Jessie as we headed home on December first, "Two highlights, actually. The lifeboat drill, because I kept picturing Mickey and Minnie going down as Jack and Rose."

"And number one?"

"Eating Donald Duck for Thanksgiving," she and Gladys answered in unison.

HOME AT PRINCETON I was unsure whether to be worried or relieved no contact from Silas Kingston or anyone else Agency-involved had been attempted. I chose to reason—which also might have been a tad willingly misguided self-deception, since no one tried a Shakespearean sea change on my life en route and back from Disney Island—perhaps Silas's black cloud had cleared. Still, without the sun that once filled my sky, my world was empty. And it was cold, as if I lay on the bottom of the sea where my own father surely waits.

I returned to Langley the next morning and resumed my job without incident or anomaly.

40

Decemnber 16, 2002. Amy Kim informs me that TIME MACHINE is complete, out of testing, ready to go. I tell her I will let the team know; for her to plan for a New Year's Eve insertion into Havana, preceded by a one-week deployment prep and rehearsal.

I advised her: "As you will be making the installation, I'll be requiring a polygraph. If there is anything at all disqualifying, anything at all you are holding back, Amy, my legal advice would be to pass on the polygraph and remove yourself from mission consideration. Know I am only, and at my utmost, going to protect you."

"I'm not hiding anything. You have my word."

I relayed this to Lynn Kingston who agreed to the timetable, thanked me for my service, indicating she would thereon take over all operational aspects.

Bullshit brush-off "thereon" deception language.

I tried to float above it all, but "all" being my life—

and its meaning—

and my heart—

and my soul—

and the year anniversary of me-and-Nina blinking on the horizon... Fuck it, I'm proud my buoyancy lasted the six days it did. But by lunch on December 21, four days floating to Christmas, if a balloon were conscious, mine burned like the remains of the Hindenburg after meeting its Lakehurst pin.

Christmas shopping—that'll cheer you up.

I drove out to Tysons Corner, the only thing on my mind was that I had zero intention of calling Nina.

"God bless you, merry gentlemen! May nothing you dismay!"

I'd tuned to the pop station Jessie likes. The one that plays Christmas music twenty-four seven the minute after the last jack-o'-lantern is smashed and, hellbent, we all ride out the other side of Halloween's covered bridge on a Currier and Ives sleigh into the frost and deepening snow. Not liking the new lyrics, I switched it off.

No reason on Earth, no prickling instinct: I put up the hypothesis and found no argument for or against calling. Anyway, what could I possibly say to fix things?

Nothing. That's what.

In fifteen days, she'd be launched on her new and undercover chosen life in Havana. And that's why it was a waste of time to think of her.

Winter, the season that pulls dying fall into its skeletal death grip, had arrived with piercing cold. I found the mall and parked my car near Jessie and Gladys's favorite: Nordstrom. I hurried through a gritty stream of ice crystals that blew inside a cloud descended to earth, foggy and bleak.

I'd relinquished my right to call Nina; gave myself my own word I would not call her. And who am I to break a personal bond?

I won't. Although she *had* asked—*"Russell, call me?"*

Or maybe it was simply "call me"? But without the question mark? Definitely without the Russell. She hadn't said Pintao. And if she'd wanted me to call her, she would have. I know her too well—that's exactly what she would have done. No doubt. It's what I live for, what she calls me when she's loving on me.

I was inside the department store without remembering having crossed the parking lot.

But would she have? I mean, said Pintao. In Lynn's office? After all, we'd only shared it—with sweet fondest, I might add, always—as a term of our endearment, a pet name between us we both privately cherished. That wouldn't be like Nina. Especially if she'd phrased it as a question. But had it been a question? Frankly, I couldn't recollect; I think I hadn't been listening. And that's the thing about mishearings; not having heard, might it have been a statement of desire? Remarkably without question.

Buy gifts. Consume. Get the plastic bits, ones and zeros, mass-creating information flowing through the electronic holiday veins.

"Happy holidays. May I direct you to a department, sir?"

"Merry Christmas, what? What business is it of yours?"

"You look a little lost. If you were looking for something special…?"

I couldn't find one thing to like about the oily clerk showing me his greasy teeth.

"I make it a point never to give anything special at Christmas, and not to interfere with other people's."

"People's what?"

"Business."

"I work here. This is my business." He measured me with the ruler of his eyes. "Are you feeling okay, sir?"

I huffed to the escalator. Made a point of stepping onto it with indignant authority, hands clutched behind my back like a prince, and almost toppled as it attempted to lurch away without me, a fool.

I reminded myself I was here for Jessie and Gladys. I wouldn't buy Nina a gift. What right did she have to expect one?

What if she buys me something? A little going-away thing before she posts to Cuba and I have nothing? How's that gonna look? My God, it would prove my infidelity worse than my little romp with must-not-even-think-her-name, LK. Lynn Kingston.

My God, such freedom to have Nina off my mind. I practiced all kinds of thoughts that had nothing to do with her and ascended. How liberating to find I could specifically and deliberately remove Nina from each of them.

Here's a thought. With Nina peeking over the top. Remove her. Guess what? Still a thought. Appropriate thinking remains without her. Nina.

I stumbled, failing to notice that I had come to the top of the moving stairs. Transformed my teeter into a little Astaire-like leap-and-land totter.

Eat your heart out, Jeremy Harker.

Crowds of shoppers rushed round tables, racks, wall displays, and cash registers, neckties and scarves and cashmere awhirl as others pushed from behind, anxious to join the Operation SANTA fray.

"You're blocking the escalator!"

"C'mon, man! Move it!"

Why, for fifty-two years I've put up with being pushed around?! You take or you get took. I wasn't going to let Nina, the only woman I've ever genuinely loved, be the one who took me. Then I got an idea. An awful idea.

Curious if I'd had a seizure and not known it, I caught up with my breath across the mall and inside the Pandora store.

Hadn't Jessie asked for a charm bracelet?

"May I see another tray of rings? Maybe that one?"

"It's the last, I'm afraid, and they're a bit for the Def Leppard crowd."

I cupped my ear. "The which?"

"Aw. Deaf joke. Hmm. Inappropriate, no? If I could recommend something custom?"

"No time. No time. No time for custom anything. This snake one will do. I like it."

Foggier yet, and colder, I hustled to my car and leaped inside.

When you have a hands-free car phone, you can throw that wonderful, awful idea, right in someone like Nina's face.

"You waited long enough," she said, having answered before the first ring ended. "I thought you pussied out."

"I called you every day."

"I didn't get any messages. No missed calls."

"Figured I'd say the wrong thing if I, in point of fact, dialed."

She said nothing. She didn't even laugh a little.

"I wanted to figure it out. Right."

She let the silence hang. I watched it swing over the trapdoor I'd kicked open with my call.

"You've always been good at puzzles," she said.

"I've never been good at life. I've let it pass by me when I wasn't looking. Look, I always say the wrong thing at the right time for it to be the worst thing I can possibly say, so I'm going to say all the wrong things right up front, but by pointing out that they're the wrong things—owning it—I think I can negate their wrongness—"

I heard her exhale. "I'm not sure this is your best idea."

"Dammit. Let me screw it up worse if it isn't! I'm me. I'm how I am. And if saying the wrong thing loses you forever, then I deserve it and can accept it as what's right. But if saying the wrong thing turns out to be the *right* thing and I never tried, and you left for Cuba and I was never going to see you again—well, that's not going to fit into my plans for the rest of my life."

"You've made plans?"

"That's why I'm calling you!"

Another silence, longer than the conversation we'd already had and then, with a kind of mercy, she said, "You were in LA for your appointment. Is this about your diagnosis? Should I be standing?"

"I... Shouldn't you ask if you should sit?"

I'd never described the content of my seizures to her. To anyone. I'd wanted so much for them to be real, to be an instrument of time. Winding and resetting life.

"You're scaring me," she whispered. "Say something."

"I'm well. It's gone. No cancer, my epilepsy, everything."

Her voice sprung tight. "I'm glad for you."

"What I figured out is that time is the least thing that matters because every moment with you is a forever moment with me, and the weight of them all put together, on who I am and what it is to be alive, has more unmovable mass than an entire galaxy. And this moment, just to be able to talk to you—because it is the present and real—this moment outweighs the past and the future combined.

"If we'd have never met again after New York, my life would have already been perfect and complete. Just having met you one time, I experienced the whole of it and all that is real and true. And if that was the best I'd ever gotten, the best I'll ever get, the best intended for me, then I am blessed I was put on this Earth to have experienced it and I need nothing more."

"That's rather dismissive."

"How's that dismissive?!"

"You're short-selling all the last year we've had, Cuba before that, and… Jesus, *Pint—You*, this phone call right now!"

"I betrayed that. All of it. I betrayed you. I betrayed myself and every bit of honesty and promise I offered you. Every expectation you had in me I stole from you and made vile. I'm not calling to be forgiven, only to confess I did a spiteful, despicable, hurtful, selfish thing to you; there's no silver lining—no gold-star lesson. Unforgiveable is what it was, and to dig into any reasoning, or second chancing, or what I learned, is only another injury to you. Completely fucked-up behavior I'm sorry for because it was meant to hurt, and it did. I killed what we had by doing it, and I don't deserve you back because of that."

"Anything else?"

"You are a perfect and wonderful and unique gift given to this world, this life we all live in and share. You are brave and you are selfless, and you are loving; you spread happiness and compassion and hope in every tiny thing you do. It ripples from you in ways and rays you can't possibly know, but I've had the blessing to warm in that radiance beside you. Everyone is always a little bit better for having encountered you, and I admire that, and would give my life for it just so that wherever you are, whoever you are with, in whatever moment you are in: you could continue being exactly Nina."

"So's you know, I had my own revenge fuck."

God dammit! I knew this was a bad idea!

"Good. I deserve it."

She waited.

"Is it going somewhere?" I prompted.

Did I hear her chuckle, throaty and derisive? I think she whispered, *Oh, Pintao*, but I do know she said this: "I only got as far as making up the revenge-fuck part. You were supposed to flip out. Say the wrong thing and hang up on me. You always ruin everything."

Hands-free, I clutched the Pandora box in my pocket.

"I could say another wrong thing. Want to hear it?"

"Is it worse than the buttering up you just lathered me with?"

"It's dumber."

"How dumb?"

"*Stupido* dumb. If I'd started with it, you'd've hung up on me."

"You sure you want to do this?"

"Happy to."

"Okay, say it."

"I have known every minute my heart and soul are yours forever. The plan I was talking about? I've seen the future. I *know* we're supposed to end up happily married and in love for the rest of our lives, and when we go into an old folks' home, it will be hand in hand, and we'll sit at a big table every morning with a bunch of other drooling, wrinkly people and argue if soft-boiled or poached eggs can ever be better than waffles, even though they only serve the same oatmeal slop every day anyway, so we oughta just get back together and prepare for the inevitable, side by side. You need allies in those places—"

Her laughter was the loud, clear, wry, bell-like sound I'd come to love.

"Nina?"

"Stop."

"Are you available for me to take you out to dinner tonight?"

"Nothing you can do or stay will stop me from going to Havana."

"I want you to go to Havana. If I had a chance to protect and to save my father from something—or to merely see him again—nothing, not even you, could have stopped me. What I'm trying to say—wrong would be I'm jealous, but also right—I'm happy and proud and fully support you doing this. In fact, that's why I want to take you to dinner. You know, in medieval days when knights went off into battle, their maiden would give them a token, sometimes a lock of hair, sometimes a handkerchief, sometimes a garter to protect them and symbolize their faithfulness their dedication—"

"Are you going to give me your garter, princess?"

"What can I say?" I said. "You've always been my knight in shining armor."

I finished with that, and she finished with yes; she didn't have anything planned and so it began. I dropped by Butterfield 9, glorious in gold and silver Christmas decorations, and set our reservation. On the way home, I called Jessie to break the good news.

"Gladys!" she shouted. "He's doing it!... He *says* tonight!"

And then I was home. The warning light dark. The front door, dead bolt popped.

I'm a little lamb who's lost in the woods...

The dripping wine.

The body.

The blood.

Nina abducted in violence equal in force to the seizure that hit me like a bullet to the head as I fled. I held no doubt our operation's security had not been breached. If it had, the Cubans would have *allowed* TIME MACHINE's deployment, stolen the technology, and turned it against us until such a time as we caught on, at which point they would have exposed us to international embarrassment in yet another blundering espionage failure against the ever vigilant, eternally mighty Fidel.

Silas Kingston had never forgotten me. I negotiated my escape from the police, knowing beyond a doubt, like Bishop and like Muir before him, Nina had fallen victim to KALEIDOSCOPE.

41

I HEADED NORTH UP 14TH STREET, my wipers hacking furiously at the ice needles that flew faster and stronger by the minute. I needed a liquor store. I needed one badly. Can't be helped. From earlier days of prior habits, spirits shrieked inside my head to be allowed comfort from the storm. I knew once past Monroe, all the way to Spring Road, there are plenty. I'd not picked up a tail and about five blocks farther, I found a bottle shop I'd patronized plenty of times. I knew it had a side lot with a public phone. Even with the ice storm, a call-back runner for the block's crack crew slapped mismatched mittens on wet black vinyl warm-up pants over rust corduroys and stomped unlaced, used-up, hand-me-down Jordan's alongside the graffiti-covered stand. Lean, and with eyes already dead, he was not yet fifteen. And he was exceedingly short. I went straight for the phone.

"Outta service."

"Beat it, b—"

They say during a life-threatening occurrence perception is altered and everything goes into slow-motion effect. Mental activity and thought velocity increase by 100 percent. Time and actual experience of it expands and extends. From the first studies from the late nineteenth century conducted on falling Swiss mountain climbers, Formula One race-car drivers in the latter half of the twentieth, and the most recent, conducted by me with a froze-ass gangbanger, moved the proof needle from 95, to 98, to 100 percent.

What was I about to call him that wouldn't get me killed?

I'd stopped myself from stupidly saying Boy. (What works in snowy Christmas 1840s London, does not work in modern-day anywhere Christmas America.)

They seem to like the N-word with each other. Suicide for me, though.

Man. *Might draw fire for mocking; age/height.*

Dude. *Too white.*

Brother. *See Man.*

Bae. *Nina calls me that occasionally. I have no idea why; better not.*

Have heard on television, a Halloween kinda spooky Boo. *I'll go for that, and heard my words transforming in super-slow sound—*

"Beeeaat iit bbbo—

Eh, shit, Boo = *spooky! Am I nuts?! Already begun the* Boy-*twisted-diphthong-*Boo-*dip-it-again-super-speed all helixing up:*

"Beat it, Beau."

His eyes flashed. Of all the words I could have chosen, this caught him most off guard.

"Do I look like my baby-boy-brutha Beau?! I's LaDarion muthafucka. My mama send yo' ass from Services, bitch?"

Curious, but now nonthreatening, he blocked the phone, tried to grab the receiver. I grabbed his wrist.

"Hate to have this go the wrong way," I said, and pressed a hundred-dollar bill I'd readied into his wet, fuzzy palm. His eyes jumped from the money to my face as I released him.

"You be wan'in' rock?"

"That's six minutes' rent while I take care of a quick call."

His teeth chattered. Melted ice ran rivulets down his frost blown face. I yanked off his Redskins hat.

"Hey!"

Gave him the wool watch cap from my pocket. I wouldn't need it where I was headed.

"Keep it, mate."

"Maze me, mista'. Why you wanna help this po' brutha?"

"Christmas magic."

He reached into his crotch to hide the money. He stepped off a couple yards. "Be quick. Some rollin' Thirteenth Street niggas see you…" He spread his hands to demonstrate my fate was out of them.

I pulled all my change, dumped it—quarters, nickels, dimes—on the metal rim of the phone box and dialed the number from memory. The recorded operator asked for a dollar-fifty for the first five minutes. Dollar-sixty-five was all I had. I dumped it in.

"You have fifteen cents to overtime," the robot voice returned—God I hate robots—then put me through.

"Hello?" came Amy's curious voice, and I risked it all.

"Stick. Stone," I said.

"'Waters of March,'" she answered and waited.

I couldn't risk using any trigger-words that would be caught by NSA-Echelon and get the call computer-flagged for human processing/analysis.

"Tour's moved up to the same date as last year's performance."

"Launching from?"

"Your duet partner's studio. Grab your instrument and get there immediately. Do not speak to your agent."

"Has our sponsor changed?" I heard a twinge of fear.

"Don't think so, but your road manager's been taken out by a bad flu."

I heard her catch her breath. "Who's coming on tour with me?"

"I'll be road manager. You good?"

I shouldn't have asked, and she shouldn't have answered, but she did. "You know I'd do anything to go with you."

Except she didn't say *you*. She said, *him* because that's the way we both knew Muir ultimately influenced everything we did and both of us lived with that. I returned the phone to its cradle.

"Merry Christmas, yo!" the boy gangsta chased me to my car gripping his waistband. "But don't be thinkin' this lid and that bill gone to change my O-G life!"

I stopped at the door, remembering something Nathan once told me. How Heinz Trettin might have killed the woman who would have cured cancer—

Our business is collateral damage. That foot off the sidewalk caught by our escaping car.

—and suddenly understood that what was collateral didn't always have to be damage.

"It won't, but one decision you'll make one day will be linked to what's happened between us and that will change the fate of the entire world."

He laughed. "You awready high, mo-fo!"

"And you'll laugh when you remember me when it happens. Merry Christmas, my good fellow!"

I started my car, swung into the left-turn lane and U-turned around the center island. I randomized my route doing my best SDR, making sure my head and tail were clear, stair-stepping blocks across town for the Rock Creek Parkway that would deliver me to Dulles. Even if they weren't directly on me, Silas would have the airport staked out, watching for my vehicle. I'd have to let them have it. They'd find blood evidence, but that wouldn't matter to his spooks. They'd want me and that's what I would deny them.

I pulled into the hourly parking lot and took the first handi-capped spot, speed now my best and only ally. No one pulled in after me. I took half a minute retrieving the magnetized box from beneath my seat and the unmarked and untraceable padlock key from inside it. I sprinted into the enclosed walkway, into the single-level terminal that handled both departures and arrivals, losing myself in the holiday crowd, moving horizontally until I was mingling with the international arrivals. I found a town car operator who didn't look too rushed on his pickup and moved beside him.

I stood too close and knew he watched me as I took the $250 cash I'd earlier pulled from an ATM for our dinner. I pinned it to my credential with my thumb.

"I need a quick drop-off less than a mile from the airport."

I slid the cash, the CIA logo on my ID case clear to see.

"You're not fucking around. Is it dangerous?"

"No. But I'll double this on my card once we're moving."

It didn't take him a second's thought. "Sign me up a patriot. Hell, yeah."

I gave him instructions and he left with the cash. Six minutes later, I broke for the sidewalk into a thick knot of exiting travelers piling into arriving cars in the curling ice. The limo driver rolled in on the outside lane between two similar town cars busy loading passengers. I slipped between the pair and into my guy's back seat. He pulled into the flow of airport traffic.

"Where to?"

I gave him the address, then instructions of how we'd get there to break any tail I might be carrying.

"Thought you said this was safe?"

I handed him my American Express. "Take twenty for the ride, five hundred for the tip."

He handled the SDR like a champ. Let me off, back into the ice storm, on a deserted street of warehouses and brick-walled industrial buildings one block over from where my escape hatch waited.

"Any time you need another ride like this one..." He offered me a business card I didn't want.

"What makes you think I picked you at random?" I cocked a finger gun at him and shut the door.

He zoomed off. I waited another minute and a half. Certain the street was empty, and he'd not swung around to looky-loo, I crossed lanes, jogged to the next corner, and went up the block until I arrived at the next street. Turned and went half another block. The road was vacant, no windows in any of the dark buildings. Why I'd selected this place over others in the area. Found the gate I was looking for. I punched in my code on the keypad and entered a cramped industrial park of concrete bunkers, corners weakly lit by orange security lights but mostly dark and freezing before me. I jogged into the veil of frozen needles blowing into my vapor-billowing face.

THE METAL RATTLED as I hauled open the door to my garage unit, which stood at the center of an inner alley that ran the middle of the *EZ Stow'N'Go* facility. Just high enough to duck inside, and I slipped beneath, shuffling it down behind me. Moved in darkness to the right wall and activated a pull-top military sleeve lantern. Besides the lantern, there were only three other things inside the unit: a garment bag on a hook, a floor safe bolted to the foundation, and a silver 1999 Ford Explorer with clean plates and VIN. Most common color, most common make. I changed into loose-fitting, heavy jeans, four-layer T-shirt, denim shirt, flannel and leather windbreaker—a pants-shirt combo smuggled out of our disguise division and designed and constructed to add an illusory twenty-five pounds in weight-gain. I tugged on some cowboy boots that, with heel and insole, added three inches to my height and changed my movement profile. An outside pocket on the garment bag contained a device like a shaving brush; with a twist of the handle, it released a powder I applied to my head that thickened and whitened my hair. The final piece of the simple, though proven-effective, disguise was a well-worn, high-crown western businessman's Stetson. Not to wear, but to carry as a distraction to tap against my thigh to draw observers' eyes away from the face to the hand.

From inside my safe, I grabbed the keys, wallet, money belt with $9,750 in various denominations (bulked me up a bit more), and a new passport that matched the vehicle, wallet, and linked to a dummy life that self-sustained a remote farmhouse in rural Pennsylvania. I left Jessie's, Gladys's, and Nina's escape kits in the safe, shut and locked the steel door.

I folded the garment bag and buckled it into a piece of shoulder-strapped luggage that could go carry-on. I threw open the garage gate. Made a quick scan and confirmed I was still alone. Got behind the wheel of the Explorer and switched on the ignition. I pulled out. Closed and secured the unit. Drove out of the facility heading for Reagan Airport.

I activated a never-before-used Motorola flip phone clipped into the car phone mount. An older model, it didn't work hands-free, but I knew Aunt Linda's telephone number by heart. Tapped it in.

She answered after a couple rings. "Merry Christmas."

"Just me. Gotta say goodbye. Merry Christmas," I said and disconnected.

She had the number committed to memory and now knew I was on my way, and that I would arrive alone. While I was confident no one could track me by my phone, we had to assume if there was a net, and if the net were wide, Linda's line would be flagged for intercept. If that were the case, I hoped Silas would think I was in fear and running. If not, and Silas attempted to put someone on Linda, he knew as well as anyone she would have one hundred tricks up her sleeve to thwart any surveillance, and a hundred more to cause permanent damage to anyone Silas might find foolish enough to involve themselves with her in person. Suffice it to say, Linda had a long, dear friendship with our nation's most recent Attorney General, Janet Reno, who would bend over backward to help out a bachelor girl in trouble. I booked a 10:50 p.m. flight through San Francisco to Fresno, trusting that Linda would have the charter plane booked and waiting. I checked my watch.

Almost half past nine. I had one more stop to make, I pulled off the highway at the Crystal City exit before Reagan International. Making sure mine was the only vehicle on the off ramp, I unrolled the window and tossed the phone into the storm as I turned onto 15th Street. I turned onto South Bell, to 20th, to Crystal Drive and pulled into the lot for the twenty-four-hour Kinko copy center. I took the envelope of Nina photos inside and faxed them to the only remaining person I could trust, dead and unknown to Silas Kingston.

I WAITED IN THE AMERICAN AIRLINES TERMINAL to board, three gates away from my own, confident I was unobserved. Once I thought I saw Amy Kim rushing down the concourse, but as the woman neared, she revealed herself as someone else. I refused to allow myself any thoughts about Amy compromising me, about the Chinese red flags, about her failing in any way. I blocked all fantasies of Nina and the horrors I could surmise now happening to her. The strongest person I have ever known, if she could hold out long enough for Amy and I to deploy TIME MACHINE and return hard results on Cuban–Venezuelan intelligence, whatever had motivated Silas Kingston to expose her would be of less value than the active electronic eavesdropping system in place and its sudden and immeasurable value would compel him to save Nina to protect it. Not only from the Cubans, but from me.

Linda, who'd helped train Silas, and knew Silas Kingston better than any of us, but whose blood loyalty to Muir was unquestionable, would act as our cutout. Our relay station and guarantor to negotiate with this man who had now become my mortal foe.

AT 4 P.M. THE FOLLOWING DAY, in cold, open-sky California winter darkness, I drove my rental car into the foothills along the towering Sierra Nevada range. I rolled along the dirt lane to Linda's cabin, swinging around the last curve past her firepit and the tall stand of memorial pines where I discovered the negotiation had been made without me. Another rental car, another cottage, another master spy mocking me from the rail.

I withheld any sign of emotion as I clamped my Stetson on my head and climbed out of the vehicle.

Silas Kingston called from Linda's porch, "Masterful tradecraft. Cowboy. If it hadn't been for Amy's call to me, you'd have moseyed away right under my nose."

Where Muir's hair had been wheatfield gold and full and fine, Silas Kingston's was darkest brown, coarse and wavy, tight against his skull like the profile on a Roman coin. They were opposites in every way. Silas's sinister eyes, hazel but with too much white, old-fashioned and studious; Muir's: cornflower blue, little white at all, and brimming always with daring delight. Both men were tall, well over six feet, but where Muir had been rugged and muscular, Silas was sinuous and lean. I had always pictured Muir as a mighty immovable stone; seeing Silas usurping his atomic pace, I now could see the Counterintelligence chief, architect of the violent and mysterious KALEIDOSCOPE, as the tree that, having fallen as an insubstantial seed into a crack, had grown to rend that boulder in two. Muir had been sixty-five that day I'd arrived at his beach house insecure within my youth. Ten years younger than I, Silas Kingston's youth threatened those insecurities more than any of the old man's cruelties.

One other difference: Muir was dead and Silas alive.

"I'm going to kill you," I said.

"Waste of thought. Waste of time. You have a fighting chance to save your girl. Now get inside, get out of your Woody costume, clean up, and take your medicine."

I draw Muir's Sig-Sauer and shoot him dead, a bullet through Silas Kingston's heart.

At least, if you believe science, some other conscious form of me in some other parallel dimension did precisely that and I'm proud of that guy, but in this blown-out corner of the snowcapped High Sierras, the event that is Muir's gun remains at home; here, fully was I disarmed in hand and heart. I did as he'd known I would do from the start. I slunk up the heavy wooden steps only to catch the riser heel of my cowboy boot and stumble.

"Shit," I said.

"What?" said Silas.

"I left my shoes in my storage unit."

"I'll get you a new pair. Least I can do."

There Silas met me, putting a hand across my back to take my shoulder. Friendly gesture. Also a control.

42

"SATAN, FATHER OF ETERNAL MATTER, trembling lest the spark of life should glow in you, has ordered an unceasing movement of the atoms that compose you, and so you shift and change forever. I, the spirit of the universe, I alone am immutable and eternal."

These last words Amy spoke on Earth did not belong to Amy Kim. They belonged to Nina. But they were not her words even after Nina had spoken them one million times at a million places and in a million voices around the globe since October 17, 1896. And, when the Nina I will ever love heard her words as recited by Amy to me, my Nina did not know the words of the other Nina were, in truth, the words of a long dead Russian. Nor did she remember she had once heard another Cuban Nina speak them in Havana at a time when she was a girl foolishly in love with a young hero of the Revolution: a man who discarded her, ruined and barren, and whom I now serve in betrayal of the United States of America.

The expression I read in Trigorin's face when he suddenly recognized Nina was the enchantment found in the faces of children on Christmas morning who recognize Santa in the plate crumbs of missing cookies. The white film on the sides of an empty milk glass. Trigorin laughed and saw my shame complete.

NO ONE KNOWS WHO ERECTED AUNT LINDA'S CABIN or when. Muir said it was already one hundred years old when he spent summers there as a boy; his Aunt Linda told him it burgeoned, a toadstool under an ancient full moon. Although modest in size, it had been constructed of mountain limestone quarried and cut by nineteenth-century Basque immigrants, Spanish shepherds whose flocks ranged the high pastures in summers but who sheltered out the harshest winters in the frigid high desert of Lone Pine. My own exploration back during my training with Linda in the early 1970s settled the question to my own satisfaction when I came upon an old stone grave marker which read: "Sultan Zaharra, Artzain Leiala." Old Sultan, Faithful Sheherd. The head of a dog carved beneath the words followed by the year 1848.

Except for basic communication technologies, a coat of fresh paint, and the odd bit of restuffing every five to ten now-and-thens, Linda's cabin was a time capsule unchanged for generations. No effort had ever been made to disguise its dual purpose as a sanctum devoted to the arcana of international espionage and as a springboard for outdoor adventure and discovery. It was ever apparent that the dual personalities of Linda's cabin were in constant competition for your attention—one that drew you in and the other that booted you out. Shelves and tables overflowed in books and manuals and exotic texts: improvised weaponry through the ages; sixteenth-century Italian poison recipes; tools for surreptitious entry focused on the Industrial Revolution modern lock; memo binders that recounted escape and evasion techniques from two world wars; Cold War magnetic tape reels trailed ribbon—true and secret roads—across piles of old minefield maps, and code keys and onetime pads abounded like a crossword puzzler's dream come true... Yet, just as plentiful, boots and jackets by the door, camp stools and sticks, rifles, archery, rods and reels, easels and paint boxes—I remembered them all—binoculars, a telescope the width of a pail, a baseball, bat and gloves, an old paper kite awaiting a scarf for a tail and a hand on its string.

Linda, her thick white hair pulled in a baker's bun, braced against a heavy table in the main room. She stood like a general, studying Cuban architectural plans and electrical schematics with a pair of Agency windbreaker boys. In the last corner, was a Christmas tree. A Plasticville station of Muir's boyhood the only gift beneath; the child's train buzzed round and round the trunk and never stopped as long as I was there.

"Hello, Russell. I'll have no complaints," said Linda. "His arrival"—a tip of her head at Silas—"though unannounced, is where we've arrived and how we will proceed. Close your mouth, open your ears, and get to business while we still have the stiletto edge."

Like I have any other choice?

A collection of paintings of assorted sizes shared the walls with mounted animal heads. I noticed a deft watercolor of a brown trout below the rippling surface of a brook. Exceptional, really. Lifelike enough that if you looked too closely, your eyes would get tail-splashed. "I did that," I remarked, claiming my rightful place in the hierarchy of Linda's decade's long admiration.

"I did that." Silas indicated a snarling taxidermized mountain lion.

"Your head's gonna look great beside it," I snarled.

"All right, Aiken, enough of your nonsense. Let me disavow you of the notion I had anything to do with Nina's unfortunate circumstances. I am glad you weren't with her, or you wouldn't be here now to fulfill the destiny Muir left you and that I now will offer and assume responsibility for."

"Muir hated you."

"Then this might surprise you. Though he fell short of his potential, Nathan Muir was the only CIA officer I've ever admired. I'm not in this for accolades, I'm in it to see freedom victorious."

"Over how many bodies?"

"As long as I can see over the pile, don't much care. Mr. Aiken: I hold out my hand once. The moment I withdraw it, I won't give a penny for your life."

I asked after Amy. Was told she was working in the cellar, rehearsing the TIME MACHINE installation, Helen Keller to her Anne Sullivan handler in darkness.

Silas Kingston took me through the back to the stone patio that, raised on broad pillars, covered the outside doorway to the stone-house cellar. We sat in carved pine rockers. He said I would reunite with Amy only after I agreed to my part of his new operation. Though he never mentioned KALEIDOSCOPE, he left me no doubt Operation SANTA SLAY now fell under its purview. Cuba and Venezuela were now only cover for the true intentions of TIME MACHINE.

"Neither Havana nor Caracas have ever been or will ever be a direct threat against the United States. Indirectly, however, they supply over eighty percent of stolen US secrets to our actual enemy. A lucrative business for them we want to enhance and increase."

"Russia," I said. "Aha."

"That old bear's got no teeth. China, Aiken. Always has been, always will be. And the dragon grows more powerful daily. Teeth, claws, and brimstone fire. They will be the greatest threat to America and the world this twenty-first century will know. Because of this, you will be taking Nina's place in securing the feedback loop TIME MACHINE allows us to triangulate Beijing via Cuba and Venezuela's dealings with the Chinese Communist Party as the PRC attempts to extend their Sino sphere of influence in Latin America."

"If this doesn't save Nina, I ain't interested."

You were right, Muir. It did make the dictionary and feels good saying it.

"This is the *only* way to save Nina. But we must move quickly before she breaks on TIME MACHINE."

"She'll give that up before she gives up her father," I said.

"No, TIME MACHINE will be last. Not because she'd hold out if tortured for it, but because they do not believe we know of their secret Havana–Caracas line, do not believe we're mounting an eavesdropping op, and won't have a direction of interrogation in that area."

I understood what he meant. "They won't ask about a listening device because they don't think we have any reason to eavesdrop on something we don't know about. Making their goal with Nina exposure of her network—"

"HUMINT."

"I prefer to think of human intelligence as living, breathing people. So how does my taking her place save Nina?"

"You'll betray her father to General Trigorin. In fact, you'll be betraying everything you stand for and have sworn to uphold."

He detailed his plan for me. Amy and I would enter Cuba. I would present myself as a hopeless, lovesick, pathetic turncoat, willing to betray my country's best-protected foreign agent for Nina's freedom. Their focus on me and upon rolling up the HOUNDFOX network would provide Amy Kim cover to tap their secret communication lines and open us up to a much better intel stream.

"They'll kill HOUNDFOX," I said, not liking the empty sound of my voice, the hollowness where honor and conviction should have echoed in indignation.

In my heart, I've already sold him out.

"That is my plan. Only way to seal the deal."

Nina would hate me for eternity. I would be everything evil to her. I would be Satan to her universe. And yet, Nina would live.

"What would happen to me?"

"We'd see to it you were tried here in absentia and convicted of treason. You would apply for asylum in Cuba. They would televise your treason, probably trot you into the public eye any time they wanted to embarrass us."

"But they'd get everything I know. Everything I've ever done. They'd see 'the big board,' er, so to speak."

Silas Kingston gave me a patient look like a master to his dog. "Ms. Hofmeyr has briefed me on your entire record. Some I've gone through myself—I've missed nothing. Clever ops. Some even pretty. But there isn't a thing you've ever done for the Agency that means all that much to our nation's security. We can't all be our fathers."

"What do you know about my father?"

"Everything you don't. So, spill the beans. Go for it. And if you're smart, string 'em along. Get a beach house, an umbrella drink, and a lobster in the bargain. We won't come after you. You have my word."

If I did nothing, both Nina and her father would die when Nina revealed him. She couldn't hold out; no one does. If it's she or I to pull that trigger, well, I had no choice. And it would ripple from there: I do nothing, TIME MACHINE is lost and with it, Amy Kim; Lynn Kingston is ruined.

"The truth—that my defection is a deception operation—it goes Top Secret on my jacket? Correct? One day it gets declassified that I acted as a patriot. I must insist on that."

Still giving me the dog look, but now the one reserved for the runt of the litter before the drop into the bucket of water, the towel over the top. "That would defeat my purposes here."

"You're telling me the Agency won't know. Ever."

Silas Kingston's eyes twinkled. "I'll know. Right next to Muir in that admiration of mine."

The sound of a scraping door below us caused Silas to rise to his feet. Amy and a female officer near my own age, with a face that could sink a thousand ships, exited, and headed around to the front door.

"She's anxious to see you," he said. "Terribly upset she had to play it this way. Would it make you feel better if I told you why she informed on you?"

"I know exactly why."

"Hm. Not surprised. If you'd only come to me earlier, you wouldn't be in this bind." He jerked his thumb back at the inside. "Be friendly to Ms. Kim and encouraging. She doesn't know your part and don't tell her. You have too much sway on the women in your life—again, I could've used you. Oh, well. Don't, or all of you go down hard. I never fuck around."

Back inside, Amy was already working with Linda, memorizing her map drawn from the old architectural plans. I heard Linda mention two names: Ambassador Smith and Flo Pritchett. I could not place them. Twice Amy caught my eye, frightened and pathetic. I returned her my most reassuring smile. A dog slurping up his own vomit.

We ate, standing at opposite ends of the main room. She never took her sad eyes from mine, which only comforted and shone back with my affection. The Helen of Troll female officer was given charge of getting us to San Francisco International, where we would board separate aircraft to Mexico City and then, separate flights to Havana.

"I need to make one call."

"Absolutely not," said Silas.

"Tough shit. I'm calling Gladys Jlassi—you know who she is; she still has clearance and can be trusted. I will say goodbye and one day she will tell my daughter. You can check the number. You can dial it. You can confirm it's her. Or you can shoot me now."

Of all of them, it was Amy's minder whose hand posted inside her jacket, her flat gaze marking Silas for the order to take me up on my offer.

Silas burned. "What's her number?"

I gave it.

Linda said, "That is Nathan's old number to his Princeton brownstone."

Silas had one of his officers confirm location and account holder/billing through NSA. When it checked out, he dialed.

"Gladys?" he said when it was answered.

"Yes, who is this?"

Silas hit the speaker button and passed me the portable receiver.

"It's Russell. I'm saying goodbye. Tell Jessie. Care for Nina— she'll need you. Nothing else can be done—"

Silas disconnected. "No one likes a long goodbye."

Especially, I thought, when it's one that routes through Princeton directly to my half-sister on Captiva Island.

PART FOUR

ACCEPTION

"'I will live in the Past, the Present, and the Future!'
Scrooge repeated, as he scrambled out of bed.
'The Spirits of all Three shall strive within me.'"

— CHARLES DICKEN, *A Christmas Carol*

43

. . . I HAVE MADE MY CONFESSION. Nothing left to chance. Nothing left to give. The shutters have been opened across from my balcony, across the Calle Obispo. I have no doubt, General Trigorin, you will find Comandante Alejandro Alvarez. I trust, after you do, that according to your word, his daughter Nina will regain her freedom.

Of my own free will and by my signature, under penalty of perjury, all applicable laws and statutes of the Republic of Cuba, I solemnly swear to the legal binding over me, I affirm this document to be the truth as I know it, unabbreviated, unfiltered, and without outside influence sworn to this day: December 25, 2002, *Hotel Florida, Havana, Cuba.*

Signed: Russell Aiken

Legal Counsel, CIA Office of General Counsel, the Central Intelligence Agency, United States of America, resigned.

A FIST POUNDED ON THE DOOR of my hotel-suite prison. A startled shout rose from the kitchen, followed by cross words between my guards. The fat one emerged, rumpled and pissed off from the long night past.

"¡Siéntate!" He ordered I sit.

I settled on the sofa. My heart raced. All my plans, failed dreams, and desperate hopes waited for the answer brought me through that door.

Nina's childhood lover, General Trigorin, left his security detail in the hallway and stepped inside. He regarded me with set jaw and smirking eyes. Unlike my meeting with him yesterday, to which he'd worn a gray Brioni suit that cost more than most

Cubans see in their lifetime, this Christmas morning, he wore his field uniform. Starched brown tunic, dark green epaulets of four gold stars, billowed paratrooper pants. Commanding and proud, his graying blond hair was covered by a ball cap embroidered with a general's star and golden oak leaves. Polyester, unstructured, and flat-billed, it made him unintentionally comical. Though even to grin would mean Nina's and my death.

"I can report, Mister Aiken, your assistance has led to a regrettable but satisfactory conclusion with regard to the traitor Alvarez." His words were measured. They were without emotion. His tone was quiet. It was serene.

Trigorin took a seat in an orange upholstered chair across from me. He crossed his legs. Beach sand scattered from the tread of his hi-gloss combat boots. I noticed something flat and square of weathered metal half-concealed in his hand. A mother-of-pearl rim. My heart constricted. Nina's treasure. The empty, sea-delivered picture frame she once dreamed would carry her wedding photo with the man now seated across from me.

The frame I'd hoped these last eleven years would one day honor us.

He placed it face down on the coffee table beside the pages of my treasonous confession. Placed between the velvet Pandora box with Nina's ring, and the inkwell I had carried to the window.

He considered my manuscript. The pages were filled; the inkwell sat empty.

He riffled the pages of my document. "Plenty to say. I'm glad. I look forward to a most careful study."

Trigorin fished a Bolivar Robusto from his pocket and set to lighting it.

The other pinch-faced guard came from the kitchen with coffee. One for the general. Nothing for me.

"And the *comandante*?" I said.

He gestured I take the frame. I flipped it over. The photograph that filled the secret, empty space hollowed from Nina's childhood heart showed Nina bracketed by her mother and her father gathered around a heavily iced cake; she leans in to blow out nine birthday candles.

"How did you get this?" I said, knowing how already, more surprised by the absence of bloodstains on its surface.

"When we located my old friend, the traitor Alvarez, he resisted arrest, firing on my security forces before taking his own life. He was holding it when we found him."

Trigorin filled his mouth with smoke, savored it, exhaled.

"And the reason you're sharing it with me?"

He gauged me with his small, dark eyes. "You are to return this to Nina. Proof of your loyalty to her after this 'tragedy.' Proof to your CIA."

I wanted to believe my guilt had been complete when I surrendered to General Trigorin twenty-four hours earlier, surrendering my country, my shame, misery, cowardice, my ineffectuality against Silas Kingston, my humiliation at falling short of Muir. Clear-sighted, I'd volunteered the destruction of my character by the ultimate corruption of my identity and ensured my crime of murder that would turn the heart of the woman I love to prolonged suffering and lifelong hatred for all of who I am and what I'd done.

I wanted to believe my guilt profound and altogether owned, and I'd shaken Trigorin's hand to insure it all. I wanted to own my indecency and live in the poverty of my dishonor. My guilt, in toto, predicated by my unreluctant acceptance to remain in disgrace upon the Cuban isle; to dine the rest of my days unnourished on the bones served at the traitors' table. I could have borne this, knowing that were it to overwhelm me, I could give all those who loathed me, a Christmas gift of suicide.

The idea that Trigorin would go back on his word and for some wild reason ask me to return to my home, overwhelmed my perfect guilt by its emotional futility. I hated to think it, but what Trigorin seemed to propose was a wash-all-my-sins-away guilt-free pass.

"I'm sorry, I don't understand. Is she safe? I want to see her."

"In due time." He lifted my confession. Weighed it before my eyes. "You understand what this and those bona fides you provided on surrender give me?"

I didn't answer. Guilt can only be discerned when one openly acknowledges the moral wrong of his betrayal; he can only find peace when that betrayal is publicly exposed and he is allowed to face punishment.

"You will return to the CIA. To your work. To your world. But you will, until your death, serve a different master. You will belong to me. You will be 'our man in Washington.' My agent inside Langley's impregnable walls. Step out of line, this handwritten and signed confession, the recordings of your initial surrender at my offices, our meeting with your offer of treason, along with the proof of Alvarez's death—your Agency's longest running Cuban spy—will go to your superiors, to your Congress, to your *casa blanca*, at the same time they will go to the American and international press. Let there be no doubt you will be charged with and convicted of treason, branded to the world the vilest of men: a coward, a murderer, a traitor. The Americans will execute you."

He paused to blow away his ash, turn his cigar, blow on its cherry end a second time. So alike and unlike Muir and his cigarettes. He smoked, blew fumes, and peered at me through the cloud of blue.

*Guilt: devastating, soul-twisted, incessant torture of remorse—
just words. Unintelligent. Useless. Random letters easily rearranged:*
write "love" instead; scout freedom to taunt rasing stress. *To what
earthly purpose but to prove I am a fool to think I know guilt. As easily
would I return to Nina to claim love and outward happiness—my
crime disguised, unknown—than my guilt unassuaged and, forced into
continuous betrayal, would grow malignant inside of me, worse than
any word I could possibly spell.*

But I would return to Nina!

And what has the CIA done for me or for those I've loved?

*Silas Kingston made my case for me. "There isn't a thing you've ever
done for the Agency that means all that much to our nation's security."*

The Agency has always been the author of all our suffering.
I offered my life to save Nina's—and wouldn't this still be
exactly that?

Without the recrimination.

Without her ever having to know.

The ultimate sacrifice for love—not even Muir could fault me.

*What's it he said? "With a good lie, a lie we tend with a garden-
er's care to keep alive, everyone ends up better and the thing called life
grows more meaningful."*

Well, love-on-ya, old man.

"If you betray this trusted arrangement I offer you, Mr. Aiken,
I further promise you this: while you await trial, your family and
everyone you love will pay with their lives. You will know the pain
of causing the death of your loved ones before you are executed by
your government, and you will carry that with you beyond death.
You are a believer; you know I speak the truth." He fingertipped
a flake of tobacco leaf from the tip of his pink piggy tongue. "Play
this right"—he picked up the ring box—"and who knows? The
hero still may get the girl."

He grinned, ever so slightly, reading in my countenance not only that he had my slavish and shameful obedience, but had identified the object of my desires as once having been his own, and in that, pinpointed my human frailty that made shallowness and fear better virtues than truth and selfless pain.

He asks I become Charlie March.

Muir killed Charlie March.

No… he didn't, exactly, did he?

I said, "Before any future between us is discussed, I've met my side of our initial agreement with my surrender and with that confession. In exchange, your promise was Nina's freedom. I will have that now."

Trigorin gave orders to my guards. His grin spread across hidden teeth. "All of this"—he gestured to the suite, his open palm lowering to end on me—"I fault myself. Had I remembered that pretty face when I approved her seizure, I would have taken Nina's father without need of you. But I can love the symmetry. Not only do I own you now and forever, but we share the most intimate of things two real men can share. Like me back then, you too, now, will be lying to her every time you fuck her. We can both agree, a man will say anything to keep a good piece of ass—even a half-breed Cubana mulatta."

He wasn't trying to provoke me; he knew the depth of my indignity. He was twisting the knife in my wounded soul to test the limits of my abasement. Before I could react, the fat guard entered, pale-faced, with sweat glistening his brow. He spoke to the general in faltering words.

I didn't need translation to know what he was saying. I leaped to my feet and barged toward the kitchen, where the direct feed from Nina's captivity streamed.

"*¡Détente!*" The guard commanded I stop.

"*¡Basta, idiota!*" Trigorin snapped and pressed after me.

The monitor, where at intervals I'd been allowed to observe Nina in her captivity, ran with the silent snowstorm of a lost signal as the other two guards cursed and struggled to reconnect.

I wheeled on Trigorin. "You son of a bitch."

The general appeared as alarmed as I.

"I assure you: they would not have lifted a finger against Nina without my order."

"Then where is she? What's happened?!"

He held a quick discussion with his men before addressing me. "People have attempted contact by radio and telephone. We have agents on the way."

"Fuck you. Our deal's off. You might as well shoot me now, as her safety was all I had to live for."

"*Tranquilo, señor. Por favor.* I am in the dark as much as you. No order was given to finish her. Your own people must have intervened."

"I'm not moving a fucking inch until I see her safe."

General Trigorin clutched both my shoulders, both to transfer confidence and to demonstrate his power over me. "My agents would not execute her without my direct order. If she escaped that room, they would not have killed her. Therefore, she is alive. So now, if she has gone from our care—rescued, which I strongly believe is the accurate assessment—you, my new friend, get back to CIA with the picture frame, with your story of Alvarez's heroism, and verify his sacrifice made to keep his network secret."

"I thought you said he *did* keep it secret."

Trigorin's eyes sparkled. "What she did not reveal in questioning will remain in place for you and me to use to my future design."

I could see his logic, his need for my swift return to set in place. I had no other card to play. "If she has been killed?"

He crushed out his cigar in an overflowing ashtray. He twisted the butt. "You have no alternative but to do as I say."

He gave orders to my guards, handed me Nina's treasured frame and Pandora's box, then turned me over to a two-man plainclothes detail waiting for me outside the door.

"*Feliz Navidad,* Mr. Aiken."

Halfway out, I turned back into the room. I went back to retrieve Muir's fountain pen. My fingers wrapped around it, pulling the empty inkwell into my palm and out of sight.

44

I ARRIVE IN HAVANA TWO DAYS EARLIER. Back in time. The afternoon of December 23, 2002. My identity kit, provided by Silas Kingston, is clean for Cuba and does not mark me as ever having traveled here before. I check in at the Hotel Nacional and make my SDR, ascertaining my surveillance is in place but passive—confirming my Canadian passport and my stated purpose of "leisure" as the reason for my visit have not raised red flags that I am any kind of security threat, known or unknown. I find my way to the Iglesia Santo Cristo del Buen Viaje.

The *caja pobre* is missing from its stand. I enter the nave and observe Amy Kim at prayer alone in the church. Casual acknowledgment, as is done between strangers; threat/no-threat fight or flight. We ignore one another, she more quickly than I, as men naturally track sexuality at a conscious level with strangers, reproductive fitness at the unconscious, for five seconds longer than females.

Believe it or not, they train us to fake this longer look.

I take a tourist pamphlet and make a modest show of interest in the artwork, artifacts, the stained glass it describes. Amy finishes her prayers. She heads for the narthex. She pauses to light two votive candles and waits five seconds between the two, signaling she has soft surveillance, but it is safe to initiate contact.

We time our exits simultaneously, so we are forced to recognize each other again in a natural way as I hold open the door for her. For the benefit of her watchers, we acknowledge each other on the front steps as tourists do. I make no attempt at visual identification of her tail. We exchange informal small talk before

I start off. Behind me, Amy fumbles with a tourist map. She frustrates, acts confused, calls after me.

I ignore her and cross the street to the park plaza. I don't look back as she looks around, looks at her map one last time, and jogs in my direction, calling me again.

I turn, puzzled. Embarrassed, she approaches me with her map. I give a friendly smile and wait for her to join me. We gather our heads over her map.

"I'm so sorry," she whispers. "He wouldn't let me tell you—"

"It's done. You followed *our* protocol and came to the church."

She points at the map. We both look around, then back at the paper.

I say, "Silas doesn't know, does he?"

"No."

I pantomime showing her a route; off her confusion, I make a show of offering to take her.

Still clutching her map, occasionally referring to it, Amy Kim falls into step beside me. By the look of us, we are two strangers bonded over shared language, shared experience of visitors to an exotic foreign island. People are passing, but she hasn't signaled they are her minders.

"Silas flipped you with your parents."

"They're not my parents."

"I know," I tell her. "Your parents were Chinese. You were adopted."

For an instant, Amy breaks character. Her eyes flash with alarm. "How long have you known?"

"I was worried about you. After our last meeting, I did my own research."

We move unhurriedly through a light crowd, putting as many individuals as possible in our wake. Her performance is curious about her surroundings, friendly to me, but also a little shy. Pitch perfect.

"My parents—adopted parents—never told me. I've not asked since finding out. I don't care. My whole life I lived their lie."

We jaywalk through traffic on the other side of the square.

She continues, "I can understand if you hate me for letting DDC Kingston use that to compromise me. Compromise you."

"I could never hate you. I've come to believe Muir: you're Jewel. I mean, you came to represent her to him. You're his Jewel returned in a new and brilliant, independent way."

She smiles to fight back emotion neither of us can afford.

"Jewel was innocent," she says. "Muir killed her anyway."

"I know. That's the thing I can't stop thinking about," I say. "What he's wanted from this. From the moment he attached us together. Me to trust you without reserve, no matter what. If we succeed in my plan, if you're willing to trust me without reservation, you and I are going to erase the stain of Muir's past."

Amy looks at her watch. She holds it with two fingers of her other hand, telling me the Cuban couple coming up on us are her surveillance.

I quickly pointed out a cross street. "Here's your stop. If you keep walking that way, you'll find what you're looking for." Which would be something that would have to present itself to her along the way.

We exchange goodbyes. I watch her, a fond, crooked smile shaping my face, and call after her. "Hey, wait up!"

She turns, quizzical. I trot her way. I ask, for all to hear, "You can say no if you want, but do you have any dinner plans?"

Amy takes a long time deciding before shyly shaking her head. "Not really."

"Would you like to make plans with me? My treat? Purely social."

She relaxes her shoulders. Innocent. Pleasant. She happily tells me her hotel. I tell her I'll be there with a taxi at 8:30 p.m.

"Would nine be all right? I'll need time to get ready," she flirts.

"Sure," I say and leave.

Her request for an extra half hour to get ready, though unplanned, did not seem unusual; a calm of confidence swept over me for the first time since the horror of Nina's house.

THE DINING ROOM AT THE MELIA COHIBA VARADERO, like the rest of the hotel, had been fully remodeled and upgraded from Old World timeless sophistication to retro twenty-first-century deco since I'd last dined there with Nina. Given a window seat with a soft-lit view of the roll of waves on silvery sand, Amy and I sat in low-backed angular chairs with sweeping armrests at an elegantly adorned table. Beautiful linens and flatware, crystal, and flowers. She looked magnificent in a tight, white sheath dress, red heels, red lipstick. She'd curled and teased her hair, full and feminine and strong. Her wild black tresses framed a pair of opalescent pearl earrings. She'd become another woman entirely. The candles flickered, warming Amy's features, which, cast with what I could only describe as deep sorrow, worried me.

I'd confirmed that the TIME MACHINE packet had been smuggled in successfully; Amy was ready to proceed with the installation, committed to whatever changes to the OPLAN I chose. Whatever troubled Amy was not mission oriented.

HOUNDFOX had yet to arrive. Assuming he'd received his signal when he'd passed the church that afternoon, we would soon make contact and confirm our after-dinner meet. I decided to use our meal to allow Amy an opportunity to open up more fully on her personal concerns, which I determined had everything to do with the unforeseen, unwanted shock she'd experienced with

Silas Kingston's revelation about her birth and her bloodline. Maybe if we talked about it, I could coax Amy out of her sadness into discovering something comforting, something good in her altered identity.

Our appetizers arrived, salad for Amy, ceviche for me. I squeezed extra lime over the raw salmon and shellfish. I asked, "About your birth parents. I get how disconcerting a revelation something like that might be—hugely unfair. Do you have a way to track them down? Might be interesting. You never know."

"I don't need to."

"Why?"

"When China instituted their one-child policy, the vast majority of girl babies wound up killed or abandoned."

"Sure. Sadly. Boys being of more economic and social value in Chinese society. But they didn't with you, and it did lead to your adoption."

"International adoptions from China weren't allowed until 1991. I appreciate the compliment, but I was born in 1979. The first year of the one-child policy."

She mixed her lettuce with her fork, watching the dressing spread, not bothering to eat.

"They must have gone to heroic effort to get you out. At least they wanted to see you had a better life than they could provide."

Her fork stopped moving. She looked at me. "They sold me to the Triads. They were arrested for black-market profiteering. They were separated, and they were imprisoned. My birth mother died of influenza. My father, so the evidence shows, killed himself when he learned of her death."

This isn't going the right way. "Ego up, Dumbo."

"I'm sorry. That doesn't sound so good. But your *parents*—you got to them, you got America—they love you. They provided for

you a wonderful life filled with opportunity. Your genius blossomed. A bad set of circumstances you or they had no control over
were made right, many times over."

Jessie, Jessie, Jessie.

She offered me a false but thankful grin.

"What's your happiest childhood memory?" I stabbed some
shrimp.

Her smile broadened, truth finding its way into it. I was glad.
The seafood was fresh and remarkable.

"My mother gave all her time to me, starting me in school
and math and science tutoring as early as I can remember. Long
before kindergarten. I loved it and it was plenty—I had no extra
time for anything—but structured social play was important. They
knew that. For my full development."

I was pleased to see her begin to eat.

"You had friends? Similar friends?"

"Not really. First, we tried music—"

"Aha. Your guitar!"

"I taught myself guitar in college. No, but we tried drawing.
Then dance. I was terrible at those. But theater class; I loved acting.
I liked it so much I worked extra hard in my scholastic studies,
doing everything twice as fast as my peers to allow for more time
with my children's theater class at our church. I loved it so much.
And you know something: I was good. The teacher suggested my
parents get me an agent for commercials, but they wouldn't hear
of it. Instead, the woman, Miss Kovacs, she got me a spot with an
older-age performing group. They were larger and funded by the
city arts council; they came with a more experienced director. That
led to my parents acquiescing to a once-a-week acting coach."

She paused to look out the window and I could see her happiness mirrored back in the glass.

"I had no idea you were an actress."

She sighed. "I was the best in every class and my instructors would move me on to better coaches each year, and by middle school, I'd done small parts with Cleveland Reparatory and Cincinnati. By high school, I was starring in every production. For a Korean, uh, Chinese, I was getting roles that would traditionally never go to an Asian over a white or a black girl. You'd think I'd have had rivals, but everyone loved me. Not for me, but for the roles I brought to life."

She briefly squeezed my hand across the table, and while the sorrow was still in her eyes, she gave a little laugh. "I can't believe I'm telling you this."

"It's a delightful story."

She chuckled. "Oh, it's not."

"I'll be the judge of that," I said through food. "Go on."

"Until Nathan, it was the only thing in my life I ever loved. And there was talk I had potential for scholarships. I auditioned for Julliard and was invited for a callback. London Academy of Music and Art too. Both told me if I passed the live audition, I would receive a full scholarship—and they told me I *would* pass. I did all this on the side. Secretly from my parents. I'd known, of course, in their plan for me, I was to go to an Ivy League school and study computer science and physics and all that, but there was a little tiny spark of hope inside this starry-eyed Indiana girl—God, it sounds so slow-witted and sad—who really thought, I *really believed it*: if I could land something big, get that kind of recognition for the one thing I loved from a top academy..."

She stopped herself. She sipped her wine. When next she spoke, the dream was gone.

"At my high school, which had a strong program—best in the entire tri-state area—we were set to perform Chekov, *The Seagull*, for our spring production. I'd been allowed to select it the year before, and I'd memorized and rehearsed for the role of Nina. Isn't that funny? My greatest ambition was once to be 'Nina'?"

I was unfamiliar with the play, but not the déjà vu sensation spinning in my brain. I urged my mind to grip reality; prayed I'd not go into seizure.

"I don't know the play," I said through gritted teeth.

I've learned to fear coincidence. The uncertain fate I abhorred, the "gut instinct" that in training at the Farm they hammer into us to always trust, had once again joined me wraithlike, grave, and silent, behind my shoulder. I refused to look.

Her teeth sparkled. "Well, that's not the point. Just a coincidence. It could have been any play. When tryouts came, I was not permitted to audition for the lead role or any other role. I was devastated. I didn't understand. My private teacher had arranged with several major schools—parental-approved Ivy League schools—who'd seen my tape, to have scouts at my performance. He'd paid out of his own pocket. So, I asked my theater instructor, and he told me the truth. He was crushed. My parents had come to the school and demanded I not be allowed to participate on stage but only in crew. He'd tried to fight it and took it all the way to the district. They would not allow me to take the opportunity from another girl to shine when my future was not to include theater. I pleaded with my parents and was punished severely for my impertinence, and for being disrespectful. Worse, they made me believe I was a fool for ever having believed I would have a future in 'playacting;' if they'd known how thoughtless I was and vain—disloyal—they would have moved me to some other extra-curricular activity where I might have rid my misplaced passion for 'fooling around and pretending' into something of more concrete benefit to my family, church, and country."

"Once you got to Princeton, you could have taken theater there."

"You don't get it. I was a disappointment to my parents. They beat into me that they had sacrificed their lives to get me where I was. Literally beat me. They had given themselves nothing so that I might have everything. I had brought them shame. To regain their love, I applied myself with twice the focus and intensity on my math and sciences. If Nathan hadn't picked me out of the crowd for the Agency and made the school force me to take his courses…" Her shoulders slumped. "I guess I'd never know the truth."

"Know what truth? About your real parents? Their sacrifice?"

Two things caught my eye: our waiters coming with our entrees, and Comandante Alejandro Alvarez with a dusky middle-aged woman on his arm walking to their table.

"The truth about today. This whole trip—that I still own the stage and it owns me."

I returned the hand squeeze. "And that was just the matinee. Tonight will be the performance of a lifetime."

"Yes," she said as her eyes engaged the waiter, complimenting him with a kind look as she watched her lobster be presented before her. "It will have to be."

She caught my eye. She looked glad. Grateful. Complete. I didn't see what I should have. "I wouldn't have it any other way," she said, and asked a blessing over our supper, thankful for our food and our lives. She supplicated for my continued safety and for those we loved and missed. We ate.

WE MET HOUNDFOX in the sea- and chemical-fragrant pool shed as I had before. The passage of eleven years since last I'd seen him, the eve of his wife's fall to cancer, had aged him poorly. His eyes were permanently red where they should have been white, and the limbal rings surrounding his irises, gone milky gray, made the brown centers, lustrous before, dull like farmed-out soil beneath a cloudy sky. His laugh lines, once uplifted like bird wings, drooped; any flight of happiness gone from a world he looked only dimly upon.

"The years have been good to you," he said, clasping my hand. "I am happy for you and Nina, who loves you truly. Where is she? Why is she not here?"

I told him everything. It pained him as a father, but he took the wound, mortal as it might be, like a soldier. Having ignored Amy, he now considered her. "She will install the device?"

"She will."

He offered Amy a handshake. "I am sorry for my rudeness. My daughter has bragged in her elliptical fashion of your talents. But your marvelous beauty was unexpected. Especially seeing you with the man I'd hoped to one day call son." He looked back at me. "I am clear of her purpose, yours you've not explained."

"I've come to bury you."

He showed teeth, calculated to resemble a smile. "This is an assassination?"

"No. Never. I was not supposed to meet you at all but to turn traitor and expose you to General Trigorin."

"Same difference, no?"

I studied him, hunting his features for Nina and found her in his cheeks, the thrust of his jaw, the tilt of his nose. I'd known my answer to his question, and why I was with him at this moment, before I'd left Lone Pine. Only now did I admit it aloud.

"I'm not here out of some sense of fair play, or for your absolution before I commit a crime against you. I'm here because my heart belongs to Nina and hers to mine, and I know where her heart must lead me."

He arched a gray eyebrow with practiced charm. "After the childish games *nenita* played with your heart?"

"I cheated on her."

"You had every right."

I showed him Nina's ring. I told him how I'd been on my way to propose to her, how she would have said yes. He agreed she would have.

"Amy will go through with the installation," I said. "*Comandante*, I'd prefer you to be the master of your own fate. This is the hardest thing I'll ever have to say, but we both know Nina would want more than anything else that I protect you. All else. I've come to exfiltrate you."

Alejandro raised his eyebrows, eyes twinkling with irony. He leaned in and took my hand. He closed the box still open in my hand and closed my hand over the box. "*Y así, eres mi hijo.*" And like that, you are my son.

He gazed into my eyes and didn't say another word for a long time. Then, as if he'd set a clock and punched the timer that would measure his finitude, he spoke at length:

"*Entiende, hijo*, she is my future to die for. It should never work the other way around. In this case, I will see to it, and you have no say. In May 1958, I stood with Fidel when he told Cuba: 'Personally, I do not aspire to any post and I consider that there is sufficient proof that I fight for the good of my people, without any personal or egotistic ambition soiling my conduct. After the revolution, we will convert the movement into a political party and we will fight with the arms of the constitution and the law. Not even then will I aspire to the presidency because I am only thirty-one years old.' You may wonder why I memorized this. Though some say that even then he was lying to us all, that he'd known his real purpose for Cuba and himself from the beginning, I have always believed his early words in my heart. I've stood by them even as he faltered. I still believe he was genuine and pure in his heart and in his words. I have endeavored my whole life to continue what we started as outlaws in the hills. I fight Fidel to save Fidel. But this Cuba he's constructed does not want prosperity, or peace, or civil liberties, even comfort for its citizens, the poor, and the powerless. This Castro I've never known has always and only ever desired to hold on to power, wealth, and luxury. Nenita would give her life gladly for her father, but her father would not be worthy of her loyalty and sacrifice were he not willing to first give his life to the future hopes of the country he'd taught her to love more. I will say no more on my decision. It is final. The only duty I have remaining is to make sure you are successful in saving *mi hija*."

"Sir, I promise you, that is already in motion."

"But it will not be successful to me until your ring is upon her finger."

We went over each step of what would happen to me. What would be required by Amy. She made difficult requests, but Nina's father took them and promised full effort by his network to her needs. There would be much to do between now and Christmas, from the moment I presented myself at Trigorin's DGI Department M compound until the moment my interrogation would end with the report of HOUNDFOX's death. Somewhere in the middle, I would have to achieve the impossible, and once and for all and, above all: in reality, I would have to travel time.

45

A BRIEF TALE OF TREASON. A strange traveler knocks on a castle gate. When the watchman answers, the man says he has come from a foreign land with a sack of stolen gold and jewels to present to the king. To prove himself, he gives the watchman a diamond.

There isn't a single version of this story where the guy gets told to take his treasure, shove it and shove off. By the same token, there isn't a version in which treachery isn't involved and at the least, one or the other—stranger or king—does not get burned. That's why we start kids out as early as possible with the fairytales where trade and commerce, technology, mass populations, wars, and terrorism, and WMDs aren't yet at stake.

You're invited inside the gates. Though you're told you are considered suspect and naturally mistrusted, you are treated politely and urged to be honest, advised that if your gold turns out to be painted tin, your life will turn out to be worth even less.

So be it. Because if the gold turns out to be real, the king will always take it and will always strive to obtain more. At this point, the king believes he's found his golden goose, only in this stranger's case, the king was the goose I'd battled past, present, and future to pull from the window and cook him for my Christmas feast.

THE FIRST STEP IN THE DEFECTION PROCESS is confrontational, meant to scare away the fakers or provoke the loonies. Second step: prove your identity. Typically, you surrender appropriate documentation and allow for its verification. I spent that period in a sparse but not uncomfortable windowless office. Treated politely,

I was served coffee and given a pad of paper to make a short declaration of intent. You don't meet anyone of importance at this time. There's no good cop, bad cop.

This process took three hours, at which point a video camera was brought into my room and attached to a tripod. Twenty minutes later, an intelligence officer in a mildly impressive military uniform took over. He switched on the recorder. He introduced himself. Advised me on the serious nature of my actions both to the Republic of Cuba and the United States of America.

He offered me the opportunity to change my mind.

He read my statement, although I knew that hidden cameras had been filming me since I'd approached the compound, and that cameras had recorded my writing of my statement—intel analysts reading it in real-time for the content of my words, forensic graphologists analyzing my psychology in how I'd shaped and spaced my letters.

He finishes reading. He lights a cigarillo. And he offers one to me. I decline.

He interviews me on my motives for defection—this is the first time the word *defection* is used—which I've already written down. It leads to a serious conversation of the international legality of the term. This goes round and round pro forma for another hour.

I am asked to sign the declaration of intent. He signs it, stamps it. Photographs of it and of me are taken at every step, the last like a prizewinner holding a cardboard sweepstakes check. He leaves with the document. I remain in the room. I am watched by my profilers for an hour, analyzing my activity, posture, biometrics for any clues of deception.

The intelligence officer brings in a polygraph team. I'm read another statement about the voluntary nature of the lie-detector test. I am offered another chance to change my mind and leave the country. I am told again these are my international rights and I refuse these rights. I sign another assertation. I am asked to renounce my citizenship with full knowledge that in doing so I am now entirely open to Cuban law and prosecution without any form of US or international representation.

I agree and sign documents to this effect.

At this point I have committed sixteen Title 18 *U.S. Criminal Code* violations, ten of them to the fullest degree and deserving of maximum punishment, which is death.

Now the polygraph is an interesting situation. As much for ferreting out my deception, it is equally important for covering my interrogator's ass if all this goes wrong. Since one doesn't get this far without it having been ascertained you are, in fact, an officer of an enemy intelligence service—bona fides proven—the results of this interrogation will always move you to the next step *whether you are found to be truthful or deceptive*. So, in this manner it is only a formality; either/or you are exceedingly valuable and can be used and abused in any number of ways against your former nation with impunity.

All of us are trained in methods of obscuring, even cheating the flutter box's results. In all honesty and of my own free will, I was defecting as Silas had ordered outside of CIA knowledge or consent. Due to the quality of my three tests, I got bumped up to VIP treatment.

THEY MOVED ME FROM THE STERILE OFFICE in the forbidding security building to an elegant reception area inside another building that received with opulence and muzzled with authority. Within five minutes, I was introduced to General Trigorin. Having seen his photograph, his commanding nature and mature good looks were not unexpected. His charisma, however, took me by surprise. It's not that I instantly wanted to like him, it's that he filled the space around him with an air that made me, and I would undoubtedly guess everyone who encountered him, want Trigorin to like them.

We discussed the nature of my decision and our line of work as if we were talking college football. Rivalry mixed with tradition, nostalgia, and the desire for fair play in mutual competition. A crock of shit he made smell of gardenias. He showed concern for my motivations. Claimed I'd not been straight, which I'd intentionally not been, and he wasn't surprised with that at all. I told him my motivation was solely to save the life of the woman I loved. He sympathized. Had assumed this the case. Indeed, had known about it—"Your sense of romantic tragedy bleeds through your handwriting." He understood romance and, though he did not ascribe to it, as a Latino, he believed in the power of a lover's sacrifice.

He was gross and yet I babbled at him as if he were my lover. He assumed I knew what now would follow but coached me through the next steps: my sequester at the Hotel Florida and my full written confession. He urged I write as I feel and as best as I may; to allow myself to verge on delirium and hold nothing back in emotion as I would unbind myself of technical, practical, or, as he put it, *material útil*—"useful" material.

"But the timing of your revelation of this HOUNDFOX you offer—as his arrest protects this soulmate of yours—will be in your hands alone."

46

I LAY ASIDE MY PEN.

One of the three remaining Cuban agents comes into the room to collect my document. I step away from the table. Along with what I've written, he takes the box of pads. About to take my pen, he returns it to me. I place it on the coffee table. I feel dirty keeping it; I've written Muir out of it, all he stood for and hoped for me, and the ink it has delivered is brown, impossible to forge, and it is dry. The agent leaves to the kitchen.

The inkwell I'd insisted they hunt down in the night and deliver me, beckons, unopened, from the hollow of my left hand. I position my face out of view from the overhead camera. I hear the air conditioner cycle on. I wait for any reaction, but my minders have not noticed or do not care. I breathe deeply five full breaths of night air before closing the balcony doors.

My eyes swim.

My hands shake.

I fumble off the inkwell cap.

"Drink me," I whisper a final counted, countdown breath.

I open it and swallow the contents and by this do I take my freedom.

ALREADY COMING AWAKE, the methylphenidate boost I'd swallowed before the induction of the remifentanil/propofol incapacitating agent counteracted the anesthetic effects of the gas-flow through the air ducts. I focused on Amy Kim, who, framed by the balcony doors opened once more, stared back at me through the faceplate of the oxygen mask she'd put over my head. She helped me to my feet as the air and the stimulant returned me to full consciousness. She indicated I follow to the kitchen doorway.

My three Cuban guards slumped unconscious in their chairs. I propped each of them into sitting positions, tilting their heads to ensure regular breathing, while Amy stopped and reset the decks running digital tape of the hotel suite to the moment before I drank the antidote ink and the gas knocked out the guards. Earlier access and modifications to the cameras and their internal processors, along with the planting of the inkwell antidote, and the sleeping-gas delivery system rigged into the Hotel Florida interrogation suite—grueling and dangerous for Amy and her HOUNDFOX helpmates—had transpired simultaneous with my surrender processing at DGI Compound M. While Amy double-checked her work, I watched Nina sleeping on the remote display from Washington. True to Trigorin's promise, Nina had not been interrogated or any more abused since I'd begun my confession. For our plan to work, the recordings would later have to match between the Hotel Florida and the feed from Nina. That was out of Amy's and my control. I prayed for Nina's safety, our reunion, and our future together in peace and love without danger.

We returned to the living room and left through the balcony doors, across a horizontal extension ladder braced by a tall and muscular Cuban agent of the HOUNDFOX network in the apartment window on the far side of the Calle Obispo. Once we were inside, Alvarez's agent waved to a compatriot on the roof the Hotel Florida who monitored the gas-flow into the suite's air conditioning and signaled the time with a show of fingers.

"We have under two hours," said Amy.

I followed her across the room. She paused only long enough to sling a canvas saddlebag over her shoulder before leading me through the door. I heard the lock set behind us by the Cuban agent as we moved swiftly for the stairs.

A two-tone white-on-blue 1956 Buick Roadmaster Riviera waited in the dark, engine idling, a trail of exhaust vapor rising behind it. Without looking back, the grandmotherly driver offered a small automatic over the front bench seat. My primary duty would be independent verification of success of TIME MACHINE's installation, but we'd also agreed I would provide security for Amy during the installation beneath the Embassy of Venezuela. Security we both understood meant the weapon would be used to provide Amy the handful of seconds needed to initiate the self-destruction of TIME MACHINE before we would inevitably lose or take our own lives.

We flew along the Malecón, along the sea, traffic gentle in the hushed Christmas hours before daybreak. We turned up Calle 18 where the International School of Havana now stood shuttered for the holidays on a property where in 1930, the Cuban–American Telephone & Telegraph Company (a fully owned subsidiary of US Bell South in Atlanta) had operated a switching house. In those days, the traffic from the six separate US submarine trunk cables—six lines spooled Key West to Havana Harbor, four in 1921, the last two in 1930 and 1941—came together to link into the local cable system of the Compañia Telefónica Cuba. With Castro and the revolution, the six US cable huts in Havana Harbor were destroyed and the Compañia Telefónica Cuba, freed from American tentacles, was nationalized.

The switching house was closed in 1959. Razed in 1961. Twelve years later, the International School was erected on the abandoned and overgrown lot. However, while the communists had leveled the original building, they never bothered to collapse and fill the underground maintenance tunnels that ran back to

the Cuban telephone system. They were—or so Castro's tele-
communication engineers asserted—spokes of a broken wagon
wheel dead-ended where the lines had gone above ground and
joined the Havana system. Those lines were cut, and the concrete
coupling recesses were sealed.

None of Castro's telephonic engineers had worked for the
overthrown President Fulgencio Batista, nor had they ever met
Florence Pritchett. "Flo" Pritchett—sometime fashion editor,
sometime model, sometime singer and radio personality. A lover
of JFK in 1944, actors Errol Flynn and Robert Walker in 1946
and 1948, David O. Selznick on and off for years, and in 1956 she
accompanied her husband, Earl E. T. Smith, to Havana where he
would serve as the last US Ambassador to Cuba, and where she
would become the lover of Cuban dictator Batista.

For their tri-weekly trysts, Flo would enter the Bell Telephone
tunnels at the Calle 18 switching station and travel underground
to a luxury apartment inside a government villa at number 512
Calle 20. Not long after Castro's takeover, this villa became the
Venezuelan Embassy. The exit from the secret tunnel was sealed
and secured, and Venezuela was assured the electrical, fiber-optic,
cable, telephonic, digital communication grid from their embassy
into the Havana grid was inaccessible and unassailable.

Havana being Havana, and Cubans being Cuban, Ambassador
Smith was assured something along those lines about his wife
as well.

The Buick *abuela* wished us a *"¡Muera Fidel!"* and let us out
on a dark lane behind the school. Amy led me into the campus—
security lights vandalized, gates unlocked by another hidden hand
of the HOUNDFOX network—and, after waiting the passage of
the night watchman across the main hall courtyard, she located
from memory an architectural oddity. Trash and leaf-strewn, it

appeared an old concrete stairway at the end of a cramped and long-neglected space between two buildings. Long untrodden, these stairs descended to a reinforced steel door that, likewise, hadn't been opened in decades.

Amy descended the stairway. She ignored the small, stamped-metal, rusted sign in Spanish above the door that read *"Eléctrico—Peligroso—No Entrada"* withdrew an aerosol lubricant from her bag and sprayed the hinges and the lock. While she timed the chemical set on her wristwatch, I waited halfway down, eyes level with the courtyard, gun ready, and watched for a chance return of the watchman. A full minute passed. I glanced back and observed her working the lock with a lock pick, and entertained a stray thought on the usefulness of Linda's library.

"Open," she whispered.

We cleared refuse from the stairwell, to prevent the noise of brushing and crunching leaves, and pulled open the heavy door.

"Quickly now," she said, and led me inside with a halogen penlight.

She scampered through the school's archaic and now unused steam heating and electrical plant to a floor-to-ceiling gordian knot of thickly painted 8", 10", and foot-and-a-half steel piping. She wedged around behind it.

Waist high in the concrete wall was a two-foot-by-two-foot iron door. Its surface and frame entirely rusted, the small door waited, long forgotten, in the concrete side wall. It resembled an old-fashioned fuse-box panel door of zero modern utility.

Amy lubricated and opened it.

A few feet beyond the hatch revealed a blank concrete wall.

"Dead end," I said.

Amy slipped through the hatch hole and stood in the space between the two walls. She signaled me inside. I followed her into the narrow space. She closed the hatch behind us. She directed her light left and illuminated a wooden ladder unused for more than half a century. It extended up the inner wall, which Amy's light further revealed plateaued to open onto an overhead concrete passageway that ran obliquely—if my sense of direction was accurate—away from the school property.

The tunnel system was dry and still. Dusted like an ancient crypt.

Amy moved into it with the speed and instinct of a rabbit in its warren, and I hustled to keep pace with her. With each cross-passage turn, each dogleg, the successive tunnel compartments widened overhead, climbed long inclines, or descended short steps: angles that matched the island's contours away from the shore. In this manner, we traveled beneath the double southwest-running lanes of Quinta Avenida, beneath the park esplanade of the boulevard's center divider, and under the double northeast-running lanes of the avenue's opposing side until we turned into a dead end. Exposed from where they passed across the space from one wall conduit to the other, hung a heavy tangle of electrical wiring, telephone and trunk lines, and bundles of cable.

Amy laid open her saddlebag and switched light sources, trading her penlight for a halogen head lamp, which she strapped around her forehead like the diadem of an Egyptian goddess. I checked my watch. We'd been gone from the hotel for thirty minutes. Amy removed her jacket and spread it on the floor. What looked like a decorative geometric-patterned, black-on-white silk inner lining, when torn out and folded high corner to low, became an electrical schematic. She withdrew TIME MACHINE and her tools and went to work.

I waited at the mouth of that final passageway, peering back into blackness, worried that if pursuit came with night vision, my gun and I would be useless. But the installation took less than twenty minutes and Amy was soon again beside me.

I went back past her, verified TIME MACHINE active and functioning. "Ready to go?" I asked.

Her expression was set, serious. She took my hands. "I'm staying," she said, her voice oddly muffled.

"That makes no sense." I noticed the pearl from one of her earrings was missing from its setting. "What do you mean?"

She said, "My L pill is in the faux pearl." Her grip tightened as she sensed I was about to pull free. "It's between my teeth. You won't get it from my mouth without me biting it."

"You're not making any sense, Amy. This is a brilliant success. There's no surprise waiting to jump us when we emerge. We are going to make it."

"I know all that. I'm not worried for you."

"Then why would you want to swallow cyanide?"

"People kill themselves when they weigh what they have to live for against what they'd like to die for."

"Amy, don't get all matter-of-fact with me about something insane. This is stress—adrenaline, fear. I will get you home. I'll get you out. We'll change your identity—you can be that actress or anyone you want."

"Charlie March, Aunt Linda, Joshua, Bishop. Muir. Even faithful you, Russell—they never let anyone out. No one escapes the Agency. All we can look forward to is what Nathan said: being hunted to our last quivering corner. After my success with this"—she indicated TIME MACHINE—"I'll always be their forever girl."

"Please. You don't want to do this." But by saying it aloud between us, we both knew I was wrong and now only wasting time that belonged singularly to me.

She released one of my hands. If I grabbed her, I had no doubt she'd bite the cyanide. My heart hammered.

Flop on the floor! Fake a seizure!

Instead, I watched her reach for her throat. She plucked off her necklace. Let the chain fall, tinkling on the cement. She placed the pendant in my hand.

"Remember you gave me some of Muir's ashes?"

"Yes."

"They're inside the pendant I've worn over my heart. He'd once made me promise that when he died, I would take on the responsibility of delivering his ashes to the Moon. It's where he wanted his remains. He said, 'Quiet and peaceful and able to watch over the globe I once pulled the handle and spun.' He wanted to give me an impossible task to distract me from my grief."

I stared at her face. Her tragic, lovely face, and in that tragedy, I saw Muir. An angel of death? Wings of mercy? I shuddered. She told me she had cut and burned a lock of her hair and combined her ashes with Muir's, mixed with a drop of her blood earlier that extra half hour while getting ready. She told me where she would have me lay their remains to rest. I tried to reason with her, but she covered my mouth. I stopped. I wasn't crying—haven't since I was eleven, well, maybe fifteen—so I don't know why she wiped my cheeks when she said: "What you said about me—about Jewel. You weren't entirely correct."

I tried again, gently pulling her. "I know you're hurting, but you don't have to do this now. Do it once we get home. I won't stop you. We'll bury you together. But don't die here alone and unclaimed. Muir would never allow it."

"Shhh, Russell. It's perfect for me. You must let me finish telling you. The CIA means nothing to me. My life is not the life I wanted— I wanted to be an actress, and you gave me my greatest performance. Here. On this beautiful island stage. I won't be Silas Kingston's puppet, or my adopted parents' project any longer. The only parent I ever truly had was Nathan Muir, so I'm *not* Jewel. Nathan didn't want to replace her, he wanted to replace her child, his child, the one he lost. You of all people know this—why he never entirely claimed Tom."

I did know.

There is no better time machine than the human mind. It never imagines darkness, but conceives of light yet to reach us, manipulates the improbable from the impossible, converting information into influence, and affects future outcome before it arrives. We do it without conscious thought.

"I know with all my being that the soul of that child is the soul I was born with. I won't be dying when you leave me, I'll be going home. Now go."

I didn't move.

She hissed, "Go!"

I took the penlight. She explained to me how she had reset the chipset in the cameras inside the hotel suite to overclock the entire recording. She told me how to reset them on real-time so that—when the gas is shut off and they reactivate the moment the guards reawaken—the two hours I will have spent will not appear in the tape. The guards will simply appear to shake off sleep, but never be seen to lose consciousness and I will appear at the window as if I never drank the antidote.

"No time will have passed, and it will be Christmas Day when you stand at that window, Russell. You'll have done it all in a night without having left your room."

Afraid to kiss her cheek and accidentally crack the cyanide capsule between her teeth, I kissed her hand. As I made my way back through the tunnels, I heard her voice, softly echoing through the tomb, reciting lines from the play she'd never gotten to perform:

"All men and beasts, lions, eagles, and quails, horned stags, geese, spiders, silent fish that inhabit the waves, starfish from the sea, and creatures invisible to the eye—in one word, life—all, all life, completing the dreary round imposed upon it, has died out at last. A thousand years have passed since the earth last bore a living creature on her breast, and the unhappy moon now lights her lamp in vain. No longer are the cries of storks heard in the meadows, or the drone of beetles in the groves of limes. All is cold, cold. All is void, void, void. All is terrible, terrible... The bodies of all living creatures have dropped to dust, and eternal matter has transformed them into stones and water and clouds; but their spirits have flowed together into one, and that great world-soul am I!"

47

WHEN TRIGORIN'S CUBAN AGENTS sent to free Nina arrived at the secluded house on Brick Church Road in Withernsea, they found the primary kidnapper—whose athletic shoes had left prints in lime juice, wine, and blood on Nina's floors—they found him between his Land Rover and the thrown pizza boxes he'd lost when his heart gave out due to the .338 Lapua Magnum round fired through it from a Russian Lobaev sniper rifle sited on a wooded hill one hundred yards away. They found the first interrogator halfway out the front door, his blue tracksuit stained red front to back by the 9mm round drilled through him point-blank by a suppressed Glock as he'd stepped outside to look for his partner late with their dinner delivery. They suspected what they'd find before they reached the basement, and their suspicions were confirmed when they entered: the third Cuban double-tapped in the head, and the American spy they'd been sent to release no longer present. They collected the equipment and with it, all indications of the three dead men's purpose and anything that might identify their corpses.

They loaded into their minivan.

They drove away.

TRIGORIN NEVER MENTIONED THIS as I went to work for him inside Langley, but I am certain he decided it bolstered the Agency illusion that the HOUNDFOX network remained protected. To prove my loyalty, my first business as a double agent involved the exposure of seven of those "protected" HOUNDFOX agents in Cuba to be turned or otherwise used to Trigorin's advantage.

These agents were provided to me by Lynn Kingston as having been identified by Nina as agents who'd played both sides or had proven themselves untrustworthy or criminal in other ways and written off the network as expendable. Other agents in Miami and Washington whom Nina had previously trusted, were revealed to me as Cuban assets and were soon turned by Lynn Kingston's operation to unwittingly run counterespionage against Havana.

As for the five YELLOW BIRD Chinese I'd turned over, one of them had been a legitimate DIANA RED asset, faithful, brave, and true; six months before Havana, he'd died in his sleep of natural causes. The other four, however, I'd embedded in my document to act as a kind of litmus test for the trust and faith Trigorin put into me and my work. These individuals, thought to be allies at the time, had worked YELLOW BIRD. Only years later was it discovered they'd also worked for the enemy throughout, responsible for a dozen dissident captures and deaths. Over the first two years of my treason to Cuba, word came to me from East Asian Analysis, one after the other, that each of these former enemies of DIANA RED were arrested and executed by the CCP.

My word to Havana was better than theirs to Beijing.

AN UNNAMED GOLD STAR was carved into the Memorial Wall in the Old Headquarters building and Amy's sacrifice was written in the Book of Honor with a date, but her name left blank for reasons of national security. I lay Amy Kim's death directly at the feet of Silas Kingston. I triangulated the bases of oversight to ensnare him, presenting the facts against him to my boss, the CIA General Counsel; to the Office of the CIA Inspectors General; to the Seventh Floor Office of Director George Tenet.

I was classified out of Amy's records and heard nothing on the matter again.

Silas Kingston never interviewed or debriefed me on how I'd confounded KALEIDOSCOPE's plans for TIME MACHINE. Lynn Kingston, who drowns family demons and childhood secrets about her deceased mother in a deepening dark well of alcohol (hauntings more terrifying than any green marbles of my own), ran the TIME MACHINE op for many years and to remarkable success. While I have no idea who runs the burst transmitter in Havana, I, Russell Aiken, am the ghost in the machine. I am the feedback loop that backstops, adjusts, amplifies, and influences Amy's time-holes as the crossword puzzles she'd envisioned; unwanted of my ambitions, I facilitate the CIA's most successful deception against Cuba ever achieved. Santa—returned to Cuba alive and well—runs sleigh-bell rings around Fidel Castro.

And yet, KALEIDOSCOPE still lingers. Magnifies. Unseen, but everywhere at once. Of this, I am certain. Early on in my working relationship with Trigorin, as he mined useful/actionable intel from my confession, he made the unusual and dangerous request for a face-to-face meeting. The biggest difficulty for me was setting my time and travel to appear as if I were hiding it from the Agency and behaving the traitor Trigorin believed me. This brought me in roundabout fashion to the Berlin Tegel Airport, Terminal A, and a private room inside the Swissair first-class lounge.

"I must have everything you know about KALEIDOSCOPE," he said.

With one single sentence, the line between loyalty and treason—or to a finer personal distinction, false treason and true treason—blurred.

"I must stand by what I provided in my statement. Further, KALEIDOSCOPE is not a CIA operation I have ever been able to confirm."

I didn't know Trigorin; in total I'd spent less than eight hours in his company. Yet sitting across from him over drinks, watching him smoke, he could have been any man—a total stranger—and I would have identified what I saw in his face. Extreme stress triggered by fear.

"I'll put it another way," I said. "We have, and I'm sure your DI have as well, a shorthand way of protecting classified information while acknowledging it without acknowledgment. We say 'we cannot confirm or deny.' Within the CIA, my inquiries on KALEIDOSCOPE came back from the highest level with a significantly different answer. Its existence was unequivocally denied."

He accepted my answer with a nod, but his hand showed a slight tremor as he rolled the ash tip of his cigar in his ashtray. He drained the whiskey he'd only sipped. It didn't appear to make him feel any better, but it was decisive. I was sure he'd settled an internal argument.

"That said," I continued, "KALEIDOSCOPE is real, and the Russian KALAYDOSKOP is real as well. I also believe we would be smart—"

"We leave this beast out of our business arrangement." His eyes bore into mine, leaving me no doubt were I to do otherwise, I would not survive.

"That's what I was going to say as well." I didn't have to say another word. "But…"

I held only hatred and disgust for the man before me. We were enemies on every level. I worked every day under his belief I spied for him so I could do the opposite and one day brutally destroy him. I kept General Trigorin in my constant prayers for the divine guidance that would lead me to that achievement.

"*But?* Be exceedingly careful what you next say," he warned.

But KALEIDOSCOPE blurs lines.

"You and I are enemies because our nations are enemies and because we have personal history that in an earlier age would demand I challenge you to a duel."

I watched a sly grin curl around the corner of his mouth. *"Por supuesto."* Of course.

"I believe there is someone within my organization— they don't know it yet—but they are uniquely suited to destroy KALEIDOSCOPE. Agreed: you and I will not involve that program in any way in any of our business. However, if you did ever develop evidence of its activity against you, your nation and its people, were you to get that to me, I would, at the appropriate time, funnel it to the individual who will go to war on behalf of all of us—and I mean worldwide—to destroy it."

He wet his lips with a dart of his tongue. He drained the drink I hadn't touched without asking and stood. He offered his hand. I filled with revulsion, shaking it, but he leaned in and whispered in my ear: "I have your word: *our* business does not include this. Ever."

"You have my word," I said.

He remained close. He did this to transfer an envelope from his breast pocket into mine.

The envelope sits unopened within my safe inside my *EZ Stow'N'Go* escape hatch. At the appropriate time (if ever that time arrives), I will hand it over to Lynn Kingston. We shall see.

As for my epilepsy? Dr. Rashmi's diagnosis it is curing itself seems to be more the rule than the exception. My medication dosage is as low as it's ever been, and my attacks are increasingly rare. The déjà vu remains but the sensations of *presque vu*, of imminent and powerful epiphany, accompanied by hallucinatory revelation—the tolling bells of my active mind breaking apart the tower-reality that contains them—have diminished almost entirely. And yet, I cling to the hope that as I had once communed with Muir across space-time, I might one day yet, overhearing my own thoughts, recognize the man most elusive and unresolved to the influences of my brain and the physics of my nature.

Is my father dead?

Of this I feel certain, although my certainty stands challenged by the unassuageable knowledge Dan Aiken/van Eyck did not die in a fiery crash among sunflowers along a Kansas highway in September 1969. I know not only by Joshua's claim, but because I have journeyed to my own proof. I have seen the man who died in Kansas. Not in hallucination, but with Lara's uncomfortable approval, I've beaten my last living sister in court, exhumed the body, and confirmed this by DNA exam; the man buried as my father is no relation to me or my sisters.

"We can't all be our fathers."

"What do you know about my father?" I beg of Silas Kingston over and over in memory.

"Everything you don't."

ALL THIS WAS YET TO COME the Christmas Day I returned from Havana.

As I passed through baggage claim, I passed a one-legged man who brush-passed me a room key envelope for the Arlington Hilton on North Stafford Street. Aware I would be under surveillance by Trigorin's watchers, I took a cab to the hotel and booked my own room. I timed my elevator ride to take advantage of a crowded car where I hit a high-floor button neither my level nor the level corresponding to the key Bishop slipped into my pocket. I made the intentional mistake of getting off with a group of guests on the wrong floor. When the man who'd followed me from the airport got off as well, I "realized" my mistake and quickly jumped back on before surveillance could rejoin me. I hit the floor corresponding to the airport-passed key and followed its number to the suite at the end of the corridor.

I inserted the plastic key into its slot and withdrew it. The electronic lock disengaged. I gently pushed open the door. My half-sister, Lara, looked up from the sitting room. She beamed at the sight of me, doing nothing to disguise the shudder of relief that washed over her. We moved for each other at once, meeting halfway in an embrace.

"Merry Christmas, Lara."

"It is now," she said. She crushed me into her.

"Where is she?"

"She's napping with baby Jack." Her soft eyes shone with hopeful anticipation. "Sometimes, the best care for a damaged soul is to care for the life of an innocent."

She softly opened the master-bedroom door. Jack, three-and-a-half months of life already blocked behind him, lay swaddled and asleep in a bassinet pulled alongside Nina in the bed.

Nina's eyelids fluttered. *"Buenos…"* She focused on my face. "Sorry I missed our date."

I stepped forward—Lara back, closing the door—and withdrew the ring box from my pocket.

"Bright side of it all," she said, "you saved yourself from buying an extra Christmas present."

"I've been a tad busy…"

"Holiday crunch?"

My face warmed to my smile. I kneeled beside the bed, but down by her knees, the sleeping baby blocked me from reaching her. I pivoted around the other side of the bassinet, but she wasn't helping, and I couldn't stretch far enough to take her hand.

"If you're so intent on kneeling, you could do it up here," she said. "Or it might be nice'n'cozy, baby, if you could get your balls back and lie down beside me."

After I untangled my shoelace from the bassinet caster, I climbed onto the bed. I balanced shakily on both knees. I opened the box.

"And what remained in Pandora's Box was hope," said Nina.

"Actually, it's 'jar.'"

"It's beautiful."

The ring dazzled in the light, and I forgot my whole memorized, Mary-what's-it, James Bond, De Beers, Oppenheimer perfect proposal.

"*¿Te comieron la lengua los ratones?*" Did the mouse eat your tongue?

I didn't want to say the wrong thing. Not now. It was the best line, so I gave it my best shot: "Marry me for once—"

No! Idiot! "*Forever is worthless without you—*"

"—and-all-for-less— I mean, worthless— I mean, forever, what it's worth."

Nina cocked her head. I tried not to lose my optimistic face at the close sight of her swelling cuts and unspeakable bruises.

"You don't look so sure… Do you love me, Pintao?"

The third time, and her voice was music. It was heaven's call in the silence predictive space between her words.

"I love you, Nina."

Nina sighed as one who has completed an arduous task with magnificent effort. "Stop wasting Christmas, you glorious fool, and get that rock on my finger."

I took her hand. The baby bleated. We stifled laughter as I slipped the ring over her slender ring finger. "Aw, Russell, you remembered."

"Pintao," I corrected and released her right hand. I had remembered the appropriate Cuban matrimonial custom.

My nephew—soon to be "our" nephew—fussed louder until, with a knock, Lara entered and took him. Nina and I were left alone. Not once did Nina ask about her father and I, respecting this, kept silence on the death of Comandante Alejandro Alvarez. We celebrated the rest of Christmas in succor and privacy.

IT WAS DETERMINED AT LANGLEY the circumstances of Amy's death would be hidden forever from her parents. They were informed by George Mason University she had been working in conjunction with the US military. There had been an accident, and Amy Kim had perished in a lab fire. When her father hired an attorney and went to the university and the press for answers, the FBI went to her father's house and warned Mr. and Mrs. Kim their daughter was a patriot casualty in the War on Terror and any further effort on their part to seek information would see them also casualties of war under Bush the Second's Patriot Act. There was a burial without a body, and it was a sad and bitter show in early February which the Agency Nine-Twelvers secretly witnessed, but none of us who worked with her and had loved her for who she was, participated.

Anyway, we had already commemorated her as she'd requested, back in Lone Pine on New Year's Eve.

IN THE HIGH SIERRAS, IT SNOWED CHRISTMAS DAY, and the next, and it would snow again at nightfall on the first day of 2003. But on New Year's Eve, the alpine sky reached into space, and the cold of the galaxy falling from the heavens reddened our noses and burned our cheeks with frost. The moon was full and crisply delineated over the snow-covered peak of California's Everest,

Mount Whitney, ablaze with diamond white reflection of the unseen sun in a sky of the deepest black-blue that matched the color of Nina's glowing skin. A bonfire blazed in Aunt Linda's pit and the trick of firelight made the trunks of her regal memorial pines appear to sway and dance in welcome of the five-foot sugar pine Nina and I had helped Aunt Linda remove from the hillside where, for years, she cultivated her pine nursery, "Unhappily, but in case."

Loading the tree in the back of Linda's rusted F150, I had the urge to ask her if she had one picked out for me. Linda grinned. "I've earmarked three or four over the years for you, dear-heart, but they twist unnaturally, grow sideways or into shrubs, or disease and perish. Every one of them for some strange reason."

So maybe that's a good thing?

Amy's tree, young though it was, had grown healthy and true; transplanted, its limbs strained precociously between her impressive companions, and we all agreed it was a proud and eager little tree indeed. The firelight threw shadows through its striving branches and those, low hanging from heroes gone before, patterned themselves as grasping hands and welcoming hugs of light and shadow. I added Amy's and Nathan's ashes around the root ball, then Nina gave Joshua Rosen—who had come bearing the gift of Amy's-once-Muir's black cat for Linda—Nina gave him the shovel and he filled in the dirt, and softly gave the Hebrew *El Malei Rachamim* prayer for Amy's soul.

In the circle of the bonfire, I read aloud from Chekov. The Nina monologue from *The Seagull*. I didn't add a single rhyme.

"'In me is the spirit of the great Alexander, the spirit of Napoleon, of Caesar, of Shakespeare, and of the tiniest leech that swims. In me the consciousness of man has joined hands with the instinct of the animal; I understand all, all, all, and each life lives again in me.'"

From the atomic to the particulate; from the playwright to all the audiences over time, touching him through the words touching them, touching us through Amy touching me; from the very first of the single-celled organisms all life arises from; from the sun and the Earth that created each other to create it. From all of that in block time: the bonfire gave an explosive crack and threw embers. Three of them, large and bright, rose high in an entwining phoenix helix and our expressions grew explicit and relaxed at Amy, Jewel, and Nathan among us.

"'I am alone,'" I continued reading. "'Once in a hundred years my lips are opened, my voice echoes mournfully across the desert earth, and no one hears. And you, poor lights of the marsh, you do not hear me. You are engendered at sunset in the putrid mud, and flit wavering about the lake till dawn, unconscious, unreasoning, unwarmed by the breath of life. Satan, father of eternal matter, trembling lest the spark of life should glow in you, has ordered an unceasing movement of the atoms that compose you, and so you shift and change forever. I, the spirit of the universe, I alone am immutable and eternal… Like a captive in a dungeon deep and void, I know not where I am, nor what awaits me. One thing only is not hidden from me: in my fierce and obstinate battle with Satan, the source of the forces of matter, I am destined to be victorious in the end. Matter and spirit will then be one at last in glorious harmony, and the reign of freedom will begin on Earth.'"

BISHOP, LARA, BABY JACK (AND THE PERSIAN CAT) all stayed with Aunt Linda while the rest of us had four rooms in a local motel—Nina and I, Gladys and Jessie, Joshua and Wendy Rosen, Bill and

Nanette Carver. A fifth room had been reserved for our special guest and her wife for the next night; they would arrive in the morning by private plane and limousine as Nina had insisted this be a double celebration.

"Worst idea ever," I'd argued. "Muir warned me against ruining this holiday the first time I got married New Year's Eve. I distinctly remember him telling me it'd be me who'd end up dead on the moon."

Nina gave a throaty chuckle, more tiger's purr than laugh.

"Yeah. I agreed with Muir. It *was* stupid of you to marry that bitch on New Year's Eve."

"You knew?"

"Shut d'fuck up," she mocked. "What? You think I'm lying? You're just jealous he told me more things than he ever told you."

"Am not."

Am so.

She draped her arms around my neck. She put her nose tip to mine and seduced me with her eyes. "Baby, New Year's Day is the most boring holiday in the book. Our marriage not only buries her once and for all, it kicks off every one of the every-years we're gonna have, forever and ever, Amen. Now kiss me and say yes like I did."

"Yes."

Adding curiouser to the curiouser, Nina surprised me. My Dr. Rashmi Patel was licensed in California to perform civil ceremonies as a unitarian minister and had been performing them for domestic partnerships in Laguna, Los Angeles, and Big Sur since 1999.

Nina and I slept in while Gladys and Jessie went up the hill early to help Tom and Lara decorate for the ceremony on Linda's broad stone patio deck. When it was time, standing beneath a forest-found and decorated bower beside Tom Bishop—my past, present, future best man—I looked into my lifesaving doctor's loving eyes in a moment of clarity.

"It's all so unreal," I said.

"Go with all God gives you, Russell. You can't back out of the operation now." She gave me a wink, then at the sound of a guitar, her eyes lifted past me. I turned. Aunt Linda played a song on Amy's guitar made popular the year Linda lost her leg to the Gestapo. 'Long Ago and Far Away.'

In that way, and in that place, that space, that eternal instant of time in its four-dimensional block of ever-when, Nina and I were married. We were completed and found completeness in our love.

WORDS IN A CROSSWORD PUZZLE: strip away the clues.

Next, remove direction.

Next, the boxes.

The letters float. Collide. Pair and repair. By chance, some create other words—a brief accident of apparent allusory meaning. Consciousness strives to pattern and find, but without anchor, the unpairing continues, stripping it to lonely singularity—any meaning found in organization is an accident, like gas molecules trapped in a demon box, and chaos is the true order of all.

We did not do.

We did not say.

We did not meet.

We were not moving.

We stopped feeling, stopped hearing, stopped seeing.

To dream perchance to live; we become better than our word.

AFTER THE WEDDING WAS OVER, after the reception dinner prepared with Lara's usual flair, after we stayed up late with stories and songs and the sharing of dreams, snow quietly fell and those of us staying in town made our way off Linda's mythic hill.

Nina and I consummated our marriage, wild and sleek of bracing arms, round shifting knees, muscled thighs, of clutching hand and grasping fingers. Long, firm and matching lengths. The soft small spots. Groaning. Arching. Grabbing more, more, more. Exhalations of forge-fire hearts and the hard-tempoed abandon of release. She twisted over beneath me and emerged alongside me, sheened and dark.

She kissed my cheek.

I kissed her mouth.

She said, "Tell me now. I'm ready. Tell me about my father."

I told Nina of my last meeting with HOUNDFOX. And some of what I didn't remember—his Castro speech—she knew by heart, and when I went to my bag, withdrew one of two items I'd hidden at the bottom, Nina wept sad joy to see her treasure, long ago thrown from the sea, changed into an icon of love for her family. All she'd once had, now preserved in time as all she now carried and could and would now never lose.

"I never dreamed how perfectly the picture meant for it would find its way to its frame. And look," she said as she pulled the faded and forever unknown photo from the sea from its place behind her father's print. "He knew to let the other spirits stay."

We'll find a photo of us together one day and then we'll know…

Nina set her treasure against the cheap bedside lamp and gazed at it until she fell into a deep and grateful sleep.

I gently rose and dressed for the weather and the rough work ahead of me. I laced my boots. I went back to my bag. I lifted out the other item I'd hidden at the bottom, heavy in my hand. I stuffed it into my jacket pocket and left the room.

I drove my rental car through horizontal snow back to Linda's lodge: eldritch, still, hushed inside the night. I walked around to the back beneath the deck where we had wed. I approached the cellar door, and it opened.

"Some things you can't come back from. I can do this for you," said Bishop, waiting in the shadows just inside. His breath blossomed like mine in frozen clouds.

"Some fatalities come in certain shapes and some in others," I said.

The gag in the mouth of the man in the back of the room muffled his shrieks. His Bruno Magli shoes, long since ruined, scraped and scuffed the limestone floor, legs kicking like those of a filthy bird of prey ensnared in hunter's wire unable to rise to flight.

"Nina would not be alive if he hadn't told me how to find her," Bishop softly cautioned.

The prisoner agreed. His noises grew more urgent.

I looked at him, his brown skin and handsome face gray and dirty, his clothing torn and soiled from days as Bishop's prisoner. Urine stains showed as frost at his crotch and striped his trouser legs. "Strange thing is, I'd almost have a drop of pity if he'd doubled and betrayed us all, if betraying Nina—and by extension, Amy and Lynn Kingston—had been merely part of this wretched game of spies we live."

I walked over to the Cuban–American former DEA agent where he sat and thrashed his legs and torqued his shoulders, his arms chained back behind him to a post that rose to support the landing above where I'd married Nina hours earlier. He'd been there all that time, a beating heart beneath the floor where we'd stood and celebrated our future. His vulture eyes blazed with hatred and with fear.

"But for lust and jealousy, won't lovers revolt now?" I backed myself with my peculiar safety net of words. "Fucker."

I pulled Muir's Sig-Sauer from my pocket and finally got the gun to work.

BRIEFLY, PERHAPS, A NEW PATTERN of across and down presents itself; new answers to find new clues; we map new questions from the graph and that becomes our story, learning it after it has already been told. The beginning of life and life's ending are unique to every human and, by extension, every living thing, universally shared in totality and universally original, unique in singular experience. These are the string theories spooled, measured, and cut by Muir's Three Fates.

It is naïve and, plainly, it is crazy to think that a brand-new pack of playing cards organized by suit and numerical order when first ordered can ever be shuffled at random any number of times to end up, one more time, returned to perfect order. And yet, it is precisely, inevitably, and definitively possible. The probability is so astronomically unfavorable that we cannot predict the number of shuffles this would take—one thousand people buying one thousand lottery tickets playing one thousand and one nights at eight random numbers who one time all pick the same numbers at the same time and that time being the same time those numbers come up as the winner.

Maybe it's one hundred people, not one thousand.

Maybe it's not even Lotto but love, but truth and lies and where the twain meet luck.

Real and imagined.

Forward and backward.

And the precise nature of everything that renders random events naught.

NOTHING IS RANDOM for the living and the dead. I fired one round into Victor Rubio's chest and exercised Nathan Muir's last lesson reserved from me till now: to make all he was into all who I am. Rubio spasmed, trembled, bled.

A scratch of movement commanded my attention. The tap of her cane preceded Aunt Linda, emerging phantomlike from the rear of the cellar. She shuffled behind Victor Rubio and slipped her stiletto from her boot. She buried her fingers in his hair like so much wool and yanked back his head. Like the Basque shepherds who had built her home used the cellar as an abattoir and laid the limestone floor for such a purpose as this, she pulled his neck taut and slit his throat.

I WENT BACK TO NINA, found home inside her arms, and she didn't waken enough to know I'd ever been gone.

Afterword & Acknowledgments

While there is no listening device in the US intelligence arsenal codenamed *TIME MACHINE*, through its fictional development for this book, I've attempted to capture the true and fascinating process many equally incredible devices developed by the Office of Technical Services follow from inception to deployment. Without question, the OTS "Wizards of Langley" (aptly dubbed by CIA Directorate of Science and Technology historian Jeffrey T. Richelson) are bombarded with what at first can only be described as magic wand, crystal ball, and other supernatural requests. Through preternatural thinking and applied science, they regularly convert these requests into astounding realities. The process is fascinating; theoretical analysis is applied to the swirl of fantastic desire; scientific principles are paired to every what-if facet of each wish and the unknown is assigned knowable parameters. Through this, they design the achievable.

TIME MACHINE's journey, from Russell Aiken hallucinatory dreamworld to Amy Kim hard-wired reality, travels from the mind's conception of time and time's relationship to ancient physics, through brain functions that process time within the framework of relativistic mechanics, into the contemplation of consciousness's relationship to quantum physics, to arrive at the conversion of quantum information theory into applied espionage. This intellectual voyage would not have been possible without my reliance on the works of several brilliant, penetrating, and transforming scientific works. I list them in the order I read them and drew from their wisdom: *The River of Consciousness*, by Oliver Sacks (Vintage, 2017); *The Order of Time*, by Carlo Rovelli

(Penguin, 2017); *Your Brain is a Time Machine: The Neuroscience and Physics of Time*, by Dean Buonomano (Norton, 2017); *Reality is Not What It Seems*, by Carlo Rovelli (Penguin, 2014); *About Time: Einstein's Unfinished Revolution* (Simon & Schuster,1995) and *The Demon in the Machine: How Hidden Webs of Information are Solving the Mystery of Life* (University of Chicago, 2019), by Paul Davies; *The Conscious Mind: In Search of a Fundamental Theory* (Oxford, 1990) by David Chalmers; and *Conscious: A Brief Guide to the Fundamental Mystery of the Mind*, by Annaka Harris (Harper, 2019).

This book owes a debt of gratitude to these scientists and theorists. Without the combined genius of these authors, *Aiken in Check* would have been impossible to write. In that I have attempted to accurately portray the essence of their scientific and philosophical arguments in my characters' thoughts and dialogue, I acknowledge here that everything I get right in this book belongs to these authors, not to me. That said, I am nagged by an Aiken-like fear I may not have applied any of it correctly and missed the point entirely. If so, let me be clear: every theoretical mistake, philosophical fallacy, or scientific foolishness found between the covers of this book is mine and mine alone.

Brain mechanics and time science are not the only areas where I have relied on the genius of others for my characters' inge-nuity. The Aiken Trilogy is presented as three written narratives composed by a manic first-person narrator, Russell Aiken. Filtered through the lens of his innate hypergraphia that is complicated by his various afflictions—alcoholism, a brain tumor, and epilepsy— I faced a unique challenge of mapping the effects each of these diseases have on the underlying behavioral condition. Once again, without neurologist Alice Weaver Flaherty's captivating, compas-sionate, and insightful book, *The Midnight Disease: The Drive to*

Write, Writer's Block, and the Creative Brain (2004, Mariner) to lead my research and provoke my imagination, Russell Aiken's sentence, paragraph, argument constructions, and free associations (and what incites these), his manic moods, his Wernicke's aphasic speech pathologies, and his hallucinations would have been untranslatable from my imagination.

Through the understanding of his condition, I was confronted with the challenge of manifesting his symptomatic compulsions in his writing style. I would not have been able to realistically accomplish (to any degree of seemingly natural skill), his incessant wordplay and puzzles, his word mathematics, word patterning, transforming, fragmenting, ordering and other lexical games, along with the numerical and literary codes he embeds throughout his three texts without the skillful work of Dimitri Borgmann in his *Language on Vacation* (Scribner's, 1965), and Ross Eckler's marvelous *Making the Alphabet Dance: Recreational Wordplay* (St. Martin's, 1996). Of all the dozens of palindromic words, phrases, and constructions woven into these three novels, I created only two.

One of two words, one of four.

I marvel at the brilliance of scores of puzzlers who have over many generations created and shared many others in magazines and newspapers, websites, and blogs since Henry Peacham introduced the palindrome in 1638. I'd like to say no one has out-mastered Dimitri Martin's 1993 224-word palindrome poem "Dammit I'm Mad," but when I just went to check that, I discovered I was wrong. I found his 500-word follow-up "Sexes."

My mention of literary codes deserves a more detailed explanation and an umbrella acknowledgment to three towering intellects. The late, great literary critic Harold Bloom and his masterpiece *The Anatomy of Influence: Literature as a Way of Life*

(Yale, 2011); likewise, the departed Umberto Eco and his seminal work, *A Theory of Semiotics* (1976; Indiana University) in which he set out "to explore the theoretical possibility and the social function of a unified approach to every phenomenon of signification and/or communication;" and the latest writings by renowned professor of physics and mathematics at Colombia University, Brian Greene, who explores the linkage between quantum physics and human imagination in his *Until the End of Time: Mind, Matter, and Our Search for Meaning in an Evolving Universe* (Knopf, 2020).

The influence of great language builds upon the self-fulfilling paradox of why language is great in the first place. The language of humans lives before each of us, lives longer than us—no matter how much of it we use or try to use up—for it is infinite; we can never say it or write it all down, because like the ouroboros Aiken obsesses over, its beginning and its ending is the same. All the language we do manage to get on paper will live longer than all mankind as it attaches to and reflects the eternal. And the insects destined to outlast us won't care to do anything with it, won't care to understand or translate it, or even know what it is, but it will have made humanity immortal long after the anthill is dashed into dust.

In 1640, Ben Johnson said that for a man to write well, the first of three necessities is that we read. In 1951, William Faulkner agreed: "Read everything—trash, classics, good and bad, and see how they do it... Then write." It's a trend, useful and important enough, that we're reminded to it this century by Stephen King: "Read a lot, write a lot,' is the great commandment." Aiken is comfortable in writing from his influences in *Muir's Gambit*. They define and hold him to his confessional parameters, uniquely combined and filtered through his subconscious; all that he has read creates his voice at its most unique. Parapets to his hidden fortress that shape his inner life. However, by *Aiken in Check*, these influences become his desperate code, fastidiously and archly buried in this text, to delegitimize his entire confession as having not been written—as Trigorin orders him—by himself whatsoever and at all. The entire trilogy circles back to the greater puzzle of information influence and how we manipulate it, and it manipulates us.

As Nathan Muir says, "In the end, it's not how you play the game, it's how the game plays you."

CPSIA information can be obtained
at www.ICGtesting.com
Printed in the USA
BVHW041018061022
648824BV00014B/383/J

9 798985 597462